PENGUIN TWENTIETH-CENTURY CLASSICS

AARON'S ROD

David Herbert Lawrence was born at Eastwood, Nottingham-shire, in 1885, fourth of the five children of a miner and his middle-class wife. He attended Nottingham High School and Nottingham University College. His first novel, *The White Peacock*, was published in 1911, just a few weeks after the death of his mother to whom he had been abnormally close. At this time he finally ended his relationship with Jessie Chambers (the Miriam of *Sons and Lovers*) and became engaged to Louie Burrows. His career as a schoolteacher was ended in 1911 by the illness which was ultimately diagnosed as tuberculosis.

In 1912 Lawrence eloped to Germany with Frieda Weekley, the German wife of his former modern languages tutor. They were married on their return to England in 1914. Lawrence was now living, precariously, by his writing. His greatest novels, *The Rainbow* and *Women in Love*, were completed in 1915 and 1916. The former was suppressed, and he could not find a publisher for the latter.

After the war Lawrence began his 'savage pilgrimage' in search of a more fulfilling mode of life than industrial Western civilization could offer. This took him to Sicily, Ceylon, Australia and, finally, New Mexico. The Lawrences returned to Europe in 1925. Lawrence's last novel, *Lady Chatterley's Lover*, was banned in 1928, and his paintings confiscated in 1929. He died in Vence in 1930 at the age of 44.

Lawrence spent most of his short life living. Nevertheless he produced an amazing quantity of work – novels, stories, poems, plays, essays, travel books, translations, letters. After his death Frieda wrote: 'What he had seen and felt and known he gave in his writing to his fellow men, the splendour of living, the hope of more and more life ... a heroic and immeasurable gift.'

D. H. LAWRENCE

Aaron's Rod

PENGUIN BOOKS

PENGUIN BOOKS

Published by the Penguin Group
27 Wrights Lane, London W8 5TZ, England
Viking Penguin Inc., 40 West 23rd Street, New York, New York 10010, USA
Penguin Books Australia Ltd, Ringwood, Victoria, Australia
Penguin Books Canada Ltd, 2801 John Street, Markham, Ontario, Canada L3R 1B4
Penguin Books (NZ) Ltd, 182–190 Wairau Road, Auckland 10, New Zealand

Penguin Books Ltd, Registered Offices: Harmondsworth, Middlesex, England

First published in Great Britain by William Heinemann Ltd 1922
Published in Penguin Books in Great Britain 1950
11 13 15 17 19 20 18 16 14 12

First published in the United States of America by
Thomas Seltzer, Inc. 1922
Viking Compass Edition published 1961
Published in Penguin Books in the United States of America 1976

Made and printed in Great Britain by
BPCC Hazell Books
Aylesbury, Bucks, England
Member of BPCC Ltd.
Set in Monotype Garamond

Contents

Contents

Introduction

BY RICHARD ALDINGTON

LAWRENCE'S novels were produced either with much care
and frequent re-writings or else hastily improvised and thrown
off in an incredibly short time. *The White Peacock*, *Sons and
Lovers*, *The Rainbow* and *Lady Chatterley's Lover* belong to the
former group; *The Lost Girl*, *Aaron's Rod* and *Kangaroo* to the
latter. He may have had some idea of what he intended to do
in *The Lost Girl*, but the other two were wholly improvisations,
begun at random, with no more coherence and structure than
the very important ones of Lawrence's compelling personality
and brilliant writing. In a sense we might think of these
improvised novels as mere pot-boilers, though Lawrence himself considered everything he wrote was important. This may
be true of *The Lost Girl*, in spite of its wonderfully eloquent
ending, but Lawrence put so much of himself into the other
two that they rise above the humble pot-boiler. How carelessly *Aaron's Rod* was written may be judged from one or
two details, pointed out long ago by Mr Middleton Murry. A
girl introduced on Page 37 as Josephine Hay becomes
Josephine Ford on Page 38. He forgets that his character
Lilly has not been in the war, and at another point defiantly
challenges the reader to prove that a simple person like Aaron
could not have thought all the Lawrentian subtleties attributed
to him.

Aaron's Rod was begun in the early part of 1918, and is
referred to in an undated letter to Lady Cynthia Asquith
(March 1918, in fact) as the novel 'which is as blameless as
Cranford' of which he had done 150 pages. After writing
eleven chapters he threw it aside. To understand them the
reader must realize that they are improvised variations on

Lawrence's own experience. In October 1917 the Lawrences were expelled from Cornwall by the military authority under the absurd suspicion of espionage. They arrived in London penniless and homeless, and were looked after by a few friends and admirers, who of course themselves came under suspicion. But to do Lawrence a good turn, as so often is the case with gifted artists, was to arouse bitter resentment at having to be under an obligation, and provoked his satirical malice.

Once safely over this difficulty and lodged in a Berkshire cottage, Lawrence most amusingly but unfairly passed the time by satirizing the very people who had loyally stood by him in his troubles. Lilly, who is as obviously Lawrence himself as Tanny is Mrs Lawrence, contemptuously rejects all these people and turns to Aaron, who is obviously intended to be Mr Middleton Murry, with whom Lawrence had bitterly quarrelled in Cornwall and with whom he was to quarrel again even more bitterly. But, in spite of their incompatibilities, Lawrence was really more attached to Mr Murry than to any other of his men friends, and was always willing to forget how bitterly he had hurt his friend in the hope of a reconciliation. This was always hopeless, because what Lawrence wanted was not a friend but an utterly obedient and subservient disciple. If *Aaron's Rod* can be said to have a theme it is the gratification of this always frustrated longing for power in Lawrence whereby at the end Aaron is left with the choice between disintegration or accepting Lilly submissively as his Master.

The opening of the book makes use of Lawrence's memories of Christmas as a child, his 1917 Christmas with his family, and above all his intimacies with the London friends who had helped him. The chapter *At The Opera* is founded on the fact that in December 1917 he was invited to a box by Lady Cynthia Asquith, but he did not take any of his other acquaintances, as in the novel. The curious chapter, *A Punch in the Wind*, is also founded on fact. I remember Jim Bricknell in real life, and it is true that he got so angry with Lawrence's taunting during a self-invited visit in the country that he gave him a punch in the chest. The chapter in which Lilly looks after the sick Aaron is probably founded on recollections of a week-end in 1915, when Mr Murry arrived at the Lawrences' cottage with a heavy cold, and Lawrence enjoyed himself fussily nursing his best friend.

It is easy to see why Lawrence abandoned the book when he did. Those early chapters have little or nothing of his peculiar daimon, none of that thrilling eloquence and passionate poetry and subtle physical emotion of which he alone had the secret. Here, and indeed throughout the book, we have a dilution of what he called his philosophy, but chiefly we have the satirical Lawrence, not at his best, but almost at the level of spiteful gossip. Chapter followed chapter, marking time and getting nowhere. Lilly is obviously part of Aaron's story, but what on earth has Aaron to do with Jim Bricknell and Josephine and Julia, whom he meets most casually? They are part of Lilly's life, but not of Aaron's. They only exist, unnecessarily, to show that for Lilly Aaron's Rod was bigger than all the others.

So the book was dropped, and remained untouched for three years, when Lawrence took it up again at Ebersteinburg, and rapidly wrote the longer portion which finishes it. Meanwhile, much had happened to him. In November, 1919, he had left England and made his way through the post-war chaos to northern Italy, Florence, and on south; and Aaron for no particular reason except Lawrence's convenience follows his route and shares his experiences – not with his own character and temperament, but with Lilly-Lawrence's. During the latter part of the book Aaron so often becomes Lilly that when the two meet the effect is almost that of the Teutonic Doppelgänger.

Yet it is this part of the book which soars from the comparative commonplace of the opening on to a level more commensurate with Lawrence's genius. He was a man full of curiosity and a remarkable power of enjoying life, and was always – until he was plainly dying – stimulated by travel, seeing new places and meeting new people. True, the book remains satirical, and some of the portraits of English people in Italy, being easily identified from salient traits which were exaggerated into caricature, gave much offence. In these caricatures Lawrence is just as unfair, as censorious and as self-righteous as in his London scenes, but the stimulus of travel awoke his verve and made the Italian scenes, particularly the Florentine ones, much more lively and amusing. The scenes at Novara (Turin, in real life) with Sir William and Lady Franks are fascinating but full of the uninteresting, too naturalistic (by half) dialogue Lawrence would not learn to prune. But the descriptions of Florence are in Lawrence's finest mood, and the caricature of James Argyle is masterly and irresistibly funny to anyone who knew the original. Since 'little Algy Constable' is now dead, alas, there is no harm in revealing that the original was the faithful friend of Oscar Wilde, Reggy Turner, and the cruel phrase about his 'flapping his eyelids like some crazy owl' is magically exact. Poor Reggy did have that habit of screwing up and unscrewing his eyes with disconcerting speed and for no apparent reason – it was only Lawrence who could catch it perfectly in a jeering phrase.

As to the end of the book, it is labelled, with unconscious veracity, *Words*. There we have the final appeal of Lilly-Lawrence to Aaron-Murry for 'submission' and 'obedience'. I can never read the end of this book which otherwise has in it so much beauty and wisdom without a smile. Listen:

'There was a long pause. Then Aaron looked up into Lilly's face. It was dark and remote-seeming. It was like a Byzantine eikon at the moment.

"And whom shall I submit to?"

'"Your soul will tell you," replied the other.'

And Echo murmured: 'David Herbert Lawrence'.

CHAPTER I

The Blue Ball

THERE was a large, brilliant evening star in the early twilight, and underfoot the earth was half frozen. It was Christmas Eve. Also the War was over, and there was a sense of relief that was almost a new menace. A man felt the violence of the nightmare released now into the general air. Also there had been another wrangle among the men on the pit-bank that evening.

Aaron Sisson was the last man on the little black railway-line climbing the hill home from work. He was late because he had attended a meeting of the men on the bank. He was secretary to the Miners' Union for his colliery, and had heard a good deal of silly wrangling that left him nettled.

He strode over a stile, crossed two fields, strode another stile, and was in the long road of colliers' dwellings. Just across was his own house: he had built it himself. He went through the little gate, up past the side of the house to the back. There he hung a moment, glancing down the dark, wintry garden.

'My father – my father's come!' cried a child's excited voice, and two little girls in white pinafores ran out in front of his legs.

'Father, shall you set the Christmas Tree?' they cried. 'We've got one!'

'Afore I have my dinner?' he answered amiably.

'Set it now. Set it now. We got it through Fred Alton.'

'Where is it?'

The little girls were dragging a rough, dark object out of a corner of the passage into the light of the kitchen door.

'It's a beauty!' exclaimed Millicent.

11

'Yes, it is,' said Marjory.

'I should think so,' he replied, striding over the dark bough. He went to the back kitchen to take off his coat.

'Set it now, father. Set it now,' clamoured the girls.

'You might as well. You've left your dinner so long, you might as well do it now before you have it,' came a woman's plangent voice, out of the brilliant light of the middle room.

Aaron Sisson had taken off his coat and waistcoat and his cap. He stood bare-headed in his shirt and braces, contemplating the tree.

'What am I to put it in?' he queried. He picked up the tree, and held it erect by the topmost twig. He felt the cold as he stood in the yard coat-less, and he twitched his shoulders.

'Isn't it a beauty!' repeated Millicent.

'Ay! – lop-sided though.'

'Put something on, you two!' came the woman's high imperative voice, from the kitchen.

'We aren't cold,' protested the girls from the yard.

'Come and put something on,' insisted the voice.

The man started off down the path; the little girls ran grumbling indoors. The sky was clear; there was still a crystalline, non-luminous light in the under air.

Aaron rummaged in his shed at the bottom of the garden, and found a spade and a box that was suitable. Then he came out to his neat, bare, wintry garden. The girls flew towards him, putting the elastic of their hats under their chins as they ran. The tree and the box lay on the frozen earth. The air breathed dark, frosty, electric.

'Hold it up straight,' he said to Millicent, as he arranged the tree in the box. She stood silent and held the top bough; he filled in round the roots.

When it was done, and pressed in, he went for the wheelbarrow. The girls were hovering excited round the tree. He dropped the barrow and stooped to the box. The girls watched him hold back his face – the boughs pricked him.

'Ay!' he replied, with a little grunt.

12

Then the procession set off – the trundling wheelbarrow, the swinging, hissing tree, the two excited little girls. They arrived at the door. Down went the legs of the wheelbarrow on the yard. The man looked at the box.

'Where are you going to have it?' he called.

'Put it in the back kitchen,' cried his wife.

'You'd better have it where it's going to stop. I don't want to hawk it about.'

'Put it on the floor against the dresser, father. Put it there,' urged Millicent.

'You come and put some paper down, then,' called the mother hastily.

The two children ran indoors; the man stood contemplative in the cold, shrugging his uncovered shoulders slightly. The open inner door showed a bright linoleum on the floor, and the end of a brown sideboard on which stood an aspidistra.

Again with a wrench Aaron Sisson lifted the box. The tree pricked and stung. His wife watched him as he entered staggering, with his face averted.

'Mind where you make a lot of dirt,' she said.

He lowered the box with a little jerk on to the spread-out newspaper on the floor. Soil scattered.

'Sweep it up,' he said to Millicent.

His ear was lingering over the sudden, clutching hiss of the tree-boughs.

A stark white incandescent light filled the room and made everything sharp and hard. In the open fire-place a hot fire burned red. All was scrupulously clean and perfect. A baby was cooing in a rockerless wicker cradle by the hearth. The mother, a slim, neat woman with dark hair, was sewing a child's frock. She put this aside, rose, and began to take her husband's dinner from the oven.

'You stopped confabbing long enough to-night,' she said.

'Yes,' he answered, going to the back kitchen to wash his hands.

In a few minutes he came and sat down to the table. The doors were shut close, but there was a draught, because the settling of the mines under the house made the doors not fit. Aaron moved his chair, to get out of the draught. But he still sat in his shirt and trousers.

He was a good-looking man, fair, and pleasant, about thirty-two years old. He did not talk much, but seemed to think about something. His wife resumed her sewing. She was acutely aware of her husband, but he seemed not very much aware of her.

'What were they on about to-day, then?' she said.

'About the throw-in.'

'And did they settle anything?'

'They're going to try it – and they'll come out if it isn't satisfactory.'

'The butties won't have it, I know,' she said.

He gave a short laugh, and went on with his meal.

The two children were squatted on the floor by the tree. They had a wooden box, from which they had taken many little newspaper packets which they were spreading out like wares.

'Don't open any. We won't open any of them till we've taken them all out – and then we'll undo one in our turns. Then we s'll both undo equal,' Millicent was saying.

'Yes, we'll take them *all* out first,' re-echoed Marjory.

'And what are they going to do about Job Arthur Freer? – Do they want him?'

A faint smile came on her husband's face.

'Nay, I don't know what they want. Some of 'em want him – whether they're a majority, I don't know.'

She watched him closely.

'Majority! I'd give 'em majority. They want to get rid of you, and make a fool of you, and you want to break your heart over it. Strikes me you need something to break your heart over.'

He laughed silently.

'Nay,' he said. 'I s'll never break my heart.'

'You'll go nearer to it over that, than over anything else: just because a lot of ignorant monkeys want a monkey of their own sort to do the Union work, and jabber to them, they want to get rid of you, and you eat your heart out about it. More fool you, that's all I say – more fool you. If you cared for your wife and children half what you care about your Union, you'd be a lot better pleased in the end. But you care about nothing but a lot of ignorant colliers, who don't know what they want except it's more money just for themselves. Self, self, self – that's all it is with them – and ignorance.'

'You'd rather have self without ignorance?' he said, smiling finely.

'I would, if I've got to have it. But what I should like to see is a man that has thought for others, and isn't all self and politics.'

Her colour had risen, her hand trembled with anger as she sewed. A blank look had come over the man's face, as if he did not hear or heed any more. He drank his tea in a long draught, wiped his moustache with two fingers, and sat looking abstractedly at the children.

They had laid all the little packets on the floor, and Millicent was saying:

'Now I'll undo the first, and you can have the second. I'll take this – '

She unwrapped the bit of newspaper and disclosed a silvery ornament for a Christmas tree; a frail thing like a silver plum, with deep rosy indentations on each side.

'Oh!' she exclaimed. 'Isn't it *lovely!*'

Her fingers cautiously held the long bubble of silver and glowing rose, cleaving to it with a curious, irritating possession. The man's eyes moved away from her. The lesser child was fumbling with one of the little packets.

'Oh' – a wail went up from Millicent – 'You've taken one! – You didn't wait.' Then her voice changed to a motherly admonition, and she began to interfere. 'This is the way to do it, look! Let me help you.'

But Marjory drew back with resentment.

'Don't, Millicent! – Don't!' came the childish cry. But Millicent's fingers itched.

At length Marjory had got out her treasure – a little silvery bell, with a glass drop hanging inside. The bell was made of frail glassy substance, light as air.

'Oh, the bell!' rang out Millicent's clanging voice. 'The bell! It's my bell. My bell! It's mine! Don't break it, Marjory. Don't break it, will you?'

Marjory was shaking the bell against her ear. But it was dumb, it made no sound.

'You'll break it, I know you will. You'll break it. Give it *me* – ' cried Millicent, and she began to take away the bell. Marjory set up an expostulation.

'*Let her alone!*' said the father.

Millicent let go as if she had been stung, but still her brassy, impudent voice persisted:

'She'll break it. She'll break it. It's *mine* – '

'You undo another,' said the mother, politic.

Millicent began with hasty, itching fingers to unclose another package.

'Aw – aw, mother, my peacock – aw, my peacock, my green peacock!' Lavishly she hovered over a sinuous greenish bird, with wings and tail of spun glass, pearly, and body of deep electric green.

'It's *mine* – my green peacock! It's mine, because Marjory's had one wing off, and mine hadn't. My green peacock that I love! I love it!' She swung it softly from the little ring on its back. Then she went to her mother.

'Look, mother, isn't it a beauty?'

'Mind the ring doesn't come out,' said her mother. 'Lovely!' The girl passed on to her father.

'Look, father, don't you love it!'

'Love it?' he re-echoed, ironical over the word love.

She stood for some moments, trying to force his attention. Then she went back to her place.

Marjory had brought forth a golden apple, red on one cheek, rather garish.

'Oh!' exclaimed Millicent feverishly, instantly seized with desire for what she had not got, indifferent to what she had. Her eye ran quickly over the packages. She took one.

'Now!' she exclaimed loudly, to attract attention. 'Now! What's this? – What's this? What will this beauty be?'

With finicky fingers she removed the newspaper. Marjory watched her wide-eyed. Millicent was self-important.

'The blue ball!' she cried in a climax of rapture. 'I've got *the blue ball*.'

She held it gloating in the cup of her hands. It was a little globe of hardened glass, of a magnificent full dark blue colour. She rose and went to her father.

'It was *your* blue ball, wasn't it, father?'

'Yes.'

'And you had it when you were a little boy, and now I have it when I'm a little girl.'

'Ay,' he replied drily.

'And it's never been broken all those years.'

'No, not yet.'

'And perhaps it never will be broken?'

To this she received no answer.

'Won't it break?' she persisted. 'Can't you break it?'

'Yes, if you hit it with a hammer,' he said.

'Aw!' she cried. 'I don't mean that. I mean if you just drop it. It won't break if you drop it, will it?'

'I daresay it won't.'

'But *will* it?'

'I sh'd think not.'

'Should I try?'

She proceeded gingerly to let the blue ball drop. It bounced dully on the floor-covering.

'Oh – h – h!' she cried, catching it up. 'I love it.'

'Let *me* drop it,' cried Marjory, and there was a performance of admonition and demonstration from the elder sister.

But Millicent must go further. She became excited.

'It won't break,' she said, 'even if you toss it up in the air.'

She flung it up, it fell safely. But her father's brow knitted slightly. She tossed it wildly: it fell with a little splashing explosion: it had smashed. It had fallen on the sharp edge of the tiles that protruded under the fender.

'*Now* what have you done!' cried the mother.

The child stood with her lip between her teeth, a look, half of pure misery and dismay, half of satisfaction, on her pretty, sharp face.

'She wanted to break it,' said the father.

'No, she didn't! What do you say that for!' said the mother. And Millicent burst into a flood of tears.

He rose to look at the fragments that lay splashed on the floor.

'You must mind the bits,' she said, 'and pick 'em all up.' He took one of the pieces to examine it. It was fine and thin and hard, lined with pure silver, brilliant. He looked at it closely. So – this was what it was. And this was the end of it. He felt the curious soft explosion of its breaking still in his ears. He threw his piece in the fire.

'Pick all the bits up,' he said. 'Give over! give over! Don't cry any more.'

The good-natured tone of his voice quieted the child, as he intended it should.

He went away into the back kitchen to wash himself. As he was bending his head over the sink before the little mirror, lathering to shave, there came from outside the dissonant voices of boys, pouring out the dregs of carol-singing.

'While Shep – ep – ep – ep herds watched – '

He held his soapy brush suspended for a minute. They called this singing! His mind flitted back to early carol music. Then again he heard the vocal violence outside.

'Aren't you off there!' he called out in masculine menace. The noise stopped, there was a scuffle. But the feet returned and the voices resumed. Almost immediately the door opened, boys were heard muttering among themselves. Millicent had given them a penny. Feet scraped on the yard, then went thudding along the side of the house, to the street.

To Aaron Sisson this was home, this was Christmas: the

unspeakably familiar. The war over, nothing was changed. Yet everything changed. The scullery in which he stood was painted green, quite fresh, very clean, the floor was red tiles. The wash-copper of red bricks was very red, the mangle with its put-up board was white-scrubbed, the American oilcloth on the table had a gay pattern, there was a warm fire; the water in the boiler hissed faintly. And in front of him, beneath him as he leaned forward shaving, a drop of water fell with strange, incalculable rhythm from the bright brass tap into the white enamelled bowl, which was not half full of pure, quivering water. The war was over, and everything just the same. The acute familiarity of this house, which he had built for his marriage twelve years ago, the changeless pleasantness of it all seemed unthinkable. It prevented his thinking.

When he went into the middle room to comb his hair he found the Christmas tree sparkling, his wife was making pastry at the table, the baby was sitting up propped in cushions.

'Father,' said Millicent, approaching him with a flat blue-and-white angel of cotton-wool, and two ends of cotton – 'tie the angel at the top.'

'Tie it at the top?' he said, looking down.

'Yes. At the very top – because it's just come down from the sky.'

'Ay, my word!' he laughed. And he tied the angel.

Coming downstairs after changing he went into the icy cold parlour, and took his music and a small handbag. With this he retreated again to the back kitchen. He was still in trousers and shirt and slippers: but now it was a clean white shirt, and his best black trousers, and new pink and white braces. He sat under the gas-jet of the back kitchen, looking through his music. Then he opened the bag, in which were sections of a flute and a piccolo. He took out the flute, and adjusted it. As he sat he was physically aware of the sounds of the night: the bubbling of water in the boiler, the faint sound of the gas, the sudden crying of the baby in the next room, then noises outside, distant boys shouting, distant rags of carols, fragments of voices of men. The whole country was roused and excited.

The little room was hot. Aaron rose and opened a square ventilator over the copper, letting in a stream of cold air which was grateful to him. Then he cocked his eye over the sheet of music spread out on the table before him. He tried his flute. And then at last, with the odd gesture of a diver taking a plunge, he swung his head and began to play. A stream of music, soft and rich and fluid, came out of the flute. He played beautifully. He moved his head and his raised bare arms with slight, intense movements, as the delicate music poured out. It was sixteenth-century Christmas melody, very limpid and delicate.

The pure, mindless, exquisite motion and fluidity of the music delighted him with a strange exasperation. There was something tense, exasperated to the point of intolerable anger, in his good-humoured breast, as he played the finely-spun peace-music. The more exquisite the music, the more perfectly he produced it, in sheer bliss; and at the same time, the more intense was the maddened exasperation within him.

Millicent appeared in the room. She fidgetted at the sink. The music was a bugbear to her, because it prevented her from saying what was on her own mind. At length it ended, her father was turning over the various books and sheets. She looked at him quickly, seizing her opportunity.

'Are you going out, father?' she said.

'Eh?'

'Are you going out?' She twisted nervously.

'What do you want to know for?'

He made no other answer, and turned again to the music. His eye went down a sheet – then over it again – then more closely over it again.

'Are you?' persisted the child, balancing on one foot. He looked at her, and his eyes were angry under knitted brows.

'What are you bothering about?' he said.

'I'm not bothering – I only wanted to know if you were going out,' she pouted, quivering to cry.

'I expect I am,' he said quietly.

She recovered at once, but still with timidity asked:

'We haven't got any candles for the Christmas tree – shall *you* buy some, because mother isn't going out?'

'Candles!' he repeated, setting his music and taking up the piccolo.

'Yes – shall you buy us some, father? Shall you?'

'Candles!' he repeated, putting the piccolo to his mouth and blowing a few piercing, preparatory notes.

'Yes, little Christmas-tree candles – blue ones and red ones, in boxes – shall you, father?'

'We'll see – if I see any –'

'But *shall* you?' she insisted desperately. She wisely mistrusted his vagueness.

But he was looking unheeding at the music. Then suddenly the piccolo broke forth, wild, shrill, brilliant. He was playing Mozart. The child's face went pale with anger at the sound. She turned, and went out, closing both doors behind her to shut out the noise.

The shrill, rapid movement of the piccolo music seemed to possess the air, it was useless to try to shut it out. The man went on playing to himself, measured and insistent. In the frosty evening the sound carried. People passing down the street hesitated, listening. The neighbours knew it was Aaron practising his piccolo. He was esteemed a good player: was in request at concerts and dances, also at swell balls. So the vivid piping sound tickled the darkness.

He played on till about seven o'clock: he did not want to go out too soon, in spite of the early closing of the public houses. He never went with the stream, but made a side current of his own. His wife said he was contrary. When he went into the middle room to put on his collar and tie, the two little girls were having their hair brushed, the baby was in bed, there was a hot smell of mince-pies baking in the oven.

'You won't forget our candles, will you father?' asked Millicent, with assurance now.

'I'll see,' he answered.

His wife watched him as he put on his overcoat and hat. He was well-dressed, handsome-looking. She felt there was a curious glamour about him. It made her feel bitter. He had an unfair advantage – he was free to go off, while she must stay at home with the children.

'There's no knowing what time you'll be home,' she said.

'I shan't be late,' he answered.

'It's easy to say so,' she retorted, with some contempt. He took his stick, and turned towards the door.

'Bring the children some candles for their tree, and don't be so selfish,' she said.

'All right,' he said, going out.

'Don't say *All right* if you never mean to do it,' she cried, with sudden anger, following him to the door.

His figure stood large and shadowy in the darkness.

'How many do you want?' he said.

'A dozen,' she said. 'And holders, too, if you can get them,' she added, with barren bitterness.

'Yes – all right,' he turned and melted into the darkness. She went indoors, worn with a strange and bitter flame.

He crossed the fields towards the little town, which once more fumed its lights under the night. The country ran away, rising on his right hand. It was no longer a great bank of darkness. Lights twinkled freely here and there, though forlornly, now that the war-time restrictions were removed. It was no glitter of pre-war nights, pit-heads glittering far-off with electricity. Neither was it the black gulf of the war darkness: instead, this forlorn sporadic twinkling.

Everybody seemed to be out of doors. The hollow dark countryside re-echoed like a shell with shouts and calls and excited voices. Restlessness and nervous excitement, nervous hilarity were in the air. There was a sense of electric sur-charge everywhere, frictional, a neurasthenic haste for excite-ment.

Every moment Aaron Sisson was greeted with Good-night – Good-night, Aaron – Good-night, Mr Sisson. People carrying parcels, children, women, thronged home on the dark paths. They were all talking loudly, declaiming loudly about what they could and could not get, and what this or the other had cost.

When he got into the main street, the only street of shops, it was crowded. There seemed to have been some violent but quiet contest, a subdued fight, going on all the afternoon and evening: people struggling to buy things, to get things. Money was spent like water, there was a frenzy of money-spending. Though the necessities of life were in abundance, still the people struggled in frenzy for cheese, sweets, raisins, pork-stuff, even for flowers and holly, all of which were scarce, and for toys and knick-knacks, which were sold out. There was a wild grumbling, but a deep satisfaction in the fight, the struggle. The same fight and the same satisfaction in the fight was witnessed whenever a tram-car stopped, or when it heaved its way into sight. Then the struggle to mount on board became desperate and savage, but stimulating. Souls surcharged with hostility found now some outlet for their feelings.

As he came near the little market-place he bethought himself of the Christmas-tree candles. He did not intend to trouble himself. And yet, when he glanced in passing into the sweet-shop window, and saw it bare as a board, the very fact that he probably *could not* buy the things made him hesitate, and try.

'Have you got any Christmas-tree candles?' he asked as he entered the shop.

'How many do you want?'

'A dozen.'

'Can't let you have a dozen. You can have two boxes – four in a box – eight. Sixpence a box.'

'Got any holders?'

'Holders? Don't ask. Haven't seen one this year.'

'Got any toffee – ?'

'Cough-drops – twopence an ounce – nothing else left.'

'Give me four ounces.'

He watched her weighing them in the little brass scales.

'You've not got much of a Christmas show,' he said.

'Don't talk about Christmas, as far as sweets is concerned. They ought to have allowed us six times the quantity – there's plenty of sugar, why didn't they? We s'll have to enjoy ourselves with what we've got. We mean to, anyhow.'

'Ay,' he said.

'Time we had a bit of enjoyment, *this* Christmas. They ought to have made things more plentiful.'

'Yes,' he said, stuffing his package in his pocket.

Royal Oak

THE war had killed the little market of the town. As he passed the market place on the brow, Aaron noticed that there were only two miserable stalls. But people crowded just the same. There was a loud sound of voices, men's voices. Men pressed round the doorways of the public-houses.

But he was going to a pub out of town. He descended the dark hill. A street-lamp here and there shed parsimonious light. In the bottoms, under the trees, it was very dark. But a lamp glimmered in front of the 'Royal Oak'. This was a low, white house sunk three steps below the highway. It was darkened, but sounded crowded.

Opening the door, Sisson found himself in the stone passage. Old Bob, carrying three cans, stopped to see who had entered – then went on into the public bar on the left. The bar itself was a sort of little window-sill on the right: the pub was a small one. In this window-opening stood the landlady, drawing and serving to her husband. Behind the bar was a tiny parlour or den, the landlady's preserve.

'Oh, it's you!' she said, bobbing down to look at the new-comer. None entered her bar-parlour unless invited.

'Come in,' said the landlady.

There was a peculiar intonation in her complacent voice, which showed she had been expecting him, a little irritably.

He went across into her bar-parlour. It would not hold more than eight or ten people, all told – just the benches along the walls, the fire between – and two little round tables.

'I began to think you weren't coming,' said the landlady, bringing him a whisky.

She was a large, stout, high-coloured woman, with a fine

profile, probably Jewish. She had chestnut-coloured eyes, quick, intelligent. Her movements were large and slow, her voice laconic.

'I'm not so late, am I?' asked Aaron.

'Yes, you *are* late, I should think.' She looked up at the little clock. 'Close on nine.'

'I did some shopping,' said Aaron, with a quick smile.

'Did you indeed! That's news, I'm sure. May we ask what you bought?'

This he did not like. But he had to answer.

'Christmas-tree candles, and toffee.'

'For the little children? Well, you've done well for once! I must say I recommend you. I didn't think you had so much in you.'

She sat herself down in her seat at the end of the bench, and took up her knitting. Aaron sat next to her. He poured water into his glass, and drank.

'It's warm in here,' he said, when he had swallowed the liquor.

'Yes, it is. You won't want to keep that thick, good overcoat on,' replied the landlady.

'No,' he said, 'I think I'll take it off.'

She watched him as he hung up his overcoat. He wore black clothes, as usual. As he reached up to the pegs, she could see the muscles of his shoulders, and the form of his legs. Her reddish-brown eyes seemed to burn, and her nose, that had a subtle, beautiful Hebraic curve, seemed to arch itself. She made a little place for him by herself, as he returned. She carried her head thrown back, with dauntless self-sufficiency.

There were several colliers in the room, talking quietly. They were the superior type all, favoured by the landlady, who loved intellectual discussion. Opposite, by the fire, sat a little, greenish man – evidently an Oriental.

'You're very quiet all at once, Doctor,' said the landlady in her slow, laconic voice.

'Yes. May I have another whisky, please?'

She rose at once, powerfully energetic.

'Oh, I'm sorry,' she said. And she went to the bar.

'Well,' said the little Hindu doctor, 'and how are things going now, with the men?'

'The same as ever,' said Aaron.

'Yes,' said the stately voice of the landlady. 'And I'm afraid they will always be the same as ever. When will they learn wisdom?'

'But what do you call wisdom?' asked Sherardy, the Hindu. He spoke with a little childish lisp.

'What do I call wisdom?' repeated the landlady. 'Why, all acting together for the common good. That is wisdom in my idea.'

'Yes, very well, that is so. But what do you call the common good?' replied the little doctor, with childish pertinence.

'Ay,' said Aaron, with a laugh, 'that's it.'

The miners were all stirring now, to take part in the discussion.

'What do I call the common good?' repeated the landlady. 'That all people should study the welfare of other people, and not only their own.'

'They are not to study their own welfare?' said the doctor.

'Ah, that I did not say,' replied the landlady. 'Let them study their own welfare, and that of others also.'

'Well then,' said the doctor, 'what is the welfare of a collier?'

'The welfare of a collier,' said the landlady, 'is that he shall earn sufficient wages to keep himself and his family comfortable, to educate his children, and to educate himself; for that is what he wants, education.'

'Ay, happen so,' put in Brewitt, a big, fine, good-humoured collier. 'Happen so, Mrs Houseley. But what if you haven't got much education, to speak of?'

'You can *always* get it,' she said patronizing.

'Nay – I'm blest if you can. It's no use tryin' to educate a man over forty – not by book-learning. That isn't saying he's a fool, neither.'

'And what better is them that's got education?' put in another man. 'What better is the manager, or th'under-manager, than we are? – Pender's yaller enough i' th' face.'

'He is that,' assented the men in chorus.

'But because he's yellow in the face, as you say, Mr Kirk,' said the landlady largely, 'that doesn't mean he has no advantages higher than what you have got.'

'Ay,' said Kirk. 'He can make more money than I can – that's about a' as it comes to.'

'He can make more money,' said the landlady. 'And when he's made it, he knows better how to use it.'

''Appen so, an' a'! – What does he do, more than eat and drink and work? – an' take it out of hisself a sight harder than I do, by th' looks of him. – What's it matter, if he eats a bit more or drinks a bit more –'

'No,' reiterated the landlady. 'He not only eats and drinks. He can read, and he can converse.'

'Me an' a' – ,' said Tom Kirk, and the men burst into a laugh. 'I can read – an' I've had many a talk an' conversation with you in this house, Mrs Houseley – am havin' one at this minute, seemingly.'

'*Seemingly*, you are,' said the landlady ironically. 'But do you think there would be no difference between your conversation and Mr Pender's, if he were here, so that I could *enjoy* his conversation?'

'An' what difference would there be?' asked Tom Kirk. 'He'd go home to his bed just the same.'

'*There*, you are mistaken. He would be the better, and so should I, a great deal better, for a little genuine conversation.'

'If it's conversation as ma'es his behind drop –' said Tom Kirk.

'An' puts th' bile in his face –' said Brewitt.

There was a general laugh.

'I can see it's no use talking about it any further,' said the landlady, lifting her head dangerously.

'But look here, Mrs Houseley, do you really think it makes

much difference to a man, whether he can hold a serious conversation or not?' asked the doctor.

'I do indeed, all the difference in the world. To me, there is no greater difference, than between an educated man and an uneducated man.'

'And where does it come in?' asked Kirk.

'But wait a bit, now,' said Aaron Sisson. 'You take an educated man – take Pender. What's his education for? What does he scheme for? What does he contrive for? What does he talk for.

'For all the purposes of his life,' replied the landlady.

'Ay, an' what's the purpose of his life?' insisted Aaron Sisson.

'The purpose of his life,' repeated the landlady, at a loss. 'I should think he knows that best himself.'

'No better than I know it – and you know it,' said Aaron.

'Well,' said the landlady, 'if you know, then speak out. What is it?'

'To make more money for the firm – and so make his own chance of a rise better.'

The landlady was baffled for some moments. Then she said:

'Yes, and suppose that he does. Is there any harm in it? Isn't it his duty to do what he can for himself? Don't you try to earn all you can?'

'Ay,' said Aaron. 'But there's soon a limit to what I can earn. It's like this. When you work it out, everything comes to money. Reckon it as you like, it's money on both sides. It's money we live for, and money is what out lives is worth – nothing else. Money we live for, and money we are when we're dead: that or nothing. An' it's money as is between the masters and us. There's a few educated ones got hold of one end of the rope, and all the lot of us hanging on to th' other end, an' we s'll go on pulling our guts out, time in, time out –'

'But they've got th' long end o' th' rope, th' masters has,' said Brewitt.

'For as long as one holds, the other will pull,' concluded Aaron Sisson philosophically.

29

'An' I'm almighty sure o' that,' said Kirk.

There was a little pause.

'Yes, that's all there is in the minds of *you men*!' said the landlady. 'But what can be done with the money: that you never think of – the education of the children, the improvement of conditions –'

'Educate the children, so that they can lay hold of the long end of the rope, instead of the short end,' said the doctor, with a little giggle.

'Ay, that's it,' said Brewitt. 'I've pulled at th' short end, an' my lads may do th' same.'

'A selfish policy,' put in the landlady.

'Selfish or not, they may do it.'

'Till the crack o' doom,' said Aaron, with a glistening smile.

'Or the crack o' th' rope,' said Brewitt.

'Yes, and *then what*?' cried the landlady.

'Then we s'll all drop on our backsides,' said Kirk.

There was a general laugh, and an uneasy silence.

'All I can say of you men,' said the landlady, 'is that you have a narrow, selfish policy. Instead of thinking of the children, instead of thinking of improving the world you live in –'

'We hang on, British bulldog breed,' said Brewitt.

There was a general laugh.

'Yes, and little wiser than dogs, wrangling for a bone,' said the landlady.

'Are we to let t'other side run off wi' th' bone, then, while we sit on our stunts an' yowl for it?' asked Brewitt.

'No indeed. There can be wisdom in everything. It's what you *do* with the money, when you've got it,' said the landlady, 'that's where the importance lies.'

'It's Missis as gets it,' said Kirk. 'It doesn't stop wi' us.'

'Ay, it's the wife as gets it, ninety per cent,' they all concurred.

'And who *should* have the money, indeed, if not your wives? They have everything to *do* with the money. What idea have *you*, but to waste it!'

'Women waste nothing – they couldn't if they tried,' said Aaron Sisson.

There was a lull for some minutes. The men were all stimulated by drink. The landlady kept them going. She herself sipped a glass of brandy – but slowly. She sat near to Sisson – and the great fierce warmth of her presence enveloped him particularly. He loved so to luxuriate, like a cat, in the presence of a violent woman. He knew that to-night she was feeling very nice to him – a female glow that came out of her to him. Sometimes when she put down her knitting, or took it up again from the bench beside him, her fingers just touched his thigh, and the fine electricity ran over his body, as if he were a cat tingling at a caress.

And yet he was not happy – nor comfortable. There was a hard, opposing core in him, that neither the whisky nor the woman could dissolve or soothe, to-night. It remained hard, nay became harder and more deeply antagonistic to his surroundings, every moment. He recognized it as a secret malady he suffered from: this strained, unacknowledged opposition to his surroundings, a hard core of irrational, exhausting withholding of himself. Irritating, because he still *wanted* to give himself. A woman and whisky, these were usually a remedy – and music. But lately these had begun to fail him. No, there was something in him that would not give in – neither to the whisky, nor the woman, nor even the music. Even in the midst of his best music, it sat deep established in him, this obstinate black dog, and growled and was never cajoled. He knew of its presence – and was a little uneasy. For, of course, he *wanted* to let himself go; to feel rosy and loving and all that. But at the very thought, the black dog showed its teeth.

Still he kept the beast at bay – with all his will he kept himself as it were genial. He wanted to melt and be rosy, happy.

He sipped his whisky with gratification, he luxuriated in the presence of the landlady, very confident of the strength of her liking for him. He glanced at her profile – that fine throwback of her hostile head, wicked in the midst of her philanthropy; that subtle, really very beautiful delicate curve of her nose, that moved him exactly like a piece of pure sound. But to-night it did not overcome him. There was a devilish little cold eye in his brain that was not taken in by what he saw.

A terrible obstinacy located itself in him. He saw the fine, rich-coloured, secretive face of the Hebrew woman, so loudly self-righteous, and so dangerous, so destructive, so lustful – and he waited for his blood to melt with passion for her. But not to-night. To-night his heart was hard and cold as ice. The very danger and lustfulness of her, which had so pricked his sense, now left him colder. He disliked her at her tricks. He had come to her once too often. To her and to every woman. Bah, the love game! And the whiskey that was to help the game. He had drowned himself once too often in the whisky and in love. Now he floated like a corpse in both, with a cold, hostile eye.

And at least half of his inward fume was anger because he could no longer drown. Nothing would have pleased him better than to have felt his senses swimming and flowing into darkness. But impossible! Cold, with a cold white fury inside him, he floated wide-eyed and apart as a corpse. He though of the gentle love of his first married years, and became only whiter and colder, set in a more intense obstinacy. A wave of revulsion lifted him.

He became aware that he was deadly antagonistic to the landlady, that he disliked the whole circumstances. A cold, diabolical consciousness detached itself from his state of semi-intoxication.

'Is it pretty much the same out there in India?' he asked of the doctor, suddenly.

The doctor started, and attended to him on his own level.

'Probably,' he answered, 'it is worse.'

'Worse!' exclaimed Aaron Sisson. 'How's that?'

'Why, because, in a way the people of India have an easier time even than the people of England. Because they have no responsibility. The British Government takes the responsibility. And the people have nothing to do, except their bit of work – and talk perhaps about national rule, just for a pastime.'

'They have to earn their living?' said Sisson.

'Yes,' said the little doctor, who had lived for some years among the colliers, and become quite familiar with them. 'Yes, they have to earn their living – and then no more. That's why the British Government is the worst thing possible for them. It is the worst thing possible. And not because it is a bad government. Really, it is not a bad government. It is a good one – and they know it – much better than they would make for themselves, probably. But for that reason it is so very bad.'

The little Oriental laughed a queer, sniggering laugh. His eyes were very bright, dilated, completely black. He was looking into the ice-blue, pointed eyes of Aaron Sisson. They were both intoxicated – but grimly so. They looked at each other in elemental difference.

The whole room was now attending to this new conversation, which they all accepted as serious. For Aaron was considered a special man, a man of peculiar understanding, even though as a rule he said little.

'If it is a good government, doctor, how can it be so bad for the people?' said the landlady.

The doctor's eyes quivered for the fraction of a second, as he watched the other man. He did not look at the landlady.

'It would not matter what kind of mess they made – and they would make a mess, if they governed themselves, the people of India. They would probably make the greatest muddle possible – and start killing one another. But it wouldn't matter if they exterminated half the population, so long as they did it themselves, and were responsible for it.'

Again his eyes dilated, utterly black, to the eyes of the other man, and an arch little smile flickered on his face.

'I think it would matter very much indeed,' said the landlady. 'They had far better *not* govern themselves.'

She was, for some reason, becoming angry. The little greenish doctor emptied his glass, and smiled again.

'But what difference does it make,' said Aaron Sisson, 'whether they govern themselves or not? They only live till they die, either way.' And he smiled faintly. He had not really listened to the doctor. The terms 'British Government', and 'bad for the people – good for the people,' made him malevolently angry.

The doctor was nonplussed for a moment. Then he gathered himself together.

'It matters,' he said, 'it matters. People should always be responsible for themselves. How can any people be responsible for themselves? How can any people be responsible for another race, for a race which is even older than they are, and not at all little children?'

Aaron Sisson watched the other dark face, with its utterly exposed eyes. He was in a state of semi-intoxicated anger and clairvoyance. He saw in the black, void, glistening eyes of the Oriental only the same danger, the same menace which he saw in the landlady. Fair, wise, even benevolent words: always the human good speaking, and always underneath, something hateful, something detestable and murderous. Wise speech, and good intentions – they were invariably maggoty with these secret lustful inclinations to destroy the man in a man. Whenever he heard anyone holding forth: the landlady, this doctor, the spokesman at the miners' meeting – or the all-benevolent newspaper – his soul curdled with revulsion as from something foul. Even the infernal goodwill and love of his wife. To hell with good-will. It was more hateful than ill-will. All righteous bullying, like poison-gas!

The landlady looked at the clock.

'Ten minutes to, gentlemen,' she said, coldly. For she too knew that Aaron was spoiled for her for that night.

The men began to take their leave, shakily. The little doctor seemed to evaporate. The landlady helped Aaron on with his coat. She saw the curious whiteness round his nostrils and his eyes, the fixed hellish look on his face.

34

'You'll eat a mince-pie in the kitchen with us, for luck?' she said to him, detaining him till last.

But he turned laughing to her.

'Nay,' he said. 'I must be getting home.'

He turned and went straight out of the house. Watching him, the landlady's face became yellow with passion and rage.

'That little poisonous Indian viper,' she said aloud, attributing Aaron's mood to the doctor. Her husband was noisily bolting the door.

Outside it was dark and frosty. A gang of men lingered in the road near the closed door. Aaron found himself among them, his heart bitterer than steel.

The men were dispersing. He should take the road home. But the devil was in it, if he could take a stride in the homeward direction. There seemed a wall in front of him. He veered. But neither could he take a stride in the opposite direction. So he was destined to veer round, like some sort of weather-cock, there in the middle of the dark road outside the Royal Oak.

But as he turned, he caught sight of a third exit. Almost opposite was the mouth of Shottle Lane, which led off under trees, at right angles to the high-road, up to New Brunswick Colliery. He veered towards the off-chance of this opening, in a delirium of icy fury, and plunged away into the dark lane, walking slowly, on firm legs.

CHAPTER 3

The Lighted Tree

IT is remarkable how many odd or extraordinary people there are in England. We hear continual complaints of the stodgy dullness of the English. It would be quite as just to complain of their freakish, unusual characters. Only *en masse* the metal is all Britannia.

In an ugly little mining town we find the odd ones just as distinct as anywhere else. Only it happens that dull people invariably meet dull people, and odd individuals always come across odd individuals, no matter where they may be. So that to each kind society seems all of a piece.

At one end of the dark, tree-covered Shottle Lane stood the 'Royal Oak' public house; and Mrs Houseley was certainly an odd woman. At the other end of the lane was Shottle House, where the Bricknells lived; the Bricknells were odd, also. Alfred Bricknell, the old man, was one of the partners in the colliery firm. His English was incorrect, his accent broad Derbyshire, and he was not a gentleman in the snobbish sense of the word. Yet he was well-to-do, and very stuck-up. His wife was dead.

Shottle House stood two hundred yards beyond New Brunswick Colliery. The colliery was embedded in a plantation, whence its burning pit-hill glowed, fumed, and stank sulphur in the nostrils of the Bricknells. Even war-time efforts had not put out this refuse-fire. Apart from this, Shottle House was a pleasant, square house, rather old, with shrubberies and lawns. It ended the lane in a dead-end. Only a field-path trekked away to the left.

On this particular Christmas Eve Alfred Bricknell had only two of his children at home. Of the others, one daughter was unhappily married, and away in India weeping herself thinner; another was nursing her babies in Streatham. Jim, the hope of the house, and Julia, now married to Robert Cunningham, had come home for Christmas.

The party was seated in the drawing-room, that the grown-up daughters had made very fine during their periods of courtship. Its walls were hung with fine grey canvas, it had a large, silvery-grey, silky carpet, and the furniture was covered with dark green silky material. Into this reticence pieces of futurism, Omega cushions and Van-Gogh-like pictures exploded their colours. Such *chic* would certainly not have been looked for up Shottle Lane.

The old man sat in his high grey arm-chair very near an enormous coal fire. In this house there was no coal-rationing. The finest coal was arranged to obtain a gigantic glow such as a coal-owner may well enjoy, a great, intense mass of pure red fire. At his fire Alfred Bricknell toasted his tan, lambs-wool-lined slippers.

He was a large man, wearing a loose grey suit, and sprawling in the large grey arm-chair. The soft lamplight fell on his clean, bald, Michelangelo head, across which a few pure hairs glittered. His chin was sunk on his breast, so that his sparse but strong-haired white beard, in which every strand stood distinct, like spun glass, lithe and elastic, curved now upwards and inwards, in a curious curve returning upon him. He seemed to be sunk in stern, prophet-like meditation. As a matter of fact, he was asleep after a heavy meal.

Across, seated on a pouffe on the other side of the fire, was a cameo-like girl with neat black hair done tight and bright in the French mode. She had strangely-drawn eyebrows, and her colour was brilliant. She was hot, leaning back behind the shaft of old marble of the mantelpiece, to escape the fire. She wore a simple dress of apple-green satin, with full sleeves and ample skirt and a tiny bodice of green cloth. This was Josephine Hay, the girl Jim was engaged to.

Jim Bricknell himself was a tall big fellow of thirty-eight. He sat in a chair in front of the fire, some distance back, and stretched his long legs far in front of him. His chin, too, was sunk on his breast, his young forehead was bald, and raised in odd wrinkles, he had a silent half-grin on his face, a little tipsy, a little satyr-like. His small moustache was reddish.

Behind him a round table was covered with cigarettes, sweets, and bottles. It was evident Jim Bricknell drank beer for choice. He wanted to get fat – that was his idea. But he couldn't bring it off: he was thin, though not too thin, except to his own thinking.

His sister Julia was bunched up in a low chair between him and his father. She, too, was a tall stag of a thing, but she sat hunched up like a witch. She wore a wine-purple dress, her arms seemed to poke out of the sleeves, and she had dragged her brown hair into straight, untidy strands. Yet she had real beauty. She was talking to the young man, who was not her husband: a fair, pale, fattish young fellow in pince-nez and dark clothes. This was Cyril Scott, a friend.

The only other person stood at the round table pouring out red wine. He was a fresh, stoutish young Englishman in khaki, Julia's husband. Robert Cunningham was a lieutenant about to be demobilized, when he would become a sculptor once more. He drank red wine in large throatfuls, and his eyes grew a little moist. The room was hot and subdued, everyone was silent.

'I say,' said Robert suddenly, from the rear, 'anybody have a drink? Don't you find it rather hot?'

'Is there another bottle of beer there?' said Jim, without moving, too settled even to stir an eyelid.

'Yes – I think there is,' said Robert.

'Thanks – don't open it yet,' murmured Jim.

'Have a drink, Josephine?' said Robert.

'No thank you,' said Josephine, bowing slightly.

Finding the drinks did not go, Robert went round with the cigarettes. Josephine Ford looked at the white rolls.

'Thank you,' she said, and taking one, suddenly licked

her rather full, dry red lips with the rapid tip of her tongue. It was an odd movement, suggesting a snake's flicker. She put her cigarette between her lips, and waited. Her movements were very quiet and well bred; but perhaps too quiet, they had the dangerous impassivity of the Bohemian, Parisian or American, rather than English.

'Cigarette, Julia?' said Robert to his wife.

She seemed to start or twitch, as if dazed. Then she looked up at her husband with a queer smile, puckering the corners of her eyes. He looked at the cigarettes, not at her. His face had the blunt, voluptuous gravity of a young lion, a great cat. She kept him standing for some moments impassively. Then suddenly she hung her long, delicate fingers over the box, in doubt, and spasmodically jabbed at the cigarettes, clumsily raking one out at last.

'Thank you, dear – thank you,' she cried, rather high, looking up and smiling once more. He turned calmly aside, offering the cigarettes to Scott, who refused.

'Oh!' said Julia, sucking the end of her cigarette. 'Robert is so happy with all the good things – aren't you, dear?' she sang, breaking into a hurried laugh. 'We aren't used to such luxurious living, we aren't – *are we, dear*? No, we're not such swells as this, we're not. Oh *Robbie*, isn't it all right, isn't it just all right!' She tailed off into her hurried, wild, repeated laugh. 'We're so happy in a land of plenty, *aren't we, dear*?'

'Do you mean I'm greedy, Julia?' said Robert.

'Greedy! Oh, greedy! – he asks if he's greedy! No, you're not greedy, Robbie, you're not greedy. I want you to be happy.'

'I'm quite happy,' he returned.

'Oh, he's happy! Really! – he's happy! Oh, what an accomplishment! Oh, my word!' Julia puckered her eyes and laughed herself into a nervous, twitching silence.

Robert went round with the matches. Julia sucked her cigarette.

'Give us a light, Robbie, if you *are* happy!' she cried.

'It's coming,' he answered.

Josephine smoked with short, sharp puffs. Julia sucked wildly at her light. Robert returned to his red wine. Jim Bricknell suddenly roused up, looked round on the company, smiling a little vacuously and showing his odd, pointed teeth.

'Where's the beer?' he asked, in deep tones, smiling full into Josephine's face, as if she were going to produce it by some sleight of hand. Then he wheeled round to the table, and was soon pouring beer down his throat as down a pipe. Then he dropped supine again. Cyril Scott was silently absorbing gin and water.

'I say,' said Jim, from the remote depths of his sprawling. 'Isn't there something we could do to while the time away?'

Everybody suddenly laughed – it sounded so remote and absurd.

'What, play bridge or poker or something conventional of that sort?' said Josephine in her distinct voice, speaking to him as if he were a child.

'Oh, damn bridge,' said Jim in his sleep-voice. Then he began pulling his powerful length together. He sat on the edge of his chair-seat, leaning forward, peering into all the faces and grinning.

'Don't look at me like that – so long –' said Josephine, in her self-contained voice. 'You make me uncomfortable.' She gave an odd little grunt of a laugh, and the tip of her tongue went over her lips as she glanced sharply, half fur-tively, round the room.

'I like looking at you,' said Jim, his smile becoming more malicious.

'But you shouldn't, when I tell you not,' she returned.

Jim twisted round to look at the state of the bottles. The father also came awake. He sat up.

'Isn't it time,' he said, 'that you all put away your glasses and cigarettes, and thought of bed?'

Jim rolled slowly round towards his father, sprawling in the long chair.

'Ah, Dad,' he said, 'to-night's the night! To-night's some

night, Dad. You can sleep any time –' his grin widened – 'but there aren't many nights to sit here – like this – eh?'

He was looking up all the time into the face of his father, full and nakedly lifting his face to the face of his father, and smiling fixedly. The father, who was perfectly sober, except for the contagion from the young people, felt a wild tremor go through his heart as he gazed on the face of his boy. He rose stiffly.

'You want to stay?' he said. 'You want to stay! Well then – well then, I'll leave you. But don't be long.' The old man rose to his full height, rather majestic. The four younger people also rose respectfully – only Jim lay still prostrate in his chair, twisting up his face towards his father.

'You won't stay long,' said the old man, looking round a little bewildered. He was seeking a responsible eye. Josephine was the only one who had any feeling for him.

'No, we won't stay long, Mr Bricknell,' she said gravely.

'Good-night, Dad,' said Jim, as his father left the room.

Josephine went to the window. She had rather a stiff, *poupée* walk.

'How is the night?' she said, as if to change the whole feeling in the room. She pushed back the thick grey silk curtains. 'Why?' she exclaimed. 'What is that light burning? A red light?'

'Oh, that's only the pit-bank on fire,' said Robert, who had followed her.

'How strange! Why is it burning now?'

'It always burns, unfortunately – it is most consistent at it. It is the refuse from the mines. It has been burning for years, in spite of all efforts to the contrary.'

'How very curious! May we look at it?' Josephine now turned the handle of the French windows, and stepped out.

'Beautiful!' they heard her voice exclaim from outside. In the room, Julia laid her hand gently, protectively over the hand of Cyril Scott.

'Josephine and Robert are admiring the night together!' she said, smiling with subtle tenderness to him.

41

'Naturally! Young people always do these romantic things,' replied Cyril Scott. He was twenty-two years old, so he could afford to be cynical.

'Do they? Don't you think it's nice of them?' she said gently removing her hand from his. His eyes were moist with pleasure.

'I do. I envy them enormously. One only needs to be sufficiently naive,' he said.

'One does, doesn't one!' cooed Julia.

'I say, do you hear the bells?' said Robert, poking his head into the room.

'No, dear! Do you?' replied Julia.

'Bells! Hear the bells! Bells!' exclaimed the half-tipsy and self-conscious Jim. And he rolled in his chair in an explosion of sudden, silent laughter, showing his mouthful of pointed teeth, like a dog. Then he gradually gathered himself together, found his feet, smiling fixedly.

'Pretty cool night!' he said aloud, when he felt the air on his almost bald head. The darkness smelt of sulphur.

Josephine and Robert had moved out of sight. Julia was abstracted, following them with her eyes. With almost supernatural kneeness she seemed to catch their voices from the distance.

'Yes, Josephine, *wouldn't* that be *awfully* romantic!' she suddenly called shrilly.

The pair in the distance started.

'What –!' they heard Josephine's sharp exclamation.

'What's that? What would be romantic?' said Jim, as he lurched up and caught hold of Cyril Scott's arm.

'Josephine wants to make a great illumination of the grounds of the estate,' said Julia, magniloquent.

'No – no – I didn't say it,' remonstrated Josephine.

'What Josephine said,' explained Robert, 'was simply that it would be pretty to put candles on one of the growing trees, instead of having a Christmas tree indoors.'

'Oh Josephine, how sweet of you!' cried Julia.

Cyril Scott giggled.

'Good egg! Champion idea, Josey, my lass. Eh? What!' cried Jim. 'Why not carry it out – eh? Why not? Most attractive.' He leaned forward over Josephine, and grinned.

'Oh no!' expostulated Josephine. 'It all sounds so silly now. No. Let us go indoors and go to bed.'

'*No!* Josephine dear – *no!* It's a *lovely* idea!' cried Julia. 'Let's get candles and lanterns and things –'

'Let's!' grinned Jim. 'Let's, everybody – let's!'

'Shall we really?' asked Robert. 'Shall we illuminate one of the fir-trees by the lawn.'

'Yes! How lovely!' cried Julia. 'I'll fetch the candles.'

'The women must put on warm cloaks,' said Robert.

They trooped indoors for coats and wraps and candles and lanterns. Then, lighted by a bicycle lamp, they trooped off to the shed to twist wire round the candles for holders. They clustered round the bench.

'I say,' said Julia, 'doesn't Cyril look like a pilot on a stormy night! Oh I say!' and she went into one of her hurried laughs.

They all looked at Cyril Scott, who was standing sheepishly in the background, in a very large overcoat, smoking a large pipe. The young man was uncomfortable, but assumed a stoic air of philosophic indifference.

Soon they were busy round a prickly fir-tree at the end of the lawn. Jim stood in the background vaguely staring. The bicycle lamp sent a beam of strong white light deep into the uncanny foliage, heads clustered and hands worked. The night above was silent, dim. There was no wind. In the near distance they could hear the panting of some engine at the colliery.

'Shall we light them as we fix them,' asked Robert, 'or save them for one grand rocket at the end?'

'Oh, as we do them,' said Cyril Scott, who had lacerated his fingers and wanted to see some reward.

A match spluttered. One naked little flame sprang alight among the dark foliage. The candle burned tremulously naked. They all were silent.

'We ought to do a ritual dance! We ought to worship the tree,' sang Julia, in her high voice.

'Hold on a minute. We'll have a little more illumination,' said Robert.

'Why, yes. We want more than one candle,' said Josephine.

But Julia had dropped the cloak in which she was huddled, and with arms slung asunder was sliding, waving, crouching in a *pas seul* before the tree, looking like an animated bough herself.

Jim, who was hugging his pipe in the background, broke into a short, harsh, cackling laugh.

'Aren't we fools!' he cried. 'What? Oh God's love, aren't we fools!'

'No – why?' cried Josephine, amused but resentful.

But Jim vouchsafed nothing further, only stood like a Red Indian, gripping his pipe.

The beam of the bicycle-lamp moved and fell about the hands and faces of the young people, and penetrated the recesses of the secret trees. Several little tongues of flame clipped sensitive and ruddy on the naked air, sending a faint glow over the needle foliage. They gave a strange, perpendicular aspiration in the night. Julia waved slowly in her tree dance. Jim stood apart, with his legs straddled, a motionless figure.

The party round the tree became absorbed and excited as more ruddy tongues of flame pricked upward from the dark tree. Pale candles became evident, the air was luminous. The illumination was becoming complete, harmonious.

Josephine suddenly looked round.

'Why – y – y!' came her long note of alarm.

A man in a bowler hat and a black overcoat stood on the edge of the twilight.

'What is it?' cried Julia.

'*Homo sapiens*!' said Robert, the lieutenant. 'Hand the light, Cyril.'

He played the beam of light full on the intruder: a man in a bowler hat, with a black overcoat buttoned to his throat, a pale, dazed, blinking face. The hat was tilted at a slightly jaunty angle over the left eye, the man was well-featured. He did not speak.

'Did you want anything?' asked Robert, from behind the light.

Aaron Sisson blinked, trying to see who addressed him. To him they were all illusory. He did not answer.

'Anything you wanted?' repeated Robert, military, rather peremptory.

Jim suddenly doubled himself up and burst into a loud, harsh cackle of laughter. Whoop! he went, and doubled himself up with laughter. Whoop! whoop! he went, and fell on the ground, and writhed with laughter. He was in that state of intoxication when he could find no release from maddening self-consciousness. He knew what he was doing, he did it deliberately. And yet he was also beside himself, in a sort of hysterics. He could not help himself, in exasperated self-consciousness.

The others all began to laugh, unavoidably. It was a contagion. They laughed helplessly and foolishly. Only Robert was anxious.

'I'm afraid he'll wake the house,' he said, looking at the doubled-up figure of Jim writhing on the grass and whooping loudly.

'No – no!' cried Josephine, weak with laughing in spite of herself. 'No – it's too long – I'm like to die laughing –'

Jim embraced the earth in his convulsions. Even Robert shook quite weakly with laughter. His face was red, his eyes full of dancing water. Yet he managed to articulate:

'I say, you know, you'll bring the old man down.' Then he went off again into spasms.

'Hu! Hu!' whooped Jim, subsiding. 'Hu!' he rolled over on his back, and lay silent. The others also became weakly silent.

'What's amiss?' said Aaron Sisson, breaking this spell. They all began to laugh again, except Jim, who lay on his back looking up at the strange sky.

45

'What're you laughing at?' repeated Aaron.

'We're laughing at the man on the grass,' replied Josephine. 'I think he's drunk a little too much.'

'Or not enough,' put in Cyril Scott. He twigged Jim's condition.

'Ay,' said Aaron, standing mute and obstinate.

'Did you want anything?' Robert enquired once more.

'Eh?' Aaron looked up, 'Me? No, not me.' A sort of inertia kept him rooted. The young people looked at one another and began to laugh, rather embarrassed.

'Another!' said Cyril Scott cynically.

They wished the stranger would go away. There was a pause.

'What do you reckon stars are?' asked the sepulchral voice of Jim. He still lay flat on his back on the grass.

Josephine went to him and pulled at his coat.

'Get up,' she said. 'You'll take cold. Get up now, we're going indoors.'

'What do you reckon stars are?' he persisted.

Aaron Sisson stood on the edge of the light, smilingly staring at the scene, like a boy out of his place, but stubbornly keeping his ground.

'Get up now,' said Josephine. 'We've had enough.' But Jim would not move.

Robert went with the bicycle lamp and stood at Aaron's side.

'Shall I show you a light to the road – you're off your track,' he said. 'You're in the grounds of Shottle House.'

'I can find my road,' said Aaron. 'Thank you.'

Jim suddenly got up and went to peer at the stranger, poking his face close to Aaron's face.

'Right-o,' he remarked. 'You're not half a bad sort of chap. Cheery-o! What's your drink?'

'Mine – whisky,' said Aaron.

'Come in and have one. We're the only sober couple in the bunch – what?' cried Jim.

Aaron stood unchanged, static in everything. Jim took

him by the arm affectionately. The stranger looked at the flickering tree, with its tiers of lights.

'A Christmas tree,' he said, jerking his head and smiling.

'That's right, old man,' said Jim, seeming thoroughly sober now. 'Come indoors and have a drink.'

Aaron Sisson negatively allowed himself to be led off. The others followed in silence, leaving the tree to flicker the night through. The stranger stumbled at the open window-door.

'Mind the step,' said Jim affectionately.

They crowded to the fire, which was still hot. The newcomer looked round vaguely. Jim took Aaron's bowler hat and gave him a chair. He sat without looking round, a remote, abstract look on his face. He was very pale, and seemed inwardly absorbed.

The party threw off their wraps and sat around. Josephine turned to Aaron Sisson, who sat with a glass of whisky in his hands, rather slack in his chair, in his thickish overcoat. He did not want to drink. His hair was blond, quite tidy, his mouth and chin handsome, but a little obstinate, his eyes inscrutable. His pallor was not natural to him. Though he kept the appearance of a smile, underneath he was hard and opposed. He did not wish to be with these people, and yet, mechanically, he stayed.

'Do you feel quite well?' Josephine asked him.

He looked at her quickly.

'Me?' he said. He smiled faintly. 'Yes, I'm all right.' Then he dropped his head again and seemed oblivious.

'Tell us your name,' said Jim affectionately.

The stranger looked up.

'My name's Aaron Sisson, if it's anything to you,' he said.

Jim began to grin.

'It's a name I don't know,' he said. Then he named all the party present. But the stranger hardly heeded, though his eyes looked curiously from one to the other, slow, shrewd, clairvoyant.

'Were you on your way home?' asked Robert, huffy.

The stranger lifted his head and looked at him.

'Home!' he repeated. 'No. The other road.' He indicated the direction with his head, and smiled faintly.

'Beldover?' inquired Robert.

'Yes.'

He had dropped his head again, as if he did not want to look at them.

To Josephine, the pale, impassive, blank-seeming face, the blue eyes with the smile which wasn't a smile, and the continual dropping of the well-shaped head was curiously affecting. She wanted to cry.

'Are you a miner?' Robert asked, *de haut en bas*.

'No,' cried Josephine. She had looked at his hands.

'Men's checkweightman,' replied Aaron. He had emptied his glass. He put it on the table.

'Have another?' said Jim, who was attending fixedly, with curious absorption, to the stranger.

'No,' cried Josephine, 'no more.'

Aaron looked at Jim, then at her, and smiled slowly, with remote bitterness. Then he lowered his head again. His hands were loosely clasped between his knees.

'What about the wife?' said Robert – the young lieutenant. 'What about the wife and kiddies? You're a married man, aren't you?'

The sardonic look of the stranger rested on the subaltern.

'Yes,' he said.

'Won't they be expecting you?' said Robert, trying to keep his temper and his tone of authority.

'I expect they will.'

'Then you'd better be getting along, hadn't you?'

The eyes of the intruder rested all the time on the flushed subaltern. The look on Aaron's face became slowly satirical.

'Oh, dry up the army touch,' said Jim contemptuously, to Robert. 'We're all civvies here. We're all right, aren't we?' he said loudly, turning to the stranger with a grin that showed his pointed teeth.

Aaron gave a brief laugh of acknowledgment.

'How many children have you?' sang Julia from her distance.

'Three.'

'Girls or boys?'

'Girls.'

'All girls? Dear little things! How old?'

'Oldest's eight – youngest nine months –'

'So small!' sang Julia, with real tenderness now.

Aaron dropped his head.

'But you're going home to them, aren't you?' said Josephine, in whose eyes the tears had already risen. He looked up at her, at her tears. His face had the same pale, perverse smile.

'Not to-night,' he said.

'But why? You're wrong!' cried Josephine.

He dropped his head and became oblivious.

'Well!' said Cyril Scott, rising at last with a bored exclamation, 'I think I'll retire.'

'Will you?' said Julia, also rising. 'You'll find your candle outside.'

She went out. Scott bade good-night, and followed her. The four people remained in the room, quite silent. Then Robert rose and began to walk about, agitated.

'Don't you go back to 'em. Have a night out. You stop here to-night,' Jim said suddenly, in a quiet, intimate tone.

The stranger turned his head and looked at him, considering.

'Yes?' he said. He seemed to be smiling coldly.

'Oh, but!' cried Josephine. 'Your wife and your children! Won't they be awfully bothered? Isn't it awfully unkind to them?'

She rose in her eagerness. He sat turning up his face to her. She could not understand his expression.

'Won't you go home to them?' she said, hysterical.

'Not to-night,' he replied quietly, again smiling.

'You're wrong!' she cried. 'You're wrong!'

And so she hurried out of the room in tears.

'Er – what bed do you propose to put him in?' asked Robert, rather officer-like.

'Don't propose at all, my lad,' replied Jim ironically – he did not like Robert. Then to the stranger he said: 'You'll be all right on the couch in my room? – it's a good couch, big enough, plenty of rugs –' His voice was easy and intimate.

Aaron looked at him, and nodded.

They had another drink each, and at last the two set off, rather stumbling, upstairs. Aaron carried his bowler hat with him.

Robert remained pacing in the drawing-room for some time. Then he went out, to return in a little while. He extinguished the lamps and saw that the fire was safe. Then he went to fasten the window-doors securely. Outside he saw the uncanny glimmer of candles across the lawn. He had half a mind to go out and extinguish them – but he did not. So he went upstairs and the house was quiet. Faint crumbs of snow were falling outside.

When Jim woke in the morning Aaron had gone. Only on the floor were two packets of Christmas-tree candles, fallen from the stranger's pockets. He had gone through the drawing-room door, as he had come. The housemaid said that while she was cleaning the grate in the dining-room she heard someone go into the drawing-room: a parlourmaid had even seen someone come out of Jim's bedroom. But they had both thought it was Jim himself, for he was an unsettled house-mate.

There was a thin film of snow, a lovely Christmas morning.

CHAPTER 4

The Pillar of Salt

OUR story will not yet see daylight. A few days after Christmas, Aaron sat in the open shed at the bottom of his own garden, looking out on the rainy darkness. No one knew he was there. It was some time after six in the evening.

From where he sat, he looked straight up the garden to the house. The blind was not drawn in the middle kitchen, he could see the figures of his wife and one child. There was a light also in the upstairs window. His wife was gone upstairs again. He wondered if she had the baby ill. He could see her figure vaguely behind the lace curtains of the bedroom. It was like looking at his home through the wrong end of a telescope. Now the little girls had gone from the middle room: only to return in a moment.

His attention strayed. He watched the light falling from the window of the next-door house. Uneasily, he looked along the whole range of houses. The street sloped down-hill, and the backs were open to the fields. So he saw a curious succession of lighted windows, between which jutted the intermediary back premises, scullery and outhouse, in dark little blocks. It was something like the keyboard of a piano: more still, like a succession of musical notes. For the rectangular planes of light were of different intensities, some bright and keen, some soft, warm, like candle-light, and there was one surface of pure red light, one or two were almost invisible, dark green. So the long scale of lights seemed to trill across the darkness, now bright, now dim, swelling and sinking. The effect was strange.

And thus the whole private life of the street was threaded in lights. There was a sense of indecent exposure, from so many backs. He felt himself almost in physical contact with this contiguous stretch of back premises. He heard the familiar sound of water gushing from the sink into the grating, the dropping of a pail outside the door, the clink of a coal shovel, the banging of a door, the sound of voices. So many houses cheek by jowl, so many squirming lives, so many back yards, back doors giving on to the night. It was revolting.

Away in the street itself, a boy was calling the newspaper: – *'ning Post! – 'ning Po-o-ost!* It was a long, melancholy howl, and seemed to epitomize the whole of the dark, wet, secretive, thickly-inhabited night. A figure passed the window of Aaron's own house, entered, and stood inside the room talking to Mrs Sisson. It was a young woman in a brown mackintosh and a black hat. She stood under the incandescent light, and her hat nearly knocked the globe. Next door a man had run out in his shirt-sleeves: a young, dark-headed collier running to the gate for a newspaper, running bareheaded, coatless, slippered, in the rain. He had got his news-sheet, and was returning. And just at that moment the young man's wife came out, shading her candle with a lading tin. She was going to the coal-house for some coal. Her husband passed her on the threshold. She could be heard breaking the bits of coal and placing them on the dustpan. The light from her candle fell faintly behind her. Then she went back, blown by a swirl of wind. But again she was at the door, hastily standing her iron shovel against the wall. Then she shut the back door with a bang. These noises seemed to scrape and strike the night.

In Aaron's own house, the young person was still talking to his wife. Millicent came out, sheltering a candle with her hand. The candle blew out. She ran indoors, and emerged again, her white pinafore fluttering. This time she performed her little journey safely. He could see the faint glimmer of her candle emerging secretly from the closet.

The young person was taking her leave. He could hear her sympathetic – 'Well – good-night I hope she'll be no worse. Good-night, Mrs Sisson!' She was gone – he heard the windy bang of the street-gate. Presently Millicent emerged again, flitting indoors.

So he rose to his feet, balancing, swaying a little before he started into motion, as so many colliers do. Then he moved along the path towards the house, in the rain and darkness, very slowly edging forwards.

Suddenly the door opened. His wife emerged with a pail. He stepped quietly aside, on to his side garden, among the sweet herbs. He could smell rosemary and sage and hyssop. A low wall divided his garden from his neighbour's. He put his hand on it, on its wetness, ready to drop over should his wife come forward. But she only threw the contents of her pail on the garden and retired again. She might have seen him had she looked. He remained standing where he was, listening to the trickle of rain in the water-butt. The hollow countryside lay beyond him. Sometimes in the windy darkness he could see the red burn of New Brunswick bank, or the brilliant jewels of light clustered at Bestwood Colliery. Away in the dark hollow, nearer, the glare of the electric power station disturbed the night. So again the wind swirled the rain across all these hieroglyphs of the countryside, familiar to him as his own breast.

A motor-car was labouring up the hill. His trained ear attended to it unconsciously. It stopped with a jar. There was a bang of the yard-gate. A shortish, dark figure in a bowler hat passed the window. Millicent was drawing down the blind. It was the doctor. The blind was drawn, he could see no more.

Stealthily he began to approach the house. He stood by the climbing rose of the porch, listening. He heard voices upstairs. Perhaps the children would be downstairs. He listened intently. Voices were upstairs only. He quietly opened the door. The room was empty, save for the baby, who was cooing in her cradle. He crossed to the hall. At the foot of the stairs he could hear the voice of the Indian doctor: 'Now, little girl, you must just keep still and warm in bed, and not cry for the moon.' He said '*de* moon' just as ever. Marjory must be ill.

So Aaron quietly entered the parlour. It was a cold, clammy room, dark. He could hear footsteps passing outside on the asphalt pavement below the window, and the wind howling with familiar cadence. He began feeling for something in the darkness of the music-rack beside the piano. He touched and felt – he could not find what he wanted. Perplexed, he turned and looked out of the window. Through the iron railing of the front wall he could see the little motor-car sending its straight beams of light in front of it, up the street.

He sat down on the sofa by the window. The energy had suddenly left all his limbs. He sat with his head sunk, listening. The familiar room, the familiar voice of his wife and his children – he felt weak as if he were dying. He felt weak, like a drowning man who acquiesces in the waters. His strength was gone, he was sinking back. He would sink back to it all, float henceforth like a drowned man.

So he heard voices coming nearer from upstairs, feet moving. They were coming down.

'No, Mrs Sisson, you needn't worry,' he heard the voice of the doctor on the stairs. 'If she goes on as she is, she'll be all right. Only she must be kept warm and quiet – warm and quiet – that's the chief thing.'

'Oh, when she has those bouts I can't bear it.' Aaron heard his wife's voice.

They were downstairs. Their feet click-clicked on the tiled passage. They had gone into the middle room. Aaron sat and listened.

'She won't have any more bouts. If she does, give her a few drops from the little bottle, and raise her up. But she won't have any more,' the doctor said.

'If she does, I s'll go off my head, I know I shall.'

'No you won't. No you won't do anything of the sort. You won't go off your head. You'll keep your head on your shoulders, where it ought to be,' protested the doctor.

'But it nearly drives me mad.'

'Then don't let it. The child won't die, I tell you. She will be all right, with care. Who have you got sitting up with her? You're not to sit up with her to-night, I tell you. Do you hear me?'

'Miss Smitham's coming in. But it's no good – I shall have to sit up. I shall *have* to.'

'I tell you you won't. You obey *me*. I know what's good for you as well as for her. I am thinking of you as much as of her.'

'But I can't bear it – all alone.' This was with the beginning of tears. There was a dead silence – then a sound of Millicent weeping with her mother. As a matter of fact, the doctor was weeping too, for he was an emotional, sympathetic soul, over forty.

'Never mind – never mind – you aren't alone,' came the doctor's matter-of-fact voice, after a loud nose-blowing. 'I am here to help you. I will do whatever I can – whatever I can.'

'I can't bear it. I can't bear it,' wept the woman. Another silence, another nose-blowing, and again the doctor:

'You'll *have* to bear it – I tell you there's nothing else for it. You'll have to bear it – but we'll do our best for you. I will do my best for you – always – *always* – in sickness or out of sickness – There!'

He pronounced *there* oddly, not quite *dhere*.

'You haven't heard from your husband?' he added.

'I had a letter' – sobs – 'from the bank this morning.'

'*From de bank?*,'

'Telling me they were sending me so much per month, from him, as an allowance, and he was quite well, but he was travelling.'

'Well then, why not let him travel? You can live.'

'But to leave me *alone!*' there was burning indignation in her voice. 'To go off and leave me with every responsibility, to leave me with all the burden.'

'Well, I wouldn't trouble about him. Aren't you better off without him?'

'I am. I am,' she cried fiercely. 'When I got that letter this morning, I said, *May evil befall you, you selfish demon*. And I hope it may.'

'Well – well, well – well, don't fret. Don't be angry, it won't make it any better, I tell you.'

'Angry! I *am* angry. I'm worse than angry. A week ago I hadn't a grey hair in my head. Now look here –' There was a pause.

'Well – well, well – well, never mind. You will be all right, don't you bother. Your hair is beautiful anyhow.'

'What makes me so mad is that he should go off like that – never a word – coolly takes his hook. I could kill him for it.'

'Were you ever happy together?'

'We were all right at first. I know I was fond of *him*. But he'd kill anything. He kept himself back, always kept himself back, couldn't give himself –'

There was a pause.

'Ah well,' sighed the doctor. 'Marriage is a mystery. I'm glad I'm not entangled in it.'

'Yes, to make some woman's life a misery. I'm sure it was death to live with him, he seemed to kill everything off inside you. He was a man you couldn't quarrel with, and get it over. Quiet – quiet in his tempers, and selfish through and through. I've lived with him twelve years – I know what it is. Killing! You don't know what he was –'

'I think I knew him. A fair man? Yes?' said the doctor.

'Fair look at. There's a photograph of him in the parlour – taken when he was married – and one of me. Yes, he's fair-haired.'

Aaron guessed that she was getting a candle to come into the parlour. He was tempted to wait and meet them – and accept it all again. Devilishly tempted, he was. Then he thought of her voice, and his heart went cold. Quick as thought he obeyed his first impulse. He felt behind the couch, on the floor where the curtains fell. Yes – the bag was there. He took it at once. In the next breath he stepped out of the room and tip-toed into the passage. He retreated to the far end, near the street door, and stood behind the coats that hung on the hall-stand.

At that moment his wife came into the passage, holding a candle. She was red-eyed with weeping, and looked frail.

'Did you leave the parlour door open?' she asked of Millicent, suspiciously.

'No,' said Millicent from the kitchen.

The doctor, with his soft, Oriental tread, followed Mrs Sisson into the parlour. Aaron saw his wife hold up the candle before his portrait, and begin to weep. But he knew her. The doctor laid his hand softly on her arm, and left it there, sympathetically. Nor did he remove it when Millicent stole into the room, looking very woe begone and important. The wife wept silently, and the child joined in.

'Yes, I know him,' said the doctor. 'If he thinks he will be happier when he's gone away, you must be happier too, Mrs Sisson. That's all. Don't let him triumph over you by making you miserable. You enjoy yourself as well. You're only a girl.'

But a tear came from his eye, and he blew his nose vigorously on a large white silk handkerchief, and began to polish his *pince-nez*. Then he turned, and they all bundled out of the room.

The doctor took his departure. Mrs Sisson went almost immediately upstairs, and Millicent shortly crept after her. Then Aaron, who had stood motionless as if turned to a pillar of salt, went quietly down the passage and into the living room. His face was very pale, ghastly-looking. He caught a glimpse of himself in the mirror over the mantel, as he passed, and felt weak, as if he were really a criminal. But his heart did not relax, nevertheless. So he hurried into the night, down the garden, climbed the fence into the field, and went away across the field in the rain, towards the high-road.

He felt sick in every fibre. He almost hated the little handbag he carried, which held his flute and piccolo. It seemed a burden just then – a millstone round his neck. He hated the scene he had left – and he hated the hard, inviolable heart that stuck unchanging in his own breast.

Coming to the high-road, he saw a tall, luminous tramcar roving along through the rain. The trams ran across country from town to town. He dared not board, because people knew him. So he took a side road, and walked in a detour for two miles. Then he came out on the high-road again, and waited for a tram-car. The rain blew on his face. He waited a long time for the last car.

At the Opera

A FRIEND had given Josephine Ford a box at the opera for one evening: our story continues by night. The box was large and important, near the stage. Josephine and Julia were there, with Robert and Jim – also two more men. The women sat in front of the box, conspicuously. They were both poor, they were rather excited. But they belonged to a set which looked on social triumphs as a downfall that one allows oneself. The two men, Lilly and Struthers, were artists, the former literary, the latter a painter. Lilly sat by Josephine in front of the box: he was her little lion of the evening.

Few women can sit in front of a big box, on a crowded and noisy opera night, without thrilling and dilating. There is an intoxication in being thus thrust forward, conspicuous and enhanced, right in the eye of the vast crowd that lines the hollow shell of the auditorium. Thus even Josephine and Julia leaned their elbows and poised their heads regally, looking condescendingly down upon the watchful world. They were two poor women, having nothing to do with society. Half Bohemians.

Josephine was an artist. In Paris she was a friend of a very fashionable dressmaker and decorator, master of modern elegance. Sometimes she designed dresses for him, and sometimes she accepted from him a commission to decorate a room. Usually at her last sou, it gave her pleasure to dispose of costly and exquisite things for other people, and then be rid of them.

This evening her dress was a simple, but a marvellously poised thing of black and silver: in the words of the correct journal. With her tight, black, bright hair, her arched brows, her dusky-ruddy face and her bare shoulders; her strange equanimity, her long, slow, slanting looks; she looked foreign and frightening, clear as a cameo, but dark, far off. Julia was the English beauty, in a lovely blue dress. Her hair was becoming untidy on her low brow, her dark blue eyes wandered and got excited, her nervous mouth twitched. Her high-pitched, sing-song voice and her hurried laugh could be heard in the theatre. She twisted a beautiful little fan that a dead artist had given her.

Not being fashionable, they were in the box when the overture began. The opera was Verdi – *Aïda*. If it is impossible to be in an important box at the opera without experiencing the strange intoxication of fashionable pre-eminence, it is just as impossible to be there without some feeling of horror at the sight the stage presents.

Josephine leaned her elbow and looked down: she knew how arresting that proud, rather stiff bend of her head was, She had some aboriginal American in her blood. But as she looked, she pursed her mouth. The artist in her forgot everything, she was filled with disgust. The sham Egypt of *Aïda* hid from her nothing of its shame. The singers were all colour-washed, deliberately colour-washed to a bright orange tint. The men had oblong dabs of black wool under their lower lip; the beard of the mighty Pharaohs. This oblong dab shook and wagged to the singing.

The vulgar bodies of the fleshy women were unendurable. They all looked such good meat. Why were their haunches so prominent? It was a question Josephine could not solve. She scanned their really expensive brilliant clothing. It was *nearly* right – nearly splendid. It only lacked that last subtlety which the world always lacks, the last final clinching which puts calm into a sea of fabric, and yet is the opposite pole to machine fixity.

But the leading tenor was the chief pain. He was large, stout, swathed in a cummerbund, and looked like a eunuch. This fattish, emasculated look seems common in stage heroes – even the extremely popular. The tenor sang bravely, his mouth made a large coffin-shaped, yawning gap in his orange face, his little beard fluttered oddly, like a tail. He turned up his eyes to Josephine's box as he sang – that being the regulation direction. Meanwhile his abdomen shook as he caught his breath, the flesh of his fat naked arms swayed.

Josephine looked down with the fixed gravity of a Red Indian, immovable, inscrutable. It was not till the scene was ended that she lifted her head as if breaking a spell, sent the point of her tongue rapidly over her dried lips, and looked round into the box. Her brown eyes expressed shame, fear, and disgust. A curious grimace went over her face – a grimace only to be expressed by the exclamation *Merde!* But she was mortally afraid of society, and its fixed institutions. Rapidly she scanned the eyes of her friends in the box. She rested on the eyes of Lilly, a dark, ugly man.

'Isn't it nasty?' she said.

'You shouldn't look so closely,' he said. But he took it calmly, easily, whilst she felt floods of burning disgust, a longing to destroy it all.

'Oh – ho – ho!' laughed Julia. 'It's so fu-nny – so funny!'

'Of course we are too near,' said Robert.

'Say you admire that pink fondant over there,' said Struthers, indicating with his eyebrows a blonde large woman in white satin with pink edging, who sat in a box opposite, on the upper tier.

'Oh the fondant – exactly – the fondant! Yes, I admire her immensely! Isn't she exactly *it!*' sang Julia.

Josephine was scanning the auditorium. So many myriads of faces – like beads on a bead-work pattern – all bead-work, in different layers. She bowed to various acquaintances – mostly Americans in uniform, whom she had known in Paris. She smiled to Lady Cochrane, two boxes off – Lady Cochrane had given her the box. But she felt rather coldly towards her.

The curtain rose, the opera wound its slow length along. The audience loved it. They cheered with mad enthusiasm.

Josephine looked down on the choppy sea of applause, white gloves clapping, heads shaking. The noise was strange and rattling. What a curious multiple object a theatre-audience was! It seemed to have a million heads, a million hands, and one monstrous, unnatural consciousness. The singers appeared before the curtain – the applause rose up like clouds of dust.

'Oh, isn't it *too wonderful!*' cried Julia. 'I am wild with excitement. Are you all of you?'

'Absolutely wild,' said Lilly laconically.

'Where is Scott to-night?' asked Struthers.

Julia turned to him and gave him a long, queer look from her dark blue eyes.

'He's in the country,' she said, rather enigmatic.

'Don't you know, he's got a house down in Dorset,' said Robert, verbally rushing in. 'He wants Julia to go down and stay.'

'Is she going?' said Lilly.

'She hasn't decided,' replied Robert.

'Oh! What's the objection?' asked Struthers.

'Well, none whatsoever, as far as can be seen, except that she can't make up her mind,' replied Robert.

'Julia's got no mind,' said Jim rudely.

'Oh! Hear the brotherly verdict!' laughed Julia hurriedly.

'You mean go down to Dorset alone?' said Struthers.

'Why not?' replied Robert, answering for her.

'And stay how long?'

'Oh – as long as it lasts,' said Robert again.

'Starting with eternity,' said Lilly, 'and working back to a fortnight.

'And what's the matter? – looks bad in the eyes of the world?'

'Yes – about that. Afraid of compromising herself –'

Lilly looked at them.

'Depends what you take the world to mean. Do you mean us in this box, or the crew outside there?' he jerked his head towards the auditorium.

'Do you think, Lilly, that we're the world?' said Robert ironically.

'Oh yes. I guess we're shipwrecked in this box, like Robinson Crusoes. And what we do on our own little island matters to us alone. As for the infinite crowds of howling savages outside there in the unspeakable, all you've got to do is to mind they don't scalp you.'

'But *won't* they?' said Struthers.

'Not unless you put your head in their hands,' said Lilly.

'I don't know –' said Jim.

But the curtain had risen, they hushed him into silence.

All through the next scene Julia puzzled herself, as to whether she should go down to the country and live with Scott. She had carried on a nervous kind of *amour* with him, based on soul sympathy and emotional excitement. But whether to go and live with him? She didn't know if she wanted to or not: and she couldn't for her life find out. She was in that nervous state when desire seems to evaporate the moment fulfilment is offered. When the curtain dropped she turned.

'You see,' she said, screwing up her eyes, 'I have to think of Robert.' She cut the word in two, with an odd little hitch in her voice – Rob-ert.'

'My dear Julia, can't you believe that I'm *tired* of being thought of,' cried Robert, flushing.

Julia screwed up her eyes in a slow smile, oddly cogitating.

'Well, who *am* I to think of?' she asked.

'Yourself,' said Lilly.

'Oh yes! Why yes! I never thought of that!' She gave a hurried little laugh. 'But then it's no *fun* to think about oneself,' she cried flatly. 'I think about Rob-ert, and Scott!' She screwed up her eyes and peered oddly at the company.

'Which of them will find you the greatest treat,' said Lilly sarcastically.

'Anyhow,' interjected Robert nervously, 'it will be something new for Scott.'

63

'Stale buns for you, old boy,' said Jim drily.

'I don't say so. But –' exclaimed the flushed, full-blooded Robert, who was nothing if not courteous to women.

'How long ha' you been married? Eh?'asked Jim.

'Six years!' sang Julia sweetly.

'Good God!'

'You see,' said Robert, 'Julia can't decide anything for herself. She waits for someone else to decide, then she puts her spoke in.'

'Put it plainly –' began Struthers.

'But don't you know, it's no *use* putting it plainly,' cried Julia.

'But *do* you want to be with Scott, out and out, or *don't* you?' said Lilly.

'Exactly!' chimed Robert. 'That's the question for you to answer, Julia.'

'I *won't* answer it,' she cried. 'Why should I?'

And she looked away into the restless hive of the theatre. She spoke so wildly that she attracted attention. But it half pleased her. She stared abstractedly down at the pit.

The men looked at one another in some comic consternation.

'Oh damn it all!' said the long Jim, rising and stretching himself. 'She's dead nuts on Scott. She's all over him. She'd have eloped with him weeks ago if it hadn't been so easy. She can't stand it that Robert offers to hand her into the taxi.'

He gave his malevolent grin round the company, then went out. He did not reappear for the next scene.

'Of course, if she loves Scott –' began Struthers.

Julia suddenly turned with wild desperation, and cried:

'I like him tremendously – tre-men-dous-ly! He *does* understand.'

'Which we don't,' said Robert.

Julia smiled her long, odd smile in their faces: one might almost say she smiled in their teeth.

'What do *you* think, Josephine?' asked Lilly.

Josephine was leaning forward. She started. Her tongue went rapidly over her lips. 'Who? I?' she exclaimed.

'Yes.'

'I think Julia should go with Scott,' said Josephine. 'She'll bother with the idea till she's done it. She loves him, really.'

'Of course she does,' cried Robert.

Julia, with her chin resting on her arms, in a position which irritated the neighbouring Lady Cochrane sincerely, was gazing with unseeing eyes down upon the stalls.

'Well then –' began Struthers. But the music struck up softly. They were all rather bored. Struthers kept on making small, half audible remarks – which was bad form, and displeased Josephine, the hostess of the evening.

When the curtain came down for the end of the act, the men got up. Lilly's wife, Tanny, suddenly appeared. She had come on after a dinner engagement.

'Would you like tea or anything?' Lilly asked.

The women refused. The men filtered out on to the crimson and white, curving corridor. Julia, Josephine and Tanny remained in the box. Tanny was soon hitched on to the conversation in hand.

'Of course,' she replied, 'one can't decide such a thing like drinking a cup of tea.'

'Of course one can't, dear Tanny,' said Julia.

'After all, one doesn't leave one's husband every day, to go and live with another man. Even if one looks on it as an experiment –'

'It's difficult!' cried Julia. 'It's difficult! I feel they all want to *force* me to decide. It's cruel.'

'Oh, men with their beastly logic, their either-this-or-that stunt, they are an awful bore. But, of course, Robert can't love you *really*, or he'd want to keep you. I can see Lilly discussing such a thing for *me*. But then you don't love Robert either,' said Tanny.

'I do! Oh, I do, Tanny! I *do* love him, I love him dearly. I think he's beautiful. Robert's beautiful. And he *needs* me. And I need him, too. I need his support. Yes, I do love him.'

'But you like Scott better,' said Tanny.

'Only because he – he's different,' sang Julia, in long tones. 'You see, Scott has his art. His art matters. And *Rob*-ert – Robert is a dilettante, don't you think – he's dilettante –' She screwed up her eyes at Tanny. Tanny cogitated.

'Of course I don't think that matters,' she replied.

'But it does, it matters tremendously, dear Tanny, tremendously.'

'Of course,' Tanny sheered off, 'I can see Scott has great attractions – a great warmth somewhere –'

'Exactly!' cried Julia. 'He *understands* –'

'And I believe he's a real artist. You might even work together. You might write his librettos.'

'Yes! – Yes! –' Julia spoke with a long, pondering hiss.

'It might be *awfully* nice,' said Tanny rapturously.

'Yes! – It might! – It might! –' pondered Julia. Suddenly she gave herself a shake. Then she laughed hurriedly, as if breaking from her line of thought.

'And wouldn't Robert be an *awfully* nice lover for Josephine! Oh, wouldn't that be splendid!' she cried, with her high laugh.

Josephine, who had been gazing down into the orchestra, turned now, flushing darkly.

'But I don't want a lover, Julia,' she said, hurt.

'Josephine, *dear*! Dear old Josephine! Don't you really! Oh, yes you do. I want one so *badly!*,' cried Julia, with her shaking laugh. 'Robert's awfully *good* to me. But we've been married six years. And it does make a difference, doesn't it, Tanny dear?'

'A great difference,' said Tanny.

'Yes, it makes a difference, it makes a difference,' mused Julia. 'Dear old *Rob*-ert – I wouldn't hurt him for worlds. I wouldn't. Do you think it would hurt Robert?'

She screwed up her eyes, looking at Tanny.

'Perhaps it would do Robert good to be hurt a little,' said Tanny. 'He's so well nourished.'

'Yes! Yes! I see what you mean, Tanny! Poor old R*ob*-ert! Oh, poor old R*ob*-ert, he's so young.'

'He *does* seem young,' said Tanny. 'One doesn't forgive it.'

'He is young,' said Julia. 'I'm five years older than he. He's only twenty-seven. Poor old Robert.'

'Robert is young, and inexperienced,' said Josephine, suddenly turning with anger. 'But I don't know why you talk about him.'

'Is he inexperienced, Josephine dear? *Is* he?' sang Julia.

Josephine flushed darkly, and turned away.

'Ah, he's not so innocent as all that,' said Tanny roughly. 'Those young young men, who seem so fresh, they're deep enough, really. They're far less innocent really than men who *are* experienced.'

'They are, aren't they, Tanny,' repeated Julia softly. 'They're old – older than the Old Man of the Seas, sometimes, aren't they? Incredibly old, like little boys who know too much – aren't they? Yes!' She spoke quietly, seriously, as if it had struck her.

Below, the orchestra was coming in. Josephine was watching closely. Julia became aware of this.

'Do you see anybody we know, Josephine?' she asked.

Josephine started.

'No,' she said, looking at her friends quickly and furtively.

'Dear old Josephine, she knows all sorts of people,' sang Julia.

At that moment the men returned.

'Have you actually come back!' exclaimed Tanny to them. They sat down without answering. Jim spread himself as far as he could, in the narrow space. He stared upwards, wrinkling his ugly, queer face. It was evident he was in one of his moods.

'If only somebody loved me!' he complained. 'If only somebody loved me I should be all right. I'm going to pieces.' He sat up and peered into the faces of the women.

'But we *all* love you,' said Josephine, laughing uneasily. 'Why aren't you satisfied!'

67

'I'm not satisfied. I'm not satisfied,' murmured Jim.

'Would you like to be wrapped in swaddling bands and laid at the breast?' asked Lilly, disagreeably.

Jim opened his mouth in a grin, and gazed long and malevolently at his questioner.

'Yes,' he said. Then he sprawled his long six foot of limb and body across the box again.

'You should try loving somebody, for a change,' said Tanny. 'You're been loved too often. Why not try and love somebody?'

Jim eyed her narrowly.

'I couldn't love *you!*,' he said, in vicious tones.

'*A la bonne heure!*' said Tanny.

But Jim sank his chin on his chest, and repeated obstinately: 'I want to be loved.'

'How may times *have* you been loved?' Robert asked him. 'It would be rather interesting to know.'

Jim looked at Robert long and slow, but did not answer.

'Did you ever keep count?' Tanny persisted.

Jim looked up at her, malevolent.

'I believe I did,' he replied.

'Forty is the age when a man should begin to reckon up,' said Lilly.

Jim suddenly sprang to his feet, and brandished his fists.

'I'll pitch the lot of you over the bloody rail,' he said. He glared at them, from under his bald, wrinkled forehead. Josephine glanced round. She had become a dusky white colour. She was afraid of him, and she disliked him intensely nowadays.

'Do you recognize anyone in the orchestra?' she asked.

The party in the box had become dead silent. They looked down. The conductor was at his stand. The music began. They all remained silent and motionless during the next scene, each thinking his own thoughts. Jim was uncomfortable. He wanted to make good. He sat with his elbows on his knees, grinning slightly, looking down. At the next interval he stood up suddenly.

'It *is* the chap – what?' he exclaimed excitedly, looking round at his friends.

'Who?' said Tanny.

'It *is* he!' said Josephine quietly, meeting Jim's eye. 'Sure!' he barked.

He was leaning forward over the ledge, rattling a programme in his hand, as if trying to attract attention. Then he made signals.

'There you are!' he exclaimed triumphantly. 'That's the chap.'

'Who? Who?' they cried.

But neither Jim nor Josephine would vouchsafe an answer.

The next was the long interval. Jim and Josephine gazed down at the orchestra. The musicians were laying aside their instruments and rising. The ugly fire-curtain began slowly to descend. Jim suddenly bolted out.

'Is it that man, Aaron Sisson?' asked Robert.

'Where? Where?' cried Julia. 'It can't be.'

But Josephine's face was closed and silent. She did not answer.

The whole party moved out on to the crimson-carpeted gangway. Groups of people stood about chatting, men and women were passing along, to pay visits or to find drinks. Josephine's party stared around, talking desultorily. And at length they perceived Jim stalking along, leading Aaron Sisson by the arm. Jim was grinning, the flautist looked unwilling. He had a comely appearance, in his white shirt – a certain comely blondness and repose. And as much a gentleman as anybody.

'Well!' cried Josephine to him. 'How do you come here?'

'I play the flute,' he answered, as he shook hands.

The little crowd stood in the gangway and talked.

'How wonderful of you to be here!' cried Julia.

He laughed.

'Do you think so?' he answered.

'Yes, I do. It seems so *far* from Shottle House and Christmas Eve. Oh, wasn't it exciting!' cried Julia.

'We've heard all about you,' said Tanny playfully.

'Oh yes,' he replied.

'Come!' said Josephine, rather irritated. 'We crowd up the gangway.' And she led the way inside the box.

Aaron stood and looked down at the dishevelled theatre.

'You get all the view,' he said.

'We do, don't we!' cried Julia.

'More than we bargain for,' said Lilly.

'Tell us what you are doing. You've got a permanent job?' asked Josephine.

'Yes – at present.'

'Ah! It's more interesting for you than at Beldover.' She had taken her seat. He looked down at her dusky young face. Her voice was always clear and measured.

'It's a change,' he said smiling.

'Oh, it must be more than that,' she said. 'Why, you must feel a whole difference. It's a whole new life.'

He smiled, as if he were laughing at her silently. She flushed.

'But isn't it?' she persisted.

'Yes. It can be,' he replied.

He looked as if he were quietly amused, but dissociated. None of the people in the box were quite real to him. He was not really amused. Julia found him dull, stupid. Tanny also was offended that he could not *perceive* her. The men remained practically silent.

'You're a chap I always hoped would turn up again,' said Jim.

'Oh yes!' replied Aaron, smiling as if amused.

'But perhaps he doesn't like us! Perhaps he's not glad that *we've* turned up,' said Julia, leaving her sting.

The flautist turned and looked at her.

'You can't *remember* us, can you?' she asked.

'Yes,' he said. 'I can remember you.'

'Oh,' she laughed. 'You *are* unflattering.'

He was annoyed. He did not know what she was getting at.

'How are your wife and children?' she asked spitefully.

'All right, I think.'

'But you've been back to them?' cried Josephine in dismay.

He looked at her, a slow, half-smiling look, but did not speak.

'Come an' have a drink. Damn the women,' said Jim uncouthly, seizing Aaron by the arm and dragging him off.

Talk

THE party stayed to the end of the interminable opera. They had agreed to wait for Aaron. He was to come round to the vestibule for them, after the show. They trooped slowly downstairs into the crush of the entrance hall. Chattering, swirling people, red carpet, palms green against cream-and-gilt walls, small whirlpools of life at the open, dark doorways, men in opera hats steering decisively about – it was the old scene. But there were no taxis – absolutely no taxis. And it was raining. Fortunately the women had brought shoes. They slipped these on. Jim rocked through the crowd, in his tall hat, looking for the flautist.

At last Aaron was found – wearing a bowler hat. Julia groaned in spirit. Josephine's brows knitted. Not that anybody cared, really. But as one must frown at something, why not at the bowler hat. Acquaintances and elegant young men in uniforms insisted on rushing up and bowing and exchanging a few words, either with Josephine, or Jim or Julia, or Lilly. They were coldly received. The party veered out into the night.

The women hugged their wraps about them, and set off sharply, feeling some repugnance for the wet pavements and the crowd. They had not far to go – only to Jim's rooms in the Adelphi. Jim was leading Aaron, holding him by the arm and slightly pinching his muscles. It gave him great satisfaction to have between his fingers the arm-muscles of a working man, one of the common people, the *fons et origo* of modern life. Jim was talking rather vaguely about Labour and Robert Smillie, and Bolshevism. He was all for revolution and the triumph of Labour.

So they arrived, mounted a dark stair, and entered a large, handsome room, one of the Adam rooms. Jim had furnished it from Heal's with striped hangings, green and white and yellow and dark purple, and with a green-and-black checked carpet, and great stripe-covered ·chairs and chesterfield. A big gas-fire was soon glowing in the handsome old fireplace, the panelled room seemed cosy.

While Jim was handing round drinks and sandwiches, and Josephine was making tea, Robert played Bach on the piano – the pianola, rather. The chairs and lounge were in a half-circle round the fire. The party threw off their wraps and sank deep into this expensive comfort of modern Bohemia. They needed the Bach to take away the bad taste that *Aïda* left in their mouths. They needed the whisky and curaçoa to rouse their spirits. They needed the profound comfort in which to sink away from the world. All the men, except Aaron, had been through the war in some way or other. But here they were, in the old setting exactly, the old Bohemian routine.

The bell rang, Jim went downstairs. He returned shortly with a frail, elegant woman – fashionable rather than Bohemian. She was cream and auburn, Irish, with a slightly-lifted upper lip that gave her a pathetic look. She dropped her wrap and sat down by Julia, taking her hand delicately.

'How are you, darling?' she asked.

'Yes – I'm happy,' said Julia, giving her odd, screwed-up smile.

The pianola stopped, they all chatted indiscriminately. Jim was watching the new-comer – Mrs Browning – with a concentrated, wolfish grin.

'I like her,' he said at last. 'I've seen her before, haven't I? – I like her awfully.'

'Yes,' said Josephine, with a slight grunt of a laugh. 'He wants to be loved.'

'Oh,' cried Clariss. 'So do I!'

'Then there you are!' cried Tanny.

'Alas no, there we aren't,' cried Clariss. She was beautiful

73

too, with her lifted upper-lip. 'We both want to be loved, and so we miss each other entirely. We run on in two parallel lines, that can never meet,' she laughed low and half sad.

'Doesn't *she* love you?' said Aaron to Jim amused, indicating Josephine. 'I thought you were engaged.'

'*Her!*' leered Jim vindictively, glancing at Josephine. '*She* doesn't love me.'

'Is that true?' asked Robert hastily, of Josephine.

'Why,' she said, 'yes. Why should he make me say out here that I don't love him!'

'Got you, my girl,' said Jim.

'Then it's no engagement?' said Robert.

'Listen to the row fools make, rushing in,' said Jim maliciously.

'No, the engagement is broken,' said Josephine.

'World coming to pieces bit by bit,' said Lilly. Jim was twisting in his chair, and looking like a Chinese dragon, diabolical. The room was uneasy.

'What gives you such a belly-ache for love, Jim?' said Lilly, 'or for being loved? Why do you want so badly to be loved?'

'Because I like it, damn you,' barked Jim. 'Because I'm in need of it.'

None of them quite knew whether they ought to take it as a joke. It was just a bit too real to be quite pleasant.

'Why are you such a baby?' said Lilly. 'There you are, six foot in length, have been a cavalry officer and fought in two wars, and you spend your time crying for somebody to love you. You're a comic.'

'Am I though,' said Jim. 'I'm losing life. I'm getting thin.'

'You don't look as if you were losing life,' said Lilly.

'Don't I? I am though. I'm dying.'

'What of? Lack of life?'

'That's about it, my young cock. Life's leaving me.'

'Better sing Tosti's "Farewell" to it.'

Jim, who had been sprawling full length in his arm-chair, the centre of interest of all the company, suddenly sprang forward and pushed his face, grinning, in the face of Lilly.

'You're a funny customer, you are,' he said.

Then he turned round in his chair, and saw Clariss sitting at the feet of Julia, with one white arm over her friend's knee. Jim immediately stuck forward his muzzle and gazed at her. Clariss had loosened her masses of thick, auburn air, so that it hung half down. Her face was creamy pale, her upper lip lifted with odd pathos. She had rose-rubies in her ears.

'I like *her*,' said Jim. 'What's her name?'

'Mrs Browning. Don't be so rude,' said Josephine.

'Browning for gravies. Any relation of Robert?'

'Oh yes! You ask my husband,' came the slow, plangent voice of Clariss.

'You've got a husband, have you?'

'Rather! Haven't I, Juley?'

'Yes,' said Julia, vaguely and wispily. 'Yes, dear, you have.'

'And two fine children,' put in Robert.

'No! You don't mean it!' said Jim. 'Who's your husband? Anybody?'

'Rather!' came the deep voice of Clariss. 'He sees to that.'

Jim stared, grinning, showing his pointed teeth, reaching nearer and nearer to Clariss who, in her frail scrap of an evening dress, amethyst and silver, was sitting still in the deep black hearthrug, her arm over Julia's knees, taking very little notice of Jim, although he amused her.

'I like you awfully, I say,' he repeated.

'Thanks, I'm sure,' she said.

The others were laughing, sprawling in their chairs, and sipping curaçoa and taking a sandwich or a cigarette. Aaron Sisson alone sat upright, smiling flickeringly. Josephine watched him, and her pointed tongue went from time to time over her lips.

'But I'm sure,' she broke in, 'this isn't very interesting for the others. Awfully boring! Don't be silly all the time, Jim, or we must go home.'

Jim looked at her with narrowed eyes. He hated her voice. She let her eyes rest on his for a moment. Then she put her cigarette to her lips. Robert was watching them both.

Josephine took her cigarette from her lips again.

'Tell us about yourself, Mr Sisson,' she said. 'How do you like being in London?'

'I like London,' said Aaron.

Where did he live? Bloomsbury. Did he know many people? No – nobody except a man in the orchestra. How had he got his job? Through an agent. Etc. Etc.

'What do you make of the miners?' said Jim, suddenly taking a new line.

'Me?' said Sisson. 'I don't make anything of them.'

'Do you think they'll make a stand against the government?'

'What for?'

'Nationalization.'

'They might, one day.'

'Think they'd fight?'

'Fight?'

'Yes.'

Aaron sat laughing.

'What have they to fight for?'

'Why, everything! What haven't they to fight for?' cried Josephine fiercely. 'Freedom, liberty, an escape from this rotten system. Won't they fight for that?'

Aaron sat smiling, slowly shaking his head.

'Nay,' he said, 'you mustn't ask me what they'll do – I've only just left them, for good. They'll do a lot of cavilling.'

'But won't they *act*?' cried Josephine.

'Act?' said Aaron. 'How, act?'

'Why, defy the government, and take things in their own hands,' said Josephine.

'They might, some time,' said Aaron, rather indifferent.

'I wish they would!' cried Josephine. 'My, wouldn't I love it if they'd make a bloody revolution.'

They were all looking now at her. Her black brows were twitching: in her black and silver dress she looked like a symbol of young disaster.

'Must it be bloody, Josephine?' said Robert.

76

'Why, yes. I don't believe in revolutions that aren't bloody,' said Josephine. 'Wouldn't I love it! I'd go in front with a red flag.'

'It would be rather fun,' said Tanny.

'Wouldn't it?' cried Josephine.

'Oh Josey, dear!' cried Julia hysterically. 'Isn't she a red-hot Bolsher! *I* should be frightened.'

'No!' cried Josephine. 'I should love it.'

'So should I,' said Jim, in a luscious sort of voice. 'What price machine-guns at the end of the Strand! That's a day to live for, what?'

'Ha! Ha!' laughed Clariss, with her deep laugh. 'We'd all Bolsh together. I'd give the cheers.'

'I wouldn't mind getting killed. I'd love it, in a real fight,' said Josephine.

'But Josephine,' said Robert; 'don't you think we've had enough of that sort of thing in the war? Don't you think it all works out rather stupid and unsatisfying?'

'Ah, but a civil war would be different. I've no interest in fighting Germans. But a civil war would be different.'

'That's a fact, it would,' said Jim.

'Only rather worse,' said Robert.

'No, I don't agree,' cried Josephine. 'You'd feel you were doing something, in a civil war.'

'Pulling the house down,' said Lilly.

'Yes,' she cried. 'Don't you hate it, the house we live in – London – England – America! Don't you hate them?'

'I don't like them. But I can't get much fire in my hatred. They pall on me rather,' said Lilly.

'Ay!' said Aaron, suddenly stirring in his chair.

Lilly and he glanced at one another with a look of recognition.

'Still,' said Tanny, 'there's got to be a clearance some day or other.'

'Oh,' drawled Clariss. 'I'm all for a clearance. I'm all for pulling the house down. Only while it stands I do want central heating and a good cook.'

'May I come to dinner?' said Jim.

'Oh yes. You'd find it rather domestic.'

'Where do you live?'

'Rather far out now – Amersham.'

'Amersham? Where's that –?'

There was a little lull. Jim gulped down a drink, standing at the sideboard. He was a tall, fine, soldierly figure, and his face, with its little sandy moustache and bald forhead, was odd. Aaron Sisson sat watching him, unconsciously.

'Hello you!' said Jim. 'Have one?'

Aaron shook his head, and Jim did not press him. It saved the drinks.

'You believe in love, don't you?' said Jim, sitting down near Aaron, and grinning at him.

'Love!' said Aaron.

'*Love!* he says,' mocked Jim, grinning at the company.

'What about it, then?' asked Aaron.

'It's life! Love is life,' said Jim fiercely.

'It's a vice, like drink,' said Lilly.

'Eh? A vice!' said Jim. 'May be for you, old bird.'

'More so still for you,' said Lilly.

'It's life. It's life!' reiterated Jim. 'Don't you agree?' He turned wolfishly to Clariss.

'Oh yes – every time – ' she drawled nonchalant.

'Here, let's write it down,' said Lilly. He found a blue pencil and printed in large letters on the old creamy marble of the mantelpiece panels: – LOVE IS LIFE.

Julia suddenly rose and flung her arms asunder wildly.

'Oh, I hate love. I hate it,' she protested.

Jim watched her sardonically.

'Look at her!' he said. 'Look at Lesbia who hates love.'

'No, but perhaps it is a disease. Perhaps we are all wrong, and we can't love properly,' put in Josephine.

'Have another try,' said Jim. 'I know what love is. I've thought about it. Love is the soul's respiration.'

'Let's have that down,' said Lilly.

LOVE IS THE SOUL'S RESPIRATION. He printed it on the old mantelpiece.

Jim eyed the letters.

'It's right,' he said. 'Quite right. When you love, your soul breathes in. If you don't breathe in, you suffocate.'

'What about breathing out?' said Robert. 'If you don't breathe out, you asphyxiate.'

'Right you are, Mock Turtle –' said Jim maliciously.

'Breathing out is a bloody revolution,' said Lilly.

'You've hit the nail on the head, said Jim solemnly.

'Let's record it then,' said Lilly. And with the blue pencil he printed:

WHEN YOU LOVE, YOUR SOUL BREATHES IN.

And then on the next line:

WHEN YOUR SOUL BREATHES OUT, IT'S A BLOODY REVOLUTION.

'I say, Jim,' he said. 'You must be busting yourself, trying to breathe in.'

'Don't you be too clever. I've thought about it,' said Jim. 'When I'm in love, I get a great inrush of energy. I actually feel it rush in – here!' He poked his finger on the pit of his stomach. 'It's the soul's expansion. And if I can't get these rushes of energy, I'm dying, and I know I am.'

He spoke the last words with sudden ferocity and desperation.

'All *I* know is,' said Tanny, 'you don't look it.'

'I *am*. I *am*,' Jim protested. 'I'm dying. Life's leaving me.'

'Maybe you're choking with love,' said Robert. 'Perhaps you've breathed in so much, you don't know how to let it go again. Perhaps your soul's got a crick in it, with expanding so much.'

'You're a bloody young sucking pig, you are,' said Jim.

'Even at that age, I've learned my manners,' replied Robert.

Jim looked round the party. Then he turned to Aaron Sisson.

'What do you make of 'em, eh?' he said.

Aaron shook his head, and laughed.

'Me?' he said.

But Jim did not wait for an answer.

'I've had enough,' said Tanny, suddenly rising. 'I think you're all silly. Besides, it's getting late.'

'She!' said Jim, rising and pointing luridly to Clariss, 'she's Love. And *he's* the working people. The hope is in these two –' He jerked a thumb to Aaron Sisson, after having indicated Mrs Browning.

'Oh, how awfully interesting. It's quite a long time since I've been a personification. I suppose you've never been one before?' said Clariss, turning to Aaron in conclusion.

'No, I don't think I have,' he answered.

'I hope personification is right. Ought it to be *allegory* or something else?' This from Clariss to Robert.

'Or a parable, Clariss,' laughed the young lieutenant.

'Good-bye,' said Tanny. 'I've been awfully bored.'

'Have you?' grinned Jim. 'Good-bye! Better luck next time.'

'We'd better look sharp,' said Robert, 'if we want to get the tube.'

The party hurried through the rainy narrow streets down to the Embankment station. Robert and Julia and Clariss were going west, Lilly and his wife, Tanny, were going to Hampstead. Josephine and Aaron Sisson were going both to Bloomsbury.

'I suppose,' said Robert, on the stairs, 'Mr Sisson will see you to your door, Josephine. He lives your way.'

'There's no need at all,' said Josephine.

The four who were going north went down to the low tube level. It was nearly the last train. The station was half deserted, half rowdy, several fellows were drunk, shouting and crowing. Down there in the bowels of London, after midnight, everything seemed horrible and unnatural.

'How I hate this London,' said Tanny. She was half Norwegian, and had spent a large part of her life in Norway, before she married Lilly.

'Yes, so do I,' said Josephine. 'But if one must earn one's

living one must stay here. I wish I could get back to Paris. But there's nothing doing for me in France. When do you go back into the country, both of you?'

'Friday,' said Lilly.

'How lovely for you! And when will you go to Norway, Tanny?'

'In about a month,' said Tanny.

'You must be awfully pleased.'

'Oh – thankful – *thankful* to get out of England –'

'I know. That's how I feel. Everything is so awful – so dismal and dreary, I find it –'

They crowded into the train. Men were still yelling like wild beasts – others were asleep – soldiers were singing.

'Have you really broken your engagement with Jim?' shrilled Tanny in a high voice, as the train roared.

'Yes, he's impossible,' said Josephine. 'Perfectly hysterical and impossible.'

'And *selfish* –' cried Tanny.

'Oh terribly –' cried Josephine.

'Come up to Hampstead to lunch with us,' said Lilly to Aaron.

'Ay – thank you,' said Aaron.

Lilly scribbled directions on a card. The hot, jaded, midnight underground rattled on. Aaron and Josephine got down to change trains.

CHAPTER 7

The Dark Square Garden

JOSEPHINE had invited Aaron Sisson to dinner at a restaurant in Soho, one Sunday evening. They had a corner to themselves, and with a bottle of burgundy she was getting his history from him.

His father had been a shaft-sinker, earning good money, but had been killed by a fall down the shaft when Aaron was only four years old. The widow had opened a shop: Aaron was her only child. She had done well in her shop. She had wanted Aaron to be a school teacher. He had served three years' apprenticeship, then suddenly thrown it up and gone to the pit.

'But why?' said Josephine.

'I couldn't tell you. I felt more like it.'

He had a curious quality of an intelligent, almost sophisticated mind, which had repudiated education. On purpose he kept the Midland accent in his speech. He understood perfectly what a personification was – and an allegory. But he preferred to be illiterate.

Josephine found out what a miner's checkweighman was. She tried to find out what sort of wife Aaron had – but, except that she was the daughter of a publican and was delicate in health, she could learn nothing.

'And do you send her money?' she asked.

'Ay,' said Aaron. 'The house is mine. And I allow her so much a week out of the money in the bank. My mother left me a bit over a thousand when she died.'

'You don't mind what I say, do you?' said Josephine.

'No, I don't mind,' he laughed.

He had this pleasant-seeming, courteous manner. But

82

he really kept her at a distance. In some things he reminded her of Robert: blond, erect, nicely built, fresh and English-seeming. But there was a curious cold distance to him, which she could not get across. An inward indifference to her – perhaps to everything. Yet his laugh was so handsome.

'Will you tell me why you left your wife and children? Didn't you love them?'

Aaron looked at the odd, round, dark muzzle of the girl. She had had her hair bobbed, and it hung in odd dark folds, very black, over her ears.

'Why I left her?' he said. 'For no particular reason. They're all right without me.'

Josephine watched his face. She saw a pallor of suffering under its freshness, and a strange tension in his eyes.

'But you couldn't leave your little girls for no reason at all–'

'Yes, I did. For no reason – except I wanted to have a bit of free room round me – to loose myself.'

'You mean you wanted love?' flashed Josephine, thinking he said *lose*.

'No, I wanted fresh air. I don't know what I wanted. Why should I know?'

'But we must know: especially when other people are going to suffer so,' said she.

'Ah well! A breath of fresh air, by myself. I felt forced to love. I feel if I go back home now, I shall be *forced* – forced to love – or care – or something.'

'Perhaps you wanted more than your wife could give you,' she said.

'Perhaps less. She's made up her mind she loves me, and she's not going to let me off.'

'Did you never love her?' said Josephine.

'Oh yes. I shall never love anybody else. But I'm damned if I want to go on being a lover, to her or anybody. That's the top and bottom of it. I don't want to *care*, when care isn't in me. And I'm not going to be forced to it.'

The fat, aproned French waiter was hovering near. Josephine let him remove the plates and the empty bottle.

'Have more wine,' she said to Aaron. 'Do?'

But he refused. She liked him because of his dead-level indifference to his surroundings. French waiters and foreign food – he noticed them in his quick, amiable-looking fashion – but he was indifferent. Josephine was piqued. She wanted to pierce this amiable aloofness of his.

She ordered coffee and brandies.

'But you don't want to get away from *everything*, do you? I myself feel so *lost* sometimes – so dreadfully alone: not in a silly sentimental fashion, because men keep telling me they love me, don't you know. But my *life* seems alone, for some reason – '

'Haven't you got relations?' he said.

'No one, now mother is dead. Nothing nearer than aunts and cousins in America. I suppose I shall see them all again one day. But they hardly count over here.'

'Why don't you get married?' he said. 'How old are you?'

'I'm twenty-five. How old are you?'

'Thirty-three.'

'You might almost be any age. I don't know why I don't get married. In a way, I hate earning my own living – yet I go on – And I like my work – '

'What are you doing now?'

'I'm painting scenery for a new play – rather fun – I enjoy it. But I often wonder what will become of me.'

'In what way?'

She was almost affronted.

'What becomes of me? Oh, I don't know! And it doesn't matter, not to anybody but myself.'

'What becomes of anybody, anyhow? We live till we die. What do you want?'

'Why, I keep saying I want to get married and feel sure of something. But I don't know – I feel dreadful sometimes – as if every minute would be the last. I keep going on and on – I don't know what for – and *it* keeps going on and on – goodness knows what it's all for.'

'You shouldn't bother yourself,' he said. 'You should just let it go on and on – '

'But I *must* bother,' she said. 'I must think and feel –'

'You've no occasion,' he said.

'How –? 'she said, with a sudden grunting, unhappy laugh. Then she lit a cigarette.

'No,' she said. 'What I should really like more than anything would be an end of the world. I wish the world would come to an end.'

He laughed, and poured his drops of brandy down his throat.

'It won't, for wishing,' he said.

'No, that's the awful part of it. It'll just go on and on. Doesn't it make you feel you'd go mad?'

He looked at her, and shook his head.

'You see it doesn't concern me,' he said. 'So long as I can float by myself.'

'But *are you satisfied!*' she cried.

'I like being by myself – I hate feeling and caring, and being forced into it. I want to be left alone –'

'You aren't very polite to your hostess of the evening,' she said, laughing a bit piqued.

'Oh, we're all right,' he said. 'You know what I mean –'

'You like your own company? Do you? Sometimes I think I'm nothing when I'm alone. Sometimes I think I surely must be nothing – nothingness.'

He shook his head.

'No,' he said. 'No. I only want to be left alone.'

'Not to have anything to do with anybody?' she queried ironically.

'Not to any extent.'

She watched him – and then she bubbled with a laugh.

'I think you're funny,' she said. 'You don't mind?'

'No – why – It's just as you see it. Jim Bricknell's a rare comic, to my eye.'

'Oh, him! – no, not actually. He's self-conscious and selfish and hysterical. It isn't a bit funny after a while.'

'I only know what I've seen,' said Aaron. 'You'd both of you like a bloody revolution, though.'

'Yes. Only when it came he wouldn't be there.'

'Would you?'

'Yes, indeed I would. I would give everything to be in it. I'd give heaven and earth for a great big upheaval – and then darkness.'

'Oh, but I don't want to die and leave all this standing. I hate it so.'

'Why do you?'

'But don't you?'

'No, it doesn't really bother me.'

'It makes me feel I can't live.'

'I can't see that.'

'But you always disagree with one!' said Josephine. 'How do you like Lilly? What do you think of him?'

'He seems sharp,' said Aaron.

'Yes! But he's more than sharp.'

'Oh yes. He's got his finger in most pies.'

'And doesn't like the plums in any of them,' said Josephine tartly.

'What does he do?'

'Writes – stories and plays.'

'And makes it pay?'

'Hardly at all. They want us to go. Shall we?'

She rose from the table. The waiter handed her her cloak, and they went out into the blowy dark night. She folded her wrap round her, and hurried forward, with short, sharp steps. There was a certain Parisian *chic* and mincingness about her, even in her walk: but underneath, a striding, savage suggestion, as if she could leg it in great strides, like some savage squaw.

Aaron pressed his bowler hat down on his brow.

'Would you rather take a bus?' she said in a high voice, because of the wind.

'I'd rather walk.'

'So would I.'

They hurried across the Charing Cross Road, where great buses rolled and rocked, crammed with people. Her heels clicked sharply on the pavement, as they walked east. They crossed Holborn, and passed the Museum. And neither of them said anything.

When they came to the corner, she held out her hand.

'Look!' she said. 'Don't come any further: don't trouble.'

'I'll walk round with you: unless you'd rather not.'

'No – but do you want to bother?'

'It's no bother.'

So they pursued their way through the high wind, and turned at last into the old, beautiful square. It seemed dark and deserted, dark like a savage wilderness in the heart of London. The wind was roaring in the great bare trees of the centre, as if it were some wild, dark grove deep in a forgotten land.

Josephine opened the gate of the Square garden with her key, and let it slam to behind him.

'How wonderful the wind is!' she shrilled. 'Shall we listen to it for a minute?'

She led him across the grass past the shrubs to the big tree in the centre. There she climbed up to a seat. He sat beside her. They sat in silence, looking at the darkness. Rain was blowing in the wind. They huddled against the big tree-trunk, for shelter, and watched the scene.

Beyond the tall shrubs and the high, heavy railings the wet street gleamed silently. The houses of the Square rose like a cliff on the inner dark sea, dimly lighted at occasional windows. Boughs swayed and sang. A taxi-cab swirled round a corner like a cat, and purred to a standstill. There was a light of an open hall door. But all far away, it seemed, unthinkably far away. Aaron sat still and watched. He was frightened, it all seemed so sinister, this dark, bristling heart of London. Wind boomed and tore like waves ripping a shingle beach. The two white lights of the taxi stared round and departed, leaving the coast at the foot of the cliffs deserted, faintly spilled with light from the high lamp. Beyond there, on the outer rim, a policeman passed solidly.

Josephine was weeping steadily all the time, but inaudibly. Occasionally she blew her nose and wiped her face. But he had not realized. She hardly realized herself. She sat near the strange man. He seemed so still and remote – so fascinating.

'Give me your hand,' she said to him, subduedly.

He took her cold hand in his warm, living grasp. She wept more bitterly. He noticed at last.

'Why are you crying?' he said.

'I don't know,' she replied, rather matter-of-fact, through her tears.

So he let her cry, and said no more, but sat with her cold hand in his warm, easy clasp.

'You'll think me a fool,' she said. 'I don't know why I cry.'

'You can cry for nothing if you like, can't you?' he said.

'Why yes, but it's not very sensible.'

He laughed shortly.

'Sensible!' he said.

'You are a strange man,' she said. But he took no notice.

'Did you ever intend to marry Jim Bricknell?' he asked.

'Yes, of course.'

'I can't imagine it,' he said.

'Why not?'

Both were watching blankly the roaring night of mid-London, the phantasmagoric old Bloomsbury square. They were still hand in hand.

'Such as you shouldn't marry,' he said.

'But why not? I want to.'

'You think you do.'

'Yes, indeed I do.'

He did not say any more.

'Why shouldn't I?' she persisted.

'I don't know – '

And again he was silent.

'You've known some life, haven't you?' he asked.

'Me? Why?'

'You seem to.'

'Do I? I'm sorry. Do I seem vicious? No, I'm not vicious. I've seen some life, perhaps – in Paris mostly. But not much. Why do you ask?'

'I wasn't thinking.'

'But what do you mean? What *are* you thinking?'

'Nothing. Nothing.'

'Don't be so irritating,' said she.

But he did not answer, and she became silent also. They sat hand in hand.

'Won't you kiss me?' came her voice out of the darkness.

He waited some moments, then his voice sounded gently, half mocking, half reproachful.

'Nay,' he said.

'Why not?'

'I don't want to.'

'Why not?' she asked.

He laughed, but did not reply.

She sat perfectly still for some time. She had ceased to cry. In the darkness her face was set and sullen. Sometimes a spray of rain blew across it. She drew her hand from his, and rose to her feet.

'I'll go in now,' she said.

'You're not offended, are you?' he asked.

'No. Why?'

They stepped down in the darkness from their perch.

'I wondered.'

She strode off for some little way. Then she turned and said:

'Yes, I think it is rather insulting.'

'Nay,' he said. 'Not it! Not it!'

And he followed her to the gate.

She opened with her key, and they crossed the road to her door.

'Good-night,' she said, turning and giving him her hand.

'You'll come and have dinner with me – or lunch – will you? When shall we make it?' he asked.

'Well, I can't say for certain. I'm very busy just now. I'll let you know.'

A policeman shed his light on the pair of them as they stood on the step.

'All right,' said Aaron, dropping back, and she hastily opened the big door, and entered.

CHAPTER 8

A Punch in the Wind

THE Lillys had a labourer's cottage in Hampshire – pleasant enough. They were poor. Lilly was a little, dark, thin, quick fellow, his wife a fine blonde. They had known Robert and Julia for some years, but Josephine and Jim were new acquaintances – fairly new.

One day in early spring Lilly had a telegram, 'Coming to see you arrive 4.30 – Bricknell.' He was surprised, but he and his wife got the spare room ready. And at four o'clock Lilly went off to the station. He was a few minutes late, and saw Jim's tall, rather elegant figure stalking down the station path. Jim had been an officer in the regular army, and still spent hours with his tailor. But instead of being a soldier he was a sort of socialist, and a red-hot revolutionary of a very ineffectual sort.

'Good lad!' he exclaimed, as Lilly came up. 'Thought you wouldn't mind.'

'Not at all. Let me carry your bag.'

Jim had a bag and a knapsack.

'I had an inspiration this morning,' said Jim. 'I suddenly saw that if there was a man in England who could save me, it was you.'

'Save you from what?' asked Lilly, rather abashed.

'Eh – ?' and Jim stopped grinning at the smaller man. Lilly was somewhat puzzled, but he had a certain belief in himself as a saviour. The two men tramped rather incongruously through the lanes to the cottage.

Tanny was in the doorway as they came up the garden path.

'So nice to see you! Are you all right?' she said.

91

'A1,' said Jim, grinning. 'Nice of you to have me.'

'Oh, we're awfully pleased.'

Jim dropped his knapsack on the broad sofa.

'I've brought some food,' he said.

'Have you! That's sensible of you. We can't get a great deal here, except just at week-ends,' said Tanny.

Jim fished out a pound of sausages and a pot of fish paste.

'How lovely the sausages,' said Tanny. 'We'll have them for dinner to-night – and we'll have the other for tea now. You'd like a wash?'

But Jim had already opened his bag, taken off his coat, and put on an old one: there before them all in the pretty cottage living-room.

'Thanks,' he said.

Lilly made the tea, and at length all sat down.

'Well, how unexpected this is – and how nice!' said Tanny.

'Jolly – eh?' said Jim. He ate rapidly stuffing his mouth too full.

'How is everybody?' asked Tanny.

'All right. Julia's gone with Cyril Scott. Can't stand that fellow, can you? What?'

'Yes, I think he's rather nice,' said Tanny. 'What will Robert do?'

'Have a shot at Josephine, apparently.'

'Really? Is he in love with her? I thought so. And she likes him too, doesn't she?' said Tanny.

'Very likely,' said Jim.

'I suppose you're jealous,' laughed Tanny.

'Me!' Jim shook his head. 'Not a bit. Like to see the ball kept rolling.'

'What have you been doing lately?'

'Been staying a few days with my wife.'

'No, really! I can't believe it.'

Jim had a French wife, who had divorced him, and two children. Now he was paying visits to this wife again: purely friendly. Tanny did most of the talking. Jim excited her, with his way of looking in her face and grinning wolfishly, and at the same time asking to be saved.

After tea he wanted to send telegrams, so Lilly took him round to the village post-office. Telegrams were a necessary part of his life. He had to be suddenly starting off to keep sudden appointments, or he felt he was a void in the atmosphere. He talked to Lilly about social reform, and so on. Jim's work in town was merely nominal. He spent his time wavering about and going to various meetings, philandering and weeping.

Lilly kept in the back of his mind the saving which James had come to look for. He intended to do his best. After dinner the three sat cosily round the kitchen fire.

'But what do you really think will happen to the world?' Lilly asked Jim, amid much talk.

'What? There's something big coming,' said Jim.

'Where from?'

'Watch Ireland, and watch Japan – they're the two poles of the world,' said Jim.

'I thought Russia and America,' said Lilly.

'Eh? What? Russia and America! They'll depend on Ireland and Japan. I know it. I've had a vision of it. Ireland on this side and Japan on the other – they'll settle it.'

'I don't see how,' said Lilly.

'*I* don't see *how* – but I had a vision of it.'

'What sort of vision?'

'Couldn't describe it.'

'But you don't think much of the Japanese, do you?' asked Lilly.

'Don't I! Don't I!' said Jim. 'What, don't you think they're wonderful?'

'No. I think they're rather unpleasant.'

'I think the salvation of the world lies with them.'

'Funny salvation,' said Lilly. 'I think they're anything but angels.'

'Do you though? Now that's funny. Why?'

'Looking at them even. I knew a Russian doctor who'd

been through the Russo-Japanese war, and who had gone a bit cracked. He said he saw the Japs rush a trench. They threw everything away and flung themselves through the Russian fire, and simply dropped in masses. But those that reached the trenches jumped in with bare hands on the Russians and tore their faces apart and bit their throats out – fairly ripped the faces off the bone. It had sent the doctor a bit mad. He said the wounded were awful – their faces torn off and their throats mangled – and dead Japs with flesh between the teeth – God knows if it's true. But that's the impression the Japanese had made on this man – it had affected his mind really.'

Jim watched Lilly, and smiled as if he were pleased.

'No – really – !' he said.

'Anyhow they're more demon than angel, I believe,' said Lilly.

'Oh, no, Rawdon, but you always exaggerate,' said Tanny.

'Maybe,' said Lilly.

'I think Japanese are fascinating – fascinating – so quick, and such *force* in them – '

'Rather! – eh?' said Jim, looking with a quick smile at Tanny.

'I think a Japanese lover would be marvellous,' she laughed riskily.

'I s'd think he would,' said Jim, screwing up his eyes.

'Do you hate the normal British as much as I do?' she asked him.

'Hate them! Hate them!' he said, with an intimate grin.

'Their beastly virtue,' said she. 'And I believe there's nobody more vicious underneath.'

'Nobody!' said Jim.

'But you're British yourself,' said Lilly to Jim.

'No, I'm Irish. Family's Irish – my mother was a Fitzpatrick.'

'Anyhow you live in England.'

'Because they won't let me go to Ireland.'

The talk drifted. Jim finished up all the beer, and they

prepared to go to bed. Jim was a bit tipsy, grinning. He asked for bread and cheese to take upstairs.

'Will you have supper?' said Lilly. He was surprised, because Jim had eaten strangely much at dinner.

'No – where's the loaf?' And he cut himself about half of it. There was no cheese.

'Bread'll do,' said Jim.

'Sit down and eat it. Have cocoa with it,' said Tanny.

'No, I like to have it in my bedroom.'

'You don't eat bread in the night?' said Lilly.

'I do.'

'What a funny thing to do.'

The cottage was in darkness. The Lillys slept soundly. Jim woke up and chewed bread and slept again. In the morning at dawn he rose and went downstairs. Lilly heard him roaming about – heard the woman come in to clean – heard them talking. So he got up to look after his visitor, though it was not seven o'clock, and the woman was busy. But before he went down, he heard Jim come upstairs again.

Mrs Short was busy in the kitchen when Lilly went down.

'The other gentleman have been down, sir,' said Mrs Short. 'He asked me where the bread and butter were, so I said should I cut him a piece. But he wouldn't let me do it. I gave him a knife and he took it for himself, in the pantry.'

'I say, Bricknell,' said Lilly at breakfast time, 'why do you eat so much bread?'

'I've got to feed up. I've been starved during this damned war.'

'But hunks of bread won't feed you up.'

'Gives the stomach something to work at, and prevents it grinding on the nerves,' said Jim.

'But surely you don't want to keep your stomach always full and heavy.'

'I do, my boy. I do. It needs keeping solid. I'm losing life, if I don't. I tell you I'm losing life. Let me put something inside me.'

'I don't believe bread's any use.'

During breakfast Jim talked about the future of the world.

'I reckon Christ's the finest thing time has ever produced,' said he; 'and will remain it.'

'But you don't want crucifixions *ad infinitum!*' said Lilly.

'What? Why not?'

'Once is enough – and have done.'

'Don't you think love and sacrifice are the finest things in life?' said Jim, over his bacon.

'Depends *what* love, and what sacrifice,' said Lilly. 'If I really believe in an Almighty God, I am willing to sacrifice for Him. That is, I'm willing to yield my own personal interest to the bigger creative interest. But it's obvious Almighty God isn't mere Love.'

'I think it is. Love and only love,' said Jim. 'I think the greatest joy is sacrificing one's self to love.'

'To *someone* you love, you mean,' said Tanny.

'No I don't. I don't mean someone at all. I mean love – love – love. I sacrifice myself to love. I reckon that's the highest man is capable of.'

'But you can't sacrifice yourself to an abstract principle,' said Tanny.

'That's just what you can do. And that's the beauty of it. Who represents the principle doesn't matter. Christ is the principle of love,' said Jim.

'But do!' said Tanny. 'It *must* be more individual. It must be *somebody* you love, not abstract love in itself. How can you sacrifice yourself to an abstraction?'

'Ha, I think Love and your Christ detestable,' said Lilly. 'A sheer ignominy.'

'Finest thing the world has produced,' said Jim.

'No. A thing which sets itself up to be betrayed! No, it's foul. Don't you see it's the Judas principle you really worship. Judas is the real hero. But for Judas the whole show would have been *manqué*.'

'Oh, yes,' said Jim. 'Judas was inevitable. I'm not sure that Judas wasn't the greatest of the disciples – and Jesus knew it. I'm not sure Judas wasn't the disciple Jesus loved.'

'Jesus certainly encouraged him in his Judas tricks,' said Tanny.

Jim grinned knowingly at Lilly.

'Then it was a nasty combination. And anything which turns on a Judas climax is a dirty show, to my thinking. I think your Judas is a rotten, dirty worm, just a dirty little self-conscious sentimental twister. And out of all Christianity he is the hero to-day. When people say Christ they mean Judas. They find him luscious on the palate. And Jesus fostered him – ' said Lilly.

'He's a profound figure, is Judas. It's taken two thousand years to begin to understand him,' said Jim, pushing the bread and marmalade into his mouth.

'A traitor is a traitor – no need to understand any further. And a system which rests all its weight on a piece of treachery makes the treachery not only inevitable but sacred. That's why I'm sick of Christianity – at any rate this modern Christ-mongery.'

'The finest thing the world has produced, or ever will produce – Christ and Judas – ' said Jim.

'Not to me,' said Lilly. 'Foul combination.'

It was a lovely morning in early March. Violets were out, and the first wild anemones. The sun was quite warm. The three were about to take out a picnic lunch. Lilly, however, was suffering from Jim's presence.

'Jolly nice here,' said Jim. 'Mind if I stay till Saturday?'

There was a pause. Lilly felt he was being bullied, almost obscenely bullied. Was he going to agree? Suddenly he looked up at Jim.

'I'd rather you went to-morrow,' he said.

Tanny, who was sitting opposite Jim, dropped her head in confusion.

'What's to-morrow?' said Jim.

'Thursday,' said Lilly.

'Thursday,' repeated Jim. And he looked up and got Lilly's eye. He wanted to say: 'Friday then?'

'Yes, I'd rather you went Thursday,' repeated Lilly.

'But Rawdon – !' broke in Tanny, who was suffering. She stopped, however.

'We can walk across country with you some way if you like,' said Lilly to Jim. It was a sort of compromise.

'Fine!' said Jim. 'We'll do that, then.'

It was lovely sunshine, and they wandered through the woods. Between Jim and Tanny was a sort of growing *rapprochement*, which got on Lilly's nerves.

'What the hell do you take that beastly personal tone for?' cried Lilly at Tanny, as the three sat under a leafless great beech-tree.

'But I'm not personal at all, am I, Mr Bricknell?' said Tanny.

Jim watched Lilly, and grinned pleasedly.

'Why shouldn't you be, anyhow?' he said.

'Yes!' she retorted. 'Why not!'

'Not while I'm here. I loathe the slimy, creepy, personal intimacy:—"*Don't you think, Mr Bricknell, that it's lovely to be able to talk quite simply to somebody? Oh, it's such a relief, after most people –* "' Lilly mimicked his wife's last speech savagely.

'But I *mean* it,' cried Tanny. 'It *is* lovely.'

'Dirty messing,' said Lilly angrily.

Jim watched the dark, irascible little man with amusement. They rose, and went to look for an inn, and beer. Tanny still clung rather stickily to Jim's side.

But it was a lovely day, the first of all the days of spring, with crocuses and wall-flowers in the cottage gardens, and white cocks crowing in the quiet hamlet.

When they got back in the afternoon to the cottage, they found a telegram for Jim. He let the Lillys see it – 'Meet you for a walk on your return journey – Lois.' At once Tanny wanted to know all about Lois. Lois was a nice girl, well-to-do middle-class, but also an actress, and she would do anything Jim wanted.

'I must get a wire to her to meet me to-morrow,' he said. 'Where shall I say?'

Lilly produced the map, and they decided on time and station at which Lois, coming out of London, should meet Jim. Then the happy pair could walk along the Thames valley, spending a night perhaps at Marlow, or some such place.

Off went Jim and Lilly once more to the post office. They were quite good friends. Having so inhospitably fixed the hour of departure, Lilly wanted to be nice. Arrived at the post office, they found it shut: half-day closing for the little shop.

'Well,' said Lilly. 'We'll go to the station.'

They proceeded to the station – found the station-master – were conducted down to the signal-box. Lilly naturally hung back from people, but Jim was hob-nob with the station-master and the signal man, quite officer-and-my-men kind of thing. Lilly sat out on the steps of the signal-box, rather ashamed, while the long telegram was shouted over the telephone to the junction town – first the young lady and her address, then the message – 'Meet me X station 3.40 to-morrow walk back great pleasure Jim.'

Anyhow that was done. They went home to tea. After tea, as the evening fell, Lilly suggested a little stroll in the woods, while Tanny prepared the dinner. Jim agreed, and they set out. The two men wandered through the trees in the dusk, till they came to a bank on the farther edge of the wood. There they sat down.

And there Lilly said what he had to say. 'As a matter of fact,' he said, 'it's nothing but love and self-sacrifice which makes you feel yourself losing life.'

'You're wrong. Only love brings it back – and wine. If I drink a bottle of burgundy I feel myself restored at the middle – right here! I feel the energy back again. And if I can fall in love – But it's becoming so damned hard – '

'What, to fall in love?' asked Lilly.

'Yes.'

'Then why not leave off trying! What do you want to poke yourself and prod yourself into love for?'

'Because I'm *dead* without it. I'm dead. I'm dying.'

'Only because you force yourself. If you drop working yourself up – '

'I shall die. I only live when I can fall in love. Otherwise I'm dying by inches. Why, man, you don't know what it was like. I used to get the most grand feelings – like a great rush of force, or light – a great rush – right here, as I've said, at the solar plexus. And it would come any time – any where – no matter where I was. And then I was all right.'

'All right for what? – for making love?'

'Yes, man, I was.'

'And now you aren't? Oh well, leave love alone, as any twopenny doctor would tell you.'

'No, you're off it there. It's nothing technical. Technically I can make love as much as you like. It's nothing a doctor has any say in. It's what I feel inside me. I feel the life going. I know it's going. I never get those inrushes now, unless I drink a jolly lot, or if I possibly could fall in love.'

'You should leave yourself and your inrushes alone.'

'But you can't. It's a sort of ache.'

'Then you should stiffen your backbone. It's your backbone that matters. You shouldn't want to abandon yourself. You shouldn't want to fling yourself all loose into a woman's lap. You should stand by yourself and learn to be by yourself. Why don't you be more like the Japanese you talk about? Quiet, aloof little devils. They don't bother about being loved. They keep themselves taut in their own selves – there, at the bottom of the spine – the devil's own power they've got there.'

Jim mused a bit.

'Think they have?' he laughed. It seemed comic to him.

'Sure! Look at them. Why can't you gather yourself there?'

'At the tail?'

'Yes. Hold yourself firm there.'

Jim broke into a cackle of a laugh, and rose. The two went through the dark woods back to the cottage. Jim staggered and stumbled like a drunken man: or worse, like a man with locomotor ataxy: as if he had no power in his lower limbs.

'Walk there – !' said Lilly, finding him the smoothest bit
of the dark path. But Jim stumbled and shambled, in a state
of nauseous weak relaxation. However, they reached the
cottage: and food and beer – and Tanny, piqued with
curiosity to know what the men had been saying privately to
each other.

After dinner they sat once more talking round the fire.
Lilly sat in a small chair facing the fire, the other two in the
arm-chairs on either side the hearth.

'How nice it will be for you, walking with Lois towards
London to-morrow,' gushed Tanny sentimentally.

'Good God,' said Lilly. 'Why the dickens doesn't he
walk by himself, without wanting a woman always there, to
hold his hand.'

'Don't be so spiteful,' said Tanny. '*You* see that you have a
woman always there, to hold *your* hand.'

'My hand doesn't need holding,' snapped Lilly.

'Doesn't it! More than most men's! But you're so beastly
ungrateful and mannish. Because I hold you safe enough all
the time, you like to pretend you're doing it all yourself.'

'All right. Don't drag yourself in,' said Lilly, detesting his
wife at that moment. 'Anyhow,' and he turned to Jim, 'it's
time you'd done slobbering yourself over a lot of little
women, one after the other.'

'Why shouldn't I, if I like it?' said Jim.

'Yes, why not?' said Tanny.

'Because it makes a fool of you. Look at you, stumbling
and staggering with no use in your legs. I'd be ashamed if I
were you.'

'Would you?' said Jim.

'I would. And it's nothing but your wanting to be loved
which does it. A maudlin crying to be loved, which makes
your knees all go ricky.'

'Think that's it?' said Jim.

'What else is it? You haven't been here a day but you must
telegraph for some female to be ready to hold your hand the
moment you go away. And before she lets go, you'll be

wiring for another. *You want to be loved*, you want to be love d – a man of your years. It's disgusting.'

'I don't see it. I believe in love – ' said Jim, watching and grinning oddly.

'Bah, love! Messing, that's what it is. It wouldn't matter if it did you no harm. But when you stagger and stumble down a road, out of sheer sloppy relaxation of your will – '

At this point Jim suddenly sprang from his chair at Lilly, and gave him two or three hard blows with his fists, upon the front of the body. Then he sat down in his own chair again, saying sheepishly:

'I knew I should have to do it, if he said any more.'

Lilly sat motionless as a statue, his face like paper. One of the blows had caught him rather low, so that he was almost winded, and could not breathe. He sat rigid, paralysed as a winded man is. But he wouldn't let it be seen. With all his will he prevented himself from gasping. Only through his parted lips he drew tiny gasps, controlled, nothing revealed to the other two. He hated them both far too much.

For some minutes there was dead silence, whilst Lilly silently and viciously fought for his breath. Tanny opened her eyes wide in a sort of pleased bewilderment, and Jim turned his face aside, and hung his clasped hands between his knees.

'There's a great silence, suddenly!' said Tanny.

'What is there to say?' ejaculated Lilly rapidly, with a spoonful of breath which he managed to compress and control into speech. Then he sat motionless again, concerned with the business of getting back his wind, and not letting the other two see.

Jim jerked in his chair, and looked round.

'It isn't that I don't like the man,' he said, in a rather small voice. 'But I knew if he went on I should have to do it.'

To Lilly, rigid and physically preoccupied, there sounded a sort of self-consciousness in Jim's voice, as if the whole thing had been semi-deliberate. He detected the sort of maudlin deliberateness which goes with hysterics, and he was colder, more icy than ever.

Tanny looked at Lilly, puzzled, bewildered, but still rather pleased, as if she demanded an answer. None being forthcoming, she said:

'Of course, you mustn't expect to say all those things without rousing a man.'

Still Lilly did not answer. Jim glanced at him, then looked at Tanny.

'It isn't that I don't like him,' he said, slowly. 'I like him better than any man I've ever known, I believe.' He clasped his hands and turned aside his face.

'Judas!' flashed through Lilly's mind.

Again Tanny looked for her husband's answer.

'Yes, Rawdon,' she said. 'You can't say the things you do without their having an effect. You really ask for it, you know.'

'It's no matter,' Lilly squeezed the words out coldly. 'He wanted to do it, and he did it.'

A dead silence ensued now. Tanny looked from man to man.

'I could feel it coming on me,' said Jim.

'Of course!' said Tanny. 'Rawdon doesn't know the things he says.' She seemed pleased that he had had to pay for them, for once.

It takes a man a long time to get his breath back, after a sharp blow in the wind. Lilly was managing by degrees. The others no doubt attributed his silence to deep or fierce thoughts. It was nothing of the kind: merely a cold struggle to get his wind back, without letting them know he was struggling: and a sheer, stock-stiff hatred of the pair of them.

'I like the man,' said Jim; 'never liked a man more than I like him.' He spoke as if with difficulty.

'The man' stuck safely in Lilly's ears.

'Oh well,' he managed to say 'It's nothing. I've done my talking and had an answer, for once.'

'Yes, Rawdy, you've had an answer, for once. Usually you don't get an answer, you know – and that's why you go so far – in the things you say. Now you'll know how you make people feel.'

'Quite!' said Lilly.

'*I* don't feel anything. I don't mind what he says,' said Jim.

'Yes, but he ought to know the things he *does* say,' said Tanny. 'He goes on, without considering the person he's talking to. This time it's come back on him. He mustn't say such personal things, if he's not going to risk an answer.'

'I don't mind what he says. I don't mind a bit,' said Jim.

'Nor do I mind,' said Lilly indifferently. 'I say what I feel. You do as you feel. There's an end of it.'

A sheepish sort of silence followed this speech. It was broken by a sudden laugh from Tanny.

'The things that happen to us!' she said, laughing rather shrilly. 'Suddenly, like a thunderbolt, we're all struck into silence!'

'Rum game, eh!' said Jim, grinning.

'Isn't it funny! Isn't life too funny!' She looked again at her husband. 'But Rawdy, you must admit it was your own fault.'

Lilly's stiff face did not change.

'Why *fault!*' he said, looking at her coldly. 'What is there to talk about?'

'Usually there's so much,' she said sarcastically.

A few phrases dribbled out of the silence. In vain Jim tried to get Lilly to thaw, and in vain Tanny gave her digs at her husband. Lilly's stiff, inscrutable face did not change, he was polite and aloof. So they all went to bed.

In the morning, the walk was to take place, as arranged, Lilly and Tanny accompanying Jim to the third station, across country. The morning was lovely, the country beautiful. Lilly liked the countryside and enjoyed the walk. But a hardness inside himself never relaxed. Jim talked a little again about the future of the world, and a higher state of Christlikeness in man. But Lilly only laughed. Then Tanny managed to get ahead with Jim, sticking to his side and talking sympathetic personalities. But Lilly, feeling it from afar, ran after them and caught them up. They were silent.

'What was the interesting topic?' he said cuttingly.

'Nothing at all!' said Tanny, nettled. 'Why must you interfere?'

'Because I intend to,' said Lilly.

And the two fell apart, as if severed with a knife. Jim walked rather sheepishly, as if cut out.

So they came at last past the canals to the wayside station: and at last Jim's train came. They all said goodbye. Jim and Tanny were both waiting for Lilly to show some sign of real reconciliation. But none came. He was cheerful and aloof.

'Good-bye,' he said to Jim. 'Hope Lois will be there all right. Third station on. Good-bye! Good-bye!'

'You'll come to Rackham?' said Jim, leaning out of the train.

'We should love to,' called Tanny, after the receding train.

'All right,' said Lilly non-committal.

But he and his wife never saw Jim again. Lilly never intended to see him: a devil sat in the little man's breast.

'You shouldn't try to make a little Jesus of yourself, coming so near to people, wanting to help them,' was Tanny's last word.

CHAPTER 9

Low-water Mark

TANNY went away to Norway to visit her people, for the first time for three years. Lilly did not go: he did not want to. He came to London and settled in a room over Covent Garden market. The room was high up, a fair size, and stood at the corner of one of the streets and the market itself, looking down on the stalls and the carts and the arcade. Lilly would climb out of the window and sit for hours watching the behaviour of the great draught-horses which brought the mountains of boxes and vegetables. Funny half-human creatures they seemed, so massive and fleshy, yet so Cockney. There was one which could not bear donkeys, and which used to stretch out its great teeth like some massive serpent after every poor diminutive ass that came with a coster's barrow. Another great horse could not endure standing. It would shake itself and give little starts, and back into the heaps of carrots and broccoli, whilst the driver went into a frenzy of rage.

There was always something to watch. One minute it was two great loads of empty crates, which in passing had got entangled, and reeled, leaning to fall disastrously. Then the drivers cursed and swore and dismounted and stared at their jeopardized loads: till a thin fellow was persuaded to scramble up the airy mountains of cages, like a monkey. And he actually managed to put them to rights. Great sigh of relief when the vans rocked out of the market.

Again there was a particular page-boy in buttons, with a round and perky behind, who nimbly carried a tea-tray from somewhere to somewhere, under the arches beside the market. The great brawny porters would tease him, and he would stop to give them cheek. One afternoon a giant lunged after him: the boy darted gracefully among the heaps of vegetables, still bearing aloft his tea-tray, like some young blue-buttoned acolyte fleeing before a false god. The giant rolled after him – when alas, the acolyte of the tea-tray slipped among the vegetables, and down came the tray. Then tears, and a roar of unfeeling mirth from the giants. Lilly felt they were going to make it up to him.

Another afternoon a young swell sauntered persistently among the vegetables, and Lilly, seated in his high little balcony, wondered why. But at last, a taxi, and a very expensive female, in a sort of silver brocade gown and a great fur shawl and ospreys in her bonnet! Evidently an assignation. Yet what could be more conspicuous than this elegant pair, picking their way through the cabbage-leaves.

And then, one cold grey afternoon in early April, a man in a black overcoat and a bowler hat, walking uncertainly. Lilly had risen and was just retiring out of the chill, damp air. For some reason he lingered to watch the figure. The man was walking east. He stepped rather insecurely off the pavements, and wavered across the setts between the wheels of the standing van. And suddenly he went down. Lilly could not see him on the floor, but he saw some vanmen go forward, and he saw one of them pick up the man's hat.

'I'd better go down,' said Lilly to himself.

So he began running down the four long flights of stone stairs, past the many doors of the multifarious business premises, and out into the market. A little crowd had gathered, and a large policeman was just rowing into the centre of the interest. Lilly, always a hoverer on the edge of public commotions, hung now hesitating on the outskirts of the crowd.

'What is it?' he said, to a rather sniffy messenger boy.

'Drunk,' said the messenger boy: except that, in unblushing Cockney, he pronounced it: 'Drank!'

Lilly hung further back on the edge of the little crowd.

'Come on here. Where d'you want to go?' he heard the hearty tones of the policeman.

'I'm all right. I'm all right,' came the testy drunken answer.

'All right, are yer! All right, and *then* some. Come on, get on your pins.'

'I'm all right! I'm all right.'

The voice made Lilly peer between the people. And sitting on the granite setts, being hauled up by a burly policeman, he saw our acquaintance Aaron, very pale in the face and a little dishevelled.

'Like me to tuck the sheets round you, shouldn't you! Fancy yourself snug in bed, don't you. You won't believe you're right in the way of traffic, will you now, in Covent Garden Market. Come on, we'll see to you.' And the policeman hoisted the bitter and unwilling Aaron.

Lilly was quickly at the centre of the affair, unobtrusive like a shadow, different from the other people.

'Help him up to my room, will you?' he said to the constable. 'Friend of mine.'

The large constable looked down on the bare-headed, wispy, unobtrusive Lilly with good-humoured suspicion and incredulity. Lilly could not have borne it if the policeman had uttered any of this Cockney suspicion, so he watched him. There was a great gulf between the public official and the odd, quiet little individual – yet Lilly had his way.

'Which room?' said the policeman, dubious.

Lilly pointed quickly round. Then he said to Aaron: –

'Were you coming to see me, Sisson? You'll come in, won't you?'

Aaron nodded rather stupidly and testily. His eyes looked angry. Somebody stuck his hat on his head for him, and made him look a fool. Lilly took it off again, and carried it for him. He turned, and the crowd eased. He watched Aaron sharply, and saw that it was with difficulty he could walk. So he caught him by the arm on the other side from the policeman, and they crossed the road to the pavement.

'Not so much of this sort of thing these days,' said the policeman.

'Not so much opportunity,' said Lilly.

'More than there was, though. Coming back to the old days, like. Working round, bit by bit.'

They had arrived at the stairs. Aaron stumbled up.

'Steady now! Steady does it!' said the policeman, steering his charge. There was a curious breach of distance between Lilly and the constable.

At last Lilly opened his own door. The room was pleasant. The fire burned warm, the piano stood open, the sofa was untidy with cushions and papers, books and papers covered the big writing desk. Beyond the screen made by the book-shelves and the piano were two beds, with washstand by one of the large windows, the one through which Lilly had climbed.

The policeman looked round curiously.

'More cosy here than in the lock-up, sir!' he said.

Lilly laughed. He was hastily clearing the sofa.

'Sit on the sofa, Sisson,' he said.

The policeman lowered his charge, with a –

'Right we are, then!'

Lilly felt in his pocket, and gave the policeman half-a-crown. But he was watching Aaron, who sat stupidly on the sofa, very pale and semi-conscious.

'Do you feel ill, Sisson?' he said sharply.

Aaron looked back at him with heavy eyes, and shook his head slightly.

'I believe you are,' said Lilly, taking his hand.

'Might be a bit o' this flu, you know,' said the policeman.

'Yes,' said Lilly. 'Where is there a doctor?' he added, on reflexion.

'The nearest?' said the policeman. And he told him 'Leave a message for you, sir?'

Lilly wrote his address on a card, then changed his mind.

'No, I'll run round myself if necessary,' he said.

And the policeman departed.

'You'll go to bed, won't you?' said Lilly to Aaron, when the door was shut. Aaron shook his head sulkily.

'I would if I were you. You can stay here till you're all right. I'm alone, so it doesn't matter.'

But Aaron had relapsed into semi-consciousness. Lilly put the big kettle on the gas stove, the little kettle on the fire. Then he hovered in front of the stupefied man. He felt uneasy. Again he took Aaron's hand and felt the pulse.

'I'm sure you aren't well. You must go to bed,' he said. And he kneeled and unfastened his visitor's boots. Meanwhile the kettle began to boil: he put a hot-water bottle into the bed.

'Let us get your overcoat off,' he said to the stupefied man. 'Come along.' And with coaxing and pulling and pushing he got off the overcoat and coat and waistcoat.

At last Aaron was undressed and in bed. Lilly brought him tea. With a dim kind of obedience he took the cup and would drink. He looked at Lilly with heavy eyes.

'I gave in. I gave in to her, else I should ha' been all right,' he said.

'To whom?' said Lilly.

'I gave in to her – and afterwards I cried, thinking of Lottie and the children. I felt my heart break, you know. And that's what did it. I should have been all right if I hadn't given in to her – '

'To whom?' said Lilly.

'Josephine. I felt, the minute I was loving her, I'd done myself. And I had. Everything came back on me. If I hadn't given in to her, I should ha' kept all right.'

'Don't bother now. Get warm and still – '

'I felt it – I felt it go, inside me, the minute I gave in to her. It's perhaps killed me.'

'No, not it. Never mind, be still. Be still, and you'll be all right in the morning.'

'It's my own fault, for giving into her. If I'd kept myself back, my liver wouldn't have broken inside me, and I shouldn't have been sick. And I knew – '

'Never mind now. Have you drunk your tea? Lie down. Lie down, and go to sleep.'

Lilly pushed Aaron down in the bed, and covered him over. Then he thrust his hands under the bedclothes and felt his feet – still cold. He arranged the water-bottle. Then he put another cover on the bed.

Aaron lay still, rather grey and peaked-looking, in a still-ness that was not healthy. For some time Lilly went about stealthily, glancing at his patient from time to time. Then he sat down to read.

He was roused after a time by a moaning of troubled breathing and a fretful stirring in the bed. He went across. Aaron's eyes were open, and dark looking.

'Have a little hot milk,' said Lilly.

Aaron shook his head faintly, not noticing.

'A little Bovril?'

The same faint shake.

Then Lilly wrote a note for the doctor, went into the office on the same landing, and got a clerk, who would be leaving in a few minutes, to call with the note. When he came back he found Aaron still watching.

'Are you here by yourself?' asked the sick man.

'Yes. My wife's gone to Norway.'

'For good?'

'No,' laughed Lilly. 'For a couple of months or so. She'll come back here: unless she joins me in Switzerland or some-where.'

Aaron was still for a while.

'You've not gone with her,' he said at length.

'To see her people? No, I don't think they want me very badly – and I didn't want very badly to go. Why should I? It's better for married people to be separated sometimes.'

'Ay – !' said Aaron, watching the other man with fever-darkened eyes.

'I hate married people who are two in one – stuck together like two jujube lozenges,' said Lilly.

'Me an' all. I hate 'em myself,' said Aaron.

'Everybody ought to stand by themselves, in the first place – men and women as well. They can come together, in the second place, if they like. But nothing is any good unless each one stands alone, intrinsically.'

'I'm with you there,' said Aaron. 'If I'd kep' myself to myself I shouldn't be bad now. Though I'm not very bad. I s'll be all right in the morning. But I did myself in when I went with another woman. I felt myself go – as if the bile broke inside me, and I was sick.'

'Josephine seduced you?' laughed Lilly.

'Ay, right enough,' replied Aaron grimly. 'She won't be coming here, will she?'

'Not unless I ask her.'

'You won't ask her, though – ?'

'No, not if you don't want her.'

'I don't.'

The fever made Aaron naive and communicative, unlike himself. And he knew he was being unlike himself, he knew that he was not in proper control of himself, so he was unhappy, uneasy.

'I'll stop here the night then, if you don't mind,' he said.

'You'll have to,' said Lilly. 'I've sent for the doctor. I believe you've got the flu.'

'Think I have?' said Aaron frightened.

'Don't be scared,' laughed Lilly.

There was a long pause. Lilly stood at the window looking at the darkening market, beneath the street-lamps.

'I s'll have to go to the hospital, if I have,' came Aaron's voice.

'No, if it's only going to be a week or a fortnight's business, you can stop here. I've nothing to do,' said Lilly.

'There's no occasion for you to saddle yourself with me,' said Aaron dejectedly.

'You can go to your hospital if you like – or back to your lodging – if you wish to,' said Lilly. 'You can make up your mind when you see how you are in the morning.'

'No use going back to my lodgings,' said Aaron.

'I'll send a telegram to your wife if you like,' said Lilly.

Aaron was silent, dead silent, for some time.

'Nay,' he said at length, in a decided voice. 'Not if I die for it.'

Lilly remained still, and the other man lapsed into a sort of semi-sleep, motionless and abandoned. The darkness had fallen over London, and away below the lamps were white. Lilly lit the green-shaded reading lamp over the desk. Then he stood and looked at Aaron, who lay still, looking sick. Rather beautiful the bones of the countenance: but the skull too small for such a heavy jaw and rather coarse mouth. Aaron half opened his eyes, and writhed feverishly, as if his limbs could not be in the right place. Lilly mended the fire, and sat down to write. Then he got up and went downstairs to unfasten the street door, so that the doctor could walk up. The business people had gone from their various holes, all the lower part of the tall house was in darkness.

Lilly waited and waited. He boiled an egg and made himself toast. Aaron said he might eat the same. Lilly cooked another egg and took it to the sick man. Aaron looked at it and pushed it away with nausea. He would have some tea. So Lilly gave him tea.

'Not much fun for you, doing this for somebody who is nothing to you,' said Aaron.

'I shouldn't if you were unsympathetic to me,' said Lilly. 'As it is, it's happened so, and so we'll let be.'

'What time is it?'

'Nearly eight o'clock.'

'Oh my Lord, the opera.'

And Aaron got half out of bed. But as he sat on the bedside he knew he could not safely get to his feet. He remained a picture of dejection.

'Perhaps we ought to let them know,' said Lilly.

But Aaron, blank with stupid misery, sat huddled there on the bedside without answering.

'I'll run round with a note,' said Lilly. 'I suppose others have had flu, beside you. Lie down!'

But Aaron stupidly and dejectedly sat huddled on the side of the bed, wearing old flannel pyjamas of Lilly's, rather small for him. He felt too sick to move.

'Lie down! Lie down!' said Lilly. 'And keep still while I'm gone. I shan't be more than ten minutes.'

'I don't care if I die,' said Aaron.

Lilly laughed.

'You're a long way from dying,' said he, 'or you wouldn't say it.'

But Aaron only looked up at him with queer, far-off, haggard eyes, something like a criminal who is just being executed.

'Lie down!' said Lilly, pushing him gently into the bed. 'You won't improve yourself sitting there, anyhow.'

Aaron lay down, turned away, and was quite still. Lilly quietly left the room on his errand.

The doctor did not come until ten o'clock: and worn out with work when he did come.

'Isn't there a lift in this establishment?' he said, as he groped his way up the stone stairs. Lilly had heard him, and run down to meet him.

The doctor poked the thermometer under Aaron's tongue and felt the pulse. Then he asked a few questions: listened to the heart and breathing.

'Yes, it's the flu,' he said curtly. 'Nothing to do but to keep warm in bed and not move, and take plenty of milk and liquid nourishment. I'll come round in the morning and give you an injection. Lungs are all right so far.'

'How long shall I have to be in bed?' said Aaron.

'Oh – depends. A week at least.'

Aaron watched him sullenly – and hated him. Lilly laughed to himself. The sick man was like a dog that is ill but which growls from a deep corner, and will bite if you put your hand in. He was in a state of black depression.

Lilly settled him down for the night, and himself went to bed. Aaron squirmed with heavy, pained limbs the night through, and slept and had bad dreams. Lilly got up to give him drinks. The din in the market was terrific before dawn, and Aaron suffered bitterly.

In the morning he was worse. The doctor gave him injections against pneumonia.

'You wouldn't like me to wire to your wife?' said Lilly.

'No,' said Aaron abruptly. 'You can send me to the hospital. I'm nothing but a piece of carrion.'

'Carrion!' said Lilly. 'Why?'

'I know it. I feel like it.'

'Oh, that's only the sort of nauseated feeling you get with flu.'

'I'm only fit to be thrown underground, and made an end of. I can't stand myself – '

He had a ghastly, grey look of self-repulsion.

'It's the germ that makes you feel like that,' said Lilly. 'It poisons the system for a time. But you'll work it off.'

At evening he was no better, the fever was still high. Yet there were no complications – except that the heart was irregular.

'The one thing I wonder,' said Lilly, 'is whether you hadn't better be moved out of the noise of the market. It's fearful for you in the early morning.'

'It makes no difference to me,' said Aaron.

The next day he was a little worse, if anything. The doctor knew there was nothing to be done. At evening he gave the patient a calomel pill. It was rather strong, and Aaron had a bad time. His burning, parched, poisoned inside was twisted and torn. Meanwhile carts banged, porters shouted, all the hell of the market went on outside, away down on the cobble setts. But this time the two men did not hear.

'You'll feel better now,' said Lilly, after the operation.

'It's done me harm,' cried Aaron fretfully. 'Send me to the hospital, or you'll repent it. Get rid of me in time.'

'Nay,' said Lilly. 'You get better. Damn it, you're only one among a million.'

Again over Aaron's face went the ghastly grimace of self-repulsion.

'My soul's gone rotten,' he said.

'No,' said Lilly. 'Only toxin in the blood.'

Next day the patient seemed worse, and the heart more irregular. He rested badly. So far, Lilly had got a fair night's rest. Now Aaron was not sleeping, and he seemed to struggle in the bed.

'Keep your courage up, man,' said the doctor sharply. 'You give way.'

Aaron looked at him blackly, and did not answer.

In the night Lilly was up time after time. Aaron would slip down on his back, and go semi-conscious. And then he would awake, as if drowning, struggling to move, mentally shouting aloud, yet making no sound for some moments, mentally shouting in frenzy, but unable to stir or make a sound. When at last he got some sort of physical control he cried: 'Lift me up! Lift me up!'

Lilly hurried and lifted him up, and he sat panting with a sobbing motion, his eyes gloomy and terrified, more than ever like a criminal who is just being executed. He drank brandy, and was laid down on his side.

'Don't let me lie on my back,' he said, terrified.

'No, I won't,' said Lilly.

Aaron frowned curiously on his nurse.

'Mind you don't let me,' he said, exacting and really terrified.

'No, I won't let you.'

And now Lilly was continually crossing over and pulling Aaron on to his side, whenever he found him slipped down on his back.

In the morning the doctor was puzzled. Probably it was the toxin in the blood which poisoned the heart. There was no pneumonia. And yet Aaron was clearly growing worse. The doctor agreed to send in a nurse for the coming night.

'What's the matter with you, man!' he said sharply to his patient. 'You give way! You give way! Can't you pull yourself together?'

But Aaron only became more gloomily withheld, retract-

ing from life. And Lilly began to be really troubled. He got a
friend to sit with the patient in the afternoon, whilst he himself went out and arranged to sleep in Aaron's room, at his
lodging.

The next morning, when he came in, he found the patient
lying as ever, in a sort of heap in the bed. Nurse had had to
lift him up and hold him up again. And now Aaron lay in a
sort of semi-stupor of fear, frustrated anger, misery and self-
repulsion: a sort of interlocked depression.

The doctor frowned when he came. He talked with the
nurse, and wrote another prescription. Then he drew Lilly
away to the door.

'What's the matter with the fellow?' he said. 'Can't you
rouse his spirit? He seems to be sulking himself out of life.
He'll drop out quite suddenly, you know, if he goes on like
this. Can't you rouse him up?'

'I think it depresses him partly that his bowels won't work.
It frightens him. He's never been ill in his life before,' said
Lilly.

'His bowels won't work if he lets all his spirit go, like an
animal dying of the sulks,' said the doctor impatiently. 'He
might go off quite suddenly – dead before you can turn
round –'

Lilly was properly troubled. Yet he did not quite know
what to do. It was early afternoon, and the sun was shining
into the room. There were daffodils and anemones in a jar,
and freezias and violets. Down below in the market were two
stalls of golden and blue flowers, gay.

'The flowers are lovely in the spring sunshine,' said Lilly.
'I wish I were in the country, don't you? As soon as you are
better we'll go. It's been a terrible cold, wet spring. But now
it's going to be nice. Do you like being in the country?'

'Yes,' said Aaron.

He was thinking of his garden. He loved it. Never in his
life had he been away from a garden before.

'Make haste and get better, and we'll go.'

'Where?' said Aaron.

'Hampshire. Or Berkshire. Or perhaps you'd like to go home? Would you?'

Aaron lay still, and did not answer.

'Perhaps you want to, and you don't want to,' said Lilly. 'You can please yourself, anyhow.'

There was no getting anything definite out of the sick man – his soul seemed stuck, as if it would not move.

Suddenly Lilly rose and went to the dressing-table.

'I'm going to rub you with oil,' he said. 'I'm going to rub you as mothers do their babies whose bowels don't work.'

Aaron frowned slightly as he glanced at the dark, self-possessed face of the little man.

'What's the good of that?' he said irritably. 'I'd rather be left alone.'

'Then you won't be.'

Quickly he uncovered the blond lower body of his patient, and began to rub the abdomen with oil, using a slow, rhythmic, circulating motion, a sort of massage. For a long time he rubbed finely and steadily, then went over the whole of the lower body, mindless, as if in a sort of incantation. He rubbed every speck of the man's lower body – the abdomen, the buttocks, the thighs and knees, down to the feet, rubbed it all warm and glowing with camphorated oil, every bit of it, chafing the toes swiftly, till he was almost exhausted. Then Aaron was covered up again, and Lilly sat down in fatigue to look at his patient.

He saw a change. The spark had come back into the sick eyes, and the faint trace of a smile, faintly luminous, into the face. Aaron was regaining himself. But Lilly said nothing. He watched his patient fall into a proper sleep.

And he sat and watched him sleep. And he thought to himself, 'I wonder why I do it. I wonder why I bother with him. Jim ought to have taught me my lesson. As soon as this man's really better he'll punch me in the wind, metaphorically if not actually, for having interfered with him. And Tanny would say he was quite right to do it. She says I want power over them. What if I do? They don't care how much power the mob has over them, the nation. Lloyd George and North-cliffe and the police and money. They'll yield themselves up to that sort of power quickly enough, and immolate themselves *pro bono publico* by the million. And what's the *bonum publicum* but the mob power? Why can't they submit to a bit of healthy individual authority? The fool would die, without me: just as that fool Jim will die in hysterics one day. Why does he last so long!

'Tanny's the same. She does nothing really but resist me: my authority, or my influence, or just *me*. At the bottom of her heart she just blindly and persistently opposes me. God knows what it is she opposes: just me myself. She thinks I want her to submit to me. So I do, in a measure natural to our two selves. Somewhere, she ought to submit to me. But they all prefer to kick against the pricks. Not that *they* get many pricks. I get them. Damn them all, why don't I leave them alone? They only grin and feel triumphant when they've insulted one and punched one in the wind.

'This Aaron will do just the same. I like him, and he ought to like me. And he'll be another Jim: he *will* like me, if he can knock the wind out of me. A lot of little Stavrogins coming up to whisper affectionately, and biting one's ear.

'But anyhow I can soon see the last of this chap: and him the last of all the rest. I'll be damned for ever if I see their Jims and Roberts and Julias and Scotts any more. Let them dance round their insipid hell-broth. Thin tack it is.

'There's a whole world besides this little gang of wastrels. Except, dear God, that they've exterminated all the peoples worth knowing. I can't do with folks who teem by the billion, like the Chinese and Japs and Orientals altogether. Only vermin teem by the billion. Higher types breed slower. I would have loved the Aztecs and the Red Indians. I *know* they hold the element in life which I am looking for – they had living pride. Not like the flea-bitten Asiatics. Even niggers are better than Asiatics, though they are wallowers. The American races – and the South Sea Islanders – the Marquesans, the Maori blood. That was the true blood. It wasn't frightened. All the rest are craven – Europeans, Asiatics, Africans – everyone at his own individual quick craven and cringing: only conceited in the mass, the mob. How I hate them: the mass-bullies, the individual Judases.

'Well, if one will be a Jesus he must expect his Judas. That's why Abraham Lincoln gets shot. A Jesus makes a Judas inevitable. A man should remain himself, not try to spread himself over humanity. He should pivot himself on his own pride.

'I suppose really I ought to have packed this Aaron off to the hospital. Instead of which here am I rubbing him with oil to rub the life into him. And I *know* he'll bite me, like a warmed snake, the moment he recovers. And Tanny will say "Quite right too," I shouldn't have been so intimate. No, I should have left it to mechanical doctors and nurses.

'So I should. Everything to its own. And Aaron belongs to this little system, and Jim is waiting to be psycho-analysed, and Tanny is waiting for her own glorification.

'All right, Aaron. Last time I break my bread for anybody, this is. So get better, my flautist, so that I can go away.

'It was easy for the Red Indians and the others to take their hook into death. They might have stayed a bit longer to help one to defy the white masses.

'I'll make some tea – '

Lilly rose softly and went across to the fire. He had to cross a landing to a sort of little lavatory, with a sink and a tap, for water. The clerks peeped out at him from an adjoining office and nodded. He nodded, and disappeared from their sight as quickly as possible, with his kettle. His dark eyes were quick, his dark hair was untidy, there was something silent and withheld about him. People could never approach him quite ordinarily.

He put on the kettle, and quietly set cups and plates on a tray. The room was clean and cosy and pleasant. He did the cleaning himself, and was as efficient and unobtrusive a house-wife as any woman. While the kettle boiled, he sat darning the socks which he had taken off Aaron's feet when the flautist arrived, and which he had washed. He preferred that no outsider should see him doing these things. Yet he preferred also to do them himself, so that he should be independent of outside aid.

His face was dark and hollow, he seemed frail, sitting there in the London afternoon darning the black woollen socks. His full brow was knitted slightly, there was a tension. At the same time, there was an indomitable stillness about him, as it were in the atmosphere about him. His hands, though small, were not very thin. He bit off the wool as he finished his darn.

As he was making the tea he saw Aaron rouse up in bed.

'I've been to sleep. I feel better,' said the patient, turning round to look what the other man was doing. And the sight of the water steaming in a jet into the teapot seemed attractive.

'Yes,' said Lilly. 'You've slept for a good two hours.'

'I believe I have,' said Aaron.

'Would you like a little tea?'

'Ay – and a bit of toast.'

'You're not supposed to have solid food. Let me take your temperature.'

The temperature was down to a hundred, and Lilly, in spite of the doctor, gave Aaron a piece of toast with his tea, enjoining him not to mention it to the nurse.

In the evening the two men talked.

'You do everything for yourself, then?' said Aaron.

'Yes, I prefer it.'

'You like living all alone?'

'I don't know about that. I never have lived alone. Tanny and I have been very much alone in various countries: but that's two, not one.'

'You miss her then?'

'Yes, of course. I missed her horribly in the cottage, when she'd first gone. I felt my heart was broken. But here, where we've never been together, I don't notice it so much.'

'She'll come back,' said Aaron.

'Yes, she'll come back. But I'd rather meet her abroad than here – and get on a different footing.'

'Why?'

'Oh, I don't know. There's something wrong with marriage altogether, I think. *Egoisme à deux* – '

'What's that mean?'

'*Egoisme à deux?* Two people, one egoism. Marriage is a self-conscious egoistic state, it seems to me.'

'You've got no children?' said Aaron.

'No. Tanny wants children badly. I don't. I'm thankful we have none.'

'Why?'

'I can't quite say. I think of them as a burden. Besides, there *are* such millions and billions of children in the world. And we know well enough what sort of millions and billions of people they'll grow up into. I don't want to add my quota to the mass – It's against my instinct – '

'Ay – !' laughed Aaron, with a curt acquiescence.

'Tanny's furious. But then, when a woman has got children, she thinks the world wags only for them and her. Nothing else. The whole world wags for the sake of the children – and their sacred mother.'

'Ay, that's *damned* true,' said Aaron.

'And myself I'm sick of the children stunt. Children are all right, so long as you just take them for what they are; young immature things like kittens and half-grown dogs, nuisances, sometimes very charming. But I'll be hanged if I can see anything high and holy about children. I should be sorry to, it would be so bad for the children. Young brats, tiresome and amusing in turns.'

'When they don't give themselves airs,' said Aaron.

'Yes, indeed. Which they do half their time. Sacred children and sacred motherhood, I'm absolutely fed stiff by it. That's why I'm thankful I have no children. Tanny can't come it over me there.'

'It's a fact. When a woman's got her children, by God,

she's a bitch in the manger. You can starve while she sits on the hay. It's useful to keep her pups warm.'

'Yes.'

'Why, you know – ' Aaron turned excitedly in the bed, 'they look on a man as if he was nothing but an instrument to get and rear children. If you have anything to do with a woman, she thinks it's because you want to get children by her. And I'm damned if it is. I want my own pleasure, or nothing: and children be damned.'

'Ah women! – *they* must be loved at any price!' said Lilly. 'And if you just don't want to love them – and tell them so – what a crime!'

'A crime!' said Aaron. 'They make a criminal of you. Them and their children be cursed. Is my life given me for nothing but to get children, and work for a woman? See them all in hell first, – they'd better die while they're children, if childhood's all that's important.'

'I quite agree,' said Lilly. 'If childhood is more important than manhood, then why live to be a man at all? Why not remain an infant?'

'Be damned and blasted to women and all their importances,' cried Aaron. 'They want to get you under, and children is their chief weapon.'

'Men have got to stand up to the fact that manhood is more than childhood – and then force women to admit it,' said Lilly. 'But the rotten whiners, they're all grovelling before a baby's napkin and a woman's petticoat.'

'It's a fact,' said Aaron. But he glanced at Lilly oddly, as if suspiciously. And Lilly caught the look. But he continued:

'And if they think you try to stand on your legs and walk with the feet of manhood, why, there isn't a blooming father and lover among them but will do his best to get you down and suffocate you – either with a baby's napkin or a woman's petticoat.'

Lilly's lips were curling, he was dark and bitter.

'Ay, it is like that,' said Aaron, rather subduedly.

'The man's spirit has gone out of the world. Men can't

123

move an inch unless they can grovel humbly at the end of the journey.'

'No,' said Aaron, watching with keen, half-amused eyes.

'That's why marriage wants readjusting – or extending – to get men on to their own legs once more, and to give them the adventure again. But men won't stick together and fight for it. Because once a woman has climbed up with her children, she'll find plenty of grovellers ready to support her and suffocate any defiant spirit. And women will sacrifice eleven men, fathers, husbands, brothers and lovers, for one baby – or for her own female self-conceit.'

'She will that,' said Aaron.

'And can you find two men to stick together, without feeling criminal, and without cringing, and without betraying one another? You can't. One is sure to go fawning round some female, then they both enjoy giving each other away, and doing a new grovel before a woman again.'

'Ay,' said Aaron.

After which Lilly was silent.

CHAPTER 10

The War Again

'ONE is a fool,' said Lilly, 'to be lachrymose. The thing to do is to get a move on.'

Aaron looked up with a glimpse of a smile. The two men were sitting before the fire at the end of a cold, wet April day: Aaron convalescent, somewhat chastened in appearance.

'Ay,' he said rather sourly. 'A move back to Guilford Street.'

'Oh, I meant to tell you,' said Lilly. 'I was reading an old Baden history. They made a law in 1528 – not a law, but a regulation – that if a man forsakes his wife and children, as now so often happens, the said wife and chiildren are at once to be despatched after him. I thought that would please you. Does it?'

'Yes,' said Aaron briefly.

'They would have arrived the next day, like a forwarded letter.'

'I should have had to get a considerable move on, at that rate,' grinned Aaron.

'Oh no. You might quite like them here.' But Lilly saw the white frown of determined revulsion on the convalescent's face.

'Wouldn't you?' he asked.

Aaron shook his head.

'No,' he said. And it was obvious he objected to the topic. 'What are you going to do about your move on?'

'Me!' said Lilly. 'I'm going to sail away next week – or steam dirtily away on a tramp called the "Maud Allen Wing".'

'Where to?'

'Malta.'

'Where from?'

'London Dock. I fixed up my passage this morning for ten pounds. I am cook's assistant, signed on.'

Aaron looked at him with a little admiration.

'You can take a sudden jump, can you?' he said.

'The difficulty is to refrain from jumping: overboard or anywhere.'

Aaron smoked his pipe slowly.

'And what good will Malta do you?' he asked, envious.

'Heaven knows. I shall cross to Syracuse, and move up Italy.'

'Sounds as if you were a millionaire.'

'I've got thirty-five pounds in all the world. But something will come along.'

'I've got more than that,' said Aaron.

'Good for you,' replied Lilly.

He rose and went to the cupboard, taking out a bowl and a basket of potatoes. He sat down again, paring the potatoes. His busy activity annoyed Aaron.

'But what's the good of going to Malta? Shall *you* be any different in yourself, in another place? You'll be the same there as you are here.'

'How am I here?'

'Why you're all the time grinding yourself against something inside you. You're never free. You're never content. You never stop chafing.'

Lilly dipped his potato into the water, and cut out the eyes carefully. Then he cut it in two, and dropped it in the clean water of the second bowl. He had not expected this criticism.

'Perhaps I don't,' said he.

'Then what's the use of going somewhere else. You won't change yourself.'

'I may in the end,' said Lilly.

'You'll be yourself, whether it's Malta or London,' said Aaron.

'There's a doom for me,' laughed Lilly. The water on the

fire was boiling. He rose and threw in salt, then dropped in the potatoes with little plops. 'But there are lots of me's. I'm not only just one proposition. A new place brings out a new thing in a man. Otherwise you'd have stayed in your old place with your family.'

'The man in the middle of you doesn't change,' said Aaron.

'Do you find it so?' said Lilly.

'Ay. Every time.'

'Then what's to be done?'

'Nothing, as far as I can see. You get as much amusement out of life as possible, and there's the end of it.'

'All right then, I'll get the amusement.'

'Ay, all right then,' said Aaron. 'But there isn't anything wonderful about it. You talk as if you were doing something special. You aren't. You're no more than a man who drops into a pub for a drink, to liven himself up a bit. Only you give it a lot of names, and make out as if you were looking for the philosopher's stone, or something like that. When you're only killing time like the rest of folks, before time kills you.'

Lilly did not answer. It was not yet seven o'clock, but the sky was dark. Aaron sat in the firelight. Even the saucepan on the fire was silent. Darkness, silence, the firelight in the upper room, and the two men together.

'It isn't quite true,' said Lilly, leaning on the mantelpiece and staring down into the fire.

'Where isn't it? You talk, and you make a man believe you've got something he hasn't got. But where is it, when it comes to? What have you got, more than me or Jim Bricknell! Only a bigger choice of words, it seems to me.'

Lilly was motionless and inscrutable like a shadow.

'Does it, Aaron!' he said, in a colourless voice.

'Yes. What else is there to it?' Aaron sounded testy.

'Why,' said Lilly at last, 'there's something. I agree, it's true what you say about me. But there's a bit of something else. There's just a bit of something in me, I think, which *isn't* a man running into a pub for a drink – '

'And what – ?'

127

The question fell into the twilight like a drop of water falling down a deep shaft into a well.

'I think a man may come into possession of his own soul at last – as the Buddhists teach – but without ceasing to love, or even to hate. One loves, one hates – but somewhere beyond it all, one understands, and possesses one's soul in patience and in peace –'

'Yes,' said Aaron slowly, 'while you only stand and talk about it. But when you've got no chance to talk about it – and when you've got to live – you don't possess your soul neither in patience nor in peace, but any devil that likes possesses you and does what it likes with you, while you fridge yourself and fray yourself out like a worn rag.'

'I don't care,' said Lilly. 'I'm learning to possess my soul in patience and in peace, and I know it. And it isn't a negative Nirvana either. And if Tanny possesses her own soul in patience and peace as well – and if in this we understand each other at last – then there we are, together and apart at the same time, and free of each other, and eternally insepar-able. I have my Nirvana – and I have it all to myself. But more than that. It coincides with her Nirvana.'

'Ah yes,' said Aaron. 'But I don't understand all that word-splitting.'

'I do though. You learn to be quite alone, and possess your own soul in isolation – and at the same time, to be perfectly *with* someone else – that's all I ask.'

'Sort of sit on a mountain top, back to back with some-body else, like a couple of idols.'

'No – because it isn't a case of sitting – or a case of back to back. It's what you get to after a lot of fighting and a lot of sensual fulfilment. And it never does away with the fight-ing and with the sensual passion. It flowers on top of them, and it would never flower save on top of them.'

'What wouldn't?'

'The possessing one's own soul – and the being together with someone else in silence, beyond speech.'

'And you've got them?'

'I've got a *bit* of the real quietness inside me.'

'So has a dog on a mat.'

'So I believe too.'

'Or a man in a pub.'

'Which I don't believe.'

'You prefer the dog?'

'Maybe.'

There was silence for a few moments.

'And I'm the man in the pub,' said Aaron.

'You aren't the dog on the mat, anyhow.'

'And you're the idol on the mountain top, worshipping yourself.'

'You talk to me like a woman, Aaron.'

'How do you talk to *me*, do you think?'

'How do I?'

'Are the potatoes done?'

Lilly turned quickly aside, and switched on the electric light. Everything changed. Aaron sat still before the fire, irritated. Lilly went about preparing the supper.

The room was pleasant at night. Two tall dark screens hid the two beds. In front, the piano was littered with music, the desk littered with papers. Lilly went out on to the landing, and set the chops to grill on the gas stove. Hastily he put a small table on the hearth-rug, spread it with a blue-and-white cloth, set plates and glasses. Aaron did not move. It was not his nature to concern himself with domestic matters – and Lilly did it best alone.

The two men had an almost uncanny understanding of one another – like brothers. They came from the same district, from the same class. Each might have been born into the other's circumstances. Like brothers, there was a profound hostility between them. But hostility is not antipathy.

Lilly's skilful housewifery always irritated Aaron: it was so self-sufficient. But most irritating of all was the little man's unconscious assumption of priority. Poor Lilly was actually unaware that he assumed this quiet predominance over others. He mashed the potatoes, he heated the plates, he warmed the red wine, he whisked eggs into the milk pudding, and served his visitor like a housemaid. But none of this detracted from the silent assurance with which he bore himself, and with which he seemed to domineer over his acquaintance.

At last the meal was ready. Lilly drew the curtains, switched off the central light, put the green-shaded electric lamp on the table, and the two men drew up to the meal. It was good food, well cooked and hot. Certainly Lilly's hands were no longer clean: but it was clean dirt, as he said.

Aaron sat in the low arm-chair at table. So his face was below, in the full light. Lilly sat high on a small chair, so that his face was in the green shadow. Aaron was handsome, and always had that peculiar well-dressed look of his type. Lilly was indifferent to his own appearance, and his collar was a rag.

So the two men ate in silence. They had been together alone for a fortnight only: but it was like a small eternity. Aaron was well now – only he suffered from the depression and the sort of fear that follows influenza.

'When are you going?' he asked irritably, looking up at Lilly, whose face hovered in that green shadow above, and worried him.

'One day next week. They'll send me a telegram. Not later than Thursday.'

'You're looking forward to going?' The question was half bitter.

'Yes. I want to get a new tune out of myself.'

'Had enough of this?'

'Yes.'

A flush of anger came on Aaron's face.

'You're easily on, and easily off,' he said, rather insulting.

'Am I?' said Lilly. 'What makes you think so?'

'Circumstances,' replied Aaron sourly.

To which there was no answer. The host cleared away the plates, and put the pudding on the table. He pushed the bowl to Aaron.

'I suppose I shall never see you again, once you've gone,' said Aaron.

'It's your choice. I will leave you an address.'

After this, the pudding was eaten in silence.

'Besides, Aaron,' said Lilly, drinking his last sip of wine, 'what do you care whether you see me again or not? What do you care whether you see anybody again or not? You want to be amused. And now you're irritated because you think I am not going to amuse you any more: and you don't know who *is* going to amuse you. I admit it's a dilemma. But it's a hedonistic dilemma of the commonest sort.'

'I don't know hedonistic. And supposing I am as you say – are you any different?'

'No, I'm not very different. But I always persuade myself there's a bit of a difference. Do you know what Josephine Ford confessed to me? She's had her lovers enough. "There isn't any such thing as love, Lilly," she said. "Men are simply afraid to be alone. That is absolutely all there is in it: fear of being alone."'

'What by that?' said Aaron.

'You agree?'

'Yes, on the whole.'

'So do I – on the whole. And then I asked her what about woman. And then she said with a woman it wasn't fear, it was just boredom. A woman is like a violinist: any fiddle, any instrument rather than empty hands and no tune going.'

'Yes – what I said before: getting as much amusement out of life as possible,' said Aaron.

'You amuse – and I'll amuse you.'

'Yes – just about that.'

'All right, Aaron,' said Lilly. 'I'm not going to amuse you, or try to amuse you any more.'

'Going to try somebody else: and Malta.'

'Malta anyhow.'

'Oh and somebody else – in the next five minutes.'

'Yes – that also.'

'Good-bye and good luck to you.'

'Good-bye and good luck to you, Aaron.'

With which Lilly went aside to wash the dishes. Aaron sat

alone under the zone of light, turning over a score of *Pelléas*. Though the noise of London was around them, it was far below, and in the room was a deep silence. Each of the men seemed invested in his own silence.

Aaron suddenly took his flute, and began trying little passages from the opera on his knee. He had not played since his illness. The noise came out a little tremulous, but low and sweet. Lilly came forward with a plate and a cloth in his hand.

'Aaron's rod is putting forth again,' he said, smiling.

'What?' said Aaron, looking up.

'I said Aaron's rod is putting forth again.'

'What rod?'

'Your flute, for the moment.'

'It's got to put forth my bread and butter.'

'Is that all the buds it's going to have?'

'Nay – that's for you to show. What flowers do you imagine came out of the rod of Moses's brother?'

'Scarlet runners, I should think, if he'd got to live on them.'

'Scarlet enough, I'll bet.'

Aaron turned unnoticing back to his music. Lilly finished the wiping of the dishes, then took a book and sat on the other side of the table.

'It's all one to you then' said Aaron suddenly, 'whether we ever see one another again?'

'Not a bit,' said Lilly, looking up over his spectacles. 'I very much wish there might be something that held us together.'

'Then if you wish it, why isn't there?'

'You might wish your flute to put out scarlet-runner flowers at the joints.'

'Ay – I might. And it would be all the same.'

The moment of silence that followed was extraordinary in its hostility.

'Oh, we shall run across one another again some time.' said Aaron.

'Sure,' said Lilly. 'More than that: I'll write you an address that will always find me. And when you write I will answer you.'

He took a bit of paper and scribbled an address. Aaron folded it and put it into his waistcoat pocket. It was an Italian address.

'But how can I live in Italy?' he said. 'You can shift about. I'm tied to a job.'

'You – with your budding rod, your flute – and your charm – you can always do as you like.'

'My what?'

'Your flute and your charm.'

'What charm?'

'Just your own. Don't pretend you don't know you've got it. I don't really like charm myself: too much of a trick about it. But whether or not, you've got it.'

'It's news to me.'

'Not it.'

'Fact, it is.'

'Ha! Somebody will always take a fancy to you. And you can live on that, as well as on anything else.'

'Why do you always speak so despisingly?'

'Why shouldn't I?'

'Have you any right to despise another man?'

'When did it go by rights?'

'No, not with you.'

'You answer me like a woman, Aaron.'

Again there was a space of silence. And again it was Aaron who at last broke it.

'We're in different positions, you and me,' he said.

'How?'

'You can live by your writing – but I've got to have a job.'

'Is that all?' said Lilly.

'Ay. And plenty. You've got the advantage of me.'

'Quite,' said Lilly. 'But why? I was a dirty-nosed little boy when you were a clean-nosed little boy. And I always had more patches on my breeches than you: neat patchtes too, my poor mother! So what's the good of talking about advantages. You had the start. And at this very moment you could buy me up, lock, stock, and barrel. So don't feel hard done by. It's a lie.'

'You've got your freedom.'

'I make it and I take it.'

'Circumstances make it for you.'

'As you like.'

'You don't do a man justice,' said Aaron.

'Does a man care?'

'He might.'

'Then he's no man.'

'Thanks again, old fellow.'

'Welcome,' said Lilly, grimacing.

Again Aaron looked at him, baffled, almost with hatred. Lilly grimaced at the blank wall opposite, and seemed to ruminate. Then he went back to his book. And no sooner had he forgotten Aaron, reading the fantasies of a certain Leo Frobenius, than Aaron must stride in again.

'You can't say there isn't a difference between your position and mine,' he said pertinently.

Lilly looked darkly over his spectacles.

'No, by God,' he said. 'I should be in a poor way otherwise.'

'You can't say you haven't the advantage – your *job* gives you the advantage.'

'All right. Then heave it out with my job, and leave me alone.'

'That's your way of dodging it.'

'My dear Aaron, I agree with you perfectly. There is no difference between us, save the fictitious advantage given to me by my job. Save for my job – which is to write lies – Aaron and I are two identical little men in one and the same little boat. Shall we leave it at that, now?'

'Yes,' said Aaron. 'That's about it.'

'Let's shake hands on it – and go to bed, my dear chap. You are just recovering from influenza, and look paler than I like.'

'You mean you want to be rid of me,' said Aaron.

'Yes, I do mean that,' said Lilly.

'Ay,' said Aaron.

And after a few minutes more staring at the score of *Pelléas*, he rose, put the score away on the piano, laid his flute beside it, and retired behind the screen. In silence, the strange dim noise of London sounding from below, Lilly read on about the Kabyles. His soul had the faculty of divesting itself of the moment, and seeking further, deeper interests. These old Africans! And Atlantis! Strange, strange wisdom of the Kabyles! Old, old dark Africa, and the world before the flood! How jealous Aaron seemed! The child of a jealous God. A jealous God! Could any race be anything but despicable, with such an antecedent?

But no, persistent as a jealous God himself, Aaron reappeared in his pyjamas, and seated himself in his chair.

'What is the difference then between you and me, Lilly?' he said.

'Haven't we shaken hands on it – a difference of jobs.'

'You don't believe that though, do you?'

'Nay, now I reckon you're trespassing.'

'Why am I? I know you don't believe it.'

'What do I believe then?' said Lilly.

'You believe you know something better than me – and that you are something better than me. Don't you?'

'Do *you* believe it?'

'What?'

'That I *am* something better than you, and that I *know* something better?'

'No, because I don't see it,' said Aaron.

'Then if you don't see it, it isn't there. So go to bed and sleep the sleep of the just and the convalescent. I am not to be badgered any more.

'Am I badgering you?' said Aaron.

'Indeed you are.'

'So I'm in the wrong, again?'

'Once more, my dear.'

'You're a God-Almighty in your way, you know.'

'So long as I'm not in anybody else's way. Anyhow, you'd be much better sleeping the sleep of the just. And I'm going out for a minute or two. Don't catch cold there with nothing on –

'I want to catch the post,' he added, rising.

Aaron looked up at him quickly. But almost before there was time to speak, Lilly had slipped into his hat and coat, seized his letters, and gone.

It was a rainy night. Lilly turned down King Street to walk to Charing Cross. He liked being out of doors. He liked to post his letters at Charing Cross post office. He did not want to talk to Aaron any more. He was glad to be alone.

He walked quickly down Villiers Street to the river, to see it flowing blackly towards the sea. It had an endless fascination for him: never failed to soothe him and give him a sense of liberty. He liked the night, the dark rain, the river, and even the traffic. He enjoyed the sense of friction he got from the streaming of people who meant nothing to him. It was like a fox slipping alert among unsuspecting cattle.

When he got back, he saw in the distance the lights of a taxi standing outside the building where he lived, and heard a thumping and hallooing. He hurried forward.

It was a man called Herbertson.

'Oh, why, there you are!' exclaimed Herbertson, as Lilly drew near. 'Can I come up and have a chat?'

'I've got that man who's had flu. I should think he is gone to bed.'

'Oh!' The disappointment was plain. 'Well, look here! I'll just come up for a couple of minutes.' He laid his hand on Lilly's arm. 'I heard you were going away. Where are you going?'

'Malta.'

'Malta! Oh, I know Malta very well. Well now, it'll be all right if I come up for a minute? I'm not going to see much more of you, apparently.' He turned quickly to the taxi. 'What is it on the clock?'

The taxi was paid, the two men went upstairs. Aaron was in bed, but he called as Lilly entered the room.

'Hullo!' said Lilly. 'Not asleep? Captain Herbertson has come in for a minute.'

'Hope I shan't disturb you,' said Captain Herbertson, laying down his stick and gloves, and his cap. He was in uniform. He was one of the few surviving officers of the Guards, a man of about forty-five, good-looking, getting rather stout. He settled himself in the chair where Aaron had sat, hitching up his trousers. The gold identity plate, with its gold chain, fell conspicuously over his wrist.

'Been to *Rosemary*,' he said. 'Rotten play, you know – but passes the time awfully well. Oh, I quite enjoyed it.'

Lilly offered him Sauterne – the only thing in the house.

'Oh yes! How awfully nice! Yes, thanks, I shall love it. Can I have it with soda? Thanks! Do you know, I think that's the very best drink in the tropics: sweet white wine, with soda. Yes – well! Well now, why are you going away?'

'For a change,' said Lilly.

'You're quite right, one needs a change now the damned thing is all over. As soon as I get out of khaki I shall be off. Malta! Yes! I've been in Malta several times. I think Valetta is quite enjoyable, particularly in winter, with the opera. Oh – er – how's your wife? All right? Yes! – glad to see her people again. Bound to be. Oh, by the way, I met Jim Bricknell. Sends you a message hoping you'll go down and stay – down at Captain Bingham's place in Surrey, you know. Awfully queer lot down there. Not my sort, no. You won't go down? No, I shouldn't. Not the right sort of people.'

Herbertson rattled away, rather spasmodic. He had been through the very front hell of the war – and like every man who had, he had the war at the back of his mind, like an obsession. But in the meantime, he skirmished.

'Yes. I was on guard the other day when the Queen gave one of her tea-parties to the blind. Awful affair. But the children are awfully nice children. Prince of Wales awfully nice, almost too nice. Prince Henry smart boy, too – oh, a smart boy. Queen Mary poured out the tea, and I handed round bread and butter. She told me I made a very good waiter. I said, "Thank you, Madam".'

The talk flowed on: about royalty and the Guards, Buckingham Palace and St James.

'Rather a nice story about Queen Victoria. Man named Joyce, something or other, often used to dine at the Palace. And he was an awfully good imitator – really clever, you know. Used to imitate the Queen. "Mr. Joyce," she said, "I hear your imitation is very amusing. Will you do it for us now, and let us see what it is like?" "Oh no, Madam! I'm afraid I couldn't do it now. I'm afraid I'm not in the humour." But she would have him do it. And it was really awfully funny. He had to do it. You know what he did. He used to take a table-napkin, and put it on with one corner over his forehead, and the rest hanging down behind, like her veil thing. And then he sent for the kettle-lid. He always had the kettle-lid, for that little crown of hers. And then he impersonated her. But he was awfully good – so clever. "Mr Joyce," she said. "We are not amused. Please leave the room." Yes, that is exactly what she said: "*We* are not amused – please leave the room." I like the *We!* don't you? And he a man of sixty or so. However, he left the room and for a fortnight or so he wasn't invited. Wasn't she wonderful – Queen Victoria?'

And so, by light transitions, to the Prince of Wales at the front, and thus into the trenches. And then Herbertson was on the subject he was obsessed by. He had come, unconsciously, for this and this only; to talk war to Lilly: or at Lilly. For the latter listened and watched, and said nothing. As a man at night helplessly takes a taxi to find some woman, some prostitute, Herbertson had almost unthinkingly got into a taxi and come battering at the door in Covent Garden, only to talk war to Lilly, whom he knew very little. But it was a driving instinct – to come and get it off his chest.

And on and on he talked, over his wine and soda. He was not conceited – he was not showing off – far from it. It was the same thing here in this officer as it was with the privates, and the same with this Englishman as with a Frenchman or a German or an Italian. Lilly had sat in a cow-shed listening to a youth in the north country: he had sat on the corn-straw that the oxen had been treading out, in Calabria, under the moon: he had sat in a farm-kitchen with a German prisoner; and every time it was the same thing, the same hot, blind, anguished voice of a man who has seen too much, experienced too much, and doesn't know where to turn. None of the glamour of returned heroes, none of the romance of war: only a hot, blind, mesmerized voice, going on and on, mesmerized by a vision that the soul cannot bear.

In this officer, of course, there was a lightness and an appearance of bright diffidence and humour. But underneath it all was the same as in the common men of all the combatant nations: the hot, seared burn of unbearable experience, which did not heal nor cool, and whose irritation was not to be relieved. The experience gradually cooled on top: but only with a surface crust. The soul did not heal, did not recover.

'I used to be awfully frightened,' laughed Herbertson. 'Now you say, Lilly, you'd never have stood it. But you would. You're nervous – and it was just the nervous ones that did stand it. When nearly all our officers were gone, we had a man come out – a man called Margeritson, from India – big merchant people out there. They all said he was no good – not a bit of good – nervous chap. No good at all. But when you had to get out of the trench and go for the Germans he was perfect – perfect. It all came to him then, at the crisis, and he was perfect.

'Some things frighten one man, and some another. Now, shells would never frighten me. But I couldn't stand bombs. You could tell the difference between our machines and the Germans. Ours was a steady noise – drrrrrrrr! but their was heavy, drrrr*ruru*drrrr*ruru*–! My word, that got on my nerves . . .

'No, I was never hit. The nearest thing was when I was knocked down by an exploding shell – several times that – you know. When you shout like mad for the men to come and dig you out, under all the earth. And my word, you do feel frightened then.' Herbertson laughed with a twinkling motion to Lilly. But between his brows there was a tension like madness.

'And a funny thing, you know – how you don't notice things. In – let me see – 1916 – the German guns were a lot better than ours. Ours were old, and when they're old you can't tell where they'll hit: whether they'll go beyond the mark, or whether they'll fall short. Well, this day our guns were firing short, and killing our own men. We'd had the order to charge, and were running forward, and I suddenly felt hot water spurting on my neck – ' He put his hand to the back of his neck and glanced round apprehensively. 'It was a chap called Innes. Oh, an awfully decent sort – people were in the Argentine. He'd been calling out to me as we were running, and I was just answering. When I felt this hot water on my neck and saw him running past me with no head – he'd got no head, and he went running past me. I don't know how far, but a long way . . . Blood, you know. Yes, well –

'Oh, I hated Chelsea – I loathed Chelsea – Chelsea was purgatory to me. I had a corporal called Wallace – he was a fine chap – oh, he was a fine chap – six foot two – and about twenty-four years old. He was my stand-back. Oh, I hated Chelsea, and parades, and drills. You know, when it's drill, and you're giving orders, you forget what order you've just given – in front of the Palace there the crowd don't notice – but it's awful for *you*. And you know you daren't look round to see what the men are doing. But Wallace was splendid. He was just behind me, and I'd hear him, quite quiet, you know, 'It's right wheel, sir.' Always perfect, always perfect – yes – well . . .

'You know you don't get killed if you don't think you will. Now I never thought I should get killed. And I never knew a man get killed if he hadn't been thinking he would. I said to Wallace I'd rather be out here, at the front, than at Chelsea. I hated Chelsea – I can't tell you how much. "Oh no, sir!" he said. "I'd rather be at Chelsea than here. I'd rather be at Chelsea. There isn't hell like this at Chelsea."

We'd had orders that we were to go back to the rear camp the next day. "Never mind, Wallace," I said. "We shall be out of this hell-on-earth to-morrow." And he took my hand. We weren't much for showing feeling or anything in the Guards. But he took my hand. And we climbed out to change. Poor fellow, he was killed – ' Herbertson dropped his head, and for some moments seemed to go unconscious, as if struck. Then he lifted his face, and went on in the same animated, chatty fashion: 'You see, he had a presentiment. I'm sure he had a presentiment. None of the men got killed unless they had a presentiment – like that, you know . . .

Herbertson nodded keenly at Lilly, with his sharp, twinkling, yet obsessed eyes. Lilly wondered why he made the presentiment responsible for the death – which he obviously did – and not *vice versa*. Herbertson implied every time, that you'd never get killed if you could keep yourself from having a presentiment. Perhaps there was something in it. Perhaps the soul issues its own ticket of death, when it can stand no more. Surely life controls life: and not accident.

'It's a funny thing what shock will do. We had a sergeant and he shouted to me. Both his feet were off – both his feet, clean at the ankle. I gave him morphia. You know officers aren't allowed to use the needle – might give the man blood poisoning. You give those tabloids. They say they act in a few minutes, but they *don't*. It's a quarter of an hour. And nothing is more demoralizing than when you have a man, wounded, you know, and crying out. Well, this man I gave him the morphia before he got over the stunning, you know. So he didn't feel the pain. Well, they carried him in. I always used to like to look after my men. So I went next morning and I found he hadn't been removed to the Clearing Station. I got hold of the doctor and I said, "Look here! Why hasn't this man been taken to the Clearing Station?" I used to get excited. But after some years they'd got used to me. "Don't get excited, Herbertson, the man's dying." "But," I said, "he's just been talking to me as strong as you are." And he had – he'd talk as strong and well as you or me, then go quiet for a bit. I said I gave him the morphia before he came round from the stunning. So he'd felt nothing. But in two hours he was dead. The doctor says that the shock does it like that sometimes. You can do nothing for them. Nothing vital is injured – and yet life is broken in them Nothing can be done – funny thing. Must be something in the brain –'

'It's obviously not the brain,' said Lilly. 'It's deeper than the brain.'

'Deeper,' said Herbertson, nodding.

'Funny thing where life is. We had a lieutenant. You know we all buried our own dead. Well, he looked as if he was asleep. Most of the chaps looked like that.' Herbertson closed his eyes and laid his face aside, like a man asleep and dead peacefully. 'You very rarely see a man dead with any other look on his face – you know the other look –' And he clenched his teeth with a sudden, momentaneous, ghastly distortion. 'Well, you'd never have known this chap was dead. He had a wound here – in the back of his head – and a bit of blood on his hand – and nothing else, nothing. Well, I said we'd give him a decent burial. He lay there waiting – and they'd wrapped him in a filthy blanket – you know. Well, I said he should have a proper blanket. He'd been dead lying there a day and a half you know. So I went and got a blanket. a beautiful blanket, out of his private kit – his people were Scotch, well-known family – and I got the pins, you know, ready to pin him up properly, for the Scots Guards to bury him. And I thought he'd be stiff, you know. But when I took him by the arms, to lift him on, he sat up. It gave me an awful shock. "Why he's alive!" I said. But they said he was dead. I couldn't believe it. It gave me an awful shock. He was as flexible as you or me, and looked as if he was asleep. You couldn't believe he was dead. But we pinned him up in his blanket. It was an awful shock to me. I couldn't believe a man could be like that after he'd been dead two days . . .

'The Germans were wonderful with the machine guns – it's a wicked thing, a machine gun. But they couldn't touch us with the bayonet. Every time the men came back they had bayonet practice, and they got awfully good. You know when you thrust at the Germans – so – if you miss him, you bring your rifle back sharp, with a round swing, so that the butt comes up and hits up under the jaw. It's one movement, following on with the stab, you see, if you miss him. It was too quick for them. But bayonet charge was worst, you know. Because your man cries out when you catch him, when you get him, you know. That's what does you . . .

'No, oh no, this was no war like other wars. All the machinery of it. No, you couldn't stand it, but for the men. The men are wonderful, you know. They'll be wiped out . . . No, it's your men who keep you going, if you're an officer . . . But there'll never be another war like this. Because the Germans are the only people who could make a war like this – and I don't think they'll ever do it again, do you?

'Oh, they were wonderful, the Germans. They were amazing. It was incredible, what they invented and did. We had to learn from them, in the first two years. But they were too methodical. That's why they lost the war. They were too methodical. They'd fire their guns every ten minutes – regular. Think of it! Of course, we knew when to run, and when to lie down. You got so that you knew almost exactly what they'd do – if you'd been out long enough. And then you could time what you wanted to do yourselves.

'They were a lot more nervous than we were, at the last. They sent up enough light at night from their trenches – you know, those things that burst in the air like electric light – we had none of that to do – they did it all for us – lit up everything. They were more nervous than we were . . . '

It was nearly two o'clock when Herbertson left. Lilly, depressed, remained before the fire. Aaron got out of bed and came uneasily to the fire.

'It gives me the bellyache, that damned war,' he said.

'So it does me,' said Lilly. 'All unreal.'

'Real enough for those that had to go through it.'

'No, least of all for them,' said Lilly sullenly. 'Not as real as a bad dream. Why the hell don't they wake up and realize it!'

'That's a fact,' said Aaron. 'They're hypnotized by it.'

'And they want to hypnotize me. And I won't be hypnotized. The war was a lie and is a lie and will go on being a lie till somebody busts it.'

'It was a fact – you can't bust that. You can't bust the fact that it happened.'

'Yes, you can. It never happened. It never happened to me. No more than my dreams happen. My dreams don't happen: they only seem.'

'But the war did happen, right enough,' smiled Aaron palely.

'No, it didn't. Not to me or to any man, in his own self. It took place in the automatic sphere, like dreams do. But the *actual man* in every man was just absent – asleep – or drugged – inert – dream-logged. That's it.'

'You tell 'em so,' said Aaron.

'I do. But it's no good. Because they won't wake up now even – perhaps never. They'll all kill themselves in their sleep.'

'They wouldn't be any better if they did wake up and be themselves – that is, supposing they are asleep, which I can't see. They are what they are – and they're all alike – and never very different from what they are now.'

Lilly stared at Aaron with black eyes.

'Do you believe in them less than I do, Aaron?' he asked slowly.

'I don't even want to believe in them.'

'But in yourself?' Lilly was almost wistful – and Aaron uneasy.

'I don't know that I've any more right to believe in myself than in them,' he replied. Lilly watched and pondered.

'No,' he said. 'That's not true – I *knew* the war was false: humanly quite false. I always knew it was false. The Germans were false, we were false, everybody was false.'

'And not you?' asked Aaron shrewishly.

'There was a wakeful, self-possessed bit of me which knew that the war and all that horrible movement was false for me.

144

And so I wasn't going to be dragged in. The Germans could have shot my mother or me or what they liked: I wouldn't have joined the *war*. I would like to kill my enemy. But become a bit of that huge obscene machine they called the war, that I never would, no, not if I died ten deaths and had eleven mothers violated. But I would like to kill my enemy: oh yes, more than one enemy. But not as a unit in a vast obscene mechanism. That, never: no, never.'

Poor Lilly was too earnest and vehement. Aaron made a fine nose. It seemed to him like a lot of words and a bit of wriggling out of a hole.

'Well,' he said, 'you've got men and nations, and you've got the machines of war – so how are you going to get out of it? League of Nations?'

'Damn all leagues. Damn all masses and groups, anyhow. All I want is to get *myself* out of their horrible heap: to get out of the swarm. The swarm to me is nightmare and nullity – horrible helpless writhing in a dream. I want to get myself awake, out of it all – all that mass-consciouness, all that mass-activity – it's the most horrible nightmare to me. No man is awake and himself. No man who was awake and in possession of himself would use poison gases: no man. His own awake self would scorn such a thing. It's only when the ghastly mob-sleep, the dream helplessness of the mass-psyche overcomes him, that he becomes completely base and obscene.'

'Ha – well,' said Aaron. 'It's the wide-awake ones that invent the poison gas, and use it. Where should we be without it?'

Lilly started, went stiff and hostile.

'Do you mean that, Aaron?' he said, looking into Aaron's face with a hard, inflexible look.

Aaron turned aside half sheepishly.

'That's how it looks on the face of it, isn't it?' he said.

'Look here, my friend, it's too late for you to be talking to me about the face of things. If that's how you feel, put your things on and follow Herbertson. Yes – go out of my room. I don't put up with the face of things here.'

Aaron looked at him in cold amazement.

'It'll do to-morrow morning, won't it?' he asked, rather mocking.

'Yes,' said Lilly coldly. 'But please go tomorrow morning.'

'Oh, I'll go all right,' said Aaron. 'Everybody's got to agree with you – that's your price.'

But Lilly did not answer. Aaron turned into bed, his satirical smile under his nose. Somewhat surprised, however, at this sudden turn of affairs.

As he was just going to sleep, dismissing the matter, Lilly came once more to his bedside, and said, in a hard voice:

'I'm *not* going to pretend to have friends on the face of things. No, and I *don't* have friends who don't fundamentally agree with me. A friend means one who is at one with me in matters of life and death. And if you're at one with all the rest, then you're their friend, not mine. So be *their* friend. And please leave me in the morning. You owe me nothing, you have nothing more to do with me. I have had enough of these friendships where I pay the piper and the mob calls the tune.

'Let me tell you, moreover, your heroic Herbertsons lost us more than ever they won. A brave ant is a damned cowardly individual. Your heroic officers are a sad sight, *afterwards*, when they come home. Bah, your Herbertson! The only justification for war is what you learn from it. And what have they learnt? Why did so many of them have presentiments, as he called it? Because they could feel inside them, there was nothing to come after. No life-courage: always death-courage. Nothing beyond this hell – only death or love-languishing – '

'What could they have seen, anyhow?' said Aaron.

'It's not what you see, actually. It's the kind of spirit you keep inside you: the life spirit. When Wallace had presentiments, Herbertson, being officer, should have said: 'None of that, Wallace. You and I, we've got to live and make life smoke.' Instead of which he let Wallace be killed, and his own heart be broken. Always the death choice. And we won't, we simply *will not* face the world as we've made it, and our own souls as we find them, and take the responsibility. We'll *never* get anywhere till we stand up man to man and face *everything* out, and break the old forms, but never let our own pride and courage of life be broken.'

Lilly broke off, and went silently to bed. Aaron turned over to sleep, rather resenting the sound of so many words. What difference did it make, anyhow. In the morning, however, when he saw the other man's pale, closed, rather haughty face, he realized that something *had* happened. Lilly was courteous and even affable: but with a curious cold space between him and Aaron. Breakfast passed, and Aaron knew that he must leave. There was something in Lilly's bearing which just showed him the door. In some surprise and confusion, and in some anger, not unmingled with humorous irony, he put his things in his bag. He put on his hat and coat. Lilly was seated rather stiffly writing.

'Well,' said Aaron. 'I suppose we shall meet again.'

'Oh sure to,' said Lilly, rising from his chair. 'We are sure to run across one another.'

'When are you going?' asked Aaron.

'In a few days' time.'

'Oh well, I'll run in and see you before you go, shall I?'

'Yes, do.'

Lilly escorted his guest to the top of the stairs, shook hands, and then returned into his own room, closing the door on himself.

Aaron did not find his friend at home when he called. He felt it was a slap in the face. But then he knew perfectly well that Lilly had made a certain call upon his, Aaron's, soul: a call which he, Aaron, did not intend to obey. Rather he curled his fine nose, worldly-wise. People who make calls on other people's souls are bound to find the door shut. If in return the soul-caller chooses to shut his worldly house-door in the face of the world-caller, well, it is nearly quits. Aaron accepted the *quid pro quo*. He was not sure whether he felt superior to his unworldly enemy or not. He rather felt he did.

More Pillar of Salt

THE opera season ended, Aaron was invited by Cyril Scott to join a group of musical people in a village by the sea. He accepted, and spent a pleasant month. It pleased the young men musically-inclined and Bohemian by profession to patronize the flautist, whom they declared marvellous. Bohemians with well-to-do parents, they could always afford to squander a little spasmodic and self-gratifying patronage. And Aaron did not mind being patronized. He had nothing else to do.

But the party broke up early in September. The flautist was detained a few days at a country house, for the amusement of the guests. Then he left for London.

In London he found himself at a loose end. A certain fretful dislike of the patronage of indifferent young men, younger than himself, and a certain distaste for regular work in the orchestra made him look round. He wanted something else. He wanted to disappear again. Qualms and emotions concerning his abandoned family overcame him. The early, delicate autumn affected him. He took a train to the Midlands.

And again, just after dark, he strolled with his little bag across the field which lay at the end of his garden. It had been mown, and the grass was already growing long. He stood and looked at the line of back windows, lighted once more. He smelled the scents of autumn, phlox and moist old vegetation and corn in sheaf. A nostalgia which was half at least revulsion affected him. The place, the home, at once fascinated him and revolted him.

Sitting in his shed, he scrutinized his garden carefully, in the starlight. There were two rows of beans, rather dishevelled. Near at hand the marrow plants sprawled from their old bed.

He could detect the perfume of a few carnations. He wondered who it was had planted the garden, during his long absence. Anyhow, there it was, planted and fruited and waning into autumn.

The blind was not drawn. It was eight o'clock. The children were going to bed. Aaron waited in his shed, his bowels stirred with violent but only half-admitted emotions. There was his wife, slim and graceful, holding a little mug to the baby's mouth. And the baby was drinking. She looked lonely. Wild emotions attacked his heart. There was going to be a wild and emotional reconciliation.

Was there? It seemed like something fearful and imminent. A passion arose in him, a craving for the violent emotional reconciliation. He waited impatiently for the children to be gone to bed, gnawed with restless desire.

He heard the clock strike nine, then half-past, from the village behind. The children would be asleep. His wife was sitting sewing some little frock. He went lingering down the garden path, stooping to lift the fallen carnations, to see how they were. There were many flowers, but small. He broke one off, then threw it away. The golden rod was out. Even in the little lawn there were asters, as of old.

His wife started to listen, hearing his step. He was filled with a violent conflict of tenderness, like a sickness. He hesitated, tapping at the door, and entered. His wife started to her feet, at bay.

'What have you come for!' was her involuntary ejaculation.

But he, with the familiar odd jerk of his head towards the garden, asked with a faint smile:

'Who planted the garden?'

And he felt himself dropping into the twang of the vernacular, which he had discarded.

Lottie only stood and stared at him, objectively. She did not think to answer. He took his hat off, and put it on the dresser. Again the familiar act maddened her.

'What have you come for?' she cried again, with a voice

full of hate. Or perhaps it was fear and doubt and even hope as well. He heard only hate.

This time he turned to look at her. The old dagger was drawn in her.

'I wonder,' he said, 'myself.'

Then she recovered herself, and with trembling hand picked up her sewing again. But she still stood at bay, beyond the table. She said nothing. He, feeling tired, sat down on the chair nearest the door. But he reached for his hat, and kept it on his knee. She, as she stood there unnaturally, went on with her sewing. There was silence for some time. Curious sensations and emotions went through the man's frame, seeming to destroy him. They were like electric shocks, which he felt she emitted against him. And an old sickness came in him again. He had forgotten it. It was the sickness of the unrecognized and incomprehensible strain between him and her.

After a time she put down her sewing, and sat again in her chair.

'Do you know how vilely you've treated me?' she said, staring across the space at him. He averted his face.

Yet he answered, not without irony:

'I suppose so.'

'And why?' she said. 'I should like to know why.'

He did not answer. The way she rushed in made him go vague.

'Justify yourself. Say why you've been so vile to me. Say what you had against me,' she demanded.

'What I *had* against her,' he mused to himself: and he wondered that she used the past tense. He made no answer.

'Accuse me,' she insisted. 'Say what I've done to make you treat me like this. Say it. You must *think* it hard enough.'

'Nay,' he said. 'I don't think it.'

This speech, by which he merely meant that he did not trouble to formulate any injuries he had against her, puzzled her.

'Don't come pretending you love me, *now*. It's too late,' she said with contempt. Yet perhaps also hope.

'You might wait till I start pretending,' he said.

This enraged her.

'You vile creature!' she exclaimed. 'Go! What have you come for?'

'To look at *you*,' he said sarcastically.

After a few minutes she began to cry, sobbing violently into her apron.

'What have I done! What have I done! I don't know what I've done that he should be like this to me,' she sobbed, into her apron. It was childish, and perhaps true. At least it was true from the childish part of her nature. He sat gloomily and uneasy.

She took the apron from her tear-stained face, and looked at him. It was true, in her moments of roused exposure she was a beautiful woman – a beautiful woman. At this moment, with her flushed, tear-stained, wilful distress, she was beautiful.

'Tell me,' she challenged. 'Tell me! Tell me what I've done. Tell me what you have against me. Tell me.'

Watching like a lynx, she saw the puzzled, hurt look in his face. Telling isn't so easy – especially when the trouble goes too deep for conscious comprehension. He couldn't *tell* what he had against her. And he had not the slightest intention of doing what she would have liked him to do, starting to pile up detailed grievances. He knew the detailed grievances were nothing in themselves.

'You *can't*,' she cried vindictively. 'You *can't*. You *can't* find anything real to bring against me, though you'd like to. You'd like to be able to accuse me of something, but you *can't*, because you know there isn't anything.'

She watched him, watched. And he sat in the chair near the door, without moving.

'You're unnatural, that's what you are,' she cried. 'You're unnatural. You're not a man. You haven't got a man's feelings. You're nasty, and cold, and unnatural. And you're a coward. You're a coward. You run away from me, without telling me what you've got against me.'

'When you've had enough, you go away and you don't care what you do,' he said, epigrammatic.

She paused a moment.

'Enough of what?' she said. 'What have you had enough of? Of me and your children? It's a nice manly thing to say. Haven't I loved you? Haven't I loved you for twelve years, and worked and slaved for you and tried to keep you right? Heavens knows where you'd have been but for me, evil as you are at the bottom. You're evil, that's what it is – and weak. You're too weak to love a woman and give her what she wants: too weak. Unmanly and cowardly, he runs away.'

'No wonder,' he said.

'No,' she cried. 'It *is* no wonder, with a nature like yours: weak and unnatural and evil. It *is* no wonder.'

She became quiet – and then started to cry again, into her apron. Aaron waited. He felt physically weak.

'And who knows what you've been doing all these months.' she wept. 'Who knows all the vile things you've been doing. And you're the father of my children – the father of my little girls – and who knows what vile things he's guilty of, all these months.'

'I shouldn't let my imagination run away with me,' he answered. 'I've been playing the flute in the orchestra of one of the theatres in London.'

'Ha!' she cried. 'It's more than that. Don't think I'm going to believe you. I know you, with your smooth-sounding lies. You're a liar, as you know. And I know you've been doing other things beside play a flute in an orchestra. You! – as if I don't know you. And then coming crawling back to me with your lies and your pretence. Don't think I'm taken in.'

'I should be sorry,' he said.

'Coming crawling back to me, and expecting to be forgiven,' she went on. 'But no – I don't forgive – and I can't forgive – never – not as long as I live shall I forgive what you've done to me.'

'You can wait till you're asked, anyhow,' he said.

'And you can wait,' she said. 'And you *shall* wait.'

She took up her sewing, and stitched steadily, as if calmly.
Anyone glancing in would have imagined a quiet domestic
hearth at that moment. He, too, feeling physically weak,
remained silent, feeling his soul absent from the scene.

Again she suddenly burst into tears, weeping bitterly.

'And the children,' she sobbed, rocking herself with grief
and chagrin. 'What have I been able to say to the children —
what have I been able to tell them?'

'What *have* you told them?' he asked coldly.

'I told them you'd gone away to work,' she sobbed, laying
her head on her arms on the table. 'What else could I tell
them? I couldn't tell them the vile truth about their father.
I couldn't tell *them* how evil you are.' She sobbed and moaned.

He wondered what exactly the vile truth would have been,
had she *started* to tell it. And he began to feel, coldly and
cynically, that among all her distress there was a luxuriating
in the violent emotions of the scene in hand, and the situation
altogether.

Then again she became quiet, and picked up her sewing.
She stitched quietly, wistfully, for some time. Then she looked
up at him — a long look of reproach, and sombre accusation,
and wifely tenderness. He turned his face aside.

'You know you've been wrong to me, don't you?' she said,
half wistfully, half menacing.

He felt her wistfulness and her menace tearing him in his
bowels and loins.

'You do know, don't you?' she insisted, still with the
wistful appeal, and the veiled threat.

'You do, or you would answer,' she said. 'You've still got
enough that's right in you, for you to know.'

She waited. He sat still, as if drawn by hot wires.

Then she slipped across to him, put her arms round him,
sank to her knees at his side, and sank her face against his
thigh.

'Say you know how wrong you are. Say you know how
cruel you've been to me,' she pleaded. But under her female
pleading and appeal he felt the iron of her threat.

'You *do* know it,' she murmured, looking up into his face as she crouched by his knee. 'You *do* know it. I can see in your eyes that you know it. And why have you come back to me, if you don't know it! Why have you come back to me? Tell me!' Her arms gave him a sharp compulsory little clutch round the waist. 'Tell me! Tell me!' she murmured, with all her appeal liquid in her throat.

But him, it half overcame, and at the same time, horrified. He had a certain horror of her. The strange, liquid sound of her appeal seemed to him like the swaying of a serpent which mesmerizes the fated, fluttering, helpless bird. She clasped her arms round him, she drew him to her, she half roused his passion. At the same time she coldly horrified and repelled him. He had not the faintest feeling, at the moment, of his own wrong. But she wanted to win his own self-betrayal out of him. He could see himself as the fascinated victim, falling to this cajoling, awful woman, the wife of his bosom. But as well, he had a soul outside himself, which looked on the whole scene with cold revulsion, and which was as unchangeable as time.

'No,' he said. 'I don't feel wrong.'

'You *do!*' she said, giving him a sharp, admonitory clutch. 'You *do*. Only you're silly, and obstinate, babyish and silly and obstinate. An obstinate little boy – you *do* feel wrong. And you *are* wrong. And you've got to say it.'

But quietly he disengaged himself and got to his feet, his face pale and set, obstinate as she said. He put his hat on, and took his little bag. She watched him curiously, still crouching by his chair.

'I'll go,' he said, putting his hand on the latch.

Suddenly she sprang to her feet and clutched him by the shirt-neck, her hand inside his soft collar, half strangling him.

'You villain,' she said, and her face was transfigured with passion as he had never seen it before, horrible. 'You villain!' she said thickly. 'What have you come here for?'

His soul went black as he looked at her. He broke her hand away from his shirt collar, bursting the stud-holes. She recoiled in silence. And in one black, unconscious movement he was gone, down the garden and over the fence and across the country, swallowed in a black unconsciousness.

She, realizing, sank upon the hearth-rug and lay there curled upon herself. She was defeated. But she too would never yield. She lay quite motionless for some time. Then she got up, feeling the draught on the floor. She closed the door, and drew down the blind. Then she looked at her wrist which he had gripped, and which pained her. Then she went to the mirror and looked for a long time at her white, strained, determined face. Come life, come death, she too would never yield. And she realized now that he would never yield.

She was faint with weariness, and would be glad to get to bed and sleep.

Aaron meanwhile had walked across the country and was looking for a place to rest. He found a cornfield with a half-built stack, and sheaves in stook. Ten to one some tramp would have found the stack. He threw a dozen sheaves together and lay down, looking at the stars in the September sky. He too would never yield. The illusion of love was gone for ever. Love was a battle in which each party strove for the mastery of the other's soul. So far, man had yielded the mastery to woman. Now he was fighting for it back again. And too late, for the woman would never yield.

But whether the woman yielded or not, he would keep the mastery of his own soul and conscience and actions. He would never yield himself up to her judgment again. He would hold himself forever beyond her jurisdiction.

Henceforth, life single, not life double.

He looked at the sky, and thanked the universe for the blessedness of being alone in the universe. To be alone, to be oneself, not to be driven or violated into something which is not oneself, surely it is better than anything. He thought of Lottie, and knew how much more truly herself she was when she was alone, with no man to distort her. And he was thankful for the division between them. Such scenes as the last were too horrible and unreal.

As for future unions, too soon to think about it. Let there be clean and pure division first, perfected singleness. That is the only way to final, living unison: through sheer, finished singleness.

Novara

HAVING no job for the autumn, Aaron fidgeted in London. He played at some concerts and some private shows. He was one of an odd quartette, for example, which went to play to Lady Artemis Hooper, when she lay in bed after her famous escapade of falling through the window of her taxi-cab. Aaron had that curious knack, which belongs to some people, of getting into the swim without knowing he was doing it. Lady Artemis thought his flute lovely, and had him again to play for her. Aaron looked at her, and she at him. She, as she reclined there in bed in a sort of half-light, well made-up, smoking her cigarettes and talking in a rather raucous voice, making her slightly rasping witty comments to the other men in the room – of course there were other men, the audience – was a shock to the flautist. This was the bride of the moment! Curious how raucous her voice sounded out of the cigarette smoke. Yet he liked her – the reckless note of the modern, social freebooter. In himself was a touch of the same quality.

'Do you love playing?' she asked him.

'Yes,' he said, with that shadow of irony which seemed like a smile on his face.

'Live for it, so to speak,' she said.

'I make my living by it,' he said.

'But that's not really how you take it?' she said. He eyed her. She watched him over her cigarette. It was a personal moment.

'I don't think about it,' he said.

'I'm sure you don't. You wouldn't be so good if you did. You're awfully lucky, you know, to be able to pour yourself down your flute.'

'You think I go down easy?' he laughed.

'Ah!' she replied, flicking her cigarette broadcast. 'That's the point. What should you say, Jimmy?' she turned to one of the men. He screwed his eyeglass nervously and stiffened himself to look at her.

'I-I shouldn't like to say, off-hand,' came the small-voiced self-conscious answer. And Jimmy bridled himself and glanced at Aaron.

'Do you find it a tight squeeze, then?' she said, turning to Aaron once more.

'No, I can't say that,' he answered. 'What of me goes down goes down easy enough. It's what doesn't go down.'

'And how much is that?' she asked, eyeing him.

'A good bit maybe,' he said.

'Slops over, so to speak,' she retorted sarcastically. 'And which do you enjoy more, trickling down your flute, or slopping over on to the lap of Mother Earth – or Miss, more probably!'

'Depends,' he said.

Having got him a few steps too far upon the personal ground, she left him to get off by himself.

So he found London got on his nerves. He felt it rubbed him the wrong way. He was flattered, of course, by his own success – and felt at the same time irritated by it. This state of mind was by no means acceptable. Wherever he was he liked to be given, tacitly, the first place – or a place among the first. Among the musical people he frequented, he found himself on a callow kind of equality with everybody, even the stars and aristocrats, at one moment, and a backstairs outsider the next. It was all just as the moment demanded. There was a certain excitement in slithering up and down the social scale, one minute chatting in a personal tête-à-tête with the most famous, or notorious, of the society beauties, and the next walking in the rain, with his flute in a bag, to his grubby lodging in Bloomsbury. Only the excitement roused all the savage sarcasm that lay at the bottom of his soul, and which burned there like an unhealthy bile.

Therefore he determined to clear out – to disappear. He had

a letter from Lilly, from Novara. Lilly was drifting about. Aaron wrote to Novara, and asked if he should come to Italy, having no money to speak of. 'Come if you want to. Bring your flute. And if you've no money, put on a good suit of clothes and a big black hat, and play outside the best café in any Italian town, and you'll collect enough to get on with.'

It was a sporting chance. Aaron packed his bag and got a passport, and wrote to Lilly to say he would join him, as invited, at Sir William Frank's. He hoped Lilly's answer would arrive before he left London. But it didn't.

Therefore behold our hero alighting at Novara, two hours late, on a wet dark evening. He hoped Lilly would be there: but nobody. With some slight dismay he faced the big, crowded station. The stream of people carried him automatically through the barrier, a porter having seized his bag, and volleyed various unintelligible questions at him. Aaron understood not one word. So he just wandered after the blue blouse of the porter.

The porter deposited the bag on the steps of the station front, fired off more questions and gesticulated into the half-illuminated space of darkness outside the station. Aaron decided it meant a cab, so he nodded and said 'Yes.' But there were no cabs. So once more the blue-bloused porter slung the big bag and the little bag on the strap over his shoulder, and they plunged into the night, towards some lights and a sort of theatre place.

One carriage stood there in the rain – yes, and it was free. 'Keb? yes – orright – sir. Whe'to? Where you go? Sir William Franks – Yes, I know. Long way go – go long way. Sir William Franks.'

The cabman spattered his few words of English. Aaron gave the porter an English shilling. The porter let the coin lie in the middle of his palm, as if it were a live beetle, and darted to the light of the carriage to examine the beast, exclaiming volubly. The cabman, wild with interest, peered down from the box into the palm of the porter, and carried on an impassioned dialogue. Aaron stood with one foot on the step.

'What you give – he? One franc?' asked the driver.

'A shilling,' said Aaron.

'One sheeling. Yes. I know that. One sheeling English' – and the driver went off into impassioned exclamations in Torinese. The porter, still muttering and holding his hand as if the coin might sting him, filtered away.

'Orright. He know – sheeling – orright. English moneys, eh? Yes, he know. You get up, sir.'

And away went Aaron, under the hood of the carriage, clattering down the wide darkness of Novara, over a bridge apparently, past huge rain-wet statues, and through more rainy half-lit streets.

They stopped at last outside a sort of park wall with trees above. The big gates were just beyond.

'Sir William Franks – there –' in a mixture of Italian and English the driver told Aaron to get down and ring the bell on the right. Aaron got down and in the darkness was able to read the name on the plate.

'How much?' said Aaron to the driver.

'Ten franc,' said the fat driver.

But it was his turn now to screw down and scrutinize the pink ten-shilling note. He waved it in his hand.

'Not good, eh? Not good moneys?'

'Yes,' said Aaron, rather indignantly. 'Good English money. Ten shillings. Better than ten francs, a good deal. Better – better –'

'Good – you say? Ten sheeling –' The driver muttered and muttered, as if dissatisfied. But as a matter of fact he stowed the note in his waistcoat pocket with considerable satisfaction, looked at Aaron curiously, and drove away.

Aaron stood there in the dark outside the big gates, and wished himself somewhere else. However, he rang the bell. There was a huge barking of dogs on the other side. Presently a light switched on, and a woman, followed by a man, appeared cautiously, in the half-opened door-way.

'Sir William Franks?' said Aaron.

'Si, signore.'

And Aaron stepped with his two bags inside the gate. Huge dogs jumped round. He stood in the darkness under the trees at the foot of the park. The woman fastened the gate – Aaron saw a door – and through an uncurtained window a man writing at a desk – rather like the clerk in an hotel office. He was going with his two bags to the open door, when the woman stopped him, and began talking to him in Italian. It was evident he must not go on. So he put down the bags. The man stood a few yards away, watchfully.

Aaron looked down at the woman and tried to make out something of what she was saying, but could not. The dogs still barked spasmodically, drops fell from the tall dark trees that rose overhead.

'Is Mr Lilly here? Mr Lilly?' he asked.

'Signore Lillee. No signore –'

And off the woman went in Italian. But it was evident Lilly was not at the house. Aaron wished more than ever he had not come, but had gone to an hotel.

He made out that the woman was asking him for his name – 'Meester – ? Meester – ?' she kept saying, with a note of interrogation.

'Sisson. Mr Sisson,' said Aaron, who was becoming impatient. And he found a visiting card to give her. She seemed appeased – said something about telephone – and left him standing.

The rain had ceased, but big drops were shaken from the dark high trees. Through the uncurtained window he saw the man at the desk reach the telephone. There was a long pause. At length the woman came back and motioned to him to go up – up the drive which curved and disappeared under the dark trees.

'Go up there?' said Aaron, pointing.

That was evidently the intention. So he picked up his bags and strode forward, from out of the circle of electric light, up the curved drive in the darkness. It was a steep incline. He saw trees and the grass slopes. There was a tang of snow in the air.

Suddenly, up ahead, a brilliant light switched on. He continued uphill through the trees along the path, towards it, and at length emerged at the foot of a great flight of steps, above which was a wide glass entrance, and an Italian man-servant in white gloves hovering as if on the brink.

Aaron emerged from the drive and climbed the steps. The man-servant came down two steps and took the little bag. Then he ushered Aaron and the big bag into a large, pillared hall, with thick Turkish carpet on the floor, and handsome appointments. It was spacious, comfortable and warm; but somewhat pretentious, rather like the imposing hall into which the heroine suddenly enters on the film.

Aaron dropped his heavy bag, with relief, and stood there, hat in hand, in his damp overcoat in the circle of light, looking vaguely at the yellow marble pillars, the gilded arches above, the shadowy distances and the great stairs. The butler disappeared – reappeared in another moment – and through an open doorway came the host. Sir William was a small, clean old man with a thin white beard and a courtly deportment, wearing a black velvet dinner jacket faced with purple silk.

'How do you do, Mr Sisson. You come straight from England?'

Sir William held out his hand courteously and benevolently, smiling an old man's smile of hospitality.

'Mr Lilly has gone away?' said Aaron.

'Yes. He left us several days ago.'

Aaron hesitated.

'You didn't expect me, then?'

'Yes, oh yes. Yes, oh yes. Very glad to see you – Well now, come in and have some dinner – '

At this moment Lady Franks appeared – short, rather plump, but erect and definite, in a black silk dress and pearls round her throat.

'How do you do? We are just at dinner.' she said. 'You haven't eaten? No – well then – would you like a bath now, or – ?'

It was evident the Franks had dispensed much hospitality: much of it charitable. Aaron felt it.

'No,' he said. 'I'll wash my hands and come straight in, shall I?'

'Yes, perhaps that would be better – '

'I'm afraid I am a nuisance – '

'Not at all – Beppe – ' and she gave instructions in Italian.

Another footman appeared, and took the big bag. Aaron took the little one this time. They climbed the broad, turning stairs, crossed another handsome lounge, gilt and ormolu and yellow silk chairs and scattered copies of *The Graphic* or of *Country Life*, then they disappeared through a doorway into a much narrower flight of stairs. Man can so rarely keep it up all the way, the grandeur.

Two black and white chambermaids appeared. Aaron found himself in a blue silk bedroom, and a footman unstrapping his bag, which he did not want unstrapped. Next minute he was beckoned and allured by the Italian servants down the corridor, and presented to the handsome, spacious bathroom, which was warm and creamy-coloured and glittering with massive silver and mysterious with up-to-date conveniences. There he was left to his own devices, and felt like a small boy finding out how it works. For even the mere turning on of the taps was a problem in silver mechanics.

In spite of all the splendours and the elaborated convenience, he washed himself in good hot water, and wished he were having a bath, chiefly because of the wardrobe of marvellous Turkish towels. Then he clicked his way back to his bedroom, changed his shirt and combed his hair in the blue silk bedroom with the Greuze picture, and felt a little dim and superficial surprise. He had fallen into country house parties before, but never into quite such a plushy sense of riches. He felt he ought to have his breath taken away. But alas, the cinema has taken our breath away so often, investing us in all the splendours of the splendidest American millionaire, or all the heroics and marvels of the Somme or the North Pole, that life has now no magnate richer than we, no hero nobler than we have been, on the film. *Connu! Connu!* Everything life has to offer is known to us, couldn't be known better, from the film.

So Aaron tied his tie in front of a big Venice mirror, and nothing was a surprise to him. He found a footman hovering to escort him to the dining-room – a real Italian footman, uneasy because milady's dinner was unsettled. He entered the rather small dining-room, and saw the people at table.

He was told various names: bowed to a young slim woman with big blue eyes and dark hair like a photograph, then to a smaller rather colourless young woman with a large nose: then to a stout, rubicund, bald colonel, and to a tall, thin, Oxford-looking major with a black patch over his eye – both these men in khaki – finally to a good-looking, well-nourished young man in a dinner-jacket, and he sat down to his soup, on his hostess's left hand. The colonel sat on her right, and was confidential. Little Sir William, with his hair and his beard white like spun glass, his manner very courteous and animated, the purple facings of his velvet jacket very impressive, sat at the far end of the table jesting with the ladies and showing his teeth in an old man's smile, a little bit affected, but pleasant, wishing everybody to be happy.

Aaron ate his soup, trying to catch up. Milady's own confidential Italian butler, fidelity itself, hovered quivering near, spiritually helping the newcomer to catch up. Two nice little entrée dishes, specially prepared for Aaron to take the place of the bygone fish and vol-au-vents of the proper dinner, testified to the courtesy and charity of his hostess.

Well, eating rapidly, he had more or less caught up by the time the sweets came. So he swallowed a glass of wine and looked round. His hostess with her pearls, and her diamond star in her grey hair, was speaking of Lilly and then of music to him.

'I hear you are a musician. That's what I should have been if I had had my way.'

'What instrument?' asked Aaron.

'Oh, the piano. Yours is the flute, Mr Lilly says. I think the flute can be so attractive. But I feel, of course, you have more range with the piano. I love the piano – and orchestra.'

At that moment, the colonel and hostess-duties distracted her. But she came back in snatches. She was a woman who reminded him a little of Queen Victoria; so assured in her own room, a large part of her attention always given to the successful issue of her duties, the remainder at the disposal of her guests. It was an old-fashioned, not unpleasant feeling: like retrospect. But she had beautiful big, smooth emeralds and sapphires on her fingers. Money! What a curious thing it is! Aaron noticed the deference of all the guests at table: a touch of obsequiousness: before the money! And the host and hostess accepted the deference, nay, expected it, as their dues. Yet both Sir William and Lady Franks *knew* that it was only money and success. They had both a certain afterthought, knowing dimly that the game was but a game, and that they were the helpless leaders in the game. They had a certain basic ordinariness which prevented their making any great hits, and which kept them disillusioned all the while. They remembered their poor and insignificant days.

'And I hear you were playing in the orchestra at Covent Garden. We came back to London last week. I enjoyed Beecham's operas so much.'

'Which do you like best?' said Aaron.

'Oh, the Russians. I think *Ivan*. It is such fine music.'

'I find *Ivan* artificial.'

'Do you? Oh, I don't think so. No, I don't think you can say that.'

Aaron wondered at her assurance. She seemed to put him just a tiny bit in his place, even in an opinion on music. Money gave her that right too. Curious – the only authority left. And he deferred to her opinion: that is, to her money. He did it almost deliberately. Yes – what did he believe in, besides money? What does any man? He looked at the black patch over the major's eye. What had he given his eye for? – the nation's money. Well, and very necessary too; otherwise we might be where the wretched Austrians are. Instead of which – how smooth his hostess's sapphires!

'Of course I myself prefer Moussorgsky,' said Aaron. 'I

think he is a greater artist. But perhaps it is just personal preference.'

'Yes. *Boris* is wonderful. Oh, some of the scenes in *Boris!*'

'And even more *Khovantchina*,' said Aaron. 'I wish we could go back to melody pure and simple. Yet I find *Khovantchina*, which is all mass music practically, gives me more satisfaction than any other opera.'

'Do you really. I shouldn't say so: oh no. But you can't mean that you would like all music to go back to melody pure and simple! Just a flute – just a pipe! Oh, Mr Sisson, you are bigoted for your instrument. I just *live* in harmony – chords, chords!' She struck imaginary chords on the white damask, and her sapphires swam blue. But at the same time she was watching to see if Sir William had still got beside his plate the white medicine *cachet* which he must swallow at every meal. Because if so, she must remind him to swallow it. However, at that very moment, he put it on his tongue. So that she could turn her attention again to Aaron and the imaginary chord on the white damask; the thing she just lived in. But the rubicund bald colonel, more rubicund after wine, most rubicund now the marsala was going, snatched her attention with a burly homage to her feminity, and shared his fear with her with a boyish gallantry.

When the women had gone up, Sir William came near and put his hand on Aaron's shoulder. It was evident the charm was beginning to work. Sir William was a self-made man, and not in the least a snob. He liked the fundamental ordinariness in Aaron, the commonness of the common man.

'Well now, Mr Sisson, we are very glad to see you: very glad indeed. I count Mr Lilly one of the most interesting men it has ever been my good fortune to know. And so for your own sake, and for Mr Lilly's sake, we are very glad to see you. Arthur, my boy, give Mr Sisson some marsala – and take some yourself.'

'Thank you, sir,' said the well-nourished young man in nice evening clothes. 'You'll take another glass yourself, sir?'

'Yes, I will, I will. I will drink a glass with Mr Sisson. Major, where are you wandering off to? Come and take a glass with us, my boy.'

'Thanks, Sir William,' drawled the young major with the black patch.

'Now, Colonel – I hope you are in good health and spirits.'

'Never better, Sir William, never better.'

'I'm very glad to hear it: very glad indeed. Try my marsala – I think it is quite good. Port is beyond us for the moment – for the moment – '

And the old man sipped his brown wine, and smiled again. He made quite a handsome picture: but he was frail.

'And where are you bound, Mr Sisson? Towards Rome?'

'I came to meet Lilly,' said Aaron.

'Ah! but Lilly has fled over the borders by this time. Never was such a man for crossing frontiers. Wonderful person, to be able to do it.'

'Where has he gone?' said Aaron.

'I think to Geneva for the moment. But he certainly talked of Venice. You yourself have no definite goal?'

'No.'

'Ah! You have not come to Italy to practise your art?'

'I shall *have* to practise it: or else – no, I haven't come for that.'

'Ah, you will *have* to practise it. Ah yes! We are all under the necessity to eat. And you have a family in England? Am I not right?'

'Quite. I've got a family depending on me.'

'Yes, then you must practise your art: you must practise your art. Well – shall we join the ladies? Coffee will no doubt be served.'

'Will you take my arm, sir?' said the well-nourished Arthur.

'Thank you, thank you,' the old man motioned him away.

So they went upstairs to where the three women were sitting in the library round the fire: chattering not very interested. The entry of Sir William at once made a stir.

The girl in white, with the biggish nose, fluttered round him. She was Arthur's wife. The girl in soft blue spread her-

self on the couch; she was the young Major's wife: and she had
a blue band round her hair. The Colonel hovered stout and
fidgety round Lady Franks and the liqueur stand. He and the
Major were both in khaki – belonging to the service on duty
in Italy still.

Coffee appeared – and Sir William doled out *crème de menthe*.
There was no conversation – only tedious words. The little
party was just commonplace and dull – boring. Yet Sir
William, the self-made man, was a study. And the young,
Oxford-like Major, with his English diffidence and his one
dark, pensive, baffled eye, was only waiting to be earnest, poor
devil.

The girl in white had been a sort of companion to Lady
Franks, so that Arthur was more or less a son-in-law. In this
capacity he acted. Aaron strayed round uneasily looking at
the books, but not to read, and at the big pictures above. It
was Arthur who fetched out little boxes containing the
orders conferred on Sir William for his war-work: and perhaps
more, for the many thousands of pounds he had spent on his
war-work.

There were three orders: one British, and quite important,
a large silver star for the breast: one Italian, smaller, and silver
and gold, and one from the State of Ruritania, in silver and
red-and-green enamel, smaller than the others.

'Come now, William,' said Lady Franks, 'you must try
them all on. You must try them all on together, and let us see
how you look.'

The little, frail old man, with his strange old man's blue
eyes and his old man's perpetual laugh, swelled out his chest
and said:

'What, am I to appear in all my vanities?' And he laughed
shortly.

'Of course you are. We want to see you,' said the white
girl.

'Indeed we do! We shouldn't mind all appearing in such
vanities – what, Lady Franks!' boomed the Colonel.

'I should think not,' replied his hostess. 'When a man has

honours conferred on him, it shows a poor spirit if he isn't proud of them.'

'Of course I am proud of them!' said Sir William.

'Well then, come and have them pinned on. I think it's wonderful to have got so much in one life-time – wonderful!' said Lady Franks.

'Oh, Sir William is a wonderful man,' said the Colonel.

'Well – we won't say so before him. But let us look at him in his orders.'

Arthur, always ready on these occasions, had taken the large and shining British star from its box, and drew near to Sir William, who stood swelling his chest, pleased, proud, and a little wistful.

'This one first,' said Arthur.

Sir William stood very still, half tremulous, like a man undergoing an operation.

'And it goes just here – the level of the heart. This is where it goes' – and carefully he pinned the large radiating ornament on the black velvet dinner-jacket of the old man.

'That is the first – and very becoming,' said Lady Franks.

'Oh, very becoming! Very becoming!' said the tall wife of the Major – she was a handsome young woman of the tall frail type.

'Do you think so, my dear?' said the old man, with his eternal smile: the curious smile of old people when they are dead.

'Not only becoming, sir,' said the Major, bending his tall slim figure forwards, 'but a reassuring sign that a nation knows how to distinguish her valuable men.'

'Quite!' said Lady Franks. 'I think it is a very great honour to have got it. The king was most gracious, too – Now the other. That goes beside it – the Italian.'

Sir William stood there undergoing the operation of the pinning-on. The Italian star being somewhat smaller than the British, there was a slight question as to where exactly it should be placed. However, Arthur decided it: and the old man stood before the company with his two stars on his chest.

'And now the Ruritanian,' said Lady Franks eagerly.

'That doesn't go on the same level with the other, Lady Franks,' said Arthur. 'That goes much lower down – about here.'

'Are you sure?' said Lady Franks. 'Doesn't it go more here?'

'No no, no no, not at all. Here! Isn't it so, Sybil?'

'Yes, I think so,' said Sybil.

Old Sir William stood quite silent, his breast prepared, peering over the facings of his coat to see where the star was going. The Colonel was called in, and though he knew nothing about it, he agreed with Arthur, who apparently did know something. So the star was pinned quite low down. Sir William, peeping down, exclaimed:

'Well, that is most curious now! I wear an order over the pit of my stomach! I think that is very curious: a curious place to wear an order.'

'Stand up! Stand up and let us look!' said Lady Franks. 'There now, isn't it handsome? And isn't it a great deal of honour for one man? Could he have expected so much, in one lifetime? I call it wonderful. Come and look at yourself, dear,' – and she led him to a mirror.

'What's more, all thoroughly deserved,' said Arthur.

'I should think so,' said the Colonel, fidgeting.

'Ah yes, nobody has deserved them better,' cooed Sybil.

'Nor on more humane and generous grounds,' said the Major, *sotto voce*.

'The effort to save life, indeed,' returned the Major's young wife: 'Splendid!'

Sir William stood naively before the mirror and looked at his three stars on his black velvet dinner-jacket.

'Almost directly over the pit of my stomach,' he said. 'I hope that is not a decoration for my greedy *appetite*.' And he laughed at the young women.

'I assure you it is in position, sir,' said Arthur. 'Absolutely correct. I will read it out to you later.'

'Aren't you satisfied? Aren't you a proud man? Isn't it

wonderful?' said Lady Franks. 'Why, what more could a man want from life? He could never *expect* so much.'

'Yes, my dear. I *am* a proud man. Three countries have honoured me –' There was a little breathless pause.

'And not more than they ought to have done,' said Sybil.

'Well! Well! I shall have my head turned. Let me return to my own humble self. I am too much in the stars at the moment.'

Sir William turned to Arthur to have his decorations removed. Aaron, standing in the background, felt the whole scene strange, childish, a little touching. And Lady Franks was so obviously trying to *console* her husband: to console the frail excitable old man with his honours. But why console him? Did he need consolation? And did she? It was evident that only the hard-money-woman in her put any price on the decorations.

Aaron came forward and examined the orders, one after the other. Just metal playthings of curious shiny silver and gilt and enamel. Heavy the British one – but only like some heavy buckle, a piece of metal merely when one turned it over. Somebody dropped the Italian cross, and there was a moment of horror. But the lump of metal took no hurt. Queer to see the things stowed in their boxes again. Aaron had always imagined these mysterious decorations as shining by nature on the breasts of heroes. Pinned-on pieces of metal were a considerable come-down.

The orders were put away, the party sat round the fire in the comfortable library, the men sipping more *crème de menthe*, since nothing else offered, and the couple of hours in front promising the tedium of small-talk of tedious people who had really nothing to say and no particular originality in saying it.

Aaron, however, had reckoned without his host. Sir William sat upright in his chair, with all the determination of a frail old man who insists on being level with the young. The new guest sat in a lower chair, smoking, that curious glimmer on his face which made him so attractive, and which only meant that he was looking on the whole scene from the outside, as it were, from beyond a fence. Sir William came almost directly to the attack.

'And so, Mr Sisson, you have no definite purpose in coming to Italy!'

'No, none,' said Aaron. 'I wanted to join Lilly.'

'But when you had joined him – ?'

'Oh nothing – stay here a time, in this country, if I could earn my keep.'

'Ah! – earn your keep? So you hope to earn your keep here? May I ask how?'

'By my flute.'

'Italy is a poor country.'

'I don't want much.'

'You have a family to provide for.'

'They are provided for – for a couple of years.'

'Oh indeed! Is that so?'

The old man got out of Aaron the detailed account of his circumstances – how he had left so much money to be paid over to his wife, and had reserved only a small amount for himself.

'I see you are like Lilly – you trust in Providence,' said Sir William.

'Providence or fate,' said Aaron.

'Lilly calls it Providence,' said Sir William. 'For my own part, I always advise Providence plus a banking account. I have every belief in Providence, plus a banking account. Providence and no banking account I have observed to be almost invariably fatal. Lilly and I have argued it. He believes in casting his bread upon the waters. I sincerely hope he won't have to cast himself after his bread, one of these days. Providence with a banking account. Believe in Providence once you have secured enough to live on. I should consider it disastrous to believe in Providence *before*. One can never be *sure* of Providence.'

'What can you be sure of, then?' said Aaron.

'Well, in moderation, I can believe in a little hard cash, and in my own ability to earn a little hard cash.'

'Perhaps Lilly believes in his own ability too.'

'No. Not so. Because he will never directly work to earn money. He works – and works quite well, I am told: but only as the spirit moves him, and never with any eye to the market. Now I call that *tempting* Providence, myself. The spirit may move him in quite an opposite direction to the market – then where is Lilly? I have put it to him more than once.'

'The spirit generally does move him dead against the market,' said Aaron. 'But he manages to scrape along.'

'In a state of jeopardy: all the time in a state of jeopardy,' said the old man. 'His whole existence, and that of his wife, is completely precarious. I found, in my youth, the spirit moved me to various things which would have left me and my wife starving. So I realized in time, this was no good. I took my spirit in hand, therefore, and made him pull the cart which mankind is riding in. I harnessed him to the work of productive labour. And so he brought me my reward.'

'Yes,' said Aaron. 'But every man according to his belief.'

'I don't see,' said Sir William, 'how a man can *believe* in a Providence unless he sets himself to the work of earning his daily bread, and making provision for future needs. That's what Providence means to me – making provision for oneself and one's family. Now Mr Lilly – and you yourself – you say you believe in a Providence that does *not* compel you to earn your daily bread, and make provision. I confess myself I cannot see it: and Lilly has never been able to convince me.'

'I don't believe in a kind-hearted Providence,' said Aaron, 'and I don't believe Lilly does. But I believe in chance. I believe, if I go my own way, without tying my nose to a job, chance will always throw something in my way: enough to get along with.'

'But on what do you base such a very unwarrantable belief?'

'I just feel like that.'

'And if you are ever quite without success – and nothing to fall back on?'

'I can work at something.'

'In case of illness, for example?'

'I can go to a hospital – or die.'

'Dear me! However, you are more logical than Lilly. He seems to believe that he has the Invisible – call it Providence if you will – on his side, and that this Invisible will never leave him in the lurch, or let him down, so long as he sticks to his own side of the bargain, and *never* works for his own ends. I don't quite see how he works. Certainly he seems to me a man who squanders a great deal of talent unworthily. Yet for some reason or other he calls this true, genuine activity, and has a contempt for actual work by which a man makes provision for his years and for his family. In the end, he will have to fall back on charity. But when I say so, he denies it, and says that in the end we, the men who work and make provision, will have to fall back on him. Well, all I can say is, that *so far* he is in far greater danger of having to fall back on me, than I on him.'

The old man sat back in his chair with a little laugh of triumph. But it smote almost devilishly on Aaron's ears, and for the first time in his life he felt that there existed a necessity for taking sides.

'I don't suppose he will do much falling back,' he said.

'Well, he is young yet. You are both young. You are squandering your youth. I am an old man, and I see the end.'

'What end, Sir William?'

'Charity – and poverty – and some not very congenial "job," as you call it, to put bread in your mouth. No, no, I would not like to trust myself to your Providence, or to your Chance. Though I admit your Chance is a sounder proposition than Lilly's Providence. You speculate with your life and your talent. I admit the nature which is a born speculator. After all, with your flute you will speculate in other people's taste for luxury, as a man may speculate in theatres or *trains de luxe*. You are the speculator. That may be your way of wisdom. But Lilly does not even speculate. I cannot see his point. I cannot see his point. Yet I have the greatest admiration for his mentality.'

The old man had fired up during this conversation – and all

the others in the room had gone silent. Lady Franks was palpably uneasy. She alone knew how frail the old man was – frailer by far than his years. She alone knew what fear of his own age, what fear of death haunted him now: fear of his own non-existence. His own old age was an agony to him: worse than an agony, a horror. He wanted to be young – to live, to live. And he was old, he was breaking up. The glistening youth of Aaron, the impetuousness of Lilly fascinated him. And both these men seemed calmly to contradict his own wealth and honours.

Lady Franks tried to turn off the conversation to the trickles of normal chit-chat. The Colonel was horribly bored – so were all the women – Arthur was indifferent. Only the young Major was implicated, troubled in his earnest and philosophic spirit.

'What I can't see,' he said, 'is the place that others have in your scheme.'

'It isn't a scheme,' said Aaron.

'Well then, your way of life. Isn't it pretty selfish, to marry a woman and then expect her to live on very little indeed, and that always precarious, just because you happen to believe in Providence or in Chance: which I think worse. What I don't see is where others come in. What would the world be like if everybody lived that way?'

'Other people can please themselves,' said Aaron.

'No they can't – because you take first choice, it seems to me. Supposing your wife – or Lilly's wife – asks for security and for provision, as Sir William says. Surely she has a right to it.'

'If I've no right to it myself – and I *have* no right to it, if I don't want it – then what right has she?'

'Every right, I should say. All the more since you are improvident.'

'Then she must manage her rights for herself. It's no good her foisting her rights on to me.'

'Isn't that pure selfishness?'

'It may be. I shall send my wife money as long as I've money to send.'

'And supposing you have none?'

'Then I can't send it – and she must look out for herself.'

'I call that almost criminal selfishness.'

'I can't help it.'

The conversation with the young Major broke off.

'It is certainly a good thing for society that men like you and Mr Lilly are not common,' said Sir William, laughing.

'Becoming commoner every day, you'll find,' interjaculated the Colonel.

'Indeed! Indeed! Well. May we ask you another question, Mr Sisson. I hope you don't object to our catechism?'

'No. Nor your judgment afterwards,' said Aaron, grinning.

'Then upon what grounds did you abandon your family? I know it is a tender subject. But Lilly spoke of it to us, and as far as I could see . . . '

'There were no grounds,' said Aaron. 'No, there weren't. I just left them.'

'Mere caprice?'

'If it's a caprice to be begotten – and a caprice to be born – and a caprice to die – then that was a caprice, for it was the same.'

'Like birth or death? – I don't follow.'

'It happened to me: as birth happened to me once – and death will happen. It was a sort of death too: or a sort of birth. But as undeniable as either. And without any more grounds.'

The old, tremulous man, and the young man, were watching one another.

'A natural event,' said Sir William.

'A natural event,' said Aaron.

'Not that you loved any other woman?'

'God save me from it.'

'You just left off loving?'

'Not even that. I went away.'

'What from?'

'From it all.'

'From the woman in particular?'

'Oh yes. Yes. Yes, that.'

176

'And you couldn't go back?'

Aaron shook his head.

'Yet you can give no reasons?'

'Not any reasons that would be any good. It wasn't a question of reasons. It was a question of her and me and what must be. What makes a child be born out of its mother, to the pain and trouble of both of them? I don't know.'

'But that is a natural process.'

'So is this – or nothing.'

'No,' interposed the Major. 'Because birth is a universal process – and yours is a specific, almost unique event.'

'Well, unique or not, it so came about. I didn't even leave off loving her – not as far as I know. I left her as I shall leave the earth when I die – because it has to be.'

'Do you know what I think it is, Mr Sisson?' put in Lady Franks. 'I think you are just in a wicked state of mind: just that. Mr Lilly too. And you must be very careful, or some great misfortune will happen to you.'

'It may,' said Aaron.

'And it will, mark my word, it will.'

'You almost wish it might, as a judgment on me,' smiled Aaron.

'Oh no, indeed. I should only be too sorry. But I feel it will, unless you are careful.'

'I'll be careful then.'

'Yes, and you can't be too careful.'

'You make me frightened.'

'I would like to make you very frightened indeed, so that you went back humbly to your wife and family.'

'It would *have* to be a big fright then, I assure you.'

'Ah, you are really heartless. It makes me angry.'

She turned angrily aside.

'Well, well! Well, well! Life! Life! Young men are a new thing to me!' said Sir William, shaking his head. 'Well, well! What do you say to whisky and soda, Colonel?'

'Why delighted, Sir William,' said the Colonel, bouncing up.

'A night-cap, and then we retire,' said Lady Franks.

Aaron sat thinking. He knew Sir William liked him: and that Lady Franks didn't. One day he might have to seek help from Sir William. So he had better placate milady. Wrinkling the fine, half mischievous smile on his face, and trading on his charm, he turned to his hostess.

'You wouldn't mind, Lady Franks, if I said nasty things about my wife and found a lot of fault with her. What makes you angry is that I know it is not a bit more her fault than mine, that we come apart. It can't be helped.'

'Oh yes, indeed. I disapprove of your way of looking at things altogether. It seems to me altogether cold and unmanly and inhuman. Thank goodness my experience of a man has been different.'

'We can't all be alike, can we? And if I don't choose to let you see me crying, that doesn't prove I've never had a bad half hour, does it? I've had many – ay, and a many.'

'Then why are you so *wrong*, so wrong in your behaviour?'

'I suppose I've got to have my bout out: and when it's out, I can alter.'

'Then I hope you've almost had your bout out,' she said.

'So do I,' said he, with a half repentant, half depressed look on his attractive face. The corners of his mouth grimaced slightly under his moustache.

'The best thing you can do is to go straight back to England, and to her.'

'Perhaps I'd better ask her if she wants me, first,' he said drily.

'Yes, you might do that too.' And Lady Franks felt she was quite getting on with her work of reform, and the restoring of woman to her natural throne. Best not go too fast, either.

'Say when,' shouted the Colonel, who was manipulating the syphon.

'When,' said Aaron.

The men stood up to their drinks.

'Will you be leaving in the morning, Mr Sisson?' asked Lady Franks.

'May I stay till Monday morning?' said Aaron. They were at Saturday evening.

'Certainly. And you will take breakfast in your room: we all do. At what time? Half past eight?'

'Thank you very much.'

'Then at half past eight the man will bring it in. Goodnight.'

Once more in his blue silk bedroom, Aaron grimaced to himself and stood in the middle of the room grimacing. His hostess's admonitions were like vitriol in his ears. He looked out of the window. Through the darkness of trees, the lights of a city below. Italy! The air was cold with snow. He came back into his soft warm bedroom. Luxurious it was. And luxurious the deep warm bed.

He was still asleep when the man came noiselessly in with the tray: and it was morning. Aaron woke and sat up. He felt that the deep warm bed, and the soft warm room had made him sleep too well: robbed him of his night, like a narcotic. He preferred to be more uncomfortable and more aware of the flight of the dark hours. It seemed numbing.

The footman in his grey house-jacket was neat and Italian and sympathizing. He gave good morning in Italian – then softly arranged the little table by the bedside, and put out the toast and coffee and butter and boiled egg and honey, with silver and delicate china. Aaron watched the soft, catlike motions of the man. The dark eyes glanced once at the blond man, leaning on his elbow on the pillow. Aaron's face had that watchful, half amused expression. The man said something in Italian. Aaron shook his head, laughed, and said:

'Tell me in English.'

The man went softly to the window curtains, and motioned them with his hand.

'Yes, do,' said Aaron.

So the man drew the buff-coloured silk curtains: and Aaron, sitting in bed, could see away beyond red roofs of a town, and in the further heaven great snowy mountains.

'The Alps,' he said in surprise.

179

'Gli Alpi, si, signore.' The man bowed, gathered up Aaron's clothes, and silently retired.

Aaron watched through the window. It was a frosty morning at the end of September, with a clear blue morning-sky, Alpine, and the watchful, snow-streaked mountain tops bunched in the distance, as if watching. There they were, lowering round, circling, waiting. They reminded him of marvellous striped sky-panthers circling round a great camp: the red-roofed city. Aaron looked, and looked again. In the near distance, under the house, elm-tree tops were yellowing. He felt himself changing inside his skin.

So he turned away to his coffee and eggs. A little silver egg-cup with a curious little frill round it: honey in a frail, iridescent glass bowl, gold-iridescent: the charm of delicate and fine things. He smiled half mockingly to himself. Two instincts played in him: the one, an instinct for fine delicate things: he had attractive hands; the other, an inclination to throw the dainty little table with all its niceties out of the window. It evoked a sort of devil in him.

He took his bath: the man brought back his things: he dressed and went downstairs. No one in the lounge: he went down to the ground floor: no one in the big hall with its pillars of yellow marble and its gold arches, its enormous, dark, bluey-red carpet. He stood before the great glass doors. Some red flowers still were blooming in the tubs on the steps, handsome: and beautiful chrysanthemums in the wide portico. Beyond, yellow leaves were already falling on the green grass and the neat drive. Everywhere was silent and empty. He climbed the wide stairs, sat in the long upper lounge where the papers were. He wanted his hat and coat, and did not know where to find them. The windows looked on to a terraced garden, the hill rising steeply behind the house. He wanted to go out.

So he opened more doors, and in a long drawing-room came upon five or six men-servants, all in the grey house-jackets, all clean-shaven, neat, with neat black hair, all with dusters or brushes or feather brooms, and all frolicking, chattering, playing like so many monkeys. They were all of the same neat, smallish size. They were all laughing. They rolled back a great rug as if it were some football game, one flew at the curtains. And they merely looked at Aaron and went on chattering, and laughing and dusting.

Surprised, and feeling that he trespassed, he stood at the window a moment looking out. The noise went on behind him. So he turned, smiling, and asked for his hat, pointing to his head. They knew at once what he wanted. One of the fellows beckoned him away, down to the hall and to the long cupboard place where hats and coats and sticks were hung. There was his hat; he put it on, while the man chattered to him pleasantly and unintelligibly, and opened for him the back door, into the garden.

CHAPTER 13

Wie es Ihnen gefällt

THE fresh morning air comes startling after a central-heated house. So Aaron found it. He felt himself dashing up the steps into the garden like a bird dashing out of a trap where it has been caught: that warm and luxurious house. Heaven bless us, we who want to save civilization. We had better make up our minds what of it we want to save. The kernel may be all well and good. But there is precious little kernel, to a lot of woolly stuffing and poisonous rind.

The gardens to Sir William's place were not imposing, and still rather war-neglected. But the pools of water lay smooth in the bright air, the flowers showed their colours beside the walks. Many birds dashed about, rather bewildered, having crossed the Alps in their migration southwards. Aaron noted with gratification a certain big magnificence, a certain reckless powerfulness in the still-blossoming, harsh-coloured, autumn flowers. Distinct satisfaction he derived from it.

He wandered upwards, up the succeeding flights of steps, till he came to the upper rough hedge, and saw the wild copse on the hill-crest just above. Passing through a space in the hedge, he climbed the steep last bit of Sir William's land. It was a little vineyard, with small vines and yellowing leaves. Everywhere the place looked neglected – but as if man had just begun to tackle it once more.

At the very top, by the wild hedge, where spindle-berries hung pink, seats were placed, and from here the view was very beautiful. The hill dropped steep beneath him. A river wound on the near side of the city, crossed by a white bridge. The city lay close clustered, ruddy on the plains, glittering in the clear air with its flat roofs and domes and square towers, strangely naked-seeming in the clear, clean air. And massive in the further nearness, snow-streaked mountains, the tiger-like Alps. Tigers prowling between the north and the south. And this beautiful city lying nearest exposed. The snow-wind brushed her this morning like the icy whiskers of a tiger. And clear in the light lay Novara, wide, fearless, violent Novara. Beautiful the perfect air, the perfect and unblemished Alp-sky. And like the first southern flower, Novara.

Aaron sat watching in silence. Only the uneasy birds rustled. He watched the city and the winding river, the bridges, and the imminent Alps. He was on the south side. On the other side of the time barrier. His old sleepy English nature was startled in its sleep. He felt like a man who knows it is time to wake up, and who doesn't want to wake up, to face the responsibility of another sort of day.

To open his darkest eyes and wake up to a new responsibility. Wake up and enter on the responsibility of a new self in himself. Ach, the horror of responsibility! He had all his life slept and shelved the burden. And he wanted to go on sleeping. It was so hateful to have to get a new grip on his own bowels, a new hard recklessness into his heart, a new and responsible consciousness into his mind and soul. He felt some finger prodding, prodding, prodding him awake out of the sleep of pathos and tragedy and spasmodic passion, and he wriggled, unwilling, oh most unwilling to undertake the new business.

In fact he ran away again. He gave a last look at the town and its white-fanged mountains, and descended through the garden, round the way of the kitchen garden and garage and stables and pecking chickens, back to the house again. In the hall still no one. He went upstairs to the long lounge. There sat the rubicund, bald, boy-like Colonel reading *The Graphic*. Aaron sat down opposite him and made a feeble conversation. But the Colonel wasn't having any. It was evident he didn't care for the fellow – Mr Aaron that is. Aaron therefore dried up, and began to sit him out, with the aid of *The Queen*. Came a servant, however, and said the Signor

Colonello was called up from the hospital, on the telephone. The Colonel once departed, Aaron fled again, this time out of the front doors, and down the steep little park to the gates.

Huge dogs and little dogs came bounding forward. Out of the lodge came the woman with the keys, smiling very pleasantly this morning. So, he was in the street. The wide road led him inevitably to the big bridge, with the violent, physical stone statue-groups. Men and women were moving about, and he noticed for the first time the littleness and the momentaneousness of the Italians in the street. Perhaps it was the wideness of the bridge and the subsequent big open boulevard. But there it was: the people seemed little upright brisk figures moving in a certain isolation, like tiny figures on a big stage. And he felt himself moving in the space between. All the northern cosiness gone. He was set down with a space round him.

Little trams flitted down the boulevard in the bright sweet light. The barbers' shops were all busy, half the Novarese at that moment ambushed in lather, full in the public gaze. A shave is nothing if not a public act, in the south. At the little outdoor tables of the cafés a very few drinkers sat before empty coffee-cups. Most of the shops were shut. It was too soon after the war for life to be flowing very fast. The feeling of emptiness, of neglect, of lack of supplies was evident everywhere.

Aaron strolled on, surprised himself at his gallant feeling of liberty: a feeling of bravado and almost swaggering careless-ness which is Italy's best gift to an Englishman. He had crossed the dividing line, and the values of life, though ostensibly and verbally the same, were dynamically different. Alas, however, the verbal and the ostensible, the accursed mechanical ideal gains day by day over the spontaneous life-dynamic, so that Italy becomes as idea-bound and as auto-matic as England: just a business proposition.

Coming to the station, he went inside. There he saw a money-changing window which was open, so he planked down a five-pound note and got two hundred and ten lire.

Here was a start. At a bookstall he saw a man buy a big time-table with a large railway map in it. He immediately bought the same. Then he retired to a corner to get his whereabouts.

In the morning he must move: where? He looked on the map. The map seemed to offer two alternatives. Milan and Genoa. He chose Milan, because of its musical associations and its cathedral. Milano then. Strolling and still strolling, he found the boards announcing Arrivals and Departures. As far as he could make out, the train for Milan left at 9.0 in the morning.

So much achieved, he left the big desolating caravanserai of the station. Soldiers were camped in every corner, lying in heaps asleep. In their grey-green uniform, he was surprised at their sturdy limbs and uniformly short stature. For the first time he saw the cock-feathers of the Bersaglieri. There seemed a new life-quality everywhere. Many worlds, not one world. But alas, the one world triumphing more and more over the many worlds, the big oneness swallowing up the many small diversities in its insatiable gnawing appetite, leaving a dreary sameness throughout the world, that means at last complete sterility.

Aaron, however, was too new to the strangeness, he had no eye for the horrible sameness that was spreading like a disease over Italy from England and the north. He plunged into the space in front of the station, and took a new wide boulevard. To his surprise it ran towards a big and over-animated statue that stood resolutely with its back to the magnificent snow-domes of the wild Alps. Wolves in the street could not have startled him more than those magnificent fierce-gleaming mountains of snow at the street-end, beyond the statue. He stood and wondered, and never thought to look who the gentleman was. Then he turned right round, and began to walk home.

Luncheon was at one o'clock. It was half-past twelve when he rang at the lodge gates. He climbed through the leaves of the little park, on a side-path, rather reluctantly towards the house. In the hall Lady Franks was discussing with Arthur a fat Pekinese who did not seem very well. She was sure the servants did not obey her orders concerning the Pekinese bitch. Arthur, who was more than indifferent, assured her they did. But she seemed to think that the whole of the male human race was in league against the miserable specimen of a she-dog. She almost cried, thinking her Queenie *might* by some chance meet with, perhaps, a harsh word or look. Queenie apparently fattened on the secret detestation of the male human species.

'I can't bear to think that a dumb creature might be ill-treated,' she said to Aaron. 'Thank goodness the Italians are better than they used to be.'

'Are they better than they used to be?'

'Oh, much. They have learnt it from us.'

She then enquired if her guest had slept, and if he were rested from his journey. Aaron, into whose face the faint snow-wind and the sun had brought a glow, replied that he had slept well and enjoyed the morning, thank you. Whereupon Lady Franks knitted her brows and said Sir William had had such a bad night. He had not been able to sleep, and had got up and walked about the room. The least excitement, and she dreaded a break-down. He must have absolute calm and restfulness.

'There's one for you and your jawing last night, Aaron, my boy!' said our hero to himself.

'I thought Sir William seemed so full of life and energy,' he said, aloud.

'Ah, did you! No, he *wants* to be. But he can't do it. He's very much upset this morning. I have been very anxious about him.'

'I am sorry to hear that.'

Lady Franks departed to some duty. Aaron sat alone before the fire. It was a huge fireplace, like a dark chamber shut in by tall, finely-wrought iron gates. Behind these iron gates of curly iron the logs burned and flickered like leopards slumbering and lifting their heads within their cage. Aaron wondered who was the keeper of the savage element, who it was that would open the iron grille and throw on another log, like meat to the lions. To be sure the fire was only to be looked at: like wild beasts in the Zoo. For the house was warm from roof to floor. It was strange to see the blue air of sunlight outside, the yellow-edged leaves falling in the wind, the red flowers shaking.

The gong sounded softly through the house. The Colonel came in heartily from the garden, but did not speak to Aaron. The Major and his wife came pallid down the stairs. Lady Franks appeared, talking domestic-secretarial business with the wife of Arthur. Arthur, well-nourished and half at home, called down the stairs. And then Sir William descended, old and frail now in the morning, shaken: still he approached Aaron heartily, and asked him how he did, and how he had spent his morning. The old man who had made a fortune: how he expected homage: and how he got it! Homage, like most things, is just a convention and a social trick. Aaron found himself paying homage too to the old man who had made a fortune. But also, exacting a certain deference in return, from the old man who had made a fortune. Getting it too. On what grounds? Youth, maybe. But mostly, scorn for fortunes and fortune-making. Did he scorn fortunes and fortune-making? Not he, otherwise whence this homage for the old man with much money? Aaron, like everybody else, was rather paralysed by a million sterling, personified in one old man. Paralysed, fascinated, overcome. All those three. Only having no final control over his own make-up, he could not drive himself into the money-making or even into the money-having habit. And he had just wit enough to threaten Sir William's golden king with his own ivory queen and knights of wilful life. And Sir William quaked.

'Well, and how have you spent your morning?' asked the host.

'I went first to look at the garden.'

'Ah, not much to see now. They have been beautiful with flowers, once. But for two and a half years the house has been a hospital for officers – and even tents in the park and garden – as many as two hundred wounded and sick at a time. We are

only just returning to civil life. And flowers need time. Yes –
yes – British officers – for two and a half years. But did you go
up, now, to the belvedere?'

'To the top – where the vines are? I never expected the
mountains.'

'You never expected the mountains? Pray, why not? They
are always there.'

'But I was never there before. I never knew they were there,
round the town. I didn't expect it like that.'

'Ah! So you found our city impressive?'

'Very! Ah very! A new world to me. I feel I've come out of
myself.'

'Yes, it is a wonderful sight – a wonderful sight – But you
have not been *into* the town?'

'Yes. I saw the men being shaved, and all the soldiers at the
station: and a statue, and mountains behind it. Oh, I've had a
full morning.'

'A full morning! That is good, that is good!' The old man
looked again at the younger man, and seemed to get life from
him, to live in him vicariously.

'Come,' said the hostess. 'Luncheon.'

Aaron sat again on his hostess's left hand. The Colonel was
more affable now it was meal-time. Sir William was again in a
good humour, chaffing the young ladies with an old man's
gallantry. But now he insisted on drawing Aaron into the
play. And Aaron did not want to be drawn. He did not one bit
want to chaffer gallantries with the young women. Between
him and Sir William there was a curious rivalry – unconscious
on both sides. The old knight had devoted an energetic,
adventurous, almost an artistic nature to the making of his
fortune and the developing of later philanthropies. He had no
children. Aaron was devoting a similar nature to anything
but fortune-making and philanthropy. The one held life to be
a storing-up of produce and a conservation of energy: the
other held life to be a sheer spending of energy and a storing-
up of nothing but experience. There they were, in opposition,
the old man and the young. Sir William kept calling Aaron into

the chaffer at the other end of the table: and Aaron kept on refusing to join. He hated long distance answers, anyhow. And in his mood of the moment he hated the young women. He had a conversation with Arthur about statues: concerning which Aaron knew nothing, and Arthur less than nothing. Then Lady Franks turned the conversation to the soldiers at the station, and said how Sir William had equipped rest-huts for the Italian privates, near the station: but that such was the jealousy and spite of the Italian Red Cross – or some such body, locally – that Sir William's huts had been left empty – standing unused – while the men had slept on the stone floor of the station, night after night, in icy winter. There was evidently much bitter feeling as a result of Sir William's philanthropy. Apparently even the honey of lavish charity had turned to gall in the Italian mouth: at least the official mouth. Which gall had been spat back at the charitable, much to his pain. It is in truth a difficult world, particularly when you have another race to deal with. After which came the beef-olives.

'Oh,' said Lady Franks, 'I had such a dreadful dream last night, such a dreadful dream. It upset me so much. I have not been able to get over it all day.'

'What was it?' said Aaron. 'Tell it, and break it.'

'Why,' said his hostess, 'I dreamed I was asleep in my room – just as I actually was – and that it was night, yet with a terrible sort of light, like the dead light before dawn, so that one could see. And my maid Giuseppina came running into my room saying: "Signora! Signora! Si alza! Subito! Signora! Vengono su!" – and I said, "Chi? Chi sono che vengono? Chi?" – "Novaresi! I Novaresi vengono su. Vengono qui!" – I got out of bed and went to the window. And there they were, in the dead light, rushing up to the house, through the trees. It was so awful, I haven't been able to forget it all day.'

'Tell me what the words are in English,' said Aaron.

'Why, she said "Get up, get up – the Novaresi, the people of Novara are coming up – vengono su – they are coming up – the Novara people – the work-people. I can't forget it. It was so real, I can't believe it didn't actually happen.'

'Ah,' said Aaron. 'It will never happen. I know, that whatever one foresees, and *feels* has happened, never happens in real life. It sort of works off through the imagining of it.'

'Well, it was almost more real to me than real life,' said his hostess.

'Then it will never happen in real life,' he said.

Luncheon passed, and coffee. The party began to disperse – Lady Franks to answer more letters, with the aid of Arthur's wife – some to sleep, some to walk. Aaron escaped once more through the big gates. This time he turned his back on the town and the mountains, and climbed up the hill into the country. So he went between the banks and the bushes, watching for unknown plants and shrubs, hearing the birds, feeling the influence of a new soil. At the top of the hill he saw over into vineyards, and a new strange valley with a winding river, and jumbled, entangled hills. Strange wild country so near the town. It seemed to keep an almost virgin wildness – yet he saw the white houses dotted here and there.

Just below him was a peasant house: and on a little loggia in the sun two peasants in white shirtsleeves and black Sunday suits were sitting drinking wine, and talking, talking. Peasant youths in black hats, their sweethearts in dark stuff dresses, wearing no hat, but a black silk or a white silk scarf, passed slowly along the little road just below the ridge. None looked up to see Aaron sitting there alone. From some hidden place somebody was playing an accordion, a jerky sound in the still afternoon. And away beyond lay the unchanging, mysterious valley, and the infolding, mysterious hills of Italy.

Returning back again another way, he lost himself at the foot of the hill in new and deserted suburb streets – unfinished streets of seemingly unfinished houses. Then a sort of boulevard where bourgeois families were taking the Sunday afternoon walk: stout papas, stout, pallid mamas in rather cheap black fur, little girls very much dressed, and long lads in short socks and round sailor caps, ribbons fluttering. Alien they felt, alien, alien, as a bourgeois crowd always does, but particularly a foreign, Sunday-best bourgeois crowd. Aaron wandered and wandered, finding the tram terminus and trying blank, unfinished street after street. He had a great disinclination to ask his way.

At last he recognized the bank and the little stream of water that ran along the street side. So he was back in time for tea. A hospital nurse was there, and two other strange women. Arthur played the part of host. Sir William came in from a walk with the dogs, but retired to his room without taking tea.

And so the evening fell. Aaron sat in the hall at some distance from the fire, which burned behind wrought-iron gates. He was tired now with all his impressions, and dispirited. He thought of his wife and children at home: of the church-bells ringing so loudly across the field beyond his garden end: of the dark-clad people trailing unevenly across the two paths, one to the left, one to the right, forking their way towards the houses of the town, to church or to chapel: mostly to chapel. At this hour he himself would be dressed in his best clothes, tying his bow, ready to go out to the public house. And his wife would be resenting his holiday departure, whilst she was left fastened to the children.

Rather tired and dispirited in this alien place, he wondered if he wished himself back. But the moment he actually *realized* himself at home, and felt the tension of barrenness which it meant, felt the curious and deadly opposition of his wife's will against his own nature, the almost nauseating ache which it amounted to, he pulled himself together and rejoiced again in his new surroundings. Her will, her will, her terrible, implacable, cunning will! What was there in the female will so diabolical, he asked himself, that it could press like a flat sheet of iron against a man all the time? The female will! He realized now that he had a horror of it. It was flat and inflexible as a sheet of iron. But also it was cunning as a snake that could sing treacherous songs.

Of two people at a deadlock, he always reminded himself, there is not one only wholly at fault. Both must be at fault. Having a detached and logical soul, he never let himself forget this truth. Take Lottie! He had loved her. He had never loved

191

any other woman. If he had had his other affairs – it was out of spite or defiance or curiosity. They meant nothing. He and Lottie had loved one another. And the love had developed almost at once into a kind of combat. Lottie had been the only child of headstrong, well-to-do parents. He also had been the only child of his widowed mother. Well then, both he and Lottie had been brought up to consider themselves the first in whatsoever company they found themselves. During the early months of the marriage he had, of course, continued the spoiling of the young wife. But this never altered the fact that, by his very nature, he considered himself as first and almost as single in any relationship. First and single he felt, and as such he bore himself. It had taken him years to realize the Lottie also felt herself first and single: under all her whimsicalness and fretfulness was a conviction as firm as steel: that she, as woman, was the centre of creation, the man was but an adjunct. She, as woman, and particularly as mother, was the first great source of life and being, and also of culture. The man was but the instrument and the finisher. She was the source and the substance.

Sure enough, Lottie had never formulated this belief inside herself. But it was formulated for her in the whole world. It is the substantial and professed belief of the whole white world. She did but inevitably represent what the whole world around her asserted: the life-centrality of woman. Woman, the life-bearer, the life-source.

Nearly all men agree to the assertion. Practically all men, even while demanding their selfish rights as superior males, tacitly agree to the fact of the sacred life-bearing priority of woman. Tacitly, they yield the worship to that which is female. Tacitly, they conspire to agree that all that is productive, all that is fine and sensitive and most essentially noble, is woman. This, in their productive and religious souls, they believe. And however much they may react against the belief, loathing their women, running to prostitutes, or beer or *anything*, out of reaction against this great and ignominious dogma of the sacred priority of women, still they do but profane the god they worship. Profaning woman, they still inversely worship her.

But in Aaron was planted another seed. He did not know it. He started off on the good old tack of worshipping his woman while his heart was honest, and profaning her in his fits of temper and revolt. But he made a bad show. Born in him was a spirit which could not worship woman: no, and would not. Could not and would not. It was not in him. In early days, he tried to pretend it was in him. But through his plaintive and homage-rendering love of a young husband was always, for the woman, discernible the arrogance of self-unyielding male. He never yielded himself: never. All his mad loving was only an effort. Afterwards, he was as devilishly unyielded as ever. And it was an instinct in her, that her man must yield to her, so that she should envelop him, yielding, in her all-beneficent love. She was quite sure that her love was all-beneficent. Of this no shadow of doubt. She was quite sure that the highest her man could ever know or ever reach, was to be perfectly enveloped in her all-beneficent love. This was her idea of marriage. She held it not as an idea, but as a profound impulse and instinct: an instinct developed in her by the age in which she lived. All that was deepest and most sacred in her feeling centred in this belief.

And he outraged her! Oh, from the first day and the first night, she felt he outraged her. True, for some time she had been taken in by his manifest love. But though you can deceive the conscious mind, you can never deceive the deep unconscious instinct. She could never understand whence arose in her, almost from the first days of marriage with him, her terrible paroxysms of hatred for him. She was in love with him: ah heaven, how maddeningly she was in love with him: a certain unseizable beauty that was his, and which fascinated her as a snake a bird. But in revulsion, how she hated him! How she abhorred him! How she despised and shuddered at him! He seemed a horrible thing to her.

And then again, oh God, the agony of her desire for him. The agony of her long, long desire for him. He was a passionate lover. He gave her, ostensibly, all she asked for. He withheld from her nothing, no experience, no degree of intimacy. She was his initiate, or he hers.

And yet, oh horror for a woman, he withheld everything from her. He withheld the very centre of himself. For a long time she never realized. She was dazed and maddened only. But as months of married experience passed into years of married torment, she began to understand. It was that, after their most tremendous and, it seemed to her, heaven-rending passion – yea, when for her every veil seemed rent and a terrible and sacred creative darkness covered the earth – then – after all this wonder and miracle – in crept a poisonous grey snake of disillusionment, a poisonous grey snake of disillusionment that bit her to madness, so that she really was a mad woman, demented.

Why? Why? He never gave himself. He never came to her, *really*. He withheld himself. Yes, in those supreme and sacred times which for her were the whole culmination of life and being, the ecstasy of unspeakable passional conjunction, he was not really hers. He was withheld. He withheld the central core of himself, like the devil and hell-fiend he was. He cheated and made play with her tremendous passional soul, her sacred sex passion, most sacred of all things for a woman. All the time, some central part of him stood apart from her, aside, looking on.

Oh, agony and horror for a passionate, fierce-hearted woman! She who loved him. She who loved him to madness. She who would have died for him. She who did die with him, many terrible and magnificent connubial deaths, in his arms, her husband.

Her husband! How bitter the word grew to her! Her husband! and him never once given, given wholly to her! Her husband – and in all the frenzied finality of desire, she never *fully* possessed him, not once. No, not once. As time went on, she learned it for inevitable. Not once!

And then, how she hated him! Cheated, foiled, betrayed, forced to love him or to hate him: never able to be at peace near him nor away from him: poor Lottie, no wonder she was as a mad woman. She was strictly as a woman demented, after the birth of her second child. For all her instinct, all her impulse, all her desire, and above all, all her *will*, was to possess her man in very fulness once: just once: and once and for all. Once, just once: and it would be once and for all.

But never! Never! Not once! Never! Not for one single solitary second! Was it not enough to send a woman mad. Was it not enough to make her demented! Yes, and mad she was. She made his life a hell for him. She bit him to the bone with her frenzy of rage, chagrin, and agony. She drove him mad too: mad, so that he beat her: mad so that he longed to kill her. But even in his greatest rages it was the same: he never finally lost himself: he remained, somewhere in the centre, in possession of himself. She sometimes wished he would kill her: or that she would kill him. Neither event happened.

And neither of them understood what was happening. How should they? They were both dazed, horrified, and mortified. He took to leaving her alone as much as was possible. But when he *had* to come home, there was her terrible will, like a flat cold snake coiled round his soul and squeezing him to death. Yes, she did not relent. She was a good wife and mother. All her duties she fulfilled. But she was not one to yield. *He* must yield. That was written in eternal letters, on the iron tablet of her will. *He* must yield. She the woman, the mother of his children, how should she ever even think to yield? It was unthinkable. He, the man, the weak, the false, the treacherous, the half-hearted, it was he who must yield. Was not hers the divine will and the divine right? Ha, she would be less than woman if she ever capitulated, abandoned her divine responsibility as woman! No, *he* must yield.

So, he was unfaithful to her. Piling reproach after reproach upon himself, he added adultery to his brutality. And this was the beginning of the end. She was more than maddened: but he began to grow silent, unresponsive, as if he did not hear her. He was unfaithful to her: and oh, in such a low way. Such shame, such shame! But he only smiled carelessly now, and asked her what she wanted. She had asked for all she got. That he reiterated. And that was all he would do.

Terrible was, that she found even his smile of insolent indifference half-beautiful. Oh bitter chain to bear! But she summoned up her strange woman's will. She fought against his fascination, the fascination he exerted over her. With fearful efforts of will she fought against it, and mastered it. And then, suddenly, horror and agony of it, up it would rush in her again, her unbearable desire for him, the longing of his contact, his quality of beauty.

That was a cross hard to bear. Yet even that she bore. And schooled herself into a fretful, petulant manner of indifference. Her odd, whimsical petulance hid a will which he, and he alone, knew to be stronger than steel, strong as a diabolical cold grey snake that presses and presses and cannot relax; nay, cannot relax. She became the same as he. Even in her moments of most passionate desire for him, the cold and snake-like tension of her will never relaxed, and the cold, snake-like eye of her intention never closed.

So, till it reached a deadlock. Each will was wound tense, and so fixed. Fixed! There was neither any relaxing nor any increase of pressure. Fixed. Hard like a numbness, a grip that was solidifying and turning to stone.

He realized, somehow, that at this terrible passive game of fixed tension she would beat him. Her fixed female soul, her wound-up female will would solidify into stone – whereas his must break. In him something must break. It was a cold and fatal deadlock, profitless. A life-automatism of fixed tension that suddenly, in him, did break. His will flew loose in a recoil away from her. He left her, as inevitably as a broken spring flies out from its hold.

Not that he was broken. He would not do her even that credit. He had only flown loose from the old centre-fixture. His will was still entire and unabated. Only he did not know: he did not understand. He swung wildly about from place to place, as if he were broken.

Then suddenly, on this Sunday evening in the strange

country, he realized something about himself. He realized that he had never intended to yield himself fully to her or to anything: that he did not intend ever to yield himself up entirely to her or to anything: that his very being pivoted on the fact of his isolate self-responsibility, aloneness. His intrinsic and central aloneness was the very centre of his being. Break it, and he broke his being. Break this central aloneness, and he broke everything. It was the great temptation, to yield himself: and it was the final sacrilege. Anyhow, it was something which, from his profoundest soul, he did not intend to do. By the innermost isolation and singleness of his own soul he would abide though the skies fell on top of one another, and seven heavens collapsed.

Vaguely he realized this. And vaguely he realized that this had been the root cause of his strife with Lottie: Lottie, the only person who had mattered at all to him in all the world: save perhaps his mother. And his mother had not mattered, no, not one-half nor one-fifth what Lottie had mattered. So it was: there was, for him, only her significance in the universe. And between him and her matters were as they were.

He coldly and terribly hated her, for a moment. Then no more. There was no solution. It was a situation without a solution. But at any rate, it was now a defined situation. He could rest in peace.

Thoughts something in this manner ran through Aaron's subconscious mind as he sat still in the strange house. He could not have fired it all off at any listener, as these pages are fired off at any chance reader. Nevertheless there it was, risen to half-consciousness in him. All his life he had *hated* knowing what he felt. He had wilfully, if not consciously, kept a gulf between his passional soul and his open mind. In his mind was pinned up a nice description of himself, and a description of Lottie, sort of authentic passports to be used in the conscious world. These authentic passports, self-describing: nose short, mouth normal, etc.; he had insisted that they should do all the duty of the man himself. This ready-made and very banal idea of himself as a really quite nice individual: eyes blue, nose short, mouth normal, chin normal: this he had insisted was really himself. It was his conscious mask.

Now at last, after years of struggle, he seemed suddenly to have dropped his mask on the floor, and broken it. His authentic self-describing passport, his complete and satisfactory idea of himself suddenly became a rag of paper, ridiculous. What on earth did it matter if he was nice or not, if his chin was normal or abnormal?

His mask, his idea of himself dropped and was broken to bits. There he sat now maskless and invisible. That was how he strictly felt: invisible and undefined, rather like Wells's *Invisible Man*. He had no longer a mask to present to people: he was present and invisible: they *could* not really think anything about him, because they could not really see him. What did they see when they looked at him? Lady Franks, for example. He neither knew nor cared. He only knew he was invisible to himself and everybody, and that all thinking about what he was like was only a silly game of Mrs Mackenzie's Dead.

So there. The old Aaron Sisson was as if painfully transmuted, as the Invisible Man when he underwent his transmutations. Now he was gone, and no longer to be seen. His visibility lost for ever.

And then what? Sitting there as an invisible presence, the preconceived world melted also and was gone. Lady Franks, Sir William, all the guests, they talked and manoeuvred with their visible personalities, manipulating the masks of themselves. And underneath there was something invisible and dying – something fading, wilting: the essential plasm of themselves: their invisible being.

Well now, and what next? Having in some curious manner tumbled from the tree of modern knowledge, and cracked and rolled out from the shell of the preconceived idea of himself like some dark, night-lustrous chestnut from the green ostensibility of the burr, he lay as it were exposed but invisible on the floor, knowing, but making no conceptions: knowing, but having no idea. Now that he was finally unmasked and exposed, the accepted idea of himself cracked and rolled aside like a broken chestnut-burr, the mask split and shattered, he was at last quiet and free. He had dreaded exposure: and behold, we cannot be exposed, for we are invisible. We cannot be exposed to the looks of others, for our very being is night-lustrous and unseeable. Like the Invisible Man, we are only revealed through our clothes and our masks.

In his own powerful but subconscious fashion Aaron realized this. He was a musician. And hence even his deepest *ideas* were not word-ideas, his very thoughts were not composed of words and ideal concepts. They too, his thoughts and his ideas, were dark and invisible, as electric vibrations are invisible no matter how many words they may purport. If I, as a word-user, must translate his deep conscious vibrations into finite words, that is my own business. I do but make a translation of the man. He would speak in music. I speak with words.

The inaudible music of his conscious soul conveyed his meaning in him quite as clearly as I convey it in words: probably much more clearly. But in his own mode only: and it was in his own mode only he realized what I must put into words. These words are my own affair. His mind was music.

Don't grumble at me then, gentle reader, and swear at me that this damned fellow wasn't half clever enough to think all these smart things, and realize all these fine-drawn-out subtleties. You are quite right, he wasn't, yet it all resolved itself in him as I say, and it is for you to prove that it didn't.

In his now silent, maskless state of wordless comprehension, he knew that he had never wanted to surrender himself utterly to Lottie: nor to his mother: nor to anybody. The last extreme of self-abandon in love was for him an act of false behaviour. His own nature inside him fated him not to take this last false step, over the edge of the abyss of selflessness. Even if he wanted to, he could not. He might struggle on the edge of the precipice like an assassin struggling with his own soul, but he could not conquer. For, according to all the current prejudice and impulse in one direction, he too had believed that the final achievement, the consummation of human life, was this flinging oneself over the precipice, down the bottomless pit of love. Now he realized that love, even in its intensest, was only an attribute of the human soul: one of its incomprehensible gestures. And to fling down the whole soul in one gesture of finality in love was as much a criminal suicide as to jump off a church tower or a mountain peak. Let a man give himself as much as he liked in love, to seven thousand extremities, he must never give himself *away*. The more generous and the more passionate a soul, the more it *gives* itself. But the more absolute remains the law, that it shall never give itself away. Give thyself, but give thyself not away. That is the lesson written at the end of the long strange lane of love.

The *idée fixe* of today is that every individual shall not only give himself, but shall achieve the last glory of giving himself away. And since this takes two – you can't even make a present of yourself unless you've got somebody to receive the present; since this last extra-divine act takes two people to perform it, you've got to take into count not only your giver but your receiver. Who is going to be the giver and who the receiver?

Why, of course, in our long-drawn-out Christian day, man is given and woman is recipient. Man is the gift, woman the receiver. This is the sacrament we live by; the holy communion we live for. That man give himself to woman in an utter and sacred abandon, all, all, all himself given, and taken. Woman, eternal woman, she is the communicant. She receives the sacramental body and spirit of the man.

And when she's got it, according to her passionate and all-too-sacred desire, completely, when she possesses her man at last finally and ultimately, without blemish or reservation in the perfection of the sacrament: then, also, poor woman, the blood and the body of which she has partaken become insipid or nauseous to her, she is driven mad by the endless meal of the marriage sacrament, poisoned by the sacred communion which was her goal and her soul's ambition.

We have pushed a process into a goal. The aim of any process is not the perpetuation of that process, but the completion thereof. Love is a process of the incomprehensible human soul: love also incomprehensible, but still only a process. The process should work to a completion, not to some horror of intensification and extremity wherein the soul and body ultimately perish. The completion of the process of love is the arrival at a state of simple, pure self-possession, for man and woman. Only that. Which isn't exciting enough for us sensationalists. We prefer abysses and maudlin self-abandon and self-sacrifice, the degeneration into a sort of slime and merge.

Perhaps, truly, the process of love is never accomplished. But it moves in great stages, and at the end of each stage a true goal, where the soul possesses itself in simple and generous singleness. Without this, love is a disease.

So Aaron, crossing a certain border-line and finding himself alone completely, accepted his loneliness or singleness as a fulfilment, a state of fulfilment. The long fight with Lottie had driven him at last to himself, so that he was quiet as a thing which has its root deep in life, and has lost its anxiety. As for considering the lily, it is not a matter of consideration. The lily toils and spins hard enough, in her own way. But without strain and that anxiety with which we try to weave ourselves a life. The lily is life-rooted, life-central. She *cannot* worry. She is life itself, a little, delicate fountain playing creatively, for as long or as short a time as may be, and unable to be anxious. She may be sad or sorry, if the north wind blows. But even then, anxious she cannot be. Whether her fountain play or cease to play, from out the cold, damp earth, she cannot be anxious. She may only be glad or sorry, and continue her way. She is perfectly herself, whatever befall; even if frosts cut her off. Happy lily, never to be saddled with an *idée fixe*, never to be in the grip of a monomania for happiness or love or fulfilment. It is not *laisser aller*. It is life-rootedness. It is being by oneself, life-living, like the much-mooted lily. One toils, one spins, one strives: just as the lily does. But like her, taking one's own life-way amidst everything, and taking one's own life-way alone. Love too. But there also, taking one's way alone, happily alone in all the wonders of communion, swept up on the winds, but never swept away from one's very self. Two eagles in mid-air, maybe, like Whitman's 'Dalliance of Eagles'. Two eagles in mid-air, grappling, whirling, coming to their intensification of love-oneness there in mid-air. In mid-air the love consummation. But all the time each lifted on its own wings: each bearing itself on its own wings at every moment of the mid-air love consummation. That is the splendid love-way.

*

The party was festive at dinner-time, the women in their finest dresses, new flowers on the table, the best wine going. It was Sunday evening. Aaron too was dressed – and Lady Franks, in black lace and pearls, was almost gay.

There were quails for dinner. The Colonel was quite happy. An air of conviviality gathered round the table during the course of the meal.

'I hope,' said Aaron, 'that we shall have some music to-night.'

'I want so much to hear your flute,' said his hostess.

'And I your piano,' he said.

'I am very weak – very out of practice. I tremble at the thought of playing before a musician. But you must not be too critical.'

'Oh,' said Aaron. 'I am not a man to be afraid of.'

'Well, we will see,' said Lady Franks. 'But I am afraid of music itself.'

'Yes,' said Aaron. 'I think it is risky.'

'Immoral! I don't see that! Music risky? Bach? Beethoven? No, I don't agree. On the contrary, I think it is most elevating – most morally inspiring. No, I tremble before it because it *is* so wonderful and elevating.'

'I often find it makes me feel diabolical,' said he.

'That is your misfortune, I am sure,' said Lady Franks. 'Please do take another – but perhaps you don't like mushrooms?'

Aaron quite liked mushrooms, and helped himself to the entrée.

'But perhaps,' said she, 'you are too modern. You don't care for Bach or Beethoven or Chopin – dear Chopin.'

'I find them all quite as modern as I am.'

'Is that so? Yes. For myself I am quite old-fashioned – though I can appreciate Strauss and Stravinsky as well, some things. But my old things – ah, I don't think the moderns are so fine. They are not so deep. They haven't fathomed life so deeply,' Lady Franks sighed faintly.

'They don't care for depths,' said Aaron.

'No, they haven't the capacity. But I like big, deep music. Oh, I love orchestra. But my instrument is the piano. I like the great masters. Bach, Beethoven. They have such faith. You were talking of faith – believing that things would work out well for you in the end. Beethoven inspires that in me too.'

'He makes you feel that all will be well with you at last?'

'Yes, he does. He makes me feel faith in my *personal* destiny. And I do feel that there is something in one's special fate. I feel that I myself have a special kind of fate, that will always look after me.'

'And you can trust to it?'

'Yes, I can. It *always* turns out right. I think something has gone wrong – and then, it always turns out right. Why, when we were in London – when we were at lunch one morning it suddenly struck me, haven't I left my fur cloak somewhere? It was rather cold, so I had taken it with me, and then never put it on. And I hadn't brought it home. I had left it somewhere. But whether in a taxi, or in a shop, or in a little show of pictures I had been to, I couldn't remember. I *could not* remember. And I thought to myself: have I lost my cloak? I went round to everywhere I could think of: no trace of it. But I didn't give it up. Something prompted me not to give it up: quite distinctly, I felt something telling me that I should get it back. So I called at Scotland Yard and gave the information. Well, two days later I had a notice from Scotland Yard, so I went. And there was my cloak. I had it back. And that has happened to me almost every time. I almost *always* get my things back. And I always feel that something looks after me, do you know: almost takes care of me.'

'But do you mean when you lose things – or in your life?'

'I mean when I lose things – or when I want to get something I want – I am very nearly always successful. And I always feel there is some sort of higher power which does it for me.'

'Finds your cloak for you.'

'Yes. Wasn't it extraordinary? I felt when I saw my cloak in Scotland Yard: There, I *knew* I should recover you. And I always feel, as I say, that there is some higher power which helps me. Do you feel the same?'

'No, not that way, worse luck. I lost a batch of music a month ago which didn't belong to me – and which I couldn't replace. But I never could recover it: though I'm sure nobody wanted it.'

'How very unfortunate. Whereas my fur cloak was just the thing that gets stolen most.'

'I wished some power would trace my music: but apparently we aren't gifted alike with guardian angels.'

'Apparently not. And that is how I regard it: almost as a gift, you know, that my fairy godmother gave me in my cradle.'

'For always recovering your property?'

'Yes – and succeeding in my undertakings.'

'I'm afraid I had no fairy godmother.'

'Well – I think I had. And very glad I am of it.'

'Why, yes,' said Aaron, looking at his hostess.

So the dinner sailed merrily on.

'But does Beethoven make you feel,' said Aaron as an afterthought, 'in the same way – that you will always find the things you have lost?'

'Yes – he makes me feel the same faith: that what I lose will be returned to me. Just as I found my cloak. And that if I enter into an undertaking, it will be successful.'

'And you life has been always successful?'

'Yes – almost always. We have succeeded with almost everything.'

'Why, yes,' said Aaron, looking at her again.

But even so, he could see a good deal of hard wornness under her satisfaction. She had had her suffering, sure enough. But none the less, she was in the main satisfied. She sat there, a good hostess, and expected the homage due to her success. And, of course, she got it. Aaron himself did his little share of shoe-licking, and swallowed the taste of boot-polish with a grimace, knowing what he was about.

The dinner wound gaily to an end. The ladies retired. Sir William left his seat of honour at the end of the table and came and sat next to Aaron, summoning the other three men to cluster near.

'Now, Colonel,' said the host, 'send round the bottle.'

With a flourish of the elbow and shoulder, the Colonel sent on the port: actually port, in those bleak, post-war days.

'Well, Mr Sisson,' said Sir William, 'we will drink to your kind Providence: providing, of course, that we shall give no offence by so doing.'

'No sir – no sir! The Providence belonged to Mr Lilly. Mr Sisson put his money on kindly Fortune, I believe,' said Arthur, who, rosy and fresh with wine, looked as if he would make a marvellous *bonne bouche* for a finely-discriminating cannibal.

'Ah, yes, indeed! A much more ingratiating lady to lift our glasses to. Mr Sisson's kindly Fortune. Fortuna gentilissima! Well, Mr Sisson, and may your Lady Fortune ever smile on you.'

Sir William lifted his glass with an odd little smirk, some touch of a strange, prim old satyr lurking in his oddly inclined head. Nay, more than satyr: that curious, rather terrible iron demon that has fought with the world and wrung wealth from it, and which knows all about it. The devilish spirit of iron itself, and iron machines. So, with his strange, old smile showing his teeth rather terribly, the old knight glowered sightlessly over his glass at Aaron. Then he drank: the strange, careful, old-man's gesture in drinking.

'But, said Aaron, 'if Fortune is a female –'

'Fortune! Fortune! Why, Fortune is a lady. What do you say, Major?'

'She has all the airs of one, Sir William,' said the Major, with the wistful grimness of his age and culture. And the young fellow stared like a crucified cyclops from his one eye: the black shutter being over the other.

'And all the graces,' capped Sir William, delighted with himself.

'Oh, quite!' said the Major. 'For some, all the airs, and for others, all the graces.'

'Faint heart ne'er won fair lady, my boy,' said Sir William. 'Not that your heart is faint. On the contrary – as we know, and your country knows. But with Lady Fortune you need another kind of stout heart – oh, quite another kind.'

'I believe it, sir: and the kind of stout heart which I am afraid I haven't got,' said the Major.

'What!' said the old man. 'Show the white feather before you've tackled the lady! Fill the Major's glass, Colonel. I am quite sure we will none of us ever say die.'

'Not likely. Not if we know it,' said the Colonel, stretching himself heartily inside his tunic. He was becoming ruddier than the cherry. All he cared about at the moment was his gay little port glass. But the Major's young cheek was hollow and sallow, his one eye terribly pathetic.

'And you, Mr Sisson,' said Sir William, 'mean to carry all before you by taking no thought for the morrow. Well now, we can only wish you success.'

'I don't want to carry all before me,' said Aaron. 'I should be sorry. I want to walk past most of it.'

'Can you tell us where to? I am intrigued, as Sybil says, to know where you will walk to. Come now. Enlighten us.'

'Nowhere, I suppose.'

'But is that satisfactory? Can you find it satisfactory?'

'Is it even true?' said the Major. 'Isn't it quite as positive an act to walk away from a situation as to walk towards it?'

'My dear boy, you can't merely walk away from a situation. Believe that. If you walk away from Rome, you walk into the

Maremma, or into the Alban Hills, or into the sea, – but you walk into something. Now, if I am going to walk away from Rome, I prefer to choose my direction, and therefore my destination.'

'But you can't,' said the Major.

'What can't you?'

'Choose. Either your direction or your destination –' The Major was obstinate.

'Really!' said Sir William. 'I have not found it so. I have not found it so. I have had to keep myself hard at work, all my life, choosing between this or that.'

'And we,' said the Major, 'have no choice, except between this or nothing.'

'Really! I am afraid,' said Sir William, 'I am afraid I am too old – or too young – which shall I say? – to understand.'

'Too young, sir,' said Arthur sweetly. 'The child was always father to the man, I believe.'

'I confess the Major makes me feel childish,' said the old man. 'The choice between this or nothing is a puzzler to me. Can you help me out, Mr Sisson? What do you make of this this-or-nothing business? I can understand neck-or-nothing –'

'I prefer the *nothing* part of it to the *this* part of it,' said Aaron grinning.

'Colonel,' said the old man, 'throw a little light on this nothingness.'

'No, Sir William,' said the Colonel, 'I am all right as I am.'

'As a matter of fact, so are we all, perfectly A 1,' said Arthur. Aaron broke into a laugh.

'That's the top and bottom of it,' he laughed, flushed with wine, and handsome. 'We're all as right as ninepence. Only it's rather nice to talk.'

'There!' said Sir William. 'We're all as right as ninepence! We're all as right as ninepence. So there we'll leave it, before the Major has time to say he is twopence short.' Laughing his strange old soundless laugh, Sir William rose and made a little bow. 'Come up and join the ladies in a minute or two,' he said. Arthur opened the door for him and he left the room.

The four men were silent for a moment – then the Colonel whipped up the decanter and filled his glass. Then he stood up and clinked glasses with Aaron, like a real old sport.

'Luck to you,' he said.

'Thanks,' said Aaron.

'You're going in the morning?' said Arthur.

'Yes,' said Aaron.

'What train?' said Arthur.

'Eight-forty.'

'Oh – then we shan't see you again. Well – best of luck.'

'Best of luck –' echoed the Colonel.

'Same to you,' said Aaron, and they all peered over their glasses and quite loved one another for a rosy minute.

'I should like to know, though,' said the hollow-cheeked young Major with the black flap over his eye, 'whether you do really mean you are all right – that it is all right with you – or whether you only say so to get away from the responsibility.'

'I mean I don't really care – I don't damn – let the devil take it all.'

'The devil doesn't want it either,' said the Major.

'Then let him leave it. I don't care one single little curse about it all.'

'Be damned! What is there to care about?' said the Colonel.

'Ay, what?' said Aaron.

'It's all the same, whether you care or don't care. So I say it's much easier not to care.' said Arthur.

'Of course it is,' said the Colonel gaily.

'And I think so too,' said Aaron.

'Right you are! We're all as right as ninepence – what? Good old sport! Here's yours!' cried the Colonel.

'We shall have to be going up,' said Arthur, wise in his generation.

As they went into the hall, Arthur suddenly put one arm round Aaron's waist, and one arm round the Colonel's, and the three did a sudden little barn-dance towards the stairs. Arthur was feeling himself quite let loose again, back in his old regimental mess.

Approaching the foot of the stairs, he let go again. He was in that rosy condition when united-we-stand. But unfortunately it is a complicated job to climb the stairs in unison. The whole lot tends to fall backwards. Arthur, therefore, rosy, plump, looking so good to eat, stood still a moment in order to find his own neatly-slippered feet. Having found them, he proceeded to put them carefully one before the other, and to his enchantment found that this procedure was carrying him magically up the stairs. The Colonel, like a drowning man, clutched feebly for the straw of the great stair-rail – and missed it. He would have gone under, but that Aaron's hand gripped his arm. So, orientating once more like a fragile tendril, he reached again for the banister rail, and got it. After which, lifting his feet as if they were little packets of sand tied to his trouser buttons, he manipulated his way upwards. Aaron was in that pleasant state when he saw what everybody else was doing and was unconscious of what he did himself. Whilst tall, gaunt, erect, like a murdered Hamlet, resurrected in khaki, with the terrible black shutter over his eye, the young Major came last.

Arthur was making a stern fight for his composure. His whole future depended on it. But do what he would, he could not get the flushed, pleased, mess-happy look off his face. The Colonel, oh awful man, did a sort of plump roly-poly cake-walk, like a fat boy, right to the very door of that sanctum-sanctorum, the library. Aaron was inwardly convulsed. Even the Major laughed.

But Arthur stiffened himself militarily and cleared his throat. All four started to compose themselves, like actors going on the stage, outside that library door. And then Arthur softly, almost wistfully, opened and held the door for the others to pass. The Colonel slunk meekly in, and sat in a chair in the background. The Major stalked in expressionless, and hovered towards the sofa where his wife sat.

There was rather a cold-water-down-your-back feeling in the library. The ladies had been waiting for coffee: Sir William was waiting too. Therefore in a little tension, half silent, the coffee was handed round. Lady Franks was discussing something with Arthur's wife. Arthur's wife was in a cream lace dress, and looking what is called lovely. The Major's wife was in amethyst chiffon with dark-red roses, and was looking blindingly beautiful. The Colonel was looking into his coffee-cup as wistfully as if it contained the illusion of tawny port. The Major was looking into space, as if there and there alone, etc. Arthur was looking for something which Lady Franks had asked for, and which he was much too flushed to find. Sir William was looking at Aaron, and preparing for another *cœur à cœur*.

'Well,' he said, 'I doubt if you will care for Milan. It is one of the least Italian of all the towns, in my opinion. Venice, of course, is a thing apart. I cannot stand, myself, that miserable specimen the modern Roman. He has most of the vices of the old Romans and none of the virtues. The most congenial town, perhaps, for a stranger, is Florence. But it has a very bad climate.'

Lady Franks rose significantly and left the room, accompanied by Arthur's wife. Aaron knew, silently, that he was summoned to follow. His hostess had her eye on him this evening. But always postponing his obedience to the cool commands of women, he remained talking, with his host in the library, and sipping *crème de menthe*. Came the ripple of the pianoforte from the open doorway down at the further end of the room. Lady Franks was playing, in the large drawing-room. And the ripple of the music contained in it the hard insistence of the little woman's will. Coldly, and decidedly, she intended there should be no more unsettling conversations for the old Sir William. Aaron was to come forthwith into the drawing-room. Which Aaron plainly understood – and so he didn't go. No, he didn't go, though the pianoforte rippled and swelled in volume. No, and he didn't go even when Lady Franks left off playing and came into the library again. There he sat, talking with Sir William. Let us do credit to Lady Franks' will-power, and admit that the talk was quite empty and distracted – none of the depths and skirmishes of the previous occasions. None the less, the talk continued. Lady

Franks retired, discomfited, to her piano again. She would never break in upon her lord.

So now Aaron relented. He became more and more distracted. Sir William wandered away like some restless, hunted soul. The Colonel still sat in his chair, nursing his last drop of *crème de menthe* resentfully. He did not care for the green toffee-stuff. Arthur was busy. The Major lay sprawled in the last stages of everything on the sofa, holding his wife's hand. And the music came pathetically through the open folding doors. Of course, she played with feeling – it went without saying. Aaron's soul felt rather tired. But she had a touch of discrimination also.

He rose and went to the drawing-room. It was a large, vacant-seeming, Empire sort of drawing-room, with yellow silk chairs along the walls and yellow silk panels upon the walls, and a huge, vasty crystal chandelier hanging from a far-away-above ceiling. Lady Franks sat at a large black Bechstein piano at one end of this vacant yellow state-room. She sat, a little plump elderly lady in black lace, for all the world like Queen Victoria in Max Beerbohm's drawing of Alfred Tennyson reading to her Victorian Majesty, with space before her. Arthur's wife was bending over some music in a remote corner of the big room.

Aaron seated himself on one of the chairs by the wall, to listen. Certainly it was a beautiful instrument. And certainly, in her way, she loved it. But Aaron remembered an anthem in which he had taken part as a boy.

> His eye is on the sparrow
> So I know He watches me.

For a long time he had failed to catch the word *sparrow*, and had heard:

> His eye is on the spy-hole
> So I know He watches me.

Which was just how it had all seemed to him, as a boy.

Now, as ever, he felt the eye was on the spy-hole. There sat the woman playing music. But her inward eye was on the spy-hole of her vital affairs – her domestic arrangements, her control of her household, guests and husband included. The other eye was left for the music, don't you know.

Sir William appeared hovering in the doorway, not at all liking the defection of Mr Aaron. Then he retreated. He seemed not to care for music. The Major's wife hovered – felt it her duty to aude, or play audience – and entered, seating herself in a breath of lilac and amethyst again at the near distance. The Major, after a certain beating about the bush, followed and sat rapt in dim contemplation near his wife. Arthur luckily was still busy with something.

Aaron, of course, made proper musical remarks in the intervals – Arthur's wife sorted out more pieces. Arthur appeared – and then the Colonel. The Colonel tip-toed beautifully across the wide blank space of the Empire room, and seated himself on a chair, rather in the distance, with his back to the wall, facing Aaron. When Lady Franks finished her piece, to everybody's amazement the Colonel clapped gaily to himself and said Bravo! as if at a Café Chantant – looking around for his glass. But there was no glass. So he crossed his neatly-khakied legs, and looked rapt again.

Lady Franks started with a *vivace* Schumann piece. Everybody listened in sanctified silence, trying to seem to like it. When suddenly our Colonel began to spring and bounce in his chair, slinging his loose leg with a kind of rapture up and down in the air, and capering upon his posterior, doing a sitting-down jig to the Schumann *vivace*. Arthur, who had seated himself at the farthest extremity of the room, winked with wild bliss at Aaron. The Major tried to look as if he noticed nothing, and only succeeded in looking agonized. His wife studied the point of her silver shoe minutely, and peeped through her hair at the performance. Aaron grimly chuckled, and loved the Colonel with real tenderness.

And the game went on while the *vivace* lasted. Up and down bounced the plump Colonel on his chair, kicking with his bright, black-patent toe higher and higher, getting quite enthusiastic over his jig. Rosy and unabashed, he was worthy of the great nation he belonged to. The broad-seated Empire chair showed no signs of giving way. Let him enjoy himself, away there across the yellow Sahara of this silk-panelled salon. Aaron felt quite cheered up.

'Well, now,' he thought to himself, 'this man is in entire command of a very important branch of the British Service in Italy. We are a great race still.'

But Lady Franks must have twigged. Her playing went rather stiff. She came to the end of the *vivace* movements, and abandoned her piece.

'I always prefer Schumann in his *vivace* moods,' said Aaron.

'Do you?' said Lady Franks. 'Oh, I don't know.'

It was now the turn of Arthur's wife to sing. Arthur seemed to get further away, if it was possible, for he was at the remotest end of the room, near the gallery doors. The Colonel became quiet, pensive. The Major's wife eyed the young woman in white lace, and seemed not to care for lace. Arthur seemed to be trying to push himself backwards through the wall. Lady Franks switched on more lights into the vast and voluminous crystal chandelier which hung like some glory-cloud above the room's centre. And Arthur's wife sang — sweet little French songs, and Ye Banks and Braes, and *Caro mio ben*, which goes without saying: and so on. She had quite a nice voice and was quite adequately trained. Which is enough said. Aaron had all his nerves on edge.

Then he had to play the flute. Arthur strolled upstairs with him, arm-in-arm, where he went to fetch his instrument.

'I find music in the home rather a strain, you know,' said Arthur.

'Cruel strain. I quite agree,' said Aaron.

'I don't mind it so much in the theatre — or even a concert — where there are a lot of other people to take the edge off — But after a good dinner — '

'It's medicine,' said Aaron.

'Well, you know, it really is, to me. It affects my inside.'

Aaron laughed. And then, in the yellow drawing-room blew into his pipe and played. He knew so well that Arthur, the Major, the Major's wife, the Colonel, and Sir William thought it merely an intolerable bore. However, he played. His hostess even accompanied him in a Mozart bit.

CHAPTER 14

XX Settembre

AARON was wakened in the morning by the soft entrance of the butler with his tray: it was just seven o'clock. Lady Franks' household was punctual as the sun itself.

But our hero roused himself with a wrench. The very act of lifting himself from the pillow was like a fight this morning. Why? He recognized his own wrench, the pain with which he struggled under the necessity to move. Why shouldn't he want to move? Why not? Because he didn't want the day in front – the plunge into a strange country, towards nowhere, with no aim in view. True, he said that ultimately he wanted to join Lilly. But this was hardly more than a sop, an excuse for his own irrational behaviour. He was breaking loose from one connection after another: and what for? Why break every tie? Snap, snap, snap went the bonds and ligatures which bound him to the life that had formed him, the people he had loved or liked. He found all his affections snapping off, all the ties which united him with his own people coming asunder. And why? In God's name, why? What was there instead?

There was nothingness. There was just himself, and blank nothingness. He had perhaps a faint sense of Lilly ahead of him: an impulse in that direction: or else merely an illusion. He could not persuade himself that he was seeking for love, for any kind of unison or communion. He knew well enough that the thought of any loving, any sort of real coming together between himself and anybody or anything, was just objectionable to him. No – he was not moving *towards* anything: he was moving almost violently away from everything. And that was what he wanted. Only that. Only let him *not* run into any sort of embrace with anything or anybody – this was what he asked. Let no new connexion be made between himself and anything on earth. Let all old connexions break. This was his craving.

Yet he struggled under it this morning as under the lid of a tomb. The terrible sudden weight of inertia! He knew the tray stood ready by the bed: he knew the automobile would be at the door at eight o'clock, for Lady Franks had said so, and he half divined that the servant had also said so: yet he lay, in a kind of paralysis in his bed. He seemed for the moment to have lost his will. Why go forward into more nothingness, away from all that he knew, all he was accustomed to and all he belonged to?

However, with a click he sat up. And the very instant he had poured his coffee from the little silver coffee-pot into his delicate cup, he was ready for anything and everything. The sense of silent adventure took him, the exhilarated feeling that he was fulfilling his own inward destiny. Pleasant to taste was the coffee, the bread, the honey – delicious.

The man brought his clothes, and again informed him that the automobile would be at the door at eight o'clock: or at least so he made out.

'I can walk,' said Aaron.

'Milady ha comandato l'automobile,' said the man softly.

It was evident that if Milady had ordered it, so it must be.

So Aaron left the still-sleeping house, and got into the soft and luxurious car. As he dropped through the park he wondered that Sir William and Lady Franks should be so kind to him: a complete stranger. But so it was. There he sat in their car. He wondered, also, as he ran over the bridge and into the city, whether this soft-running automobile would ever rouse the socialistic bile of the work-people. For the first time in his life, as he sat among the snug cushions, he realized what it might be to be rich and uneasy: uneasy, even if not afraid, lurking there inside an expensive car. Well, it wasn't much of a sensation anyhow: and riches were stuffy, like wadded upholstery on everything. He was glad to get out into the fresh air of the common crowd. He was glad to be in the bleak, not-very-busy station. He was glad to be part of common life. For the very atmosphere of riches seems to be stuffed and wadded, never any real reaction. It was terrible, as if one's very body, shoulders and arms, were upholstered and made cushiony. Ugh, but he was glad to shake off himself the atmosphere of wealth and motor-cars, to get out of it all. It was like getting out of quilted clothes.

'Well,' thought Aaron, 'if this is all it amounts to, to be rich, you can have riches. They talk about money being power. But the only sort of power it has over me is to bring on a kind of numbness, which I fairly hate. No wonder rich people don't seem to be really alive.'

The relief of escaping quite took away his self-conscious embarrassment at the station. He carried his own bags, bought a third-class ticket, and got into the train for Milan without caring one straw for the comments or the looks of the porters.

It began to rain. The train ran across the great plain of north Italy. Aaron sat in his wood-seated carriage and smoked his pipe in silence, looking at the thick, short Lombards opposite him without heeding them. He paid hardly any outward attention to his surroundings, but sat involved in himself.

In Milan he had been advised to go to the Hotel Britannia, because it was not expensive, and English people went there. So he took a carriage, drove round the green space in front of Milan station, and away into the town. The streets were busy, but only half-heartedly so.

It must be confessed that every new move he made was rather an effort. Even he himself wondered why he was struggling with foreign porters and foreign cabmen, being talked at and not understanding a word. But there he was. So he went on with it.

The hotel was small and congenial. The hotel porter answered in English. Aaron was given a little room with a tiny balcony, looking on to a quiet street. So, he had a home of his own once more. He washed, and then counted his money. Thirty-seven pounds he had: and no more. He stood on the balcony and looked at the people going by below. Life seems to be moving so quick, when one looks down on it from above.

Across the road was a large stone house with its green shutters all closed. But from the flagpole under the eaves, over the central window of the uppermost floor – the house was four storeys high – waved the Italian flag in the melancholy damp air. Aaron looked at it – the red, white and green tricolour, with the white cross of Savoy in the centre. It hung damp and still. And there seemed a curious vacancy in the city – something empty and depressing in the great human centre. Not that there was really a lack of people. But the spirit of the town seemed depressed and empty. It was a national holiday. The Italian flag was hanging from almost every house front.

It was about three o'clock in the afternoon. Aaron sat in the restaurant of the hotel drinking tea, for he was rather tired, and looking through the thin curtains at the little square outside, where people passed, little groups of dark, aimless-seeming men, a little bit poorer looking – perhaps rather shorter in stature – but very much like the people in any other town. Yet the feeling of the city was so different from that of London. There seemed a curious emptiness. The rain ceased, but the pavements were still wet. There was a tension.

Suddenly there was a noise of two shots, fired in rapid succession. Aaron turned startled to look into the quiet piazza. And to his amazement, the pavements were empty, not a soul was in sight. Two minutes before the place was busy with passers-by, and a newspaper man selling the *Corriere*, and little carriages rattling through. Now, as if by magic, nobody, nothing. It was as if they had all melted into thin air.

The waiter, too, was peeping behind the curtain. A carriage came trotting into the square – an odd man took his way alone – the traffic began to stir once more, and people reappeared as suddenly as they had disappeared. Then the waiter ran hastily and furtively out and craned his neck, peering round the square. He spoke with two youths – rather loutish youths. Then he returned to his duty in the hotel restaurant.

'What was it? What were the shots?' Aaron asked him.

'Oh – somebody shooting at a dog,' said the man negligently.

'At a dog!' said Aaron, with round eyes.

He finished his tea, and went out into the town. His hotel was not far from the cathedral square. Passing through the arcade, he came in sight of the famous cathedral with its numerous spines pricking into the afternoon air. He was not as impressed as he should have been. And yet there was something in the northern city – this big square with all the trams threading through, the little Continental trams: and the spiny bulk of the great cathedral, like a grey-purple sea-urchin with many spines, on the one side, the ornamental grass-plots and flower-beds on the other: the big shops going all along the further strands, all round: and the endless, restless, nervous drift of a north Italian crowd, so nervous, so twitchy; nervous and twitchy as the slipping past of the little yellow tram-cars; it all affected him with a sense of strangeness, nervousness, and approaching winter. It struck him the people were afraid of themselves: afraid of their own souls, and that which was in their own souls.

Turning up the broad steps of the cathedral, he entered the famous building. The sky had cleared, and the freshened light shone coloured in living tablets round the wonderful, towering, rose-hearted dusk of the great church. At some altars lights flickered uneasily. At some unseen side-altar mass was going on, and a strange ragged music fluttered out on the incense-dusk of the great and lofty interior, which was all shadow, all shadow, hung round with jewel tablets of light. Particularly beautiful the great east bay, above the great altar. And all the time, over the bog-patterned marble floor, the faint click and rustle of feet coming and going, coming and going, like shallow, uneasy water rustled back and forth in a trough. A white dog trotted pale through the under-dusk, over the pale, big-patterned floor. Aaron came to the side altar where mass was going on, candles ruddily wavering. There was a small cluster of kneeling women – a ragged handful of on-looking men – and people wandering up and wandering away, young women with neatly dressed black hair, and shawls, but without hats; fine young women in very high heels; young men with nothing to do; ragged men with nothing to do. All strayed faintly clicking over the slabbed floor, and glanced at the flickering altar where the white-surpliced boys were curtseying and the white-and-gold priest was bowing, his hands over his breast, in the candle-light. All strayed, glanced, lingered, and strayed away again, as if the spectacle were not sufficiently holding. The bell chimed for the elevation of the Host. But the thin trickle of people trickled the same, uneasily, over the slabbed floor of the vastly-upreaching, shadow-foliaged cathedral.

The smell of incense in his nostrils, Aaron went out again by a side door, and began to walk along the pavements of the cathedral square, looking at the shops. Some were closed, and had little notices pinned on them. Some were open, and seemed half-stocked with half-elegant things. Men were crying newspapers. In the cafes a few men were seated drinking vermouth. In the doorway of the restaurants waiters stood inert, looking out on the streets. The curious heart-eating *ennui* of the big town on a holiday came over our hero. He felt he must get out, whatever happened. He could not bear it.

So he went back to his hotel and up to his room. It was still only five o'clock. And he did not know what to do with himself. He lay on the bed, and looked at the painting on his bedroom ceiling. It was a terrible business in Reckitt's blue and browny gold, with awful heraldic beasts, rather worm-wriggly, displayed in a blue field.

As he lay thinking of nothing and feeling nothing except a certain weariness, or dreariness, or tension, or God-knows-what, he heard a loud hoarse noise of humanity in the distance, something frightening. Rising, he went on to his little balcony. It was a sort of procession or march of men, here and there a red flag fluttering from a man's hand. There had been a big meeting, and this was the issue. The procession was irregular, but powerful: men four abreast. They emerged irregularly from the small piazza into the street, calling and vociferating.

They stopped before a shop and clotted into a crowd, shouting, becoming vicious. Over the shop-door hung a tricolour – a national flag. The shop was closed: men began to knock at the door. They were all workmen, some in railwaymen's caps, mostly in black hats. Some wore red cotton neckties. They lifted their faces to the national flag, and as they shouted and gesticulated Aaron could see their strong teeth in their jaws. There was something frightening in their lean, strong Italian jaws, something inhuman and possessed-looking in their foreign, southern-shaped faces, so much more formed and demon-looking than northern faces. They had a demon-like fixed purpose and sharp will, and the noise of their voices was like a scraping of steel and copper weapons. Aaron wondered what they wanted. There were no women – all men; a strange male slashing sound. Vicious it was – the head of the procession clustering thick before the shop, the thick wedge of the procession beyond, flecked with red flags.

A window opened above the shop, and a frowsty-looking man, yellow-pale, was quickly and nervously hauling in the national flag. There were shouts of derision and mockery: a great overtone of derision, acrid. The flag and its owner ignominiously disappeared. And the procession moved on.

Almost every shop had a flag flying. And every one of these flags now began to disappear, quickly or slowly, sooner or later, in obedience to the command of the vicious, derisive crowd, that marched and clotted slowly down the street, having its own way.

Only one flag remained flying: the big tricolour that floated from the top storey of the house opposite Aaron's hotel. The ground floor of this house consisted of shop-premises – now closed. There was no sign of any occupant. The flag floated inert aloft.

The whole crowd had come to a stop immediately below the hotel, and all were now looking up at the green and white and red tricolour which stirred damply in the early evening light, from under the broad eaves of the house opposite. Aaron looked at the long flag, which drooped almost unmoved from the eaves-shadow, and he half expected it to furl itself up of its own accord, in obedience to the will of the masses. Then he looked down at the packed black shoulders of the mob below, and at the curious clustering pattern of a sea of black hats. He could hardly see anything but hats and shoulders, uneasily moving like boiling pitch away beneath him. But the shouts began to come up hotter and hotter. There had been a great banging of the shop door and a ringing of the bell of the guilty house-door. The crowd – the swollen head of the procession – talked and shouted, occupying the centre of the street but leaving the pavement clear. A woman in a white blouse appeared in the shop-door. She came out and looked up at the flag and shook her head and gesticulated with her hands. It was evidently not her flag: she had nothing to do with it. The leaders now turned again to the large house-door, and began to ring all the bells and to beat with their fists. But no good – there was no answer. Voices arose ragged and ironical. The woman explained again, with rapid gestures. Apparently there was nobody at home in the upper apartments – all entrances were locked – there was no caretaker to be found. Nobody owned the flag. There it hung under the broad eaves of the strong house, and didn't even know it was guilty. The woman went back into her shop and drew down the iron shutter from inside.

The crowd, nonplussed, now began to argue and shout and whistle. The voices rose in pitch and derision. Steam was getting up. There hung the gaudy flag. The mob crowded forward and filled the street in a mass below. All the rest of the street was empty and shut up. And still hung the showy rag, red and white and green, up aloft.

Suddenly there was a lull – then shouts, half-encouraging, half-derisive. And Aaron saw a smallish black figure of a youth, fair-haired, not more than seventeen years old, clinging like a monkey to the front of the house, and by the help of the heavy drain-pipe and the stonework ornamentation climbing up to the stone ledge that ran beneath the ground-floor windows, up like a sudden cat on to the projecting footing.

There he did not stop, but continued his race like some frantic lizard running up the great wall-front, working his way from the noise below as if in a frenzy of fright. It was one unending wriggling movement, sheer up the front of the impassive, heavy stone house.

The flag hung from a pole under one of the windows of the top storey – the third floor. Up went the wriggling figure of the possessed youth. The cries of the crowd below were now wild, ragged ejaculations of excitement and encouragement. The youth seemed to be lifted up, almost magically, on the intense upreaching excitement of the massed men below. He had passed the ledge of the first floor, like a lizard he wriggled up and passed the ledge or coping of the second floor, and there he was, like an upward-climbing shadow, scrambling on to the coping of the third floor. The crowd was for a second electrically still as the boy rose there erect, cleaving to the wall with the tips of his fingers.

But he did not hesitate for one breath. He was on his feet and running along the narrow coping that went across the house-front under the third-floor windows, running there on that narrow footing away above the street, straight to the flag. He had got it: he had clutched it in one hand, a handful of it. Exactly like a great flame rose the simultaneous yell of the crowd as the boy jerked and got the flag loose. He had torn it down, it was in his hand. A tremendous long yell, touched with a snarl of triumph, and searing like a puff of flame sounded as the boy remained for one moment with the flag in his fist looking down at the crowd below. His face was odd and elated and still. Then with the slightest gesture he threw the flag from him, and Aaron watched the gaudy remnant falling towards the many faces, whilst the noise of yelling rose up unheeded.

There was a great clutch and hiss in the crowd. The boy still unmoved, holding by one hand behind him, looking down from above, from his dangerous elevation, in a sort of abstraction.

And the next thing Aaron was conscious of was the sound

of trumpets. A sudden startling challenge of trumpets, and out of nowhere a sudden rush of grey-green carabinieri battering the crowd wildly with truncheons. It was so sudden that Aaron *heard* nothing any more. He only saw.

In utmost amazement he saw the sturdy, greeny-grey carabinieri, like a posse of foot-soldiers, rushing thick and wild and indiscriminate on the crowd, with a frenzied excitement which must have been based on fear: a sudden, new, excited crowd in uniform attacking the civilian crowd and laying about blindly, furiously, with truncheons. There was a seething moment in the street below. And almost instantaneously the original crowd burst into it in a frenzy of panic. The mob broke as if something had exploded inside it. A few black-hatted men fought furiously to get themselves free of the hated soldiers; in the confusion bunches of men staggered, reeled, fell, and were struggling among the legs of their comrades and of the carabinieri. But the bulk of the crowd just burst and fled, in every direction. Like drops of water they seemed to fly up at the very walls themselves. They darted into any entry, any doorway. They sprang up the walls and clambered into the ground-floor windows. They sprang up the walls on to window ledges, and then jumped down again and ran: clambering, wriggling, darting, running in every direction; some cut, blood on their faces, terror or frenzy or flight in their hearts. Not so much terror as the frenzy of running away. In a breath the street was empty.

And all the time there above on the stone coping stood the long-faced, fair-haired boy, while four stout carabinieri in the street below stood with uplifted revolvers and covered him, shouting that if he moved they would shoot. So there he stood, still looking down, still holding with his left hand behind him, covered by four revolvers. He was not so much afraid as twitchily self-conscious because of his false position.

Meanwhile down below the crowd had disappeared – melted momentaneously. The carabinieri were busy arresting the men who had fallen and been trodden underfoot, or who

223

had let themselves foolishly be taken. Perhaps half-a-dozen men: half-a-dozen prisoners: less rather than more.

The sergeant ordered these to be secured between soldiers. And last of all the youth up above, still covered by the revolvers, was ordered to come down. He turned quite quietly, and quite humbly, cautiously picked his way along the coping to the drain-pipe. He reached this pipe and began in cautious dejection to climb down. It was a real climb down.

Once in the street he was seized by the grey uniforms. The soldiers formed up. The sergeant gave the order. And away marched authority, triumphant and thankful to have got off so lightly. The dejected youth was marched away between them.

Then were heard a few scattered yells of derision and protest against the carabinieri. There were once more gangs of men and groups of youths along the street. They sent up an occasional shout or threat. But always over their shoulders, and ready to pretend it was not they who shouted. They were all cowed and hang-dog once more, and made not the slightest effort to save the youth. Nevertheless they prowled and watched ready for next time.

So, away went the prisoner and the grey-green soldiers, and the street was left to the little gangs and groups of hang-dog, discontented men, all thoroughly out of countenance. The scene was ended.

Aaron looked round, dazed. And then for the first time he noticed, on the next balcony to his own, two young men: young gentlemen, he would have said. The one was tall and handsome and well-coloured, might be Italian. But the other, with his pale thin face and his rimless monocle in his eye, he was surely an Englishman. He was surely one of the young officers shattered by the war. A look of strange, arch, bird-like pleasure was on his face at this moment: if one could imagine the gleaming smile of a white owl over the events that had just passed, this was the impression produced on Aaron by the face of the young man with the monocle. The other youth, the ruddy handsome one, had knitted his brows in mock distress, and was glancing with a look of shrewd curiosity at

Aaron, and with a look of almost self-satisfied excitement first to one end of the street, then to the other.

'But imagine, Angus, it's all over!' he said, laying his hand on the arm of the monocled young man, and making great eyes – not without a shrewd glance in Aaron's direction.

'Did you see him fall!' replied Angus, with another strange gleam.

'Yes! But was he *hurt* – ?'

'I don't know. I should think so. He fell right back out of that window on to those stones!'

'But how perfectly *awful!* Did you ever see anything like it?'

'No. It's one of the funniest things I ever did see. I saw nothing quite like it, even in the war – '

Here Aaron withdrew into his room. His mind and soul were in a whirl. He sat down in his chair, and did not move again for a great while. When he did move, he took his flute and played he knew not what. But strange, strange his soul passed into his instrument. Or passed half into his instrument. There was a big residue left, to go bitter, or to ferment into good old wine of wisdom.

He did not notice the dinner gong, and only the arrival of the chambermaid, to put the wash-table in order, sent him down to the restaurant. The first thing he saw, as he entered, was the two young Englishmen seated at a table in a corner just behind him. Their hair was brushed straight back from their foreheads, making the sweep of the head bright and impeccable, and leaving both the young faces clear as if in cameo. Angus had laid his monocle on the table, and was looking round the room with wide, light-blue eyes, looking hard, like some bird-creature, and seeming to see nothing. He had evidently been very ill: was still very ill. His cheeks and even his jaw seemed shrunken, almost withered. He forgot his dinner: or he did not care for it. Probably the latter.

'What do you think, Francis,' he said, 'of making a plan to see Florence and Siena and Orvieto on the way down, instead of going straight to Rome?' He spoke in precise, particularlyenunciated words, in a public-school manner, but with a strong twang of South Wales.

'Why Angus,' came the graceful voice of Francis, 'I thought we had settled to go straight through via Pisa.' Francis was graceful in everything – in his tall, elegant figure, in the poses of his handsome head, in the modulation of his voice.

'Yes, but I see we can go either way – either Pisa or Florence. And I thought it might be nice to look at Florence and Siena and Orvieto. I believe they're very lovely,' came the soft, precise voice of Angus, ending in a touch of odd emotion on the words 'very lovely', as if it were a new experience to him to be using them.

'I'm *sure* they're marvellous. I'm quite sure they're marvellously beautiful,' said Francis, in his assured, elegant way. 'Well then, Angus – suppose we do that, then? When shall we start?'

Angus was the nervous insister. Francis was quite occupied with his own thoughts and calculations and curiosity. For he was very curious, not to say inquisitive. And at the present moment he had a new subject to ponder.

This new subject was Aaron, who sat with his back to our new couple, and who, with his fine sharp ears, caught every word that they said. Aaron's back was broad enough, and his shoulders square, and his head rather small and fairish and well-shaped – and Francis was intrigued. He wanted to know was the man English. He *looked* so English – yet he might be – he might perhaps be Danish, Scandinavian, or Dutch. Therefore the elegant young man watched and listened with all his ears.

The waiter who had brought Aaron his soup now came very free and easy, to ask for further orders.

'What would you like to drink? Wine? Chianti? Or white wine? Or beer?' The old-fashioned 'Sir' was dropped. It is too old-fashioned now, since the war.

'What *should* I drink?' said Aaron, whose acquaintance with wines was not very large.

226

'Half-litre of Chianti: that is very good,' said the waiter, with the air of a man who knew only too well how to bring up his betters, and train them in the way they should go.

'All right,' said Aaron.

The welcome sound of these two magic words, All Right! was what the waiter most desired. 'All Right! Yes! All Right!' This is the pith, the marrow, the sum and essence of the English language to a southerner. Of course it is not *all right*. It is *Or-rye* – and one word at that. The blow that would be given to most foreign waiters, if they were forced to realize that the famous *orye* was really composed of two words, and spelt *all right*, would be too cruel, perhaps.

'Half litre Chianti. Orye,' said the waiter. And we'll let him say it.

'English!' whispered Francis melodramatically in the ear of Angus. 'I *thought* so. The flautist.'

Angus put in his monocle, and stared at the oblivious shoulders of Aaron, without apparently seeing anything.

'Yes. Obviously English,' said Angus, pursing like a bird.

'Oh, but I *heard* him,' whispered Francis emphatically.

'Quite,' said Angus. 'But quite inoffensive.'

'Oh, but Angus, my dear – he's the *flautist*. Don't you remember? The divine bit of Scriabin. At least I believe it was Scriabin. But *perfectly divine!!!* I adore the flute above all things – ' And Francis placed his hand on Angus' arm, and rolled his eyes – 'Lay this to the credit of a bottle of Lacrimae Cristi, if you like.'

'Yes. So do I,' said Angus, again looking archly through the monocle, and seeing nothing. 'I wonder what he's doing here.'

'Don't you think we might *ask* him?' said Francis, in a vehement whisper. 'After all, we are the only three English people in the place.'

'For the moment, apparently we are,' said Angus. 'But the English are all over the place wherever you go, like bits of orange peel in the street. Don't forget that, Francesco.'

'No, Angus, I don't. The point is, his flute is *perfectly divine –*

227

and he seems quite attractive in himself. Don't you think so?'

'Oh, quite,' said Angus, whose observations had got no further than the black cloth of the back of Aaron's jacket. That there was a man inside he had not yet paused to consider.

'Quite a musician,' said Francis.

'The hired sort,' said Angus, 'most probably.'

'But he *plays* – he *plays* most marvellously. *That* you can't get away from, Angus.'

'I quite agree,' said Angus.

'Well then? Don't you think we might hear him again? Don't you think we might get him to play for us? But I should love it more than anything.'

'Yes, I should too,' said Angus. 'You might ask him to coffee and a liqueur.'

'I should like to – most awfully. But do you think I might?'

'Oh, yes. He won't mind being offered a coffee and liqueur. We can give him something decent. Where's the waiter?' Angus lifted his pinched, ugly bare face and looked round with weird command for the waiter. The waiter, having not much to do, and feeling ready to draw these two weird young birds, allowed himself to be summoned.

'Where's the wine list? What liqueurs have you got?' demanded Angus abruptly.

The waiter rattled off a list, beginning with Strega and ending with cherry brandy.

'Grand Marnier,' said Angus. 'And leave the bottle.'

Then he looked with arch triumph at Francis, like a wicked bird. Francis bit his finger moodily, and glowered with handsome, dark-blue, uncertain eyes at Mr Aaron, who was just surveying the *frutta:* which consisted of two rather old pomegranates and various pale yellow apples, with a sprinkling of withered dried figs. At the moment, they all looked like a *natura morta* arrangement.

'But do you think I might – ?' said Francis moodily. Angus pursed his lips with reckless brightness.

'Why not? I see no reason why you shouldn't,' he said.

Whereupon Francis cleared his throat, disposed of his serviette, and rose to his feet, slowly but gracefully. Then he composed himself, and took on the air he wished to assume at the moment. It was a nice *dégagé* air, half naive and half enthusiastic. Then he crossed to Aaron's table, and stood on one lounging hip, gracefully, and bent forward in a confidential manner, and said:

'*Do* excuse me. But I *must* ask you if it was you we heard playing the flute so perfectly wonderfully, just before dinner.'

The voice was confidential and ingratiating. Aaron, relieved from the world's stress of seeing life anew in the rosy glow of half a litre of good old Chianti – the war was so near, but gone by – looked up at the dark blue, ingenuous, well-adapted eyes of our friend Francis, and smiling, said:

'Yes. I saw you on the balcony as well.'

'Oh, did you notice us?' plunged Francis. 'But wasn't it an extraordinary affair?'

'Very,' said Aaron. 'I couldn't make it out, could you?'

'Oh, cried Francis, 'I never try. It's all much too new and complicated for me. But perhaps you know Italy?'

'No, I don't,' said Aaron.

'Neither do we. And we feel rather stunned. We had only just arrived – and then – Oh!' Francis put up his hand to his comely brow and rolled his eyes. 'I feel perfectly overwhelmed with it still.'

He here allowed himself to sink friendlily into the vacant chair opposite Aaron's.

'Yes, I thought it was a bit exciting,' said Aaron. 'I wonder what will become of him –'

'– Of the one who climbed for the flag, you mean? No! But wasn't it perfectly marvellous! Oh incredible, quite incredible! And then your flute to finish it all! Oh! I felt it only wanted that. I haven't got over it yet. But your playing was *marvellous*, really marvellous. Do you know, I can't forget it. You are a professional musician, of course?'

'If you mean I play for a living,' said Aaron. 'I have played in orchestras in London.'

'Of course! Of course! I knew you must be a professional. But don't you give private recitals too?'

'No, I never have.'

'Oh! cried Francis, catching his breath. 'I can't believe it. But you play *marvellously!* Oh, I just loved it, it simply swept me away, after that scene in the street. It seemed to sum it all up, you know.'

'Did it,' said Aaron, rather grimly.

'But won't you come and have coffee with us at our table?' said Francis. 'We should like it most awfully if you would.'

'Yes, thank you,' said Aaron, half rising.

'But you haven't had your dessert,' said Francis, laying a fatherly detaining hand on the arm of the other man. Aaron looked at the detaining hand.

'The dessert isn't much to stop for,' he said. 'I can take with me what I want.' And he picked out a handful of dried figs.

The two went across to Angus' table.

'We're going to take coffee together,' said Francis complacently, playing the host with a suave assurance that was rather amusing and charming in him.

'Yes. I'm very glad,' said Angus. Let us give the show away: he was being wilfully nice. But he *was* quite glad to be able to be so nice. Anything to have a bit of life going: especially a bit of pleased life. He looked at Aaron's comely, wine-warmed face with gratification.

'Have a Grand Marnier,' he said. 'I don't know how bad it is. Everything is bad now. They lay it down to the war as well. It used to be quite a decent drink. What the war has got to do with bad liqueurs, I don't know.'

Aaron sat down in a chair at their table.

'But let us introduce ourselves,' said Francis. 'I am Francis – or really Franz Dekker. And this is Angus Guest, my friend.'

'And my name is Aaron Sisson.'

'What! What did you say?' said Francis, leaning forward. He too had sharp ears.

'Aaron Sisson.'

'Aaron Sisson! Oh, but how amusing! What a nice name!'

'No better than yours, is it?'

'Mine! Franz Dekker! Oh, much more amusing, *I* think,' said Francis archly.

'Oh well, it's a matter of opinion. You're the double decker, not me.'

'The double decker!' said Francis archly. 'Why, what do you mean! —' He rolled his eyes significantly. 'But may I introduce my friend, Angus Guest.'

'You've introduced me already, Francesco,' said Angus.

'So sorry,' said Francis.

'Guest!' said Aaron.

Francis suddenly began to laugh.

'May he not be Guest?' he asked, fatherly.

'Very likely,' said Aaron. 'Not that I was ever good at guessing.'

Francis tilted his eyebrows. Fortunately the waiter arrived with the coffee.

'Tell me,' said Francis, 'will you have your coffee black, or with milk?' He was determined to restore a tone of sobriety.

The coffee was sipped in sober solemnity.

'Is music your line as well, then?' asked Aaron.

'No, we're painters. We're going to work in Rome.'

'To earn your living?'

'Not yet.'

The amount of discretion, modesty, and reserve which Francis put into these two syllables gave Aaron to think that he had two real young swells to deal with.

'No,' continued Francis. 'I was only *just* down from Oxford when the war came — and Angus had been about ten months at the Slade. But I have always painted. So now we are going to work, really hard, in Rome, to make up for lost time. Oh, one has lost so much time, in the war. And such *precious* time! I don't know if ever one will even be able to make it up again.' Francis tilted his handsome eyebrows and put his head on one side with a wise distressed look.

'No,' said Angus. 'One will never be able to make it up.

What is more, one will never be able to start again where one left off. We're shattered old men, now, in one sense. And in another sense, we're just pre-war babies.'

The speech was uttered with an odd abruptness and didacticism which made Aaron open his eyes. Angus had that peculiar manner: he seemed to be haranguing himself in the circle of his own thoughts, not addressing himself to his listener. So his listener listened on the outside edge of the young fellow's crowded thoughts. Francis put on a distressed air, and let his attention wander. Angus pursed his lips and his eyes were stretched wide with a kind of pleasure, like a wicked owl which has just joyfully hooted an ill omen.

'Tell me,' said Francis to Aaron. 'Where were *you* all the time during the war?'

'I was doing my job,' said Aaron. Which led to his explaining his origins.

'Really! So your music is quite new! But how interesting!' cried Francis.

Aaron explained further.

'And so the war hardly affected you? But what did you *feel* about it, privately?'

'I didn't feel much. I didn't know what to feel. Other folks did such a lot of feeling, I thought I'd better keep my mouth shut.'

'Yes, quite!' said Angus. 'Everybody has such a lot of feelings on somebody else's behalf, that nobody ever had time to realize what they felt themselves. I know I was like that. The feelings all came on to me from the outside: like flies settling on meat. Before I knew where I was I was eaten up with a swarm of feelings, and I found myself in the trenches. God knows what for. And ever since then I've been trying to get out of my swarm of feelings, which buzz in and out of me and have nothing to do with me. I realized it in hospital. It's exactly like trying to get out of a swarm of nasty, dirty flies. And every one you kill makes you sick, but doesn't make the swarm any less.'

Again Angus pursed and bridled and looked like a pleased

wicked white owl. Then he polished his monocle on a very choice silk handkerchief, and fixed it unseeing in his left eye.

But Francis was not interested in his friend's experiences. For Francis had had a job in the War Office – whereas Angus was a war hero with shattered nerves. And let him depreciate his own experiences as much as he liked, the young man with the monocle kept tight hold on his prestige as a war hero. Only for himself, though. He by no means insisted that any one else should be war-bitten.

Francis was one of those men who, like women, can set up the sympathetic flow and make a fellow give himself away without realizing what he is doing. So there sat our friend, Aaron, amusingly unbosoming himself of all his history and experiences, drawn out by the arch, subtle attentiveness of the handsome Francis. Angus listened too with pleased amusedness on his pale, emaciated face, pursing his shrunken jaw. And Aaron sipped various glasses of the liqueur, and told all his tale as if it was a comedy. A comedy it seemed, too, at that hour. And a comedy no doubt it was. But mixed, like most things in this life. Mixed.

It was quite late before this seance broke up: and the waiter itching to get rid of the fellows.

'Well now,' said Francis as he rose from the table and settled his elegant waist, resting on one hip as usual. 'We shall see you in the morning, I hope. You say you are going to Venice. Why? Have you some engagement in Venice?'

'No,' said Aaron. 'I was only going to look for a friend – Rawdon Lilly.'

'Rawdon Lilly! Why, is he in Venice? Oh, I've heard *such* a lot about him. I should like *so* much to meet him. But I heard he was in Germany –'

'I don't know where he is.'

'Angus! Didn't we hear that Lilly was in Germany?'

'Yes, in Munich, being psycho-analysed, I believe it was.'
Aaron looked rather blank.

'But have you anything to take you to Venice? It's such a

bad climate in the winter. Why not come with us to Florence?'
said Francis.

Aaron wavered. He really did not know what to do.

'Think about it,' said Francis, laying his hand on Aaron's
arm. 'Think about it tonight. And we'll meet in the morning.
At what time.

'Any time,' said Aaron.

'Well, say eleven. We'll meet in the lounge here at eleven.
Will that suit you? All right then. It's so awfully nice meeting
you. That marvellous flute. And think about Florence. But do
come. Don't disappoint us.'

The two young men went elegantly upstairs.

CHAPTER 15

A Railway Journey

THE next day but one, the three set off for Florence. Aaron had made an excursion from Milan with the two young heroes, and dined with them subsequently at the most expensive restaurant in the town. Then they had all gone home – and had sat in the young men's bedroom drinking tea, whilst Aaron played the flute. Francis was really musical and enchanted. Angus enjoyed the novelty, and the moderate patronage he was able to confer. And Aaron felt amused and pleased, and hoped he was paying for his treat.

So behold them setting off for Florence in the early morning Angus and Francis had first-class tickets: Aaron took a third-class.

'Come and have lunch with us on the train,' said Angus. 'I'll order three places, and we can lunch together.'

'Oh, I can buy a bit of food at the station,' said Aaron.

'No, come and lunch with us. It will be much nicer. And we shall enjoy it as well,' said Angus.

'Of course! Ever so much nicer! Of course!' cried Francis. 'Yes, why not, indeed! Why should you hesitate?'

'All right then,' said Aaron, not without some feeling of constraint.

So they separated. The young men settled themselves amidst the red plush and crochet-work, looking, with their hair plastered smoothly back, quite as first-class as you could wish, creating quite the right impression on the porters and the travelling Italians. Aaron went to his third-class, further up the train.

'Well then, *au revoir*, till luncheon,' cried Francis.

The train was fairly full in the third and second classes.

However, Aaron got his seat, and the porter brought on his bags, after disposing of the young men's luggage. Aaron gave the tip uneasily. He always hated tipping – it seemed humiliating both ways. And the airy aplomb of the two young cavaliers, as they settled down among the red plush and the obsequiousness, and said 'Well then, *au revoir* till luncheon', was peculiarly unsettling: though they did not intend it so.

'The porter thinks I'm their servant – their valet,' said Aaron to himself, and a curious half-amused, half-contemptuous look flickered on his face. It annoyed him. The falsity occasioned by the difference in the price of the tickets was really humiliating. Aaron had lived long enough to know that as far as manhood and intellect went – nay, even education – he was not the inferior of the two young 'gentlemen'. He knew quite well that, as far as intrinsic nature went, they did not imagine him an inferior: rather the contrary. They had rather an exaggerated respect for him and his life-power, and even his origin. And yet – they had the inestimable cash advantage – and they were going to keep it. They knew it was nothing more than an artificial cash superiority. But they gripped it all the more intensely. They were the upper middle classes. They were Eton and Oxford. And they were going to hang on to their privileges. In these days, it is a fool who abdicates before he's forced to. And therefore:

'Well then – *au revoir* till luncheon.'

They were being so awfully nice. And inwardly they were *not* condescending. But socially, they just had to be. The world is made like that. It wasn't their own private fault. It was no fault at all. It was just the mode in which they were educated, the style of their living. And as we know, *le style c'est l'homme*.

Angus came of very wealthy iron people near Merthyr. Already he had a very fair income of his own. As soon as the law-business concerning his father's and his grandfather's will was settled, he would be well off. And he knew it, and valued himself accordingly. Francis was the son of a highly-esteemed barrister and politician of Sydney, and in his day would inherit his father's lately-won baronetcy. But Francis had not very much money: and was much more class-flexible than Angus. Angus had been born in a house with a park, and of awful hard-willed, money-bound people. Francis came of a much more adventurous, loose, excitable family, he had the colonial newness and adaptability. He knew, for his own part, that class superiority was just a trick, nowadays. Still, it was a trick that paid. And a trick he was going to play as long as it did pay.

While Aaron sat, a little pale at the gills, immobile, ruminating these matters, a not very pleasant look about his nose-end, he heard a voice:

'Oh, there you *are!* I thought I'd better come and see, so that we can fetch you at lunch time. You've got a seat? Are you quite comfortable? Is there anything I could get you? Why, you're in a non-smoker! But that doesn't matter, everybody will smoke. Are you sure you have everything? Oh, but just wait one moment – '

It was Francis, long and elegant, with his straight shoulders and his coat buttoned to show his waist, and his face so well-formed and so modern. So modern, altogether. His voice was pleasantly modulated, and never hurried. He now looked as if a thought had struck him. He put a finger to his brow, and hastened back to his own carriage. In a minute he returned with a new London literary magazine.

'Something to read – I shall have to *fly* – see you at lunch.' and he turned and elegantly hastened, but not too fast, back to his carriage. The porter was holding the door for him. So Francis looked pleasantly hurried, but by no means rushed. Oh dear no. He took his time. It was not for him to bolt and scramble like a mere Italian.

The people in Aaron's carriage had watched the apparition of the elegant youth intently. For them, he was a being from another sphere – no doubt a young milordo with power, wealth, and glamorous life behind him. Which was just what Francis intended to convey. So handsome – so very, very impressive in all his elegant calm showiness. He made such a *bella figura*. It was just what the Italians loved. Those in the first-class regions thought he might even be an Italian, he was so attractive.

The train in motion, the many Italian eyes in the carriage studied Aaron. He too was good-looking. But by no means so fascinating as the young milordo. Not half as sympathetic. No good at all at playing a role. Probably a servant of the young signori.

Aaron stared out of the window, and played the one single British role left to him, that of ignoring his neighbours, isolating himself in their midst, and minding his own business. Upon this insular trick our greatness and our predominance depends – such as it is. Yes, they might look at him. They might think him a servant or what they liked. But he was inaccessible to them. He isolated himself upon himself, and there remained.

It was a lovely day, a lovely, lovely day of early autumn. Over the great plain of Lombardy a magnificent blue sky glowed like midsummer, the sun shone strong. The great plain, with its great stripes of cultivation – without hedges or boundaries – how beautiful it was! Sometimes he saw oxen ploughing. Sometimes, oh so beautiful, teams of eight, of ten, even of twelve pale, great soft oxen in procession, plough-ing the dark velvety earth, a driver with a great whip at their head, a man far behind holding the plough-shafts. Beautiful the soft plunging motion of oxen moving forwards. Beautiful the strange, snaky lifting of the muzzles, the swaying of the sharp horns. And the soft, soft crawling motion of a team of oxen, so invisible, almost, yet so inevitable. Now and again straight canals of water flashed blue. Now and again the great lines of grey-silvery poplars rose and made avenues of lovely grey airy quadrangles across the plain. Their top boughs were spangled with gold and green leaf. Sometimes the vine-leaves were gold and red, a patterning. And the great square farm-homesteads, white, red-roofed, with their out-buildings, stood naked amid the lands, without screen or softening. There was something big and exposed about it all. No more the cosy English ambushed life: no longer the cosy littleness of the landscape. A bigness – and nothing to shelter the unshrinking spirit. It was all exposed, exposed to the sweep of plain, to the high strong sky, and to human gaze. A kind of boldness, an indifference. Aaron was impressed and fascinated. He looked with a new interest at the Italians in the carriage with him – for this same boldness and indifference and exposed gesture. And he found it in them too. And again it fascinated him. It seemed so much bigger, as if the walls of life had fallen. Nay, the walls of English life will have to fall.

Sitting there in the third-class carriage, he became happy again. The *presence* of his fellow-passengers was not so hampering as in England. In England, everybody seems held tight and gripped, nothing is left free. Every passenger seems like a parcel who is holding his string as fast as he can about him, lest one corner of the wrapper should come undone and reveal what is inside. And every other passenger is forced, by the public will, to hold himself as tight-bound also. Which in the end becomes a sort of self-conscious madness.

But here, in the third-class carriage, there was no tight string round every man. They were not all trussed with self-conscious string as tight as capons. They had a sufficient amount of callousness and indifference and natural equanimity. True, one of them spat continually on the floor, in large spits. And another sat with his boots all unlaced and his collar off, and various important buttons undone. They did not seem to care if bits of themselves did show, through the gaps in the wrapping. Aaron winced – but he preferred it to English tightness. He was pleased, he was happy with the Italians. He thought how generous and natural they were.

So the towns passed by, and the hours, and he seemed at last to have got outside himself and his old conditions. It seemed like a great escape. There was magic again in life – real magic. Was it illusion, or was it genuine? He thought it was genuine, and opened his soul as if there was no danger.

Lunch-time came. Francis summoned Aaron down the rocking train. The three men had a table to themselves, and all felt they were enjoying themselves very much indeed. Of

course Francis and Angus made a great impression again.
But in the dining car were mostly middle-class, well-to-do
Italians. And these did not look upon our two young heroes
as two young wonders. No, rather with some criticism, and
some class-envy. But they were impressed: oh, they were
impressed! How should they not be, when our young gentlemen had such an air! Aaron was conscious all the time that
the fellow-diners were being properly impressed by the flower
of civilization and the salt of the earth, namely, young, well-to-
do Englishmen. And he had a faint premonition, based on
experience perhaps, that fellow-passengers in the end never
forgive the man who has 'impressed' them. Mankind loves
being impressed. It asks to be impressed. It almost forces
those whom it can force to play a role and to make an impression. And afterwards, never forgives.

When the train ran into Bologna Station, they were still in
the restaurant car. Nor did they go at once to their seats.
Angus had paid the bill. There was three quarters of an hour's
wait in Bologna.

'You may as well come down and sit with us,' said Francis.
'We've got nobody in our carriage, so why shouldn't we all
stay together during the wait? You kept your own seat, I
suppose?'

No, he had forgotten. So when he went to look for it, it was
occupied by a stout man who was just taking off his collar
and wrapping a white kerchief round his neck. The third-class
carriages were packed. For those were early days after the war,
while men still had pre-war notions and were poor. Ten
months would steal imperceptibly by, and the mysterious
revolution would be effected. Then, the second class and the
first class would be packed, indescribably packed, crowded,
on all great trains: and the third class carriages, lo and behold,
would be comparatively empty. Oh marvellous days of bank-
ruptcy, when nobody will condescend to travel third!

However, these were still modest, sombre months immediately after the peace. So a large man with a fat neck and a
white kerchief, and his collar over his knee, sat in Aaron's seat.

Aaron looked at the man, and at his own luggage overhead. The fat man saw him looking and stared back: then stared also at the luggage overhead: and with his almost invisible north-Italian gesture said much plainer than words could have said it: 'Go to hell. I'm here and I'm going to stop here.'

There was something insolent and unbearable about the look – and about the rocky fixity of the large man. He sat as if he had insolently taken root in his seat. Aaron flushed slightly. Francis and Angus strolled along the train, outside, for the corridor was already blocked with the mad Bologna rush, and the baggage belonging. They joined Aaron as he stood on the platform.

'But where is your seat?' cried Francis, peering into the packed and jammed compartments of the third-class.

'That man's sitting in it.'

'Which?' cried Francis, indignant.

'The fat one there – with the collar on his knee.'

'But it was *your seat!*'

Francis' gorge rose in indignation. He mounted into the corridor. And in the doorway of the compartment he bridled like an angry horse rearing, bridling his head. Poising himself on one hip, he stared fixedly at the man with the collar on his knee, then at the baggage aloft. He looked down at the fat man as a bird looks down from the eaves of a house. But the man looked back with a solid, rock-like impudence, before which an Englishman quails: a jeering, immovable insolence, with a sneer round the nose and a solid-seated posterior.

'But,' said Francis in English – none of them had any Italian yet. 'But,' said Francis, turning round to Aaron, 'that was *your seat!*' and he flung his long fore-finger in the direction of the fat man's thighs.

'Yes!' said Aaron.

'And he's *taken* it – !' cried Francis in indignation.

'And he knows it too,' said Aaron.

'But – !' – and Francis looked round imperiously, as if to summon his bodyguard. But bodyguards are no longer forthcoming, and train-guards are far from satisfactory. The fat man sat on, with a sneer-grin, very faint but very effective, round his nose, and a solidly-planted posterior. He quite enjoyed the pantomime of the young foreigners. The other passengers said something to him, and he answered laconic. Then they all had the faint sneer-grin round their noses. A woman in the corner grinned jeeringly straight in Francis' face. His charm failed entirely this time: and as for his commandingness, that was ineffectual indeed. Rage came up in him.

'Oh, well – something must be done,' said he decisively. 'But didn't you put something in the seat to *reserve* it?'

'Only that *New Statesman* – but he's moved it.'

The man still sat with the invisible sneer-grin on his face, and that peculiar and immovable plant of his Italian posterior.

'Mais – cette place etait *réservée* – ' said Francis, moving to the direct attack.

The man turned aside and ignored him utterly – then said something to the men opposite, and they all began to show their teeth in a grin.

Francis was not so easily foiled. He touched the man on the arm. The man looked round threateningly, as if he had been struck.

'Cette place est réservée – par ce Monsieur –' said Francis with hauteur, though still in an explanatory tone, and pointing to Aaron.

The Italian looked him, not in the eyes, but between the eyes, and sneered full in his face. Then he looked with contempt at Aaron. And then he said, in Italian, that there was room for such snobs in the first-class, and that they had not any right to come occupying the place of honest men in the third.

'Già! Già' barked the other passengers, in the carriage.

'Loro possono andare prima classe – *prima classe*!' said the woman in the corner, in a very high voice, as if talking to deaf people, and pointing at Aaron's luggage, then along the train to the first-class carriages.

'C'è posto là,' said one of the men, shrugging his shoulders.

There was a jeering quality in the hard insolence which made Francis go very red and Angus very white. Angus stared like a death's-head behind his monocle, with death-blue eyes.

'Oh, never mind. Come along to the first-class. I'll pay the difference. We shall be much better all together. Get the luggage down, Francis. It wouldn't be possible to travel with this lot, even if he gave up the seat. There's plenty of room in our carriage – and I'll pay the extra,' said Angus.

He knew there was one solution – and only one – Money.

But Francis bit his finger. He felt almost beside himself – and quite powerless. For he knew the guard of the train would jeer too. It is not so easy to interfere with honest third-class Bolognesi in Bologna Station, even if they *have* taken another man's seat. Powerless, his brow knitted, and looking just like Mephistopheles with his high forehead and slightly arched nose, Mephistopheles in a rage, he hauled down Aaron's bag and handed it to Angus. So they transferred themselves to the first-class carriage, while the fat man and his party in the third-class watched in jeering, triumphant silence. Solid, planted, immovable, in static triumph.

So Aaron sat with the others amid the red plush, whilst the train began its long slow climb of the Apennines, stinking sulphureous through tunnels innumerable. Wonderful the steep slopes, the great chestnut woods, and then the great distances, glimpsed between the heights, Firenzuola away and beneath, Turneresque hills far off, built of heaven-bloom, not of earth. It was cold at the summit-station, ice and snow in the air, fierce. Our travellers shrank into the carriage again, and wrapped themselves round.

Then the train began its long slither downhill, still through a whole necklace of tunnels, which fortunately no longer stank. So down and down, till the plain appears in sight once more, the Arno valley. But then began the inevitable hitch that always happens in Italian travel. The train began to hesitate – to falter to a halt, whistling shrilly as if in protest: whistling pip-pip-pip in expostulation as it stood forlorn among the fields: then stealing forward again and stealthily making pace, gathering speed, till it had got up a regular spurt: then suddenly the brakes came on with a jerk, more faltering to a halt, more whistling and pip-pip-pipping, as the engine stood jingling with impatience: after which another creep and splash, and another choking off. So on till they landed in Prato station: and there they sat. A fellow passenger told them there was an hour to wait here: an hour. Something had happened up the line.

'Then I propose we make tea,' said Angus, beaming.

'Why not! Of course. Let us make tea. And I will look for water.'

So Aaron and Francis went to the restaurant bar and filled the little pan at the tap. Angus got down the red picnic case, of which he was so fond, and spread out the various arrangements on the floor of the coupé. He soon had the spirit-lamp burning, the water heating. Francis proposed that he and Aaron should dash into Prato and see what could be bought, whilst the tea was in preparation. So off they went, leaving Angus like a busy old wizard manipulating his arrangements on the floor of the carriage, his monocle beaming with bliss. The one fat fellow-passenger with a lurid striped rug over his knees watched with acute interest. Everybody who passed the doorway stood to contemplate the scene with pleasure. Officials came and studied the situation with appreciation. Then Francis and Aaron returned with a large supply of roast chestnuts, piping hot, and hard dried plums, and good dried figs, and rather stale rusks. They found the water just boiling, Angus just throwing in the tea-egg, and the fellow-passenger just poking his nose right in, he was so thrilled.

Nothing pleased Angus so much as thus pitching camp in the midst of civilization. The scrubby newspaper packets of chestnuts, plums, figs and rusks were spread out: Francis flew for salt to the man at the bar, and came back with a little paper of rock-salt: the brown tea was dispensed in the silver-fitted glasses from the immortal luncheon-case: and the picnic was in full swing. Angus, being in the height of his happiness, now sat on the seat cross-legged, with his feet under him, in the authentic Buddha fashion, and on his face the queer rapt alert look, half a smile, also somewhat Buddhistic, holding his glass of brown tea in his hand. He was as rapt and immobile as if he really were in a mystic state. Yet it was only his delight in the tea-party. The fellow-passenger peered at the tea, and said in broken French, was it good? In equally fragmentary French Francis said very good, and offered the fat passenger some. He, however, held up his hand in protest, as if to say not for any money would he swallow the hot-watery stuff. And he pulled out a flask of wine. But a handful of chestnuts he accepted.

The train-conductor, ticket-collector, and the heavy green soldier who protected them, swung open the door and stared attentively. The fellow passenger addressed himself to these new-comers, and they all began to smile good-naturedly. Then the fellow passenger – he was stout and fifty and had a brilliant striped rug always over his knees – pointed out the Buddha-like position of Angus, and the three in-starers smiled again. And so the fellow-passenger thought he must try too. So he put aside his rug, and lifted his feet from the floor, and took his toes in his hands, and tried to bring his legs up and his feet under him. But his knees were fat, his trousers in the direst extreme of peril, and he could no more manage it than if he had tried to swallow himself. So he desisted suddenly, rather scared, whilst the three bunched and official heads in the door-way laughed and jested at him, showing their teeth and teasing him. But on our gipsy party they turned their eyes with admiration. They loved the novelty and the fun. And on the thin, elegant Angus in his new London clothes they looked really puzzled, as he sat there immobile, gleaming through his monocle like some Buddha going wicked, perched cross-legged and ecstatic on the red velvet seat. They marvelled that the lower half of him could so double up, like a foot-rule. So they stared till they had seen enough. When they suddenly said 'Buon' appetito', withdrew their heads and shoulders, slammed the door, and departed.

Then the train set off also – and shortly after six arrived in

Florence. It was debated what should Aaron do in Florence. They young men had engaged a room at Bertolini's hotel, on the Lungarno. Bertolini's was not expensive – but Aaron knew that his friends would not long endure hotel life. However, he went along with the other two, trusting to find a cheaper place on the morrow.

It was growing quite dark as they drove to the hotel, but still was light enough to show the river rustling, the Ponte Vecchio spanning its little storeys across the flood, on its low heavy piers: and some sort of magic of the darkening, varied houses facing, on the other side of the stream. Of course they were all enchanted.

'I knew,' said Francis, 'we should love it.'

Aaron was told he could have a little back room and pension terms for fifteen liras a day, if he stayed at least fifteen days. The exchange was then at forty-five. So fifteen liras meant just six-shillings-and-sixpence a day, without extras. Extras meant wine, tea, butter, and light. It was decided he should look for something cheaper next day.

By the tone of the young men, he now gathered that they would prefer it if he took himself off to a cheaper place. They wished to be on their own.

'Well then,' said Francis, 'you will be in to lunch here, won't you? Then we'll see you at lunch.'

It was as if both young men had drawn in their feelers now. They were afraid of finding the new man an incubus. They wanted to wash their hands of him. Aaron's brow darkened.

> Perhaps it was right to dissemble your love
> But why did you kick me downstairs . . .

The morning then found him out early, before his friends had arisen. It was sunny again. The magic of Florence at once overcame him, and he forgot the bore of limited means and hotel costs. He went straight out of the hotel door, across the road, and leaned on the river parapet. There ran the Arno: not such a flood after all, but a green stream with shoals of pebbles in its course. Across, and in the delicate shadow of the early sun, stood the opposite Lungarno, the old flat houses, pink, or white, or grey stone, with their green shutters, some closed, some opened. It had a flowery effect, the skyline irregular against the morning light. To the right the delicate Trinità bridge, to the left the old bridge with its little shops over the river. Beyond, towards the sun, glimpses of green, sky-bloomed country: Tuscany.

There was a noise and clatter of traffic: boys pushing hand-barrows over the cobble-stones, slow bullocks stepping side by side, and shouldering one another affectionately, drawing a load of country produce, then horses in great brilliant scarlet cloths, like vivid palls, slowly pulling the long narrow carts of the district and men hu-huing! – and people calling: all the sharp, clattering morning noise of Florence.

'Oh Angus! Do come and look! *Oh* so lovely!'

Glancing up, he saw the elegant figure of Francis, in fine coloured-silk pyjamas, perched on a small upper balcony, turning away from the river towards the bedroom again, his hand lifted to his lips, as if to catch there his cry of delight. The whole pose was classic and effective: and very amusing. How the Italians would love it!

Aaron slipped back across the road, and walked away under the houses towards the Ponte Vecchio. He passed the bridge – and passed the Uffizi – watching the green hills opposite, and San Miniato. Then he noticed the over-dramatic group of statuary in the Piazza Mentana – male and physical and melo-dramatic – and then the corner house. It was a big old Floren-tine house, with many green shutters and wide eaves. There was a notice plate by the door – 'Pension Nardini.'

He came to a full stop. He stared at the notice-plate, stared at the glass door, and turning round, stared at the over-pathetic dead soldier on the arm of his over-heroic pistol-firing comrade; *Mentana* – and the date! Aaron wondered what and where Mentana was. Then at last he summoned his energy, opened the glass door, and mounted the first stairs.

He waited some time before anybody appeared. Then a maid-servant.

'Can I have a room?' said Aaron.

The bewildered, wild-eyed servant maid opened a door and showed him into a heavily-gilt, heavily-plush drawing-room with a great deal of frantic grandeur about it. There he sat and cooled his heels for half an hour. Arrived at length a stout young lady – handsome, with big dark-blue Italian eyes, but anaemic and too stout.

'Oh!' she said as she entered, not knowing what else to say.

'Good-morning,' said Aaron awkwardly.

'Oh, good-morning! English! Yes! Oh, I am so sorry to keep you, you know, to make you wait so long. I was upstairs, you know, with a lady. Will you sit?'

'Can I have a room?' said Aaron.

'A room! Yes, you can.'

'What terms?'

'Terms! Oh! Why, ten francs a day, you know, pension – if you stay – how long will you stay?'

'At least a month, I expect.'

'A month! Oh yes. Yes, ten francs a day.'

'For everything?'

'Everything. Yes, everything. Coffee, bread, honey or jam in the morning: lunch at half-past twelve; tea in the drawing-room, half-past four: dinner at half-past seven: all very nice. And a warm room with the sun – Would you like to see?'

So Aaron was led up the big, rambling old house to the top floor – then along a long corridor – and at last into a big bedroom with two beds and a red-tiled floor – a little dreary, as ever – but the sun just beginning to come in, and a lovely view on to the river, towards the Ponte Vecchio, and at the hills with their pines and villas and verdure opposite.

Here he would settle. The signorina would send a man for his bags, at half-past two in the afternoon.

At luncheon Aaron found the two friends, and told them of his move.

'How very nice for you! Ten francs a day – but that is nothing. I am so pleased you've found something. And when will you be moving in?' said Francis.

'At half-past two.'

'Oh, so soon. Yes, just as well. But we shall see you from time to time, of course. What did you say the address was? Oh yes – just near the awful statue. Very well. We can look you up any time – and you will find us here. Leave a message if we should happen not to be in – we've got lots of engagements –'

CHAPTER 16

Florence

THE very afternoon after Aaron's arrival in Florence the sky
became dark, the wind cold, and rain began steadily to fall.
He sat in his big, bleak room above the river, and watched the
pale green water fused with yellow, the many-threaded streams
fuse into one, as swiftly the surface flood came down from the
hills. Across, the dark green hills looked darker in the wet,
the umbrella pines held up in vain above the villas. But away
below, on the Lungarno, traffic rattled as ever.

Aaron went down at five o'clock to tea, and found himself
alone next a group of women, mostly Swedes or Danish or
Dutch, drinking a peculiar brown herb-brew which tasted like
nothing on earth, and eating two thick bits of darkish bread
smeared with a brown smear which hoped it was jam, but
hoped in vain. Unhappily he sat in the gilt and red, massively
ornate room, while the foreign women eyed him. Oh, bitter
to be a male under such circumstances.

He escaped as soon as possible back to his far-off regions,
lonely and cheerless, away above. But he rather liked the far-
off remoteness in the big old Florentine house: he did not
mind the peculiar dark, uncosy dreariness. It was not really
dreary: only indifferent. Indifferent to comfort, indifferent to
all homeliness and cosiness. The over-big furniture trying to
be impressive, but never to be pretty or bright or cheerful.
There it stood, ugly and apart. And there let it stand. Neither
did he mind the lack of fire, the cold sombreness of his big
bedroom. At home, in England, the bright grate and the
ruddy fire, the thick hearth-rug and the man's arm-chair, these
had been inevitable. And now he was glad to get away from it
all. He was glad not to have a cosy hearth, and his own arm-

chair. He was glad to feel the cold, and to breathe the un-warmed air. He preferred the Italian way of no fires, no heat-ing. If the day was cold, he was willing to be cold too. If it was dark, he was willing to be dark. The cosy brightness of a real home – it had stifled him till he felt his lungs would burst. The horrors of real domesticity. No, the Italian brutal way was better.

So he put his overcoat over his knee, and studied some music he had bought in Milan: some Pergolesi and the Scarlatti he liked, and some Corelli. He preferred frail, sensitive, abstract music, with not much feeling in it, but a certain limpidity and purity. Night fell as he sat reading the scores. He would have liked to try certain pieces on his flute. But his flute was too sensitive, it winced from the new strange surroundings, and would not blossom.

Dinner sounded at last – at eight o'clock, or something after. He had to learn to expect the meals always forty minutes late. Down he went, down the long, dark, lonely corridors and staircases. The dining-room was right downstairs. But he had a little table to himself near the door, the elderly women were at some little distance. The only other men were Agos-tino, the unshapely waiter, and an Italian duke, with wife and child and nurse, the family sitting all together at a table half-way down the room, and utterly preoccupied with a little yellow dog.

However, the food was good enough, and sufficient, and the waiter and the maid-servant cheerful and bustling. Every-thing felt happy-go-lucky and informal, there was no par-ticular atmosphere. Nobody put on any airs, because nobody in the Nardini took any notice if they did. The little ducal dog yapped, the ducal son shouted, the waiter dropped half-a-dozen spoons, the old women knitted during the waits, and all went off so badly that it was quite pleasant. Yes, Aaron preferred it to Bertolini's, which was trying to be efficient and correct: though not making any strenuous effort. Still, Bertolini's was much more up to scratch, there was the tension of proper standards. Whereas here at Nardini's, nothing mattered very much.

It was November. When he got up to his far-off room again, Aaron felt almost as if he were in a castle with the draw-bridge drawn up. Through the open window came the sound of the swelling Arno, as it rushed and rustled along over its gravel-shoals. Lights spangled the opposite side. Traffic sounded deep below. The room was not really cold, for the summer sun so soaks into these thick old buildings, that it takes a month or two of winter to soak it out. The rain still fell.

In the morning it was still November, and the dawn came slowly. And through the open window was the sound of the river's rushing. But the traffic started before dawn, with a bang and a rattle of carts, and a bank and jingle of tram-cars over the not-distant bridge. Oh noisy Florence! At half-past seven Aaron rang for his coffee: and got it at a few minutes past eight. The signorina had told him to take his coffee in bed.

Rain was still falling. But towards nine o'clock it lifted, and he decided to go out. A wet, wet world. Carriages going by, with huge wet shiny umbrellas, black and with many points, erected to cover the driver and the tail of the horse and the box-seat. The hood of the carriage covered the fare. Clatter-clatter through the rain. Peasants with long wagons and slow oxen, and pale-green huge umbrellas erected for the driver to walk beneath. Men tripping along in cloaks, shawls, umbrellas, anything, quite unconcerned. A man loading gravel in the river-bed, in spite of the wet. And innumerable bells ringing: but innumerable bells. The great soft trembling of the cathedral felt in all the air.

Anyhow it was a new world. Aaron went along close to the tall thick houses, following his nose. And suddenly he caught sight of the long slim neck of the Palazzo Vecchio up above, in the air. And in another minute he was passing between massive buildings, out into the Piazza della Signoria. There he stood still and looked round him in real surprise and real joy. The flat, empty square with its stone paving was all wet. The great buildings rose dark. The dark sheer front of the Palazzo Vecchio went up like a cliff, to the battlements, and the slim tower soared dark and hawk-like, crested, high above. And at the foot of the cliff stood the great naked David, white and stripped in the wet, white against the dark, warm-dark cliff of the building – and near, the heavy naked men of Bandinelli.

The first thing he had seen, as he turned into the square, was the back of one of these Bandinelli statues: a great naked man of marble, with a heavy back and strong naked flanks over which the water was trickling. And then to come immediately upon the David, so much whiter, glistening skin-white in the wet, standing a little forward, and shrinking.

He may be ugly, too naturalistic, too big, and anything else you like. But the David in the Piazza della Signoria, there under the dark great Palace, in the position Michelangelo chose for him, there standing forward stripped and exposed and eternally half-shrinking, half-wishing to expose himself, he is the genius of Florence. The adolescent, the white, self-conscious, physical adolescent: enormous, in keeping with the stark, grim, enormous palace, which is dark and bare as he is white and bare. And behind, the big, lumpy Bandinelli men are in keeping too. They may be ugly – but they are there in their place, and they have their own lumpy reality. And this morning in the rain, standing unbroken, with the water trickling down their flanks and along the inner side of their great thighs, they were real enough, representing the un-daunted physical nature of the heavier Florentines.

Aaron looked and looked at the three great naked men. David so much white, and standing forward, self-conscious: then at the great splendid front of the Palazzo Vecchio: and at the fountain splashing water upon its wet, wet figures; and the distant equestrian statue; and the stone-flagged space of the grim square. And he felt that here he was in one of the world's living centres, here, in the Piazza della Signoria. The sense of having arrived – of having reached a perfect centre of the human world: this he had.

And so, satisfied, he turned round to look at the bronze Perseus which rose just above him. Benvenuto Cellini's dark hero looked female, with his plump hips and his waist, female and rather insignificant: graceful, and rather vulgar. The clownish Bandinellis were somehow more to the point. Then all the statuary in the Loggia! But that is a mistake. It looks too much like the yard of a monumental mason.

The great naked men in the rain, under the dark-grey November sky, in the dark, strong, inviolable square! The wonderful hawk-head of the old palace! The physical, self-conscious adolescent, Michelangelo's David, shrinking and exposing himself, with his white, slack limbs! Florence, passionate, fearless Florence had spoken herself out. Aaron was fasincated by the Piazza della Signoria. He never went into the town, nor returned from it to his lodging, without contriving to pass through the square. And he never passed through it without satisfaction. Here men had been at their intensest, most naked pitch, here, at the end of the old world and the beginning of the new. Since then, always rather puling and apologetic.

Aaron felt a new self, a new life-urge rising inside himself. Florence seemed to start a new man in him. It was a town of men. On Friday morning, so early, he heard the traffic. Early, he watched the rather low, two-wheeled traps of the peasants spanking recklessly over the bridge, coming in to town. And then, when he went out, he found the Piazza della Signoria packed with men: but all, all men. And all farmers, land-owners and land-workers. The curious, fine-nosed Tuscan farmers, with their half-sardonic, amber-coloured eyes. Their curious individuality, their clothes worn so easy and reckless, their hats with the personal twist. Their curious full oval cheeks, their tendency to be too fat, to have a belly and heavy limbs. Their close-sitting dark hair. And above all, their sharp, almost acrid, mocking expression, the silent curl of the nose, the eternal challenge, the rock-bottom unbelief, and the subtle fearlessness. The dangerous, subtle, never-dying fearlessness, and the acrid unbelief. But men! Men! A town of men, in spite of everything. The one manly quality, undying, acrid fearlessness. The eternal challenge of the unquenched human soul. Perhaps too acrid and challenging to-day, when there is nothing left to challenge. But men – who existed without apology and without justification. Men who would neither justify themselves nor apologise for themselves. Just men. The rarest thing left in our sweet Christendom.

Altogether Aaron was pleased with himself, for being in Florence. Those were early days after the war, when as yet very few foreigners had returned, and the place had the native sombreness and intensity. So that our friend did not mind being alone.

The third day, however, Francis called on him. There was a tap at the bedroom door, and the young man entered, all eyes of curiosity.

'Oh, there you *are!*' he cried, flinging his hand and twisting his waist and then laying his hand on his breast. 'Such a *long* way up to you! But *miles* –! Well, how are you? Are you quite all right here? You are? I'm so glad – we've been so *rushed*, seeing people, that we haven't had a *minute*. But not a *minute!* People! People! People! Isn't it amazing how many there are, and how many one knows, and gets to know! But amazing! Endless acquaintances! – oh, and such quaint people here! so *odd!!* so *more* than odd! Oh extraordinary –!' Francis chuckled to himself over the extraordinariness. Then he seated himself gracefully at Aaron's table. 'Oh, *music!* What? Corelli! So interesting! So very *clever*, these people, weren't they! Corelli and the younger Scarlatti and all that crowd.' Here he closed the score again. 'But now – *look!* Do you want to know anybody here, or don't you? I've told them about you and of course they're dying to meet you and hear you play. But I thought it best not to mention anything about – about your being hard-up, and all that. I said you were just here on a visit. You see with this kind of people I'm sure it's much the best not to let them start off by thinking you will need them at all – or that you *might* need them. Why give yourself away, anyhow? Just meet them and take them for what they're worth – and then you can see. If they like to give you an engagement to play at some show or other – well, you can decide when the time comes whether you will accept. Much better that these kind of people shouldn't get it into their heads at once that they can hire your services. It doesn't do. They haven't enough discrimination for that. Much best make rather a favour of it, than sort of *ask* them to hire you. Don't you agree? Perhaps I'm wrong.'

Aaron sat and listened and wondered at the wisdom and the genuine kindness of the young *beau*. And more still, he wondered at the profound social disillusionment. This handsome collie dog was something of a social wolf, half showing his fangs at the moment. But with genuine kindheartedness for another wolf. Aaron was touched.

'Yes, I think that's the best way,' he said.

'You do! Yes, so do I. Oh, they are such queer people! Why is it, do you think, that English people abroad go so very *queer* – so ultra-English – *incredible!* – and at the same time so perfectly impossible? But impossible! Pathological, I assure you. And as for their sexual behaviour – oh, dear, don't mention it. I assure you it doesn't bear mention. And all quite flagrant, quite unabashed – under the cover of this fanatical Englishness. But I couldn't begin to *tell* you all the things. It's just incredible.'

Aaron wondered how on earth Francis had been able to discover and bear witness to so much that was incredible, in a bare two days. But a little gossip, and an addition of lurid imagination, will carry you anywhere.

'Well now,' said Francis. 'What are you doing today?'

Aaron was not doing anything in particular.

'Then will you come and have dinner with us – ?'

Francis fixed up the time and the place – a small restaurant at the other end of the town. Then he leaned out of the window.

'Fascinating place! Oh, fascinating place!' he said, in soliloquy. 'And you've got a superb view. Almost better than ours, I think. Well then, half-past seven. We're meeting a few other people, mostly residents or people staying some time. We're not inviting them. Just dropping in, you know – a little restaurant. We shall see you then! Well then, *a rivederci* till this evening. So glad you like Florence! I'm simply loving it – revelling. And the pictures! Oh – '

The party that evening consisted all of men: Francis and Angus, and a writer, James Argyle, and little Algy Constable, and tiny Louis Mee, and deaf Walter Rosen. They all snapped and rattled at one another, and were rather spiteful but rather amusing. Francis and Angus had to leave early. They had another appointment. And James Argyle got quite tipsy, and said to Aaron:

'But my boy, don't let yourself be led astray by the talk of such people as Algy. Beware of them, my boy, if you've a soul to save. If you've a soul to save!' And he swallowed the remains of his litre.

Algy's nose trembled a little, and his eyes blinked.

'And if you've a soul to *lose*,' he said, 'I would warn you very earnestly against Argyle.' Whereupon Algy shut one eye and opened the other so wide, that Aaron was almost scared.

'Quite right, my boy. Ha! Ha! Never a truer thing said! Ha-ha-ha.' Argyle laughed his Mephistophelian tipsy laugh. 'They'll teach you to save. Never was such a lot of ripe old savers! Save their old trouser-buttons! Go to them if you want to learn to save. Oh yes, I advise it seriously. You'll lose nothing – not even a reputation. You may lose your *soul*, of course. But that's a detail, among such a hoard of banknotes and trouser buttons. Ha-ha! What's a soul, to them –?'

'What is it to you, is perhaps the more pertinent question,' said Algy, flapping his eyelids like some crazy owl. 'It is you who specialise in the matter of soul, and we who are in need of enlightenment – '

'Yes, very true, you *are!* You *are* in need of enlightenment. A set of benighted wise virgins. Ha-ha-ha! That's good, that – benighted wise virgins! What –' Argyle put his red face near to Aaron's, and made a *moue*, narrowing his eyes quizzically as he peered up from under his level grey eyebrows. 'Sit in the dark to save the lamp-oil! And all no good to them. When the bridegroom cometh –! Ha-ha! Good that! Good, my boy! The bridegroom –' he giggled to himself. 'What about the bridegroom, Algy, my boy? Eh? What about him? Better trim your wick, old man, if it's not too late –'

'We were talking of souls, not wicks, Argyle,' said Algy.

'Same thing. Upon my soul it all amounts to the same thing. Where's the soul in a man that hasn't got a bed-fellow – eh? – asnwer me that! Can't be done, you know. Might as well ask a virgin chicken to lay you an egg. But believe me, there's far more damned chastity in the world, than anything else. Even in this town. Call it chastity, if you like. I see nothing in it but sterility. It takes a rat to praise long tails. Impotence set up the praise of chastity – believe me or not – but that's the bottom of it. The virtue is made out of the necessity. Ha-ha-ha! They can't do it, and so they make a virtue of not doing it. Like them! Like them!'

There was a pause. Argyle was in his cups, which left no more to be said. Algy, quivering and angry, looked disconcertingly round the room as if he were quite calm and collected. The deaf Jewish Rosen was smiling down his nose and saying: 'What was that last? I didn't catch that last,' cupping his ear with his hand in the frantic hope that someone would answer. No one paid any heed.

'I shall be going,' said Algy, looking round. Then to Aaron he said, 'You play the flute, I hear. May we hear you some time?'

'Yes,' said Aaron, non-committal.

'Well look here – come to tea to-morrow. I shall have some friends, and Del Torre will play the piano. Come to tea to-morrow, will you?'

'Thank you, I will.'

'And perhaps you'll bring your flute along.'

'Don't you do any such thing, my boy. Make them entertain *you*, for once. They're always squeezing an entertainment out of somebody' – and Argyle desperately emptied the remains of Algy's wine into his own glass: whilst Algy stood as if listening to something far off, and blinking terribly.

'Anyhow,' he said at length, 'you'll come, won't you? And bring your flute if you feel like it.'

'Don't you take that flute, my boy,' persisted Argyle. 'Don't think of such a thing. If they want a concert, let them buy their tickets and go to the Teatro Diana. Or to Marchesa del Torre's Saturday morning. She can afford to treat them.'

Algy looked at Argyle, and blinked.

'Well,' he said, 'I hope you'll get home all right, Argyle.'

'Thank you for your courtesy, Algy. Won't you lend me your arm?'

As Algy was small and frail, somewhat shaky: and as Argyle was a finely built, heavy man of fifty or more, the slap was unkind.

'Afraid I can't to-night. Good-night – '

Algy departed, so did little Mee, who had sat with a little delighted disapproval on his tiny, bird-like face, without saying anything. And even the Jew Rosen put away his deaf-machine and began awkwardly to take his leave. His long nose was smiling to itself complacently at all the things Argyle had been saying.

When he too had gone, Argyle arched his brows at Aaron, saying:

'Oh, my dear fellow, what a lot they are! Little Mee – look-ing like an innocent little boy. He's over seventy if he's a day. Well over seventy. Well, you don't believe me. Ask his mother – ask his mother. She's ninety-five. Old lady of ninety-five – ' Argyle even laughed himself at his own pre-posterousness.

'And then Algy – Algy's not a fool, you know. Oh, he can be most entertaining, most witty, and amusing. But he's out of place here. He should be in Kensington, dandling round the ladies' drawing-rooms and making his *mots*. They're rich, you know, the pair of them. Little Mee used to boast that he lived on eleven-and-threepence a week. Had to, poor chap. But then what does a white mouse like that need? Makes a heavy meal on a cheese-paring. Luck, you know – but, of course, he's come into money as well. Rich as Croesus, and still lives on nineteen-and-twopence a week. Though it's nearly double, of course, what it used to be. No wonder he looks anxious. They disapprove of me – oh, quite right, quite right from their own point of view. Where would their money be otherwise? It wouldn't last long if I laid hands on it – ' he made a devilish quizzing face. 'But you know, they get on my nerves. Little old maids, you know, little old maids. I'm sure I'm surprised at their patience with me. But when people are patient with you, you want to spit gall at them. Don't you? Ha-ha-ha! Poor old Algy. Did I lay it on him, to-night, or did I miss him?'

'I think you got him,' said Aaron.

'He'll never forgive me. Depend on it, he'll never forgive me. Ha-ha! I like to be unforgiven. It adds *zest* to one's intercourse with people, to know that they'll never forgive one. Ha-ha-ha! Little old maids, who do their knitting with their tongues. Poor old Algy – he drops his stitches now. Ha-ha-ha! Must be eighty, I should say.'

Aaron laughed. He had never met a man like Argyle before – and he could not help being charmed. The other man had a certain wicked whimsicality that was very attractive, when levelled against someone else, and not against oneself. He must have been very handsome in his day, with his natural dignity, and his clean-shaven strong square face. But now his face was all red and softened and inflamed, his eyes had gone small and wicked under his bushy grey brows. Still he had a presence. And his grey hair, almost gone white, was still handsome.

'And what are you going to do in Florence?' asked Argyle. Aaron explained.

'Well,' said Argyle, 'make what you can out of them, and then go. Go before they have time to do the dirty on you. If they think you want anything from them, they'll treat you like a dog, like a dog. Oh, they're very frightened of anybody who wants anything of them: frightened to death. I see nothing of them. Live by myself – see nobody. Can't stand it, you know: their silly little tea-parties – simply can't stand it, No, I live alone – and shall die alone. At least, I sincerely hope so. I should be sorry to have any of them hanging round.'

The restaurant was empty, the pale, malarial waiter – he had, of course, contracted malaria during the war – was looking purple round the eyes. But Argyle callously sat on. Aaron therefore rose to his feet.

'Oh, I'm coming, I'm coming,' said Argyle.

He got unsteadily to his feet. The waiter helped him on with his coat: and he put a disreputable-looking little curly hat on his head. Then he took his stick.

'Don't look at my appearance, my dear fellow,' said Argyle. 'I am frayed at the wrists – Look here!' He showed the cuffs of his overcoat, just frayed through. 'I've got a trunkful of clothes in London, if only somebody would bring it out to me. Ready then! Avanti!'

And so they passed out into the still rainy street. Argyle lived in the very centre of the town: in the cathedral square. Aaron left him at his hotel door.

'But come and see me,' said Argyle. 'Call for me at twelve o'clock – or just before twelve – and let us have luncheon together. What! Is that all right? Yes, come just before twelve. When? – to-morrow? To-morrow morning? Will you come to-morrow?'

Aaron said he would come on Monday.

'Monday, eh! You say Monday! Very well then. Don't you forget now. Don't you forget. For I've a memory like a vice. I shan't forget – just before twelve then. And come right up. I'm right under the roof. In Paradise, as the porter always says. Siamo nel paradiso. But he's a *crétin*. As near Paradise as I care for, for it's devilish hot in summer, and damned cold in winter. Don't you forget now – Monday, twelve o'clock.'

And Argyle pinched Aaron's arm fast, then went unsteadily up the steps to his hotel door.

The next day at Algy's there was a crowd. Algy had a very pleasant flat indeed, kept more scrupulously neat and finicking than ever any woman's flat was kept. So to-day, with its bowls of flowers and its pictures and books and old furniture, and Algy, very nicely dressed, fluttering and blinking and making really a charming host, it was all very delightful to the little mob of visitors. They were a curious lot, it is true:

everybody rather exceptional. Which, though it may be startling, is so very much better fun than everybody all alike. Aaron talked to an old, old Italian elegant in side-curls, who peeled off his grey gloves and studied his formalities with a delightful Mid-Victorian dash, and told stories about a *plaint* which Lady Surry had against Lord Marsh, and was quite incomprehensible. Out rolled the English words, like plums out of a burst bag, and all completely unintelligible. But the old *beau* was supremely satisfied. He loved talking English, and holding his listeners spell-bound.

Next to Aaron on the sofa sat the Marchesa del Torre, an American woman from the Southern States, who had lived most of her life in Europe. She was about forty years of age, handsome, well-dressed, and quiet in the buzz of the tea-party. It was evident she was one of Algy's lionesses. Now she sat by Aaron, eating nothing, but taking a cup of tea and keeping still. She seemed sad – or not well perhaps. Her eyes were heavy. But she was very carefully made up, and very well dressed, though simply: and sitting there, full-bosomed, rather sad, remote-seeming, she suggested to Aaron a modern Cleopatra brooding, Anthony-less.

Her husband, the Marchese, was a little intense Italian in a Colonel's grey uniform, cavalry, leather gaiters. He had blue eyes, his hair was cut very short, his head looked hard and rather military: he would have been taken for an Austrian officer, or even a German, had it not been for the peculiar Italian sprightliness and touch of grimace in his mobile countenance. He was rather like a gnome – not ugly, but odd.

Now he came and stood opposite to Signor di Lanti, and quizzed him in Italian. But it was evident, in quizzing the old buck, the little Marchese was hovering near his wife, in ear-shot. Algy came up with cigarettes, and she at once began to smoke, with that peculiar heavy intensity of a nervous woman.

Aaron did not say anything – did not know what to say. He was peculiarly conscious of the woman sitting next to him, her arm near his. She smoked heavily, in silence, as if abstracted, a sort of cloud on her level, dark brows. Her hair was dark, but a softish brown, not black, and her skin was fair. Her bosom would be white. Why Aaron should have had this thought, he could not for the life of him say.

Manfredi, her husband, rolled his blue eyes and grimaced as he laughed at old Lanti. But it was obvious that his attention was diverting sideways, towards his wife. Aaron, who was tired of nursing a tea-cup, placed it on a table and resumed his seat in silence. But suddenly the little Marchese whipped out his cigarette-case, and making a little bow, presented it to Aaron, saying:

'Won't you smoke?'

'Thank you,' said Aaron.

'Turkish that side – Virginia there – you see.'

'Thank you, Turkish,' said Aaron.

The little officer in his dove-grey and yellow uniform snapped his box shut again, and presented a light.

'You are new in Florence?' he said, as he presented the match.

'Four days,' said Aaron.

'And I hear you are musical.'

'I play the flute – no more.'

'Ah yes – but then you play it as an artist, not as an accomplishment.'

'But how do you know?' laughed Aaron.

'I was told so – and I believe it.'

'That's nice of you, anyhow. But you are a musician too.'

'Yes – we are both musicians – my wife and I.'

Manfredi looked at his wife. She flicked the ash off her cigarette.

'What sort?' said Aaron.

'Why, how do you mean, what sort? We are dilettanti, I suppose.'

'No – what is your instrument? The piano?'

'Yes – the pianoforte. And my wife sings. But we are very much out of practice. I have been at the war four years, and we have had our home in Rome. My wife was in Paris often, she did not wish to stay in Italy alone. And so – you see – everything goes – '

'But you will begin again?'

'Yes. We have begun already. We have music on Saturday mornings. Next Saturday a string quartette, and violin solos by a young Florentine woman – a friend – very good indeed, daughter of our Professor Tortoli, who composes – as you may know –'

'Yes,' said Aaron.

'Would you care to come and hear – ?'

'Awfully nice if you would –' suddenly said the wife, quite simply, as if she had merely been tired, and not talking before.

'I should like to very much –'

'Do come then.'

While they were making the arrangements, Algy came up in his blandest manner.

'Now Marchesa – might we hope for a song?'

'No – I don't sing any more,' came the slow, contralto reply.

'Oh, but you can't mean you say that deliberately –'

'Yes, quite deliberately –' She threw away her cigarette and opened her little gold case to take another.

'But what can have brought you to such a disastrous decision?'

'I can't say,' she replied, with a little laugh. 'The war, probably.'

'Oh, but don't let the war deprive us of this, as of everything else.'

'Can't be helped,' she said. 'I have no choice in the matter. The bird has flown –' She spoke with a certain heavy languor.

'You mean the bird of your voice? Oh, but that is quite impossible. One can hear it calling out of the leaves every time you speak.'

'I'm afraid you can't get him to do any more than call out of the leaves.'

'But – but – pardon me – is it because you don't intend there should be any more song? Is that your intention?'

'That I couldn't say,' said the Marchesa, smoking, smoking.

'Yes,' said Manfredi. 'At the present time it is because she *will* not – not because she cannot. It is her will, as you say.'

'Dear me! Dear me!' said Algy. 'But this is really another disaster added to the war list. But – but – will none of us ever be able to persuade you?' He smiled, half cajoling, half pathetic, with a prodigious flapping of his eyes.

'I don't know,' said she. 'That will be as it must be.'

'Then can't we say it must be *song* once more?'

To this sally she merely laughed, and pressed out her half-smoked cigarette.

'How very disappointing! How very cruel of – of fate and the war – and – and all the sum total of evils,' said Algy.

'Perhaps – ' here the little and piquant host turned to Aaron.

'Perhaps, Mr Sisson, your flute might call out the bird of song. As thrushes call each other into challenge, you know. Don't you think that is very probable?'

'I have no idea,' said Aaron.

'But you, Marchesa. Won't you give us hope that it might be so?'

'I have no idea, either,' said she. 'But I should very much like to hear Mr Sisson's flute. It's an instrument I like extremely.'

'There now. You see you may work the miracle, Mr Sisson. Won't you play to us?'

'I'm afraid I didn't bring my flute along,' said Aaron. 'I didn't want to arrive with a little bag.'

'Quite!' said Algy. 'What a pity it wouldn't go in your pocket.'

'Not music and all,' said Aaron.

'Dear me! What a *comble* of disappointment. I never felt so strongly, Marchesa, that the old life and the old world had collapsed. Really – I shall soon have to try to give up being cheerful at all.'

'Don't do that,' said the Marchesa. 'It isn't worth the effort.'

'Ah! I'm glad you find it so. Then I have hope.'

She merely smiled, indifferent.

The tea-party began to break up – Aaron found himself

going down the stairs with the Marchesa and her husband. They descended all three in silence, husband and wife in front. Once outside the door, the husband asked:

'How shall we go home, dear? Tram or carriage – ?' It was evident he was economical.

'Walk,' she said, glancing over her shoulder at Aaron. 'We are all going the same way, I believe.'

Aaron said where he lived. They were just across the river. And so all three proceeded to walk through the town.

'You are sure it won't be too much for you – too far?' said the little officer, taking his wife's arm solicitously. She was taller than he. But he was a spirited fellow.

'No, I feel like walking.'

'So long as you don't have to pay for it afterwards.'

Aaron gathered that she was not well. Yet she did not look ill – unless it were nerves. She had that peculiar heavy remote quality of pre-occupation and neurosis.

The streets of Florence were very full this Sunday evening, almost impassable, crowded particularly with gangs of grey-green soldiers. The three made their way brokenly, and with difficulty. The Italian was in a constant state of returning salutes. The grey-green, sturdy, unsoldierly soldiers looked at the woman as she passed.

'I am sure you had better take a carriage,' said Manfredi.

'No – I don't mind it.'

'Do you feel at home in Florence?' Aaron asked her.

'Yes – as much as anywhere. Oh yes – quite at home.'

'Do you like it as well as anywhere?' he asked.

'Yes – for a time. Paris for the most part.'

'Never America?'

'No, never America. I came when I was quite a little girl to Europe – Madrid – Constantinople – Paris. I hardly knew America at all.'

Aaron remembered that Francis had told him, the Marchesa's father had been a famous figure in Europe.

'So you feel you have no country of your own?'

'I have Italy. I am Italian now, you know.'

Aaron wondered why she spoke so muted, so numbed. Manfredi seemed really attached to her – and she to him. They were so simple with one another.

They came towards the bridge where they should part.

'Won't you come and have a cocktail?' she said.

'Now?' said Aaron.

'Yes. This is the right time for a cocktail. What time is it, Manfredi?'

'Half-past six. Do come and have one with us,' said the Italian. 'We always take one about this time.'

Aaron continued with them over the bridge. They had the first floor of an old palazzo opposite, a little way up the hill. A man-servant opened the door.

'If only it will be warm,' she said. 'The apartment is almost impossible to keep warm. We will sit in the little room.'

Aaron found himself in a quite warm room with shaded lights and a mixture of old Italian stiffness and deep soft modern comfort. The Marchesa went away to take off her wraps, and the Marchese chatted with Aaron. The little officer was amiable and kind, and it was evident he liked his guest.

'Would you like to see the room where we have music?' he said. 'It is a fine room for the purpose – we used before the war to have music every Saturday morning, from ten to twelve: and all friends might come. Usually we had fifteen or twenty people. Now we are starting again. I myself enjoy it so much. I am afraid my wife isn't so enthusiastic as she used to be. I wish something would rouse her up, you know. The war seemed to take her life away. Here in Florence are so many amateurs. Very good indeed. We can have very good chamber-music indeed. I hope it will cheer her up and make her quite herself again. I was away for such long periods, at the front. And it was not good for her to be alone. I am hoping now all will be better.'

So saying, the little, odd officer switched on the lights of the long salon. It was a handsome room in the Italian mode of the Empire period – beautiful old faded tapestry panels – reddish – and some ormolu furniture – and other things mixed in – rather conglomerate, but pleasing, all the more pleasing. It was big, not too empty, and seemed to belong to human life, not to show and shutupedness. The host was happy showing it.

'Of course the flat in Rome is more luxurious than this,' he said. 'But I prefer this. I prefer it here.' There was a certain wistfulness as he looked round, then began to switch off the lights.

They returned to the little salotta. The Marchesa was seated in a low chair. She wore a very thin white blouse, that showed her arms and her throat. She was a full-breasted, soft-skinned woman, though not stout.

'Make the cocktails then, Manfredi,' she said. 'Do you find this room very cold?' she asked of Aaron.

'Not a bit cold,' he said.

'The stove goes all the time,' she said, 'but without much effect.'

'You wear such thin clothes,' he said.

'Ah no, the stove should give heat enough. Do sit down. Will you smoke? There are cigarettes – and cigars, if you prefer them.'

'No, I've got my own, thanks.'

She took her own cigarette from her gold case.

'It is a fine room, for music, the big room,' said he.

'Yes, quite. Would you like to play for us some time, do you think?'

'Do you want me to? I mean does it interest you?'

'What – the flute?'

'No – music altogether – '

'Music altogether – ! Well! I used to love it. Now – I'm not sure. Manfredi lives for it, almost.'

'For that and nothing else?' asked Aaron.

'No, no! No, no! Other things as well.'

'But you don't like it much any more?'

'I don't know. Perhaps I don't. I'm not sure.'

'You don't look forward to the Saturday mornings?' he asked.

'Perhaps I don't – but for Manfredi's sake, of course, I do. But for his sake more than my own, I admit. And I think he knows it.'

'A crowd of people in one's house – ' said Aaron.

'Yes, the people. But it's not only that. It's the music itself – I think I can't stand it any more. I don't know.'

'Too emotional? Too much feeling for you?'

'Yes, perhaps. But no. What I can't stand is chords, you know: harmonies. A number of sounds all sounding together. It just makes me ill. It makes me feel so sick.'

'What – do you want discords? – dissonances?'

'No – they are nearly as bad. No, it's just when any number of musical notes, different notes, come together, harmonies or discords. Even a single chord struck on the piano. It makes me feel sick. I just feel as if I should retch. Isn't it strange? Of course, I don't tell Manfredi. It would be too cruel to him. It would cut his life in two.'

'But then why do you have the music – the Sundays – then?'

'Oh, I just keep out of the way as much as possible. I'm sure you feel there is something wrong with me, that I take it as I do,' she added, as if anxious: but half ironical.

'No – I was just wondering – I believe I feel something the same myself. I know orchestra makes me blind with hate or I don't know what. But I want to throw bombs.'

'There now. It does that to me, too. Only now it has fairly got me down, and I feel nothing but helpless nausea. You know, like when you are seasick.'

Her dark-blue, heavy, haunted-looking eyes were resting on him as if she hoped for something. He watched her face steadily, a curious intelligence flickering on his own.

'Yes,' he said. 'I understand it. And I know, *at the bottom*, I'm like that. But I keep myself from realizing, don't you know. Else perhaps, where should I be? Because I make my life and my living at it, as well.'

'At music! Do you! But how bad for you. But perhaps the flute is different. I have a feeling that it is. I can think of one single pipe-note – yes, I can think of it quite, quite calmly.

And I can't even think of the piano, or of the violin with its tremolo, or of orchestra, or of a string quartette – or even a military band – I can't think of it without a shudder. I can only bear drum-and-fife. Isn't it crazy of me? But from the other, from what we call music proper, I've endured too much. But bring your flute one day. Bring it, will you? And let me hear it quite alone. Quite, quite alone. I think it might do me an awful lot of good. I do really. I can imagine it.' She closed her eyes, and her strange, sing-song lapsing voice came to an end. She spoke almost like one in a trance – or a sleep-walker.

'I've got it now in my overcoat pocket,' he said, 'if you like.'

'Have you? Yes!' She was never hurried: always slow and resonant, so that the echoes of her voice seemed to linger. 'Yes – do get it. And play in the other room – quite – quite without accompaniment. Do – and try me.'

'And you will tell me what you feel?'

'Yes.'

Aaron went out to his overcoat. When he returned with his flute, which he was screwing together, Manfredi had come with the tray and the three cocktails. The Marchesa took her glass.

'Listen, Manfredi,' she said. 'Mr Sisson is going to play, quite alone in the sala. And I am going to sit here and listen.'

'Very well,' said Manfredi. 'Drink your cocktail first. Are you going to play without music?'

'Yes,' said Aaron.

'I'll just put on the lights for you.'

'No – leave it dark. There will be enough light come in from here.'

'Sure?' said Manfredi.

'Yes.'

The little soldier was an intruder at the moment. Both the others felt it so. But they bore him no grudge. They knew it was they who were exceptional, not he. Aaron swallowed his drink, and looked towards the door.

'Sit down, Manfredi. Sit still,' said the Marchesa.

'Won't you let me try some accompaniment?' said the soldier.

'No. I shall just play a little thing from memory,' said Aaron.

'Sit down, dear. Sit down,' said the Marchesa to her husband.

He seated himself obediently. The flash of bright yellow on the grey of his uniform seemed to make him like a chaffinch or a gnome.

Aaron returned to the other room, and waited awhile, to get back the spell which connected him with the woman, and gave the two of them this strange isolation, beyond the bounds of life, as it seemed.

He caught it again. And there, in the darkness of the big room, he put his flute to his lips, and began to play. It was a clear, sharp, lilted run-and-fall of notes, not a tune in any sense of the word, and yet a melody: a bright, quick sound of pure animation: a bright, quick, animate noise, running and pausing. It was like a bird's singing, in that it had no human emotion or passion or intention or meaning – a ripple and poise of animate sound. But it was unlike a bird's singing, in that the notes followed clear and single one after the other, in their subtle gallop. A nightingale is rather like that – a wild sound. To read all the human pathos into nightingales' singing is nonsense. A wild, savage, non-human lurch and squander of sound, beautiful, but entirely unaesthetic.

What Aaron was playing was not of his own invention. It was a bit of mediæval phrasing written for the pipe and the viol. It made the piano seem a ponderous, nerve-racking steam-roller of noise, and the violin, as we know it, a hateful wire-drawn nerve-torturer.

After a little while, when he entered the smaller room again, the Marchesa looked full into his face.

'Good!' she said. 'Good!'

And a gleam almost of happiness seemed to light her up. She seemed like one who had been kept in a horrible enchanted castle – for years and years. Oh, a horrible enchanted castle, with wet walls of emotions and ponderous chains of feelings and a ghastly atmosphere of must-be. She felt she had seen through the opening door a crack of sunshine, and thin, pure, light outside air, outside, beyond this dank and beastly dungeon of feelings and moral necessity. Ugh! – she shuddered convulsively at what had been. She looked at her little husband. Chains of necessity all round him: a little jailer. Yet she was fond of him. If only he would throw away the castle keys. He was a little gnome. What did he clutch the castle-keys so tight for?

Aaron looked at her. He knew that they understood one another, he and she. Without any moral necessity or any other necessity. Outside – they had got outside the castle of so-called human life. Outside the horrible, stinking human castle of life. A bit of true, limpid freedom. Just a glimpse.

'Charming!' said the Marchese. 'Truly charming! But what was it you played?'

Aaron told him.

'But truly delightful. I say, won't you play for us one of these Sundays? And won't you let me take the accompaniment? – I should be charmed, charmed, if you would.'

'All right,' said Aaron.

'Do drink another cocktail,' said his hostess.

He did so. And then he rose to leave.

'Will you stay to dinner?' said the Marchesa. 'We have two people coming – two Italian relatives of my husband. But –'

No, Aaron declined to stay to dinner.

'Then won't you come on – let me see – on Wednesday? Do come on Wednesday. We are alone. And do bring the flute. Come at half-past six, as to-day, will you? Yes?'

Aaron promised – and then he found himself in the street. It was half-past seven. Instead of returning straight home, he crossed the Ponte Vecchio and walked straight into the crowd. The night was fine now. He had his overcoat over his arm, and in a sort of trance or frenzy, whirled away by his evening's experience, and by the woman, he strode swiftly forward, hardly heeding anything, but rushing blindly on through all the crowd, carried away by his own feelings, as much as if he had been alone, and all this many people merely trees.

Leaving the Piazza Vittorio Emmanuele a gang of soldiers suddenly rushed round him, buffeting him in one direction, whilst another gang, swinging round the corner, threw him back helpless again into the midst of the first gang. For some moments he struggled among the rude, brutal little mob of grey-green coarse uniforms that smelt so strong of soldiers. Then, irritated, he found himself free again, shaking himself and passing on towards the cathedral. Irritated, he now put on his overcoat and buttoned it to the throat, closing himself in, as it were, from the brutal insolence of the Sunday night mob of men. Before, he had been walking through them in a rush of naked feeling, all exposed to their tender mercies. He now gathered himself together.

As he was going home, suddenly, just as he was passing the Bargello, he stopped. He stopped, and put his hand to his breast pocket. His letter-case was gone. He had been robbed. It was as if lightning ran through him at that moment, as if a fluid electricity rushed down his limbs, through the sluice of his knees, and out at his feet, leaving him standing there almost unconscious. For a moment unconscious and super-conscious he stood there. He had been robbed. They had put their hand in his breast and robbed him. If they had stabbed him it could hardly have had a greater effect on him.

And he had known it. He had known it. When the soldiers jostled him so evilly they robbed him. And he knew it. He had known it as if it were fate. Even as if it were fated beforehand.

Feeling quite weak and faint, as if he had really been struck by some evil electric fluid, he walked on. And as soon as he began to walk, he began to reason. Perhaps his letter-case was in his other coat. Perhaps he had not had it with him at all. Perhaps he was feeling all this, just for nothing. Perhaps it was all folly.

He hurried forward. He wanted to make sure. He wanted relief. It was as if the power of evil had suddenly seized him and thrown him, and he wanted to say it was not so, that he had imagined it all, conjured it up. He did not want to admit the power of evil – particularly at that moment. For surely a very ugly evil spirit had struck him, in the midst of that gang of Italian soldiers. He knew it – it had pierced him. It had *got* him.

But he wanted to say it was not so. Reaching the house, he hastened upwards to his far-off, lonely room, through the dark corridors. Once in his own apartment, he shut the door and switched on the light, a sensation like fear at his heart. Then he searched his other pocket. He looked everywhere. In vain.

In vain, truly enough. For he *knew* the thing was stolen. He had known it all along. The soldiers had deliberately plotted, had deliberately rushed him and taken his purse. They must have watched him previously. They must have grinned, and jeered at him.

He sat down in a chair, to recover from the shock. The pocket-book contained four hundred francs, three one-pound notes, and various letters and private effects – Well, these were lost. But it was not so much the loss as the assault on his person that caused him to feel so stricken. He felt the jeering, gibing blows they had given as they jostled him.

And now he sat, weak in every limb, and said to himself: 'Yes – and if I hadn't rushed along so full of feeling: if I hadn't exposed myself: if I hadn't got worked up with the Marchesa, and then rushed all kindled through the streets, without reserve: it would never have happened. I gave myself away: and there was someone ready to snatch what I gave. I gave myself away. It is my own fault. I should have been on my guard. I should be always on my guard: always, always, with God and the devil both, I should be on my guard. Godly or devilish, I should hold fast to my reserve and keep on the watch. And if I don't, I deserve what I get.'

But still he sat in his chair in his bedroom, dazed. One part of his soul was saying emphatically: It serves you right. It is nothing but right. It serves everybody right who rushes enkindled through the street, and trusts implicitly in mankind and in the life-spirit, as if mankind and the life-spirit were a playground for enkindled individuals. It serves you right. You have paid about twelve pounds sterling for your lesson. Fool, you might have known beforehand, and then you needn't have paid at all. You can ill afford twelve pounds sterling, you fool. But since paid you have, then mind, mind the lesson is learned. Never again. Never expose yourself again. Never again absolute trust. It is a blasphemy against life, is absolute trust. Has a wild creature ever absolute trust? It minds itself. Sleeping or waking it is on its guard. And so must you be, or you'll go under. Sleeping or waking, man or woman, God or the devil, keep your guard over yourself. Keep your guard over yourself, lest worse befall you. No man is robbed unless he incites a robber. No man is murdered unless he attracts a murderer. Then be not robbed: it lies within your own power. And be not murdered. Or if you are, you deserve it. Keep your guard over yourself, now, always and forever. Yes, against God quite as hard as against the devil. He's fully as dangerous to you . . .

Thus thinking, not in his mind but in his soul, his active living soul, he gathered his equanimity once more, and accepted the fact. So he rose and tidied himself for dinner. His face was now set, and still. His heart also was still – and fearless. Because its sentinel was stationed. Stationed, stationed for ever.

And Aaron never forgot. After this, it became essential to him to feel that the sentinel stood guard in his own heart. He felt a strange unease the moment he was off his guard. Asleep or awake, in the midst of the deepest passion or the suddenest love, or in the throes of greatest excitement or bewilderment, somewhere, some corner of himself was awake to the fact that the sentinel of the soul must not sleep: no, never, not for one instant.

CHAPTER 17

Nel Paradiso

AARON and Lilly sat on Argyle's little loggia, high up under
the eaves of the house, a sort of long attic-terrace just under
the roof, where no one would have suspected it. It was level
with the grey conical roof of the Baptistery. Here sat Aaron
and Lilly in the afternoon, in the last of the lovely autumn
sunshine. Below, the square was already cold in shadow, the
pink and white and green Baptistery rose lantern-shaped as
from some sea-shore, cool, cold and wan now the sun was
gone. Black figures, innumerable black figures, curious
because they were all on end, up on end – Aaron could not say
why he expected them to be horizontal – little black figures
up on end, like fishes that swim on their tails, wiggled end-
lessly across the piazza, little carriages on natural all-fours
rattled tinily across, the yellow little tram-cars like dogs
slipped round the corner. The balcony was so high up, that
the sound was ineffectual. The upper space, above the houses,
was nearer than the under-currents of the noisy town. Sunlight, lovely full sunlight, lingered warm and still on the balcony. It caught the facade of the cathedral sideways, like the
tips of a flower, and sideways lit up the stem of Giotto's tower,
like a lily stem, or a long, lovely pale pink and white and green
pistil of the lily of the cathedral. Florence, the flowery town.
Firenze – Fiorenze – the flowery town: the red lilies. The
Fiorentini, the flower-souled. Flowers with good roots in the
mud and muck, as should be: and fearless blossoms in the air,
like the cathedral and the tower and the David.

'I love it,' said Lilly, 'I love this place. I love the cathedral
and the tower. I love its pinkness and its paleness. The gothic
souls find fault with it, and say it is gimcrack and tawdry and

276

cheap. But I love it; it is delicate and rosy, and the dark stripes are as they should be, like the tiger marks on a pink lily. It's a lily, not a rose: a pinky white lily with dark tigery marks. And heavy too, in its own substance: earth-substance, risen from earth into the air: and even forgetting the dark, black-fierce earth – I reckon here men for a moment were themselves, as a plant in flower is for the moment completely itself. Then it goes off. As Florence has gone off. No flowers now. But it *has* flowered. And I don't see why a race should be like an aloe tree, flower once and die. Why should it? Why not flower again? Why not?'

'If it's going to, it will,' said Aaron. 'Our deciding about it won't alter it.'

'The decision is part of the business.'

Here they were interrupted by Argyle, who put his head through one of the windows. He had flecks of lather on his reddened face.

'Do you think you're wise now,' he said, 'to sit in that sun?'

'So late in the year?' laughed Lilly.

'Always fear the sun when there's an "r" in the month,' said Argyle. 'Always fear it "r" or no "r," I say. I'm frightened of it. I've been in the south, I know what it is. I tell you, I'm frightened of it. But if you think you can stand it – well – '

'It won't last much longer, anyhow,' said Lilly.

'Too long for me, my boy. I'm a shady bird, in all senses of the word, in all senses of the word. Now are you comfortable? What? Have another cushion? A rug for your knees? You're quite sure now? Well, wait just one moment till the waiter brings up a syphon, and you shall have a whiskey and soda. Precious – oh yes, very precious these days – like drinking gold. Thirty-five liras a bottle, my boy!' Argyle pulled a long face and made a noise with his lips. 'But I had this bottle given me, and luckily you've come while there's a drop left. Very glad you have! Very glad you have.'

Here he poked a little table through the window, and put a bottle and two glasses, one a tooth-glass, upon it. Then he withdrew again to finish shaving. The waiter presently hobbled up with the syphon and third glass. Argyle pushed his head through the window, that was only a little higher than the balcony. He was soon neatly shaved, and was brushing his hair.

'Go ahead, my boys, go ahead with that whiskey!' he said.

'We'll wait for you,' said Lilly.

'No, no, don't think of it. However, if you will, I shall be one minute only – one minute only. I'll put on the water for the tea now. Oh, damned bad methylated spirit they sell now! And six francs a litre! Six francs a litre! I don't know what I'm going to do, the air I breathe costs money nowadays. Just one moment and I'll be with you! Just one moment –'

In a very little while he came from the tiny attic bed-room, through the tiniest cupboard of a sitting-room under the eaves, where his books were, and where he had hung his old red Indian tapestries – or silk embroideries – and he emerged there up above the world on the loggia.

'Now then – siamo nel Paradiso, eh? Paradisal enough for you, is it?'

'The devil looking over Lincoln,' said Lilly laughing, glancing up into Argyle's face.

'The devil looking over *Florence* would feel sad,' said Argyle. 'The place is fast growing respectable. Oh, piety makes the devil chuckle. No doubt about it, no doubt whatever. There – !' he had just finished settling his tie and buttoning his waistcoat. 'How do I look, eh? Presentable? I've just had this suit turned. Clever little tailor across the way there. But he charged me a hundred and twenty francs.' Argyle pulled a face and made the little trumping noise with his lips. 'However – not bad, is it? He had to let in a bit at the back of the waistcoat and a gusset, my boy, a gusset in the trousers back. Well, well, might do worse. Is it all right?'

Lilly eyed the suit.

'Very nice. Very nice indeed. Such a good cloth! That makes all the difference.'

'Oh, my dear fellow, all the difference! This suit is eleven years old – eleven years old. But beautiful English cloth – before the war, before the war!'

'It looks quite wonderfully expensive and smart now,' said Lilly.

'Expensive and smart, eh! Ha-ha-ha! Well, it cost me a hundred and twenty francs to have it turned, and I found that expensive enough. Well now, come – ' here Argyle's voice took a new gay cheer. 'A whiskey and soda, Lilly? Say when! Oh, nonsense, nonsense! You're going to have double that. You're no lily of the valley here, remember. Not with me. Not likely. *Siamo nel paradiso*, remember.'

'But why should we drink your whiskey? Tea would do for us just as well.'

'Not likely! Not likely! When I have the pleasure of your company, my boy, we drink a glass of something, unless I am utterly stripped. Say when, Aaron.'

'When,' said Aaron.

Argyle at last seated himself heavily in a small chair. The sun had left the loggia, but was glowing still on Giotto's tower and the top of the cathedral façade, and on the remoter great red-tiled dome.

'Look at my little red monthly rose,' said Argyle. 'Wonderful little fellow! I wouldn't have anything happen to him for the world. Oh, a bacchic little chap. I made Pasquale wear a wreath of them on his hair. Very becoming they were, very. Oh, I've had a charming show of flowers. Wonderful creatures sunflowers are. They got up and put their heads over the balcony, looking down on the square below. Oh great fun, great fun! The Blessed Damosel looked down – what? Lucky thing for her she wasn't on my balcony. Ha-ha-ha! Oh, you never know, she might have enjoyed it. Never believe a woman when she says she's chaste, nor a man when he says he's a – Yes, I had a charming show of flowers, charming – zinnias, petunias, ranunculus, sunflowers, white stocks – oh charming. Look at that bit of honeysuckle. You see the berries where his flowers were! Delicious scent, I assure you.'

Under the little balcony wall Argyle had put square red-tiled pots, all round, and in these still bloomed a few pansies and asters, whilst in a corner a monthly rose hung flowers like round blood-drops. Argyle was as tidy and scrupulous in his tiny rooms and his balcony as if he were a first-rate seaman on a yacht. Lilly remarked on this.

'Do you see signs of the old maid coming out in me? Oh, I don't doubt it. I don't doubt it. We all end that way. Age makes old maids of us all. And Tanny is all right, you say? Bring her to see me.'

'All right, Argyle. Höflichkeiten.'

'What? gar keine Höflichkeiten. Wahrhaftiger Kerl, bin ich, When am I going to see Tanny? When are you coming to dine with me?

'After you've dined with us – say the day after to-morrow –'

'Right you are. Delighted – Let me look if that water's boiling.' He got up and poked half himself inside the bedroom.

'Look,' said Lilly. 'There's Del Torre!'

'Like some sort of midge, in that damned grey-and-yellow uniform. I can't stand it, I tell you. I can't stand the sight of any more of these uniforms. Like a blight on the human landscape. Like a blight. Like green-flies on rose-trees, smother-flies. Europe's got the smother-fly in these infernal shoddy militarists.'

'Del Torre's coming out of it as soon as he can,' said Lilly.

'I should think so too.'

'I like him myself – very much. Look, he's seen us! He wants to come up, Argyle.'

'What, in that uniform! I'll see him in his grandmother's crinoline first.'

'Don't be fanatical, it's bad taste. Let him come up a minute.'

'Not for my sake. But for yours, he shall.' Argyle stood at the parapet of the balcony and waved his arm. 'Yes, come up,' he said, 'come up, you little mistkäfer – what the Americans call a bug. Come up and be damned.'

Of course Del Torre was too far off to hear this exhortation. Lilly also waved to him – and watched him pass into the doorway far below.

'I'll rinse one of these glasses for him,' said Argyle.

The Marchese's step was heard on the stone stairs: then his knock.

'Come in! Come in!' cried Argyle from the bedroom, where he was rinsing the glass. The Marchese entered, grinned with his curious, half courteous greeting. 'Go through – go through,' cried Argyle. 'Go on to the loggia – and mind your head. Good heavens, mind your head in that doorway.'

The Marchese just missed the top of the doorway as he climbed the abrupt steps on to the loggia. There he greeted Lilly and Aaron with hearty handshakes.

'Very glad to see you – very glad indeed – ' he cried, grinning with excited courtesy and pleasure, and covering Lilly's hand with both his own gloved hands. 'When did you come to Florence?'

There was a little explanation. Argyle shoved the last chair – it was a luggage stool – through the window.

'All I can do for you in the way of a chair,' he said.

'Ah, that is all right,' said the Marchese. 'Well, it is very nice up here – and very nice company. Of the very best, the very best in Florence.'

'The highest, anyhow,' said Argyle grimly, as he entered with the glass. 'Have a whiskey and soda, Del Torre. It's the bottom of the bottle, as you see.'

'The bottom of the bottle! Then I start with the tail-end, yes!' He stretched his blue eyes so that the whites showed all round, and grinned a wide, gnome-like grin.

'You made that start long ago, my dear fellow. Don't play the *ingénu* with me, you know it won't work. Say when, my man, say when!'

'Yes, when,' said Del Torre. 'When did I make that start, then?'

'At some unmentionably young age. Chickens such as you soon learn to cheep.'

'Chickens such as I soon learn to cheep,' repeated Del Torre, pleased with the verbal play. 'What is cheap, please? What is *to cheap*?'

'Cheep! Cheep!' squeaked Argyle, making a face at the little

Italian, who was perched on one strap of the luggage-stool. 'It's what chickens say when they're poking their little noses into new adventures – naughty ones.'

'Are chickens naughty? Oh! I thought they could only be good!'

'Featherless chickens like yourself, my boy.'

'Oh, as for featherless. Then there is no saying what they will do – ' And here the Marchese turned away from Argyle with the inevitable question to Lilly:

'Well, and how long will you stay in Florence?'

Lilly did not know: but he was not leaving immediately.

'Good! Then you will come and see us at once . . .'

Argyle rose once more, and went to make the tea. He shoved a lump of cake – or rather panetone, good currant loaf – through the window, with a knife to cut it.

'Help yourselves to the panetone,' he said. 'Eat it up. The tea is coming at once. You'll have to drink it in your glasses, there's only one old cup.'

The Marchese cut the cake, and offered pieces. The two men took and ate.

'So you have already found Mr Sisson!' said Del Torre to Lilly.

'Ran straight into him in the Via Nazionale,' said Lilly.

'Oh, one always runs into everybody in Florence. We are all already acquainted: also with the flute. That is a great pleasure.'

'So I think. Does your wife like it too?'

'Very much indeed! She is quite *éprise*. I too shall have to learn to play it.'

'And run the risk of spoiling the shape of your mouth – like Alcibiades.'

'Is there a risk? Yes! Then I shan't play it. My mouth is too beautiful. But Mr Sisson has not spoilt his mouth.'

'Not yet,' said Lilly. 'Give him time.'

'Is he also afraid – like Alcibiades?'

'Are you, Aaron?' said Lilly.

'What?'

'Afraid of spoiling your beauty by screwing your mouth to the flute?'

'I look a fool, do I, when I'm playing?' said Aaron.

'Only the least little bit in the world,' said Lilly. 'The way you prance your head, you know, like a horse.'

'Ah well,' said Aaron, 'I've nothing to lose.'

'And were you surprised, Lilly, to find your friend here?' asked Del Torre.

'I ought to have been. But I wasn't really.'

'Then you expected him?'

'No. It came naturally though. But why did you come, Aaron? What exactly brought you?'

'Accident,' said Aaron.

'Ah no! No! There is no such thing as accident,' said the Italian. 'A man is drawn by his fate, where he goes.'

'You are right,' said Argyle, who came now with the teapot. 'A man is drawn – or driven. Driven, I've found it. Ah, my dear fellow, what is life but a search for a friend? A search for a friend – that sums it up.'

'Or a lover,' said the Marchese, grinning.

'Same thing. Same thing. My hair is white – but that is the sum of my whole experience. The search for a friend.' There was something at once real and sentimental in Argyle's tone.

'Are you not seeking any more, Lilly?' asked the Marchese. 'Do you seek nothing?'

'We married men who haven't left our wives, are we supposed to seek anything?' said Lilly. 'Aren't we perfectly satisfied and in bliss with the wonderful women who honour us as wives?'

'Ah yes, yes!' said the Marchese. 'But now we are not speaking to the world. Now we try to speak of that which we have in the centre of our hearts.'

'And what have we there?' said Lilly.

'Well – shall I say? We have unrest. We have another need. We have something that hurts and eats us, yes eats us inside. Do I speak the truth?'

'Yes. But what is the something?'

'I don't know. I don't know. But it is something in love, I think. It is love itself which gnaws us inside, like a cancer,' said the Italian.

'But why should it? Is that the nature of love?' said Lilly.

'I don't know. Truly, I don't know. But perhaps it *is* in the nature of love – I don't know. But I tell you. I love my wife – she is very dear to me. I admire her, I trust her, I believe her. She is to me much more than any woman, more even than my mother. And so, I am very happy. I am very happy, she is very happy, in our love and our marriage. But wait. Nothing has changed – the love has not changed: it is the same. And yet we are *not* happy. No, we are not happy. I know she is not happy, I know I am not –'

'Why should you be?' said Lilly.

'Yes – and it is not even happiness,' said the Marchese, screwing up his face in a painful effort of confession. 'It is not even happiness. No, I do not ask to be happy. Why should I? It is childish. But there is for both of us, I know it, something which bites us, which eats us within, and drives us, drives us, somewhere, we don't know where. But it drives us, and eats us, and eats away the life – and yet we love each other, and we must not be separate. Do you know what I mean? Do you understand me at all in what I say? I speak what is true –'

'Yes, I understand. I'm in the same dilemma myself. But what I want to hear, is *why* you think it is so. Why is it?'

'Shall I say what I think? Yes? And you can tell me if it is foolish to you. Shall I tell you? Well. Because a woman, she now first wants the man, and he must go to her because he is wanted. Do you understand? You know – supposing I go to a woman – supposing she is my wife – and I go to her, yes, with my blood all ready, because it is I who want. Then she puts me off. Then she says, not now, not now, I am tired, I am not well. I do not feel like it. She puts me off – till I am angry or sorry or whatever I am – but still my blood has gone down again, you understand, and I don't want her any more. And then she puts her arms round me, and caresses me, and makes love to me – till she rouses me once more. So, and so she rouses me – and so I come to her. And I love her, it is very good, very good. But it was she who began, it was her initiative, you know. I do not think, in all my life, my wife has loved me from *my* initiative, you know. She will yield to me – because I insist, or because she wants to be a good submissive wife who loves me. So she will yield to me. But ah, what is it, you know? What is it, a woman who allows me, and who has no answer? It is something worse than nothing – worse than nothing. And so it makes me very discontented and unbelieving. If I say to her, she says it is not true – not at all true. Then she says, all she wants is that I should desire her, that I should love her and desire her. But even that is putting *her* first. And if I come to her so, if I come to her of my own desire, then she puts me off. She puts me off, or she only allows me to come to her. Even now it is the same, after ten years, as it was at first. But now I know, and for many years I did not know –'

The little man was intense. His face was strained, his blue eyes so stretched that they showed the white all round. He gazed into Lilly's face.

'But does it matter?' said Lilly slowly, 'in which of you the desire initiates? Isn't the result the same?'

'It matters. It matters –' cried the Marchese.

'Oh, my dear fellow, how *much* it matters –' interrupted Argyle sagely.

'Ay!' said Aaron.

The Marchese looked from one to the other of them.

'It matters!' he cried. 'It matters life or death. It used to be, that desire started in the man, and the woman answered. It used to be so for a long time in Italy. For this reason the women were kept away from the men. For this reason our Catholic religion tried to keep the young girls in convents, and innocent, before marriage. So that with their minds they should not know, and should not start this terrible thing, this woman's desire over a man, beforehand. This desire which starts in a woman's head, when she knows, and which takes a man for her use, for her service. This is Eve. Ah, I hate Eve.

I hate her, when she knows, and when she *wills*. I hate her when she will make of me that which serves her desire. She may love me, she may be soft and kind to me, she may give her life for me. But why? Only because I am *hers*. I am that thing which does her most intimate service. She can see no other in me. And I may be no other to her –'

'Then why not let it be so, and be satisfied?' said Lilly.

'Because I cannot. I cannot. I would. But I cannot. The Borghesia – the citizens – the bourgeoisie, they are the ones who can. Oh yes. The bourgeoisie, the shopkeepers, these serve their wives so, and their wives love them. They are the marital maquereaux – the husband-maquereaux, you know. Their wives are so stout and happy, and they dote on their husbands and always betray them. So it is with the bourgeoise. She loves her husband so much, and is always seeking to betray him. Or she is a Madame Bovary, seeking for a scandal. But the bourgeois husband, he goes on being the same. He is the horse, and she the driver. And when she says gee-up, you know – then he comes ready, like a hired maquereau. Only he feels so good, like a good little boy at her breast. And then there are the nice little children. And so they keep the world going – But for me –' he spat suddenly and with frenzy on the floor.

'You are quite right, my boy,' said Argyle. 'You are quite right. They've got the start of us, the women: and we've got to canter when they say gee-up. I – oh, I went through it all. But I broke the shafts and smashed the matrimonial cart, I can tell you, and I didn't care whether I smashed her up along with it or not. I didn't care one single bit, I assure you. And here I am. And she is dead and buried these dozen years. Well – well! Life, you know, life. And Women. Oh, they are the very hottest hell once they get the start of you. There's *nothing* they won't do to you, once they've got you. Nothing they won't do to you. Especially if they love you. Then you may as well give up the ghost: or smash the cart behind you and her in it. Otherwise she will just harry you into submission, and make a dog of you, and cuckold you under your nose. And you'll submit. Oh, you'll submit, and go on calling her my darling. Or else, if you won't submit, she'll do for you. Your only chance is to smash the shafts, and the whole matrimonial cart. Or she'll do for you. For a woman has an uncanny, hellish strength – she's a she-bear and a wolf, is a woman, when she's got the start of you. Oh, it's a terrible experience, if you're not a bourgeois, and not one of the knuckling-under money-making sort.'

'Knuckling-under sort. Yes. That is it,' said the Marchese.

'But can't there be a balancing of wills?' said Lilly.

'My dear boy, the balance lies in that, that when one goes up, the other goes down. One acts, the other takes. It is the only way in love. And the woman are nowadays the active party. Oh yes, not a shadow of doubt about it. They take the initiative, and the man plays up. That's how it is. The man just plays up. Nice manly proceeding, what!' cried Argyle.

'But why can't man accept it as the natural order of things?' said Lilly. 'Science makes it the natural order.'

'All my – to science,' said Argyle. 'No man with one drop of real spunk in him can stand it long.'

'Yes! Yes! Yes!' cried the Italian. 'Most men want it so. Most men want only, that a woman shall want them, and they shall then play up to her when she has roused them. Most men want only this: that a woman shall choose one man out, to be her man, and he shall worship her and come up when she shall provoke him. Otherwise he is to keep still. And the woman, she is quite sure of her part. She must be loved and adored, and above all, obeyed: particularly in her sex desire. There she must not be thwarted, or she becomes a devil. And if she is obeyed, she becomes a misunderstood woman with nerves, looking round for the next man whom she can bring under. So it is.'

'Well,' said Lilly. 'And then what?'

'Nay,' interrupted Aaron. 'But do you think it's true what he says? Have you found it like this? You're married. Has your experience been different, or the same?'

'What was yours?' asked Lilly.

'Mine was the same. Mine was the same, if ever it was,' said Aaron.

'And mine was *extremely* similar,' said Argyle with a grimace.

'And yours, Lilly?' asked the Marchese anxiously.

'Not very different,' said Lilly.

'Ah!' cried Del Torre, jerking up erect as if he had found something.

'And what's your way out?' Aaron asked him.

'I'm not out – so I won't holla,' said Lilly. 'But Del Torre puts it best. What do you say is the way out, Del Torre?'

'The way out is that it should change: that the man should be the asker and the woman the answerer. It *must* change.'

'But it *doesn't*. Prrr!' Argyle made his trumping noise.

'Does it?' asked Lilly of the Marchese.

'No. I think it does not.'

'And will it ever again?'

'Perhaps never.'

'And then what?'

'Then? Why the man seeks a *pis-aller*. Then he seeks something which will give him answer, and which will not only draw him, draw him, with a terrible sexual will. So he seeks young girls, who know nothing, and so cannot force him. He thinks he will possess them while they are young, and they will be soft and responding to his wishes. But in this too he is mistaken. Because now a baby of one year, if it be a female, is like a woman of forty, so is its will made up, so it will force a man.'

'And so young girls are no good, even as a *pis-aller*.'

'No good – because they are all modern women. Every one, a modern woman. Not one who isn't.'

'Terrible thing, the modern woman,' put in Argyle.

'And then a man naturally loves his own wife too, even if it is not bearable to love her.'

'Or one leaves her, like Aaron,' said Lilly.

'And seeks another woman, so,' said the Marchese.

'Does he seek another woman?' said Lilly. 'Do you, Aaron?'

'I don't *want* to,' said Aaron. 'But – I can't stand by myself in the middle of the world and in the middle of people, and know I am quite by myself, and nowhere to go, and nothing to hold on to. I can for a day or two – But then, it becomes unbearable as well. You get frightened. You feel you might go funny – as you would if you stood on this balcony wall with all the space beneath you.'

'Can't one be alone – quite alone?' said Lilly.

'But no – it is absurd. Like Saint Simeon Stylites on a pillar. But it is absurd!' cried the Italian.

'I don't mean like Simeon Stylites. I mean can't one live with one's wife, and be fond of her: and with one's friends and enjoy their company: and with the world and everything, pleasantly: and yet *know* that one is alone? Essentially, at the very core of me, alone. Eternally alone. And choosing to be alone. Not sentimental or *lonely*. Alone, choosing to be alone, because by one's own nature one is alone. The being with another person is secondary,' said Lilly.

'One is alone,' said Argyle, 'in all but love. In all but love, my dear fellow. And then I agree with you.'

'No,' said Lilly, 'in love most intensely of all, alone.'

'Completely incomprehensible,' said Argyle. 'Amounts to nothing.'

'One man is but a part. How can he be so alone?' said the Marchese.

'In so far as he is a single individual soul, he *is* alone – *ipso facto*. In so far as I am I, and only I am I, and I am only I, in so far, I am inevitably and eternally alone, and it is my last blessedness to know it, and to accept it, and to live with this as the core of my self-knowledge.'

'My dear boy, you are becoming metaphysical, and that is as bad as softening of the brain,' said Argyle.

'All right,' said Lilly.

'And,' said the Marchese, 'it may be so by *reason*. But in the heart – ? Can the heart ever beat quite alone? Plop! Plop! Can the heart beat quite alone, alone in all the atmosphere, all the space of the universe? Plop! Plop! Plop! Quite alone in all the space?' A slow smile came over the Italian's face. 'It is impossible. It may beat *against* the heart of other men, in anger, all in pressure against the others. It may beat hard, like iron, saying it is independent. But this is only beating against the heart of mankind, not alone. But either with or against the heart of mankind, or the heart of someone, mother, wife, friend, children – so must the heart of every man beat. It is so.'

'It beats alone in its own silence,' said Lilly.

The Italian shook his head.

'We'd better be going inside, anyhow,' said Argyle. 'Some of you will be taking cold.'

'Aaron,' said Lilly. 'Is it true for you?'

'Nearly,' said Aaron, looking into the quiet, half-amused, yet frightening eyes of the other man. 'Or it has been.'

'A miss is as good as a mile,' laughed Lilly, rising and picking up his chair to take it indoors. And the laughter of his voice was so like simple, deliberate amiability, that Aaron's heart really stood still for a second. He knew that Lilly *was* alone – as far as he, Aaron, was concerned. Lilly was alone – and out of his isolation came his words, indifferent as to whether they came or not. And he left his friends utterly to their own choice. Utterly to their own choice. Aaron felt that Lilly was *there*, existing in life, yet neither asking for connexion nor preventing any connexion. He was present, he was the real centre of the group. And yet he asked nothing of them, and he imposed nothing. He left each to himself, and he himself remained just himself: neither more nor less. And there was a finality about it, which was at once maddening and fascinating. Aaron felt angry, as if he were half insulted by the other man's placing the gift of friendship or connexion so quietly back in the giver's hands. Lilly would receive no gift of friendship in equality. Neither would he violently refuse it. He let it lie unmarked. And yet at the same time Aaron knew that he could depend on the other man for help, nay almost for life itself – so long as it entailed no breaking of the intrinsic isolation of Lilly's soul. But this condition was also hateful. And there was also a great fascination in it.

CHAPTER 18

The Marchesa

So Aaron dined with the Marchesa and Manfredi. He was
quite startled when his hostess came in: she seemed like somebody else. She seemed like a demon, her hair on her brows,
her terrible modern elegance. She wore a wonderful gown of
thin blue velvet, of a lovely colour, with some kind of gauzy
gold-threaded filament down the sides. It was terribly modern,
short, and showed her legs and her shoulders and breast and
all her beautiful white arms. Round her throat was a collar of
dark-blue sapphires. Her hair was done low, almost to the
brows, and heavy, like an Aubrey Beardsley drawing. She was
most carefully made up – yet with that touch of exaggeration,
lips slightly too red, which was quite intentional, and which
frightened Aaron. He thought her wonderful, and sinister.
She affected him with a touch of horror. She sat down opposite
him, and her beautifully shapen legs, in frail, goldish stock-
ings, seemed to glisten metallic naked, thrust from out of the
wonderful, wonderful skin, like periwinkle-blue velvet. She
had tapestry shoes, blue and gold: and almost one could see
her toes: metallic naked. The gold-threaded gauze slipped at
her side. Aaron could not help watching the naked-seeming
arch of her foot. It was as if she were dusted with dark gold-
dust upon her marvellous nudity.

She must have seen his face, seen that he was *ébloui*.

'You brought the flute?' she said, in that toneless, melancholy, unstriving voice of hers. Her voice alone was the same:
direct and bare and quiet.

'Yes.'

'Perhaps I shall sing later on, if you'll accompany me. Will
you?'

'I thought you hated accompaniments.'

'Oh no – not just unison. I don't mean accompaniment. I mean unison. I don't know how it will be. But will you try?'

'Yes, I'll try.'

'Manfredi is just bringing the cocktails. Do you think you'd prefer orange in yours?'

'I'll have mine as you have yours.'

'I don't take orange in mine. Won't you smoke?'

The strange, naked, remote-seeming voice! And then the beautiful firm limbs thrust out in that dress, and nakedly dusky as with gold dust. Her beautiful woman's legs, slightly glistening, duskily. His one abiding instinct was to touch them, to kiss them. He had never known a woman exercise such power over him. It was a bare, occult force, something he could not cope with.

Manfredi came in with the little tray. He was still in uniform.

'Hello!' cried the little Italian. 'Glad to see you – Well, everything all right? Glad to hear it. How is the cocktail, Nan?'

'Yes,' she said. 'All right.'

'One drop too much peach, eh?'

'No, all right.'

'Ah,' and the little officer seated himself, stretching his gaitered legs as if gaily. He had a curious smiling look on his face, that Aaron thought also diabolical – and almost handsome. Suddenly the odd, laughing, satanic beauty of the little man was visible.

'Well, and what have you been doing with yourself?' said he. 'What did you do yesterday?'

'Yesterday?' said Aaron. 'I went to the Uffizi.'

'To the Uffizi? Well! And what did you think of it?'

'Very fine.'

'I think it is. I think it is. What pictures did you look at?'

'I was with Dekker. We looked at most, I believe.'

'And what do you remember best?'

'I remember Botticelli's Venus on the shell.'

'Yes! Yes! – ' said Manfredi. 'I like her. But I like others better. You thought her a pretty woman, yes?'

'No – not particularly pretty. But I like her body. And I like the fresh air. I like the fresh air, the summer sea-air all through it – through her as well.'

'And her face?' asked the Marchesa, with a slow ironic smile.

'Yes – she's a bit baby-faced,' said Aaron.

'Trying to be more innocent than her own common-sense will let her,' said the Marchesa.

'I don't agree with you, Nan,' said her husband. 'I think it is just that wistfulness and innocence which makes her the true Venus: the true modern Venus. She chooses *not* to know too much. And that is her attraction. Don't you agree, Aaron? Excuse me, but everybody speaks of you as Aaron. It seems to come naturally. Most people speak of me as Manfredi too, because it is easier, perhaps, than Del Torre. So if you find it easier, use it. Do you mind that I call you Aaron?'

'Not at all. I hate Misters, always.'

'Yes, so do I. I like one name only.'

The little officer seemed very winning and delightful to Aaron this evening – and Aaron began to like him extremely. But the dominating consciousness in the room was the woman's.

'*Do* you agree, Mr Sisson?' said the Marchesa. 'Do you agree that the mock-innocence and the sham wistfulness of Botticelli's Venus are her great charm?'

'I don't think she is at all charming, as a person,' said Aaron. 'As a particular woman, she makes no impression on me at all. But as a picture – and the fresh air, particularly the fresh air. She doesn't seem so much a woman, you know, as the kind of out-of-doors morning-feeling at the sea-side.'

'Quite! A sort of sea-scape of a woman. With perfectly sham innocence. Are you as keen on innocence as Manfredi is?'

'Innocence?' said Aaron. 'It's the sort of thing I don't have much feeling about.'

'Ah, I know you,' laughed the soldier wickedly. 'You are

the sort of man who wants to be Antony to Cleopatra. Ha-ha!'

Aaron winced as if struck. Then he too smiled, flattered. Yet felt he had been struck. Did he want to be Antony to Cleopatra? Without knowing, he was watching the Marchesa. And she was looking away, but knew he was watching her. And at last she turned her eyes to his, with a slow, dark smile, full of pain and fuller still of knowledge. A strange, dark, silent look of knowledge she gave him: from so far away, it seemed. And he felt all the bonds that held him melting away. His eyes remained fixed and gloomy, but with his mouth he smiled back at her. And he was terrified. He knew he was sinking towards her – sinking towards her. And he was terrified. But at the back of his mind, also, he knew there was Lilly, whom he might depend on. And also, he wanted to sink towards her. The flesh and blood of him simply melted out, in desire towards her. Cost what may, he must come to her. And yet he knew at the same time that, cost what may, he must keep the power to recover himself from her. He must have his cake and eat it.

And she became Cleopatra to him. 'Age cannot wither her, nor custom stale – ' To his instinctive, unwilled fancy, she was Cleopatra.

They went in to dinner, and he sat on her right hand. It was a smallish table, with a very few daisy-flowers: everything rather frail, and sparse. The food the same – nothing very heavy, all rather exquisite. They drank hock. And he was aware of her beautiful arms, and her bosom; her low-crowded, thick hair, parted in the centre, the sapphires on her throat, the heavy rings on her fingers: and the paint on her lips, the fard. Something deep, deep at the bottom of him hovered upon her, cleaved to her. Yet he was as if sightless, in a stupor. Who was she, what was she? He had lost all his grasp. Only he sat there, with his face turned to hers, or to her, all the time. And she talked to him. But she never looked at him.

Indeed she said little. It was the husband who talked. His manner towards Aaron was almost caressive. And Aaron liked it. The woman was silent mostly, and seemed remote. And Aaron felt his life ebb towards her. He felt the marvellousness, the rich beauty of her arms and breast. And the thought of her gold-dusted smooth limbs beneath the table made him feel almost an idiot.

The second wine was a gold-coloured Moselle, very soft and rich and beautiful. She drank this with pleasure, as one who understands. And for dessert there was a dish of cacchi – that orange-coloured, pulpy Japanese fruit – persimmons. Aaron had never eaten these before. Soft, almost slimy, of a wonderful colour and of a flavour that had sunk from harsh astringency down to that first decay-sweetness which is all autumn-rich. The Marchese loved them, and scooped them out with his spoon. But she ate none.

Aaron did not know what they talked about, what was said. If someone had taken his mind away altogether, and left him with nothing but a body and a spinal consciouness, it would have been the same.

But at coffee the talk turned to Manfredi's duties. He would not be free from the army for some time yet. On the morrow, for example, he had to be out and away before it was day. He said he hated it, and wanted to be a free man once more. But it seemed to Aaron he would be a very bored man, once he was free. And then they drifted on to talk of the palazzo in which was their apartment.

'We've got such a fine terrace – you can see it from your house where you are.' said Manfredi. 'Have you noticed it?'

'No,' said Aaron.

'Near that tuft of palm-trees. Don't you know?'

'No,' said Aaron.

'Let us go out and show it him,' said the Marchesa.

Manfredi fetched her a cloak, and they went through various doors, then up some steps. The terrace was broad and open. It looked straight across the river at the opposite Lungarno: and there was the thin-necked tower of the Palazzo Vecchio, and the great dome of the cathedral in the distance, in shadow-bulk in the cold aired night of stars. Little trams were running brilliant over the flat new bridge on the right. And from a garden just below rose a tuft of palm-trees.

'You see,' said the Marchesa, coming and standing close to Aaron, so that she just touched him, 'you can know the terrace, just by these palm trees. And you are in the Nardini just across there, are you? On the top floor, you said?'

'Yes, the top floor – one of the middle windows, I think.'

'One that is always open now – and the others shut. I have noticed it, not connecting it with you.'

'Yes, my window is always open.'

She was leaning very slightly against him, as he stood. And he knew, with the same kind of inevitability with which he knew he would one day die, that he would be the lover of this woman. Nay, that he *was* her lover already.

'Don't take cold,' said Manfredi.

She turned at once indoors. Aaron caught a faint whiff of perfume from the little orange trees in tubs round the wall.

'Will you get the flute?' she said, as they entered.

'And will you sing?' he answered.

'Play first,' she said.

He did as she wished. As the other night, he went into the big music-room to play. And the stream of sound came out with the quick wild imperiousness of the pipe. It had an immediate effect on her. She seemed to relax the peculiar, drug-like tension which was upon her at all ordinary times. She seemed to go still, and yielding. Her red mouth looked as if it might moan with relief. She sat with her chin dropped on her breast, listening. And she did not move. But she sat softly, breathing rather quick, like one who has been hurt, and is soothed. A certain womanly naturalness seemed to soften her.

And the music of the flute came quick, rather brilliant like a call-note, or like a long quick message, half command. To her it was like a pure male voice – as a blackbird's when he calls: a pure male voice, not only calling, but telling her something, telling her something, and soothing her soul to sleep. It was like the fire-music putting Brünhilde to sleep. But the pipe did not flicker and sink. It seemed to cause a natural relaxation in her soul, a peace. Perhaps it was more like waking to a sweet, morning-awakening, after a night of tormented, painful tense sleep. Perhaps more like that.

When Aaron came in, she looked at him with a gentle fresh smile that seemed to make the fard on her face look like a curious tiredness, which now she might recover from. And as the last time, it was difficult for her to identify this man with the voice of the flute. It was rather difficult. Except that perhaps, between his brows was something of a doubt, and in his bearing an aloofness that made her dread he might go away and not come back. She could see it in him, that he might go away and not come back.

She said nothing to him, only just smiled. And the look of knowledge in her eyes seemed, for the moment, to be contained in another look: a look of faith, and at last happiness. Aaron's heart stood still. No, in her moment's mood of faith and at last peace, life-trust, he was perhaps more terrified of her than in her previous sinister elegance. His spirit started and shrank. What was she going to ask of him?

'I am so anxious that you should come to play one Saturday morning,' said Manfredi. 'With an accompaniment, you know. I should like so much to hear you with the piano accompaniment.'

'Very well,' said Aaron.

'Will you really come? And will you practise with me, so that I can accompany you?' said Manfredi eagerly.

'Yes. I will,' said Aaron.

'Oh good! Oh good! Look here, come in on Friday morning and let us both look through the music.'

'If Mr Sisson plays for the public,' said the Marchesa, 'he must not do it for charity. He must have the proper fee.'

'No, I don't want it,' said Aaron.

'But you must earn money, mustn't you?' said she.

'I must,' said Aaron. 'But I can do it somewhere else.'

'No. If you play for the public, you must have your earnings. When you play for me, it is different.'

'Of course,' said Manfredi. 'Every man must have his wage. I have mine from the Italian Government –'

After a while, Aaron asked the Marchesa if she would sing.

'Shall I?' she said.

'Yes, do.'

'Then I will sing alone first, to let you see what you think of it – I shall be like Trilby – I won't say like Yvette Guilbert, because I daren't. So I will be like Trilby, and sing a little French song. Though not Malbrouk, and without a Svengali to keep me in tune.'

She went near the door, and stood with her hands by her side. There was something wistful, almost pathetic now, in her elegance.

> Derrière chez mon père
> *Vole vole mon cœur, vole!*
> Derrière chez mon père
> Il y a un pommier doux.
> *Tout doux, et iou*
> *Et iou, tout doux.*
> *Il y a un pommier doux.*
>
> Trois belles princesses
> *Vole vole mon cœur, vole!*
> Trois belles princesses
> Sont assises dessous.
> *Tout doux, et iou*
> *Et iou, tout doux.*
> *Sont assises desous.*

She had a beautiful, strong, sweet voice. But it was faltering, stumbling, and sometimes it seemed to drop almost to speech. After three verses she faltered to an end, bitterly chagrined.

'No,' she said. 'It's no good. I can't sing.' And she dropped in her chair.

'A lovely little tune,' said Aaron. 'Haven't you got the music?'

She rose, not answering, and found him a little book.

'What do the words mean?' he asked her.

She told him. And then he took his flute.

'You don't mind if I play it, do you?' he said.

So he played the tune. It was so simple. And he seemed to catch the lilt and the timbre of her voice.

'Come and sing it while I play,' he said.

'I can't sing,' she said, shaking her head rather bitterly.

'But let us try,' said he, disappointed.

'I know I can't,' she said. But she rose.

He remained sitting at the little table, the book propped up under the reading lamp. She stood at a little distance, unhappy.

'I've always been like that,' she said. 'I could never sing music, unless I had a thing drilled into me, and then it wasn't singing any more.'

But Aaron wasn't heeding. His flute was at his mouth, he was watching her. He sounded the note, but she did not begin. She was twisting her handkerchief. So he played the melody alone. At the end of the verse, he looked up at her again, and a half mocking smile played in his eyes. Again he sounded the note, a challenge. And this time, as at his bidding, she began to sing. The flute instantly swung with a lovely soft firmness into the song, and she wavered only for a minute or two. Then her soul and her voice got free, and she sang – she sang as she wanted to sing, as she had always wanted to sing, without that awful scotch, that impediment inside her own soul, which prevented her.

She sang free, with the flute gliding along with her. And oh, how beautiful it was for her! How beautiful it was to sing the little song in the sweetness of her own spirit. How sweet it was to move pure and unhampered at last in the music! The lovely ease and lilt of her own soul in its motion through the music! She wasn't aware of the flute. She didn't know there was anything except her own pure lovely song-drift. Her soul seemed to breathe as a butterfly breathes, as it rests on a leaf and slowly breathes its wings. For the first time! For the first time her soul drew its own deep breath! All her life, the breath had caught half-way. And now she breathed full, deep, to the deepest extent of her being.

And oh, it was so wonderful, she was dazed. The song

ended, she stood with a dazed, happy face, like one just coming awake. And the fard on her face seemed like the old night-crust, the bad sleep. New and luminous she looked out. And she looked at Aaron with a proud smile.

'Bravo Nan! That was what you wanted,' said her husband.

'It was, wasn't it?' she said, turning a wondering, glowing face to him.

His face looked strange and withered and gnome-like, at the moment.

She went and sat in her chair, quite silent, as if in a trance. The two men also sat quite still. And in the silence a little drama played itself between the three, of which they knew definitely nothing. But Manfredi knew that Aaron had done what he himself never could do, for this woman. And yet the woman was his own woman, not Aaron's. And so, he was displaced. Aaron, sitting there, glowed with a sort of triumph. He had performed a little miracle, and felt himself a little wonder-worker, to whom reverence was due. And as in a dream the woman sat, feeling what a joy it was to float and move like a swan in the high air, flying upon the wings of her own spirit. She was as a swan which never before could get its wings quite open, and so which never could get up into the open, where alone it can sing. For swans and storks make their music only when they are high, high up in the air. Then they can give sound to their strange spirits. And so she.

Aaron and Manfredi kept their faces averted from one another and hardly spoke to one another. It was as if two invisible hands pushed their faces apart, away, averted. And Aaron's face glimmered with a little triumph, and a little grimace of obstinacy. And the Italian's face looked old, rather monkey-like, and of a deep, almost stone-bare bitterness. The woman looked wonderingly from one man to the other – wondering. The glimmer of the open flower, the wonder-look, still lasted. And Aaron said in his heart, what a goodly woman, what a woman to taste and enjoy. Ah, what a woman to enjoy! And was it not his privilege? Had he not gained it?

His manhood, or rather his maleness, rose powerfully in

him, in a sort of mastery. He felt his own power, he felt suddenly his own virile title to strength and reward. Suddenly, and newly flushed with his own male super-power, he was going to have his reward. The woman was his reward. So it was, in him. And he cast it over in his mind. He wanted her – ha, didn't he! But the husband sat there, like a soap-stone Chinese monkey, greyish-green. So, it would have to be another time.

He rose, therefore, and took his leave.

'But you'll let us do that again, won't you?' said she.

'When you tell me, I'll come,' said he.

'Then I'll tell you soon,' said she.

So he left, and went to his own place, and there to his own remote room. As he laid his flute on the table he looked at it and smiled. He remembered that Lilly had called it Aaron's Rod.

'So you blossom, do you? – and thorn as well,' said he.

For such a long time he had been gripped inside himself, and withheld. For such a long time it had been hard and unyielding, so hard and unyielding. He had wanted nothing, his desire had kept itself back, fast back. For such a long time his desire for woman had withheld itself, hard and resistant. All his deep, desirous blood had been locked, he had wanted nobody, and nothing. And it had been hard to live, so. Without desire, without any movement of passionate love, only gripped back in recoil! That was an experience to endure.

And now came his desire back. But strong, fierce as iron. Like the strength of an eagle with the lightning in its talons. Something to glory in, something overweening, the powerful male passion, arrogant, royal, Jove's thunderbolt. Aaron's black rod of power, blossoming again with red Florentine lilies and fierce thorns. He moved about in the splendour of his own male lightning, invested in the thunder of the male passion-power. He had got it back, the male godliness, the male godhead.

So he slept, and dreamed violent dreams of strange, black strife, something like the street-riot in Milan, but more terrible. In the morning, however, he cared nothing about his dreams. As soon as it was really light, he rose, and opened his window wide. It was a grey, slow morning. But he saw neither the morning nor the river nor the woman walking on the gravel river-bed with her goose nor the green hill up to San Miniato. He watched the tuft of palm-trees, and the terrace beside it. He could just distinguish the terrace clearly, among the green of foliage. So he stood at his window for a full hour, and did not move. Motionless, planted, he stood and watched that terrace across the Arno. But like a statue.

After an hour or so, he looked at his watch. It was nine o'clock. So he rang for his coffee, and meanwhile still stood watching the terrace across. He felt his turn had come. The phoenix had risen in fire again, out of the ashes.

Therefore at ten o'clock he went over the bridge. He wrote on the back of his card a request, would she please let him have the little book of songs, that he might practise them over. The man-servant went, and came back with the request that Aaron should wait. So Aaron entered, while the man took his hat.

The man-servant spoke only French and Spanish, no English. He was a Spaniard, with greyish hair and stooping shoulders and dark, mute-seeming eyes. He spoke as little as possible. The Marchesa had inherited him from her father.

Aaron sat in the little sitting-room and waited. After a rather long time the Marchesa came in – wearing a white, thin blouse and a blue skirt. She was hardly made up at all. She had an odd, pleased, yet brooding look on her face as she gave Aaron her hand. Something brooded between her brows. And her voice was strange, with a strange, secret undertone, that he could not understand. He looked up at her. And his face was bright, and his knees, as he sat, were like the knees of the gods.

'You wanted the book of *chansons*?' she said.

'I wanted to learn your tunes,' he replied.

'Yes. Look – here it is!' And she brought him the little yellow book. It was just a hand-book, with melody and words only, no accompaniment. So she stood offering him the book, but waiting as if for something else, and standing as if with another meaning.

He opened the leaves at random.

'But I ought to know which ones you sing,' said he, rising and standing by her side with the open book.

'Yes,' she said, looking over his arm. He turned the pages one by one. '*Trois jeunes tambours*,' said she. 'Yes, that . . . Yes *En passant par la Lorraine* . . . *Auprès de ma blonde* . . . Oh, I like that one so much – ' He stood and went over the tune in his mind.

'Would you like me to play it?' he said.

'Very much,' said she.

So he got his flute, propped up the book against a vase, and played the tune, whilst she hummed it fragmentarily. But as he played, he felt that he did not cast the spell over her. There was no connexion. She was in some mysterious way withstanding him. She was withstanding him, and his male super-power, and his thunderbolt desire. She was, in some indescribable way, throwing cold water over his phoenix newly risen from the ashes of its nest in flames.

He realised that she did not want him to play. She did not want him to look at the songs. So he put the book away, and turned round, rather baffled, not quite sure what was happening, yet feeling she was withstanding him. He glanced at her face: it was inscrutable: it was her Cleopatra face once more, yet with something new and warm in it. He could not understand it. What was it in her face that puzzled him? Almost angered him? But she could not rob him of his male power, she could not divest him of his concentrated force.

'Won't you take off your coat?' she said, looking at him with strange, large dark eyes. A strange woman, he could not understand her. Yet, as he sat down again, having removed his overcoat, he felt her looking at his limbs, his physical body. And this went against him, he did not want it. Yet quite fixed in him too was the desire for her, her beautiful white arms, her whole soft white body. And such desire he would not contradict or allow to be contradicted. It was his will also.

Her whole soft white body – to possess it in its entirety, its fulness.

'What have you to do this morning?' she asked him.

'Nothing,' he said. 'Have you?' He lifted his head and looked at her.

'Nothing at all,' said he.

And then they sat in silence, he with his head dropped. Then again he looked at her.

'Shall we be lovers?' he said.

She sat with her face averted, and did not answer. His heart struck heavily, but he did not relax.

'Shall we be lovers?' came his voice once more, with the faintest touch of irony.

Her face gradually grew dusky. And he wondered very much to see it.

'Yes,' said she, still not looking at him. 'If you wish.'

'I do wish,' he said. And all the time he sat with his eyes fixed on her face, and she sat with her face averted.

'Now?' he said. 'And where?'

Again she was silent for some moments, as if struggling with herself. Then she looked at him, a long, strange, dark look, incomprehensible, and which he did not like.

'You don't want emotions? You don't want me to say things, do you?' he said.

A faint ironic smile came on her face.

'I know what all that is worth,' she said, with curious calm equanimity. 'No, I want none of that.'

'Then – ?'

But now she sat gazing on him with wide, heavy, incomprehensible eyes. It annoyed him.

'What do you want to see in me?' he asked, with a smile, looking steadily back again.

And now she turned aside her face once more, and once more the dusky colour came in her cheek. He waited.

'Shall I go away?' he said at length.

'Would you rather?' she said, keeping her face averted.

'No,' he said.

Then again she was silent.

'Where shall I come to you?' he said.

She paused a moment still, then answered:

'I'll go to my room.'

'I don't know which it is,' he said.

'I'll show it you,' she said.

'And then I shall come to you in ten minutes. In ten minutes,' he reiterated.

So she rose, and led the way out of the little salon. He walked with her to the door of her room, bowed his head as she looked at him, holding the door handle; and then he turned and went back to the drawing-room, glancing at his watch.

In the drawing-room he stood quite still, with his feet apart, and waited. He stood with his hands behind him, and his feet apart, quite motionless, planted and firm. So the minutes went by unheeded. He looked at his watch. The ten minutes were just up. He had heard footsteps and doors. So he decided to give her another five minutes. He wished to be quite sure that she had had her own time for her own movements.

Then at the end of the five minutes he went straight to her room, entered, and locked the door behind him. She was lying in bed, with her back to him.

He found her strange, not as he had imagined her. Not powerful, as he had imagined her. Strange, in his arms she seemed almost small and childish, whilst in daily life she looked a full, womanly woman. Strange, the naked way she clung to him! Almost like a sister, a younger sister! Or like a child! It filled him with a curious wonder, almost a bewilderment. In the dark sightlessness of passion, she seemed almost like a clinging child in his arms. And yet, like a child who in some deep and essential way mocked him. In some strange and incomprehensible way, as a girl-child blindly obstinate in her deepest nature, she was against him. He felt she was not his woman. Through him went the feeling, 'This is not my woman.'

When, after a long sleep, he awoke and came fully to himself, with that click of awakedness which is the end, the first shades were closing on the afternoon. He got up, and reached for his watch.

'Quarter past four,' he said.

Her eyes stretched wide with surprise as she looked at him. But she said nothing. The same strange and wide, perhaps insatiable child-like curiosity was in her eyes as she watched him. He dressed very quickly. And her eyes were wide, and she said no single word.

But when he was dressed, and bent over her to say good-bye, she put her arms round him, that seemed such frail and childish arms now, yet withal so deadly in power. Her soft arms round his neck, her tangle of hair over his face. And yet, even as he kissed her, he felt her deadly. He wanted to be gone. He wanted to get out of her arms and her clinging and her tangle of hair and her curiosity and her strange and hateful power.

'You'll come again. We'll be like this again?' she whispered.

And it was hard for him to realize that this was that other woman, who had sat so silently on the sofa, so darkly and reservedly, at the tea at Algy's.

'Yes! I will! Good-bye now!' And he kissed her, and walked straight out of the room. Quickly he took his coat and his hat, quickly, and left the house. In his nostrils was still the scent with which the bed linen was faintly scented – he did not know what it was. But now he wiped his face and his mouth, to wipe it away.

He had eaten nothing since coffee that morning, and was hungry, faint feeling. And his face, and his mind, felt withered. Curiously he felt blasted – as if blighted by some electricity. And he knew, he knew quite well he was only in possession of a tithe of his natural faculties. And in his male spirit he felt himself hating her: hating her deeply, damnably. But he said to himself: 'No, I won't hate her. I won't hate her.'

So he went on, over the Ponte Vecchio, where the jewellers' windows on the bridge were already blazing with light, on into the town. He wanted to eat something, so he decided to go to a shop he knew, where one could stand and eat good tiny rolls split into truffle or salami sandwiches, and drink marsala. So one after the other he ate little truffle rolls, and drank a few glasses of marsala. And then he did not know what to do. He did not want to eat any more. He had had what he wanted. His hunger had been more nervous than sensual.

So he went into the street. It was just growing dark and the town was lighting up. He felt curiously blazed, as if some flame or electric power had gone through him and withered his vital tissue. Blazed, as if some kind of electric flame had run over him and withered him. His brain felt withered, his mind had only one of its many-sighted eyes left open and unscorched. So many of the eyes of his mind were scorched now and sightless.

Yet a restlessness was in his nerves. What should he do? He remembered he had a letter in his pocket from Sir William Franks. Sir William had still teased him about his fate and his providence, in which he, Aaron, was supposed to trust. 'I shall be very glad to hear from you, and to know how your benevolent Providence – or was yours a Fate – has treated you since we saw you – '

So, Aaron turned away, and walked to the post office. There he took paper, and sat down at one of the tables in the writing room, and wrote his answer. It was very strange, writing thus when most of his mind's eyes were scorched, and it seemed he could hardly see to hold the pen, to drive it straight across the paper. Yet write he must. And most of his faculties being quenched or blasted for the moment, he wrote perhaps his greatest, or his innermost truth. 'I don't want my Fate or my Providence to treat me well. I don't want kindness or love. I don't believe in harmony and people loving one another. I believe in the fight and in nothing else. I believe in the fight which is in everything. And if it is a question of women, I believe in the fight of love, even if it blinds me. And if it is a question of the world, I believe in fighting it and in having it hate me, even if it breaks my legs. I want the world to hate me, because I can't bear the thought that it might love me.

Of all things love is the most deadly to me, and especially from such a repulsive world as I think this is . . . '

Well, here was a letter for a poor old man to receive. But, in the dryness of his withered mind, Aaron got it out of himself. When a man writes a letter to himself, it is a pity to post it to somebody else. Perhaps the same is true of a book.

His letter written, however, he stamped it and sealed it and put it in the box. That made it final. Then he turned towards home. One fact remained unbroken in the debris of his consciousness: that in the town was Lilly: and that when he needed, he could go to Lilly: also, that in the world was Lottie, his wife: and that against Lottie, his heart burned with a deep, deep, almost unreachable bitterness. Like a deep burn on his deepest soul, Lottie. And like a fate which he resented, yet which steadied him. Lilly.

He went home and lay on his bed. He had enough self-command to hear the gong and go down to dinner. White and abstract-looking, he sat and ate his dinner. And then, thank God, he could go to bed, alone, in his own cold bed, alone, thank God. To be alone in the night! For this he was unspeakably thankful.

CHAPTER 19

Cleopatra, but not Antony

AARON awoke in the morning feeling better, but still only a part himself. The night alone had restored him. And the need to be alone still was his greatest need. He felt an intense resentment against the Marchesa. He felt that somehow, she had given him a scorpion. And his instinct was to hate her. And yet he avoided hating her. He remembered Lilly – and the saying that one must possess oneself, and be alone in possession of oneself. And somehow, under the influence of Lilly, he refused to follow the reflex of his own passion. He refused to hate the Marchesa. He *did* like her. He *did* esteem her. And after all, she too was struggling with her fate. He had a genuine sympathy with her. Nay, he was not going to hate her.

But he could not see her. He could not bear the thought that she might call and see him. So he took the tram to Settignano, and walked away all day into the country, having bread and sausage in his pocket. He sat for long hours among the cypress trees of Tuscany. And never had any trees seemed so like ghosts, like soft, strange, pregnant presences. He lay and watched tall cypresses breathing and communicating, faintly moving and as it were walking in the small wind. And his soul seemed to leave him and to go far away, far back, perhaps, to where life was all different and time passed otherwise than time passes now. As in clairvoyance he perceived it: that our life is only a fragment of the shell of life. That there has been and will be life, human life such as we do not begin to conceive. Much that is life has passed away from men, leaving us all mere bits. In the dark, mindful silence and inflection of the cypress trees, lost races, lost language, lost human ways of feeling and of knowing. Men have known as we can no more

know, have felt as we can no more feel. Great life-realities
gone into the darkness. But the cypresses commemorate. In
the afternoon, Aaron felt the cypresses rising dark about him,
like so many high visitants from an old, lost, lost subtle
world, where men had the wonder of demons about them,
the aura of demons, such as still clings to the cypresses, in
Tuscany.

All day, he did not make up his mind what he was going to
do. His first impulse was never to see her again. And this was
his intention all day. But as he went home in the tram he
softened, and thought, nay, that would not be fair. For how
had she treated him, otherwise than generously.

She had been generous, and the other thing, that he felt
blasted afterwards, which was his experience, that was fate,
and not her fault. So he must see her again. He must not act
like a churl. But he would tell her – he would tell her that he
was a married man, and that though he had left his wife, and
though he had no dogma of fidelity, still, the years of marriage
had made a married man of him, and any other woman than
his wife was a strange woman to him, a violation. 'I will tell
her,' he said to himself, 'that at the bottom of my heart I love
Lottie still, and that I can't help it. I believe that is true. It
isn't love, perhaps. But it is marriage. I am married to Lottie.
And that means I can't be married to another woman. It isn't
my nature. And perhaps I can't bear to live with Lottie now
because I am married and not in love. When a man is married,
he is not in love. A husband is not a lover. Lilly told me that:
and I know it's true now. Lilly told me that a husband cannot
be a lover, and a lover cannot be a husband. And that women
will only have lovers now, and never a husband. Well, I am a
husband, if I am anything. And I shall never be a lover again,
not while I live. No, not for anybody. I haven't it in me. I am
a husband, and so it is finished with me as a lover. I can't be a
lover any more, just as I can't be aged twenty any more. I am
a man now, not an adolescent. And to my sorrow I am a
husband to a woman who wants a lover: always a lover. But
all women want lovers. And I can't be it any more. I don't

want to. I have finished that. Finished for ever: unless I become senile – '

Therefore next day he gathered up his courage. He would not have had courage unless he had known that he was not alone. The other man was in the town, and from this fact he derived his strength: the fact that Lilly was there. So at tea-time he went over the river, and rang at her door. Yes, she was at home, and she had other visitors. She was wearing a beautiful soft afternoon dress, again of a blue, like chicory-flowers, a pale, *warm* blue. And she had cornflowers in her belt: heaven knows where she had got them.

She greeted Aaron with some of a childish shyness. He could tell that she was glad he had come, and that she had wondered at his not coming sooner. She introduced him to her visitors: two young ladies and one old lady and one elderly Italian count. The conversation was mostly in French or Italian, so Aaron was rather out of it.

However, the visitors left fairly early, so Aaron stayed them out. When they had gone, he asked:

'Where is Manfredi?'

'He will come in soon. At about seven o'clock.'

Then there was a silence again.

'You are dressed fine to-day,' he said to her.

'Am I?' she smiled.

He was never able to make out quite what she felt, what she was feeling. But she had a quiet little air of proprietorship in him, which he did not like.

'You will stay to dinner to-night, won't you?' she said.

'No – not to-night,' he said. And then, awkwardly, he added: 'You know. I think it is better if we are friends – not lovers. You know – I don't feel free. I feel my wife, I suppose, somewhere inside me. And I can't help it – '

She bent her head and was silent for some moments. Then she lifted her face and looked at him oddly.

'Yes,' she said. 'I am sure you love your wife.'

The reply rather staggered him – and to tell the truth, annoyed him.

'Well,' he said. 'I don't know about love. But when one has been married for ten years – and I did love her – then – some sort of bond or something grows. I think some sort of connexion grows between us, you know. And it isn't natural, quite, to break it. Do you know what I mean?'

She paused a moment. Then, very softly, almost gently, she said:

'Yes, I do. I know so well what you mean.'

He was really surprised at her soft acquiescence. What *did* she mean?

'But we can be friends, can't we?' he said.

'Yes, I hope so. Why yes! I should be sorry if we couldn't be friends.'

After which speech he felt that everything was all right – everything was A1. And when Manfredi came home, the first sound he heard was the flute and his wife's singing.

'I'm so glad you've come,' his wife said to him. 'Shall we go into the sala and have real music? Will you play?'

'I should love to,' replied the husband.

Behold them then in the big drawing-room, and Aaron and the Marchese practising together, and the Marchesa singing an Italian folk-song while her husband accompanied her on the pianoforte. But her singing was rather strained and forced. Still, they were quite a little family, and it seemed quite nice. As soon as she could, the Marchesa left the two men together, whilst she sat apart. Aaron and Manfredi went through old Italian and old German music, tried one thing and then another, and seemed quite like brothers. They arranged a piece which they should play together on a Saturday morning, eight days hence.

The next day, Saturday, Aaron went to one of the Del Torre music mornings. There was a string quartette – and a violin soloist – and the Marchese at the piano. The audience, some dozen or fourteen friends, sat at the near end of the room, or in the smaller salotta, whilst the musicians performed at the further end of the room. The Lillys were there, both Tanny and her husband. But apart from these, Aaron knew nobody, and felt uncomfortable. The Marchesa gave her guests little sandwiches and glasses of wine or marsala or vermouth, as they chose. And she was quite the hostess: the well-bred and very simple, but still the conventional hostess. Aaron did not like it. And he could see that Lilly too was unhappy. In fact, the little man bolted the moment he could, dragging after him the indignant Tanny, who was so looking forward to the excellent little sandwiches. But no – Lilly just rudely bolted. Aaron followed as soon as he could.

'Will you come to dinner to-morrow evening?' said his hostess to him as he was leaving. And he agreed. He had really resented seeing her as a conventional hostess, attending so charmingly to all the other people, and treating him so merely as one of the guests, among many others. So that when at the last moment she quietly invited him to dinner next day, he was flattered and accepted at once.

The next day was Sunday – the seventh day after his coming together with the Marchesa – which had taken place on the Monday. And already he was feeling much less dramatic in his decision to keep himself apart from her, to be merely friends. Already the memory of the last time was fanning up in him, not as a warning but as a terrible incitement. Again the naked desire was getting hold of him, with that peculiar brutal powerfulness which startled him and also pleased him.

So that, by the time Sunday morning came, his recoil had exhausted itself, and he was ready again, eager again, but more wary this time. He sat in his room alone in the morning, playing his flute, playing over from memory the tunes she loved, and imagining how he and she would get into unison in the evening. His flute, his Aaron's rod, would blossom once again with splendid scarlet flowers, the red Florentine lilies. It was curious, the passion he had for her: just unalloyed desire, and nothing else. Something he had not known in his life before. Previously there had been always *some* personal quality, some sort of personal tenderness. But here, none. She did not seem to want it. She seemed to hate it, indeed. No, all he felt was stark, naked desire, without a single pretension. True enough, his last experience had been a warning to him. His desire and himself likewise had broken rather disastrously under the proving. But not finally broken. He was ready again. And with all the sheer powerful insolence of desire he looked forward to the evening. For he almost expected Manfredi would not be there. The officer had said something about having to go to Padua on the Saturday afternoon.

So Aaron went skipping off to his appointment, at seven o'clock. Judge of his chagrin, then, when he found already seated in the salotta an elderly, quite well-known, very cultured and very well connected English authoress. She was charming, in her white hair and dress of soft white wool and white lace, with a long chain of filigree gold beads, like bubbles. She was charming in her old-fashioned manner too, as if the world were still safe and stable, like a garden in which delightful culture, and choice ideas bloomed safe from wind and weather. Alas, never was Aaron more conscious of the crude collapse in the world than when he listened to this animated, young-seeming lady from the safe days of the seventies. All the old culture and choice ideas seemed like blowing bubbles. And dear old Corinna Wade, she seemed to be blowing bubbles still, as she sat there so charming in her soft white dress, and talked with her bright animation about the influence of woman in Parliament and the influence of woman in the Periclean day. Aaron listened spell-bound, watching the bubbles float round his head, and almost hearing them go pop.

To complete the party arrived an elderly littérateur who was more proud of his social not-very-important stand than of his literature. In fact he was one of those English snobs of the old order, living abroad. Perfectly well dressed for the evening, his hair and his prim face was the most well-dressed thing to be met in North Italy.

'Oh, so glad to see you, Mr ffrench. I didn't know you were in Florence again. You make that journey from Venice so often. I wonder you don't get tired of it,' cried Corinna Wade.

'No,' he said. 'So long as duty to England calls me to

Florence, I shall come to Florence. But I can *live* in no town but Venice.'

'No, I suppose you can't. Well there *is* something special about Venice: having no streets and no carriages, and moving about in a gondola. I suppose it is all much more soothing.'

'Much less nerve-racking, yes. And then there is a quality in the whole life. Of course I see few English people in Venice – only the old Venetian families, as a rule.'

'Ah yes. That must be very interesting. They are very exclusive still, the Venetian *noblesse,*' said Miss Wade.

'Oh very exclusive,' said Mr ffrench. 'That is one of the charms. Venice is really altogether exclusive. It excludes the world, really, and defies time and modern movement. Yes, in spite of the steamers on the canal, and the tourists.'

'That is so. That is so. Venice is a strange backwater. And the old families are very proud still, in these democratic days. They have a great opinion of themselves, I am told.'

'Well,' said Mr ffrench. 'Perhaps you know the rhyme:

> Veneziano gran' Signore
> Padovano buon' dottore.
> Vicenzese mangia il gatto
> Veronese tutto matto –'

'How very amusing!' said Miss Wade. '*Veneziano* gran' signore. The Venetian is a great gentleman! Yes, I know they are all convinced of it. Really, how very amusing, in these advanced days. To be born a Venetian, is to be born a great gentleman! But this outdoes divine right of kings.'

'To be born a Venetian *gentleman* is to be born a great gentleman,' said Mr ffrench, rather fussily.

'You seriously think so?' said Miss Wade. 'Well now, what do you base your opinion on?'

Mr ffrench gave various bases for his opinion.

'Yes – interesting. Very interesting. Rather like the Byzantines – lingering on into far other ages. Anna Comnena always charmed me very much. *How* she despised the flower of the north – even Tancred! And so the lingering Venetian families! And you, in your palazzo on the Grand Canal: you are a northern barbarian civilized into the old Venetian Signoria. But how very romantic a situation!'

It was really amusing to see the old maid, how she skirmished and hit out so gaily, like an old jaunty free-lance: and to see the old bachelor, how prim he was, and nervy and fussy and precious, like an old maid.

But need we say that Mr Aaron felt very much out of it. He sat and listened, with a sardonic small smile on his face and a sardonic gleam in his blue eyes, that looked so very blue on such an occasion. He made the two elderly people uncomfortable with his silence: his democratic silence, Miss Wade might have said.

However, Miss Wade lived out towards Galuzzo, so she rose early, to catch her tram. And Mr ffrench gallantly and properly rose to accompany her, to see her safe on board. Which left Aaron and the Marchesa alone.

'What time is Manfredi coming back?' said he.

'To-morrow,' replied she.

There was a pause.

'Why do you have those people?' he asked.

'Who?'

'Those two who were here this evening.'

'Miss Wade and Mr ffrench? Oh, I like Miss Wade so very much. She is so refreshing.'

'Those old people,' said Aaron. 'They licked the sugar off the pill, and go on as if everything was toffee. And we've got to swallow the pill. It's easy to be refreshing –'

'No, don't say anything against her. I like her so much.'

'And him?'

'Mr ffrench! Well, he's perhaps a little like the princess who felt the pea through three feather-beds. But he can be quite witty, and an excellent conversationalist too. Oh yes, I like him quite well.'

'Matter of taste,' said Aaron.

They had not much to say to one another. The time passed, in the pauses. He looked at his watch.

'I shall have to go,' he said.

'Won't you stay?' she said, in a small, muted voice.

'Stay all night?' he said.

'Won't you?'

'Yes,' he said quietly. Did he not feel the strength of his desire on him?

After which she said no more. Only she offered him whisky and soda, which he accepted.

'Go then,' he said to her. 'And I'll come to you. Shall I come in fifteen minutes?'

She looked at him with strange, slow dark eyes. And he could not understand.

'Yes,' she said. And she went.

And again, this night as before, she seemed strangely small and clinging in his arms. And this night he felt his passion drawn from him as if a long, live nerve were drawn out from his body, a long, live thread of electric fire.

This night he slept with a deeper obliviousness than before. But ah, as it grew towards morning, how he wished he could be alone.

They must stay together till the day was light. And she seemed to love clinging to him and curling strangely on his breast. He could never reconcile it with her who was a hostess entertaining her guests. How could she now in a sort of little ecstasy curl herself and nestle herself on his, Aaron's breast, tangling his face all over with her hair? He verily believed that this was what she really wanted of him: to curl on his naked breast, to make herself small, small, to feel his arms round her, and his slow, still, breathing lifting her, while he himself was remote, silent, in some way inaccessible. This seemed almost to make her beside herself with gratification. But why, why? Was it because he was one of her own race, and she, as it were, crept right home to him?

He did not know. He only knew it had nothing to do with him: and that, save out of *complaisance,* he did not want it. But did he not want it? – the magic feeling of phallic immortality. But at the same time it simply blasted his own central life. It simply blighted him.

And she clung to him closer. Strange, she was afraid of him! Of his actual male physique she was afraid as of a fetish. Fetish afraid, and fetish-fascinated! Or was her fear only a delightful game of cat and mouse? Or was the fear genuine, and the delight the greater: a sort of sacrilege? The fear, and the dangerous, sacrilegious power over that which she feared.

In some way she was not afraid of him at all. In some other way she used him as a mere magic implement, used him with the most amazing priestess-craft. Himself, the individual man which he was, this she ignored with an indifference that was startling to him.

He forgot, perhaps, that this was how he had treated her. His famous desire for her, what had it been but this same attempt to strike a magic fire out of her, for his own ecstasy. They were playing the same game of fire. In him, however, there was always something, all the time something hard and reckless and defiant, which stood apart. She was absolutely gone in her own incantations. She was absolutely gone, like a priestess utterly involved in her own terrible rites. And he was part of the ritual only, God and victim in one. God and victim. All the time, God and victim. When his aloof soul realized, amid the incantation, how he was being used, – not as himself, but as something quite different. God and victim; then he dilated with intense surprise, and his remote soul stood up tall and knew itself alone. He did not want it – not at all. He knew he was apart. And he looked back over the whole mystery of their love contact. Only his soul was apart.

He was aware of the strength and beauty and godlikeness that his breast was then to her – the magic. But himself, he stood far off, like Moses' sister Miriam. She would drink the one drop of his innermost heart's blood, and he would be carrion. As Cleopatra killed her lovers in the morning. Surely they knew that death was their just climax. They had approached the climax. Accept then.

But his soul stood apart, and could have nothing to do with it. If he had *really* been tempted, he would have gone on, and she might have had his central heart's blood. Yes, and thrown away the carrion. He would have been willing.

But fatally, he was not tempted. His soul stood apart and decided. At the bottom of his soul he disliked her. Or if not her, then her whole motive. Her whole life-mode. He was neither God nor victim: neither more nor less than himself. His soul, in its isolation as she lay there on his breast, chose it so with the soul's inevitability. So, there was no temptation.

When it was sufficiently light, he kissed her and left her. Quietly he left the silent flat. He had some difficulty in unfastening the various locks and bars and catches of the massive door downstairs, and began, in irritation and anger, to feel he was a prisoner, that he was locked in. But suddenly the ponderous door came loose, and he was out in the street. The door shut heavily behind him, with a shudder. He was out in the morning streets of Florence.

CHAPTER 20

The Broken Rod

THE day was rainy. Aaron stayed indoors alone, and copied music and slept. He felt the same stunned, withered feeling as before, but less intensely, less disastrously, this time. He knew now, without argument or thought, that he would never go again to the Marchesa: not as a lover. He would go away from it all. He did not dislike her. But he would never see her again. A great gulf had opened, leaving him alone on the far side.

He did not go out till after dinner. When he got downstairs he found the heavy night-door closed. He wondered: then remembered the Signorina's fear of riots and disturbances. As again he fumbled with the catches, he felt that the doors of Florence were trying to prevent his egress. However, he got out.

It was a very dark night, about nine o'clock, and deserted seeming. He was struck by the strange, deserted feeling of the city's atmosphere. Yet he noticed before him, at the foot of the statue, three men, one with a torch: a long torch with naked flames. The men were stooping over something dark, the man with the torch bending forward too. It was a dark, weird little group, like Mediaeval Florence. Aaron lingered on his doorstep, watching. He could not see what they were doing. But now, the two were crouching down; over a long dark object on the ground, and the one with the torch bending also to look. What was it? They were just at the foot of the statue, a dark little group under the big pediment, the torch-flames weirdly flickering as the torch-bearer moved and stooped lower to the two crouching men, who seemed to be kneeling.

Aaron felt his blood stir. There was something dark and mysterious, stealthy, in the little scene. It was obvious the men did not want to draw attention, they were so quiet and furtive-looking. And an eerie instinct prevented Aaron's going nearer to look. Instead, he swerved on to the Lungarno, and went along the top of the square, avoiding the little group in the centre. He walked the deserted dark-seeming street by the river, then turned inwards, into the city. He was going to the Piazza Vittorio Emmanuele, to sit in the café which is the centre of Florence at night. There he could sit for an hour, and drink his vermouth and watch the Florentines.

As he went along one of the dark, rather narrow streets, he heard a hurrying of feet behind him. Glancing round, he saw the torch-bearer coming along at a trot, holding his flaming torch up in front of him as he trotted down the middle of the narrow dark street. Aaron shrank under the wall. The trotting torch-bearer drew near, and now Aaron perceived the other two men slowly trotting behind, stealthily, bearing a stretcher on which a body was wrapped up, completely and darkly covered. The torch-bearer passed, the men with the stretcher passed too, hastily and stealthily, the flickering flames revealing them. They took no notice of Aaron, no notice of anything, but trotted softly on towards the centre of the city. Their queer, quick footsteps echoed down the distance. Then Aaron too resumed his way.

He came to the large, brilliantly-lighted café. It was Sunday evening, and the place was full. Men, Florentines, many, many men sat in groups and in twos and threes at the little marble tables. They were mostly in dark clothes or black overcoats. They had mostly been drinking just a cup of coffee – others, however, had glasses of wine or liquor. But mostly it was just a little coffee-tray with a tiny coffee pot and a cup and saucer. There was a faint film of tobacco smoke. And the men were all talking: talking, talking with that peculiar intensity of the Florentines. Aaron felt the intense, compressed sound of many half-secret voices. For the little groups and couples abated their voices, none wished that others should hear what they said.

Aaron was looking for a seat – there was no table to himself – when suddenly someone took him by the arm. It was Argyle.

'Come along now! Come and join us. Here, this way! Come along!'

Aaron let himself be led away towards a corner. There sat Lilly and a strange man: called Levison. The room was warm. Aaron could never bear to be too hot. After sitting a minute, he rose and took off his coat, and hung it on a stand near the window. As he did so he felt the weight of his flute – it was still in his pocket. And he wondered if it was safe to leave it.

'I suppose no one will steal from the overcoat pockets,' he said, as he sat down.

'My dear chap, they'd steal the gold filling out of your teeth, if you happened to yawn,' said Argyle. 'Why, have you left your valuables in your overcoat?'

'My flute,' said Aaron.

'Oh, they won't steal that,' said Argyle.

'Besides,' said Lilly, 'we should see anyone who touched it.'

And so they settled down to the vermouth.

'Well,' said Argyle, 'what have you been doing with yourself, eh? I haven't seen a glimpse of you for a week. Been going to the dogs, eh? I can see I shall have to take you in hand, and commence my work of reform. Oh, I'm a great reformer, a Zwingli and Savonarola in one. I couldn't count the number of people I've led into the right way. It takes some finding, you know. Strait is the gate – damned strait sometimes. A damned tight squeeze ...' Argyle was somewhat intoxicated. He spoke with a slight slur, and laughed, really tickled at his own jokes. The man Levison smiled acquiescent. But Lilly was not listening. His brow was heavy and he seemed abstracted. He hardly noticed Aaron's arrival.

'Did you see the row yesterday?' asked Levison.

'No,' said Aaron. 'What was it?'

'It was the Socialists. They were making a demonstration against the imprisonment of one of the railway-strikers. I was there. They went on all right, with a good bit of howling and gibing: a lot of young louts, you know. And the shopkeepers shut up shop, and nobody showed the Italian flag, of course. Well, when they came to the Via Benedetto Croce, there were a few mounted carabinieri. So they stopped the procession, and the sergeant said that the crowd could continue, could go on where they liked, but would they not go down the Via Verrocchio, because it was being repaired, the roadway was all up, and there were piles of cobbles stones. These might prove a temptation and lead to trouble. So would the demonstrators not take that road – they might take any other they liked. Well, the very moment he had finished, there was a revolver shot, he made a noise, and fell forward over his horse's nose. One of the anarchists had shot him. Then there was hell let loose, the carabinieri fired back, and people were bolting and fighting like devils. I cleared out, myself. But my God – what do you think of it?'

'Seems pretty mean,' said Aaron.

'Mean! He had just spoken them fair – they could go where they liked, only would they not go down the one road, because of the heap of stones. And they let him finish. And then shot him dead.'

'Was he dead?' said Aaron.

'Yes – killed outright, the Nazione says.'

There was a silence. The drinkers in the café all continued to talk vehemently, casting uneasy glances.

'Well,' said Argyle, 'if you let loose the dogs of war, you mustn't expect them to come to heel again in five minutes.'

'But there's no fair play about it, not a bit,' said Levison.

'Ah, my dear fellow, are you still so young and callow that you cherish the illusion of fair play?' said Argyle.

'Yes, I am,' said Levison.

'Live longer and grow wiser,' said Argyle, rather contemptuously.

'Are you a Socialist?' asked Levison.

'Am I my aunt Tabitha's dachshund bitch called Bella,' said Argyle, in his musical, indifferent voice. 'Yes, Bella's her name. And if you can tell me a demneder name for a dog, I shall listen, I assure you, attentively.'

'But you haven't got an aunt called Tabitha,' said Aaron.

'Haven't I? Oh, haven't I? I've got *two* aunts called Tabitha: if not more.'

'They aren't of any vital importance to you, are they?' said Levison.

'Not the very least in the world – if it hadn't been that my elder Aunt Tabitha had christened her dachshund bitch Bella. I cut myself off from the family after that. Oh, I turned over a new leaf, with not a family name on it. Couldn't stand Bella amongst the rest.'

'You must have strained most of the gnats out of your drink, Argyle,' said Lilly, laughing.

'Assiduously! Assiduously! I can't stand these little vermin. Oh, I am quite indifferent about swallowing a camel or two – or even a whole string of dromedaries. How charmingly Eastern that sounds! But gnats! Not for anything in the world would I swallow one.'

'*You*'re a bit of a Socialist though, aren't you?' persisted Levison, now turning to Lilly.

'No,' said Lilly. 'I was.'

'And am no more,' said Argyle sarcastically. 'My dear fellow, the only hope of salvation for the world lies in the re-institution of slavery.'

'What kind of slavery?' asked Levison.

'Slavery! *Slavery!* When I say *slavery* I don't mean any of your damned modern reform cant. I mean solid sound slavery on which the Greek and the Roman world rested. *Far* finer worlds than ours, my dear chap! Oh *far* finer. And can't be done without slavery. Simply can't be done. Oh, they'll all come to realise it, when they've had a bit more of this democratic washerwoman business.'

Levison was laughing, with a slight sneer down his nose.

'Anyhow, there's no immediate danger – or hope, if you prefer it – of the re-instituting of classic slavery,' he said.

'Unfortunately no. We are all such fools,' said Argyle.

'Besides,' said Levison, 'who would you make slaves of?'

'Everybody, my dear chap: beginning with the idealists and

the theorizing Jews, and after them your nicely-bred gentlemen, and then perhaps your profiteers and Rothschilds, and
all politicians, and ending up with the proletariat,' said Argyle.

'Then who would be the masters? – the professional classes,
doctors and lawyers and so on?'

'What? Masters? They would be the sewerage slaves, as
being those who had made most stinks.'

There was a moment's silence.

'The only fault I have to find with your system,' said
Levison, rather acidly, 'is that there would be only one master,
and everybody else slaves.'

'Do you call that a fault? What do you want with more than
one master? Are you asking for several? Well, perhaps there's
cunning in *that*. Cunning devils, cunning devils, these theorizing slaves –' and Argyle pushed his face with a devilish leer
into Aaron's face. 'Cunning devils!' he reiterated, with a slight
tipsy slur. 'Epictetus wasn't the last of 'em – nor the first. Oh,
not by any means, not by any means.'

Here Lilly could not avoid a slight spasm of amusement.

'But returning to serious conversation,' said Levison, turning his rather sallow face to Lilly. 'I think you'll agree with me
that Socialism is the inevitable next step –'

Lilly waited for some time without answering. Then he
said, with unwilling attention on the question:

'I suppose it's the logically inevitable next step.'

'Yes – logically inevitable – and humanly inevitable at the
same time. Some form of Socialism is bound to come, no
matter how you postpone it or try variations,' said Levison.

'All right, let it come,' said Lilly. 'It's not my affair, neither
to help it nor to keep it back, or even to try varying it.'

'There I don't follow you,' said Levison. 'Suppose you were
in Russia now –'

'I watch it I'm not.'

'But you're in Italy, which isn't far off. Supposing a Socialist
revolution takes place all round you. Won't that force the
problem on you? It is every man's problem,' persisted Levison.

'Not mine,' said Lilly.

'How shall you escape it?' said Levison.

'Because to me it is no problem. To Bolsh or not to Bolsh, as far as my mind goes, presents no problem. Not any more than to be or not to be. To be or not to be is simply no problem –'

'No, I quite agree, that since you are already existing, and since death is ultimately inevitable, to be or not to be is no sound problem,' said Levison. 'But the parallel isn't true of Socialism. That is not a problem of existence, but of a certain mode of existence which centuries of thought and action on the part of Europe have now made logically inevitable for Europe. And therefore there is a problem. There is more than a problem, there is a dilemma. Either we must go to the logical conclusion – or –'

'Somewhere else,' said Lilly.

'Yes – yes. Precisely! But *where* else? That's the one half of the problem: supposing you do not agree to a logical progression in human social activity. Because after all, human society through the course of ages only enacts, spasmodically but still inevitably, the logical development of a given idea.'

'Well, then, I tell you. The idea and the ideal has for me gone dead – dead as carrion –'

'Which idea, which ideal precisely?'

'The ideal of love, the ideal that it is better to give than to receive, the ideal of liberty, the ideal of the brotherhood of man, the ideal of the sanctity of human life, the ideal of what we call goodness, charity, benevolence, public spiritedness, the ideal of sacrifice for a cause, the ideal of unity and unanimity – all the lot – all the whole beehive of ideals – has all got the modern bee-disease, and gone putrid, stinking. And when the ideal is dead and putrid, the logical sequence is only stink. Which, for me, is the truth concerning the ideal of good, peaceful, loving humanity and its logical sequence in Socialism and equality, equal opportunity or whatever you like. By this time he stinketh – and I'm sorry for any Christus who brings him to life again, to stink livingly for another thirty years: the beastly Lazarus of our idealism.'

'That may be true for you –'

'But it's true for nobody else,' said Lilly. 'All the worse for them. Let them die of the bee-disease.'

'Not only that,' persisted Levison, 'but what is your alternative? Is it merely nihilism?'

'My alternative,' said Lilly, 'is an alternative for no one but myself, so I'll keep my mouth shut about it.'

'That isn't fair.'

'I tell you, the ideal of fairness stinks with the rest. I have no obligation to say what I think.'

'Yes, if you enter into conversation, you have –'

'Bah, then I didn't enter into conversation. The only thing is, I agree in the rough with Argyle. You've got to have a sort of slavery again. People are not *men*: they are insects and instruments, and their destiny is slavery. They are too many for me, and so what I think is ineffectual. But ultimately they will be brought to agree – after sufficient extermination – and then they will elect for themselves a proper and healthy and energetic slavery.'

'I should like to know what you mean by slavery. Because to me it is impossible that slavery should be healthy and energetic. You seem to have some other idea in your mind, and you merely use the word slavery out of exasperation –'

'I mean it none the less. I mean a real committal of the life-issue of inferior beings to the responsibility of a superior being.'

'It'll take a bit of knowing, who are the inferior and which is the superior,' said Levison sarcastically.

'Not a bit. It is written between a man's brows, which he is.'

'I'm afraid we shall all read differently.'

'So long as we're liars.'

'And putting that question aside: I presume that you mean that this committal of the life-issue of inferior beings to someone higher shall be made voluntarily – a sort of voluntary self-gift of the inferiors –'

'Yes – more or less – and a voluntary acceptance. For it's no pretty gift, after all. But once made it must be held fast by genuine power. Oh yes – no playing and fooling about with it. Permanent and very efficacious power.'

'You mean military power?'

'I do, of course.'

Here Levison smiled a long, slow, subtle smile of ridicule. It all seemed to him the preposterous pretentiousness of a megalomaniac – one whom, after a while, humanity would probably have the satisfaction of putting into prison, or into a lunatic asylum. And Levison felt strong, overwhelmingly strong, in the huge social power with which he, insignificant as he was, was armed against such criminal-imbecile pretensions as those above set forth. Prison or the lunatic asylum. The face of the fellow gloated in these two inevitable engines of his disapproval.

'It will take you some time before you'll get your doctrines accepted,' he said.

'Accepted! I'd be sorry. I don't want a lot of swine snouting and sniffing at me with their acceptance. Bah, Levison – one can easily make a fool of you. Do you take this as my gospel?'

'I take it you are speaking seriously.'

Here Lilly broke into that peculiar, gay, whimsical smile.

'But I should say the blank opposite with just as much fervour,' he declared.

'Do you mean to say you don't *mean* what you've been saying?' said Levison, now really looking angry.

'Why, I'll tell you the real truth,' said Lilly. 'I think every man is a sacred and holy individual, *never* to be violated. I think there is only one thing I hate to the verge of madness and that is *bullying*. To see any living creature *bullied*, in *any* way, almost makes a murderer of me. That is true. Do you believe it – ?'

'Yes,' said Levison unwillingly. 'That may be true as well. You have no doubt, like most of us, got a complex nature which –'

CRASH!

There intervened one awful minute of pure shock, when the soul was in darkness.

Out of this shock Aaron felt himself issuing amid a mass of terrible sensations: the fearful blow of the explosion, the noise of glass, the hoarse howl of people, the rushing of men, the sudden gulf, the awful gulfing whirlpool of horror in the social life.

He stood in agony and semi-blindness amid a chaos. Then as he began to recover his consciousness, he found himself standing by a pillar some distance from where he had been sitting: he saw a place where tables and chairs were all upside down, legs in the air, amid débris of glass and breakage: he saw the café almost empty, nearly everybody gone: he saw the owner, or the manager, advancing aghast to the place of débris: he saw Lilly standing not far off, white as a sheet, and as if unconscious. And still he had no idea of what had happened. He thought perhaps something had broken down. He could not understand.

Lilly began to look round. He caught Aaron's eye. And then Aaron began to approach his friend.

'What is it?' he asked.

'A bomb,' said Lilly.

The manager, and one old waiter, and three or four youths had now advanced to the place of débris. And now Aaron saw that a man was lying there – and horror, blood was running across the floor of the café. Men began now hastily to return to the place. Some seized their hats and departed again at once. But many began to crowd in – a black eager crowd of men pressing to where the bomb had burst – where the man was lying. It was rather dark, some of the lamps were broken – but enough still shone. Men surged in with that eager, excited zest of people, where there has been an accident. Grey carabinieri, and carabinieri in the cocked hat and fine Sunday uniform pressed forward officiously.

'Let us go,' said Lilly.

And he went to the far corner, where his hat hung. But Aaron looked in vain for his own hat. The bomb had fallen near the stand where he had hung it and his overcoat.

'My hat and coat?' he said to Lilly.

Lilly, not very tall, stood on tiptoe. Then he climbed on a chair and looked round. Then he squeezed past the crowd.

Aaron followed. On the other side of the crowd excited angry men were wrestling over overcoats that were mixed up with a broken marble table-top. Aaron spied his own black hat under the sofa near the wall. He waited his turn and then in the confusion pressed forward to where the coats were. Someone had dragged out his, and it lay on the floor under many feet. He managed, with a struggle, to get it from under the feet of the crowd. He felt at once for his flute. But his trampled, torn coat had no flute in its pocket. He pushed and struggled, caught sight of a section and picked it up. But it was split right down, two silver stops were torn out, and a long thin spelk of wood was curiously torn off. He looked at it, and his heart stood still. No need to look for the rest.

He felt utterly, utterly overcome – as if he didn't care what became of him any further. He didn't care whether he were hit by a bomb, or whether he himself threw the next bomb, and hit somebody. He just didn't care any more about anything in life or death. It was as if the reins of his life slipped from his hands, and he would let everything run where it would, so long as it did run.

Then he became aware of Lilly's eyes on him – and automatically he joined the little man.

Let us go,' said Lilly.

And they pushed their way through the door. The police were just marching across the square. Aaron and Lilly walked in the opposite direction. Groups of people were watching. Suddenly Lilly swerved – in the middle of the road was a large black glisten of blood, trickling horribly. A wounded man had run from the blow and fallen here.

Aaron did not know where he was going. But in the Via Tornabuoni Lilly turned towards the Arno, and soon they were on the Ponte Santa Trinità.

'Who threw the bomb?' said Aaron.

'I suppose an anarchist.'

'It's all the same,' said Aaron.

330

The two men, as if unable to walk any further, leaned on the broad parapet of the bridge and looked at the water in the darkness of the still, deserted night. Aaron still had his flute section in his hand, his overcoat over his arm.

'Is that your flute?' asked Lilly.

'Bit of it. Smashed.'

'Let me look.'

He looked, and gave it back.

'No good,' he said.

'Oh no,' said Aaron.

'Throw it in the river, Aaron,' said Lilly.

Aaron turned and looked at him.

'Throw it in the river,' repeated Lilly. 'It's an end.'

Aaron nervelessly dropped the flute into the stream. The two men stood leaning on the bridge-parapet, as if unable to move.

'We shall have to go home,' said Lilly. 'Tanny may hear of it and be anxious.'

Aaron was quite dumbfounded by the night's event: the loss of his flute. Here was a blow he had not expected. And the loss was for him symbolistic. It chimed with something in his soul: the bomb, the smashed flute, the end.

'There goes Aaron's Rod, then,' he said to Lilly.

'It'll grow again. It's a reed, a water-plant. You can't kill it,' said Lilly, unheeding.

'And me?'

'You'll have to live without a rod, meanwhile.'

To which pleasant remark Aaron made no reply.

CHAPTER 21

Words

HE went home to bed: and dreamed a strange dream. He dreamed that he was in a country with which he was not acquainted. Night was coming on, and he had nowhere to sleep. So he passed the mouth of a sort of cave or house, in which a woman, an old woman, sat. Therefore he entered, and though he could not understand the language, still his second self understood. The cave was a house: and men came home from work. His second self assumed that they were tin-miners.

He wandered uneasily to and fro, no one taking any particular notice of him. And he realized that there was a whole vast country spreading, a sort of underworld country, spreading away beyond him. He wandered from vast apartment to apartment, down narrow corridors like the roads in a mine. In one of the great square rooms, the men were going to eat. And it seemed to him that what they were going to eat was a man, a naked man. But his second self knew that what appeared to his eyes as a man was really a man's skin stuffed tight with prepared meat, as the skin of a Bologna sausage. This did not prevent his seeing the naked man who was to be eaten walk slowly and stiffly across the gangway and down the corridor. He saw him from behind. It was a big and handsome man in the prime of life, quite naked and perhaps stupid. But, of course, he was only a skin stuffed with meat, whom the grey tin-miners were going to eat.

Aaron, the dream-Aaron, turned another way, and strayed among the vast square rooms, cavern apartments. He came into one room where there were many children, all in white gowns. And they were all busily putting themselves to bed, in the many beds scattered about the room at haphazard. And each child went to bed with a wreath of flowers on its head, white flowers and pink, so it seemed. So there they all lay, in their flower-crowns in the vast space of the rooms. And Aaron went away.

He could not remember the following part. Only he seemed to have passed through many grey domestic apartments, where were all women, all greyish in their clothes and appearance, being wives of the underground tin-miners. The men were away and the dream-Aaron remembered with fear the food they were to eat.

The next thing he could recall was, that he was in a boat. And now he was most definitely two people. His invisible, *conscious* self, what we have called his second self, hovered as it were before the prow of the boat, seeing and knowing, but unseen. His other self, the palpable Aaron, sat as a passenger in the boat, which was being rowed by the unknown people of this underworld. They stood up as they thrust the boat along. Other passengers were in the boat too, women as well, but all of the unknown people, and not noticeable.

The boat was upon a great lake in the underworld country, a lake of dark blue water, but crystal clear and very beautiful in colour. The second or invisible Aaron sat in the prow and watched the fishes swimming suspended in the clear, beautiful dark-blue water. Some were pale fish, some frightening-looking, like centipedes swimming, and some were dark fish, of definite form, and delightful to watch.

The palpable or visible Aaron sat at the side of the boat, on the end of the middle seat, with his naked right elbow leaning out over the side. And now the boat entered upon shallows. The impalpable Aaron in the bows saw the whitish clay of the bottom swirl up in clouds at each thrust of the oars, whitish clayey clouds which would envelop the strange fishes in a sudden mist. And on the right hand of the course stakes stood up in the water, at intervals, to mark the course.

The boat must pass very near these stakes, almost touching. And Aaron's naked elbow was leaning right over the side. As they approached the first stake, the boatmen all uttered a strange cry of warning, in a foreign language. The flesh-and-blood Aaron seemed not even to hear. The invisible Aaron heard, but did not comprehend the words of the cry. So the naked elbow struck smartly against the stake as the boat passed.

The rowers rowed on. And still the flesh-and-blood Aaron sat with his arm over the side. Another stake was nearing. 'Will he heed, will he heed?' thought the anxious second self. The rowers gave the strange warning cry. He did not heed, and again the elbow struck against the stake as the boat passed.

And yet the flesh-and-blood Aaron sat on and made no sign. There were stakes all along this shallow part of the lake. Beyond was deep water again. The invisible Aaron was becoming anxious. 'Will he never hear? Will he never heed? Will he never understand?' he thought. And he watched in pain for the next stake. But still the flesh-and-blood Aaron sat on, and though the rowers cried so acutely that the invisible Aaron almost understood their very language, still the Aaron seated at the side heard nothing, and his elbow struck against the third stake.

This was almost too much. But after a few moments, as the boat rowed on, the palpable Aaron changed his position as he sat, and drew in his arm: though even now he was not aware of any need to do so. The invisible Aaron breathed with relief in the bows, the boat swung steadily on, into the deep, unfathomable water again.

They were drawing near a city. A lake-city, like Mexico. They must have reached a city, because when Aaron woke up and tried to piece together the dream of which these are mere fragments, he could remember having just seen an idol. An Astarte he knew it as, seated by the road, and in her open lap were some eggs: smallish hen's eggs, and one or two bigger eggs, like swan's, and one single little roll of bread. These lay in the lap of the roadside Astarte . . . And then he could remember no more.

He woke, and for a minute tried to remember what he had

been dreaming, and what it all meant. But he quickly relinquished the effort. So he looked at his watch: it was only half-past three. He had one of those American watches with luminous, phosphorescent figures and fingers. And to-night he felt afraid of its eerily shining face.

He was awake a long time in the dark – for two hours, thinking and not thinking, in that barren state which is not sleep, nor yet full wakefulness, and which is a painful strain. At length he went to sleep again, and did not wake till past eight o'clock. He did not ring for his coffee till nine.

Outside was a bright day – but he hardly heeded it. He lay profitlessly thinking. With the breaking of the flute, that which was slowly breaking had finally shattered at last. And there was nothing ahead: no plan, no prospect. He knew quite well that people would help him: Francis Dekker or Angus Guest or the Marchese or Lilly. They would get him a new flute, and find him engagements. But what was the good? His flute was broken, and broken finally. The bomb had settled it. The bomb had settled it and everything. It was an end, no matter how he tried to patch things up. The only thing he felt was a thread of destiny attaching him to Lilly. The rest had all gone as bare and bald as the dead orb of the moon. So he made up his mind, if he could, to make some plan that would bring his life together with that of his evanescent friend.

Lilly was a peculiar bird. Clever and attractive as he undoubtedly was, he was perhaps the most objectionable person to know. It was stamped on his peculiar face. Aaron thought of Lilly's dark, ugly face, which had something that lurked in it as a creature under leaves. Then the thought of the wide-apart eyes, with their curious candour and surety. The peculiar, half-veiled surety, as if nothing, nothing could overcome him. It made people angry, this look of silent, indifferent assurance. 'Nothing can touch him on the quick, nothing can really *get* him,' they felt at last. And they felt it with resentment, almost with hate. They wanted to be able to get at him. For he was so open-seeming, so very outspoken. He gave himself away so much. And he had no money to fall back on. Yet he gave himself away so easily, paid such attention, almost deference to any chance friend. So they all thought: Here is a wise person who finds me the wonder which I really am. And lo and behold, after he had given them the trial, and found their inevitable limitations, he departed and ceased to heed their wonderful existence. Which, to say the least of it, was fraudulent and damnable. It was then, after his departure, that they realized his basic indifference to them, and his silent arrogance. A silent arrogance that knew all their wisdom, and left them to it.

Aaron had been through it all. He had started by thinking Lilly a peculiar little freak: gone on to think him a wonderful chap, and a bit pathetic: progressed, and found him generous, but overbearing: then cruel and intolerant, allowing no man to have a soul of his own: then terribly arrogant, throwing a fellow aside like an old glove which is in holes at the finger-ends. And all the time, which was most beastly, seeing through one. All the time, freak and outsider as he was, Lilly *knew*. He knew, and his soul was against the whole world.

Driven to bay, and forced to choose. Forced to choose, not between life and death, but between the world and the uncertain, assertive Lilly. Forced to choose, and yet, in the world, having nothing left to choose. For in the world there was nothing left to choose, unless he would give in and try for success. Aaron knew well enough that if he liked to do a bit of buttering, people would gladly make a success of him, and give him money and success. He could become quite a favourite.

But no! If he had to give in to something: if he really had to give in, and it seemed he had: then he would rather give in to the devilish little Lilly than to the beastly people of the world. If he had to give in, then it should be to no woman, and to no social ideal, and to no social institution. No! – if he had to yield his wilful independence, and give himself, then he would rather give himself to the little, individual *man* than to any of the rest. For to tell the truth, in the man was something incomprehensible, which had dominion over him, if he chose to allow it.

As he lay pondering this over, escaping from the *cul de sac* in which he had been running for so long, by yielding to one of his pursuers: yielding to the peculiar mastery of one man's nature rather than to the quicksands of woman or the stinking bog of society: yielding, since yield he must, in some direction or other: yielding in a new direction now, to one strange and incalculable little individual: as Aaron lay so relaxing, finding a peculiar delight in giving his soul to his mind's hero, the self-same hero tapped and entered.

'I wondered,' he said, 'if you'd like to walk into the country with me: it is such a nice day. I thought you might have gone out already. But here you are in bed like a woman who's had a baby. You're all right, are you?'

'Yes,' said Aaron. 'I'm all right.'

'Miserable about your flute? Ah well, there are more flutes. Get up then.' And Lilly went to the window, and stood looking out at the river.

'We're going away on Thursday,' he said.

'Where to?' said Aaron.

'Naples. We've got a little house there for the winter – in the country, not far from Sorrento – I must get a bit of work done, now the winter is coming. And forget all about everything and just live with life. What's the good of running after life, when we've got it in us, if nobody prevents us and obstructs us?'

Aaron felt very queer.

'But for how long will you settle down –?' he asked.

'Oh, only for the winter. I am a vagrant really: or a migrant. I must migrate. Do you think a cuckoo in Africa and a cuckoo in Essex is one *and* the same bird? Anyhow, I know I must oscillate between north and south, so oscillate I do. It's just my nature. All people don't have the same needs.'

'Perhaps not,' said Aaron, who had risen and was sitting on the side of the bed.

'I would very much like to try life in another continent,

among another race. I feel Europe becoming like a cage to me.
Europe may be all right in herself. But I find myself chafing.
Another year I shall get out. I shall leave Europe. I begin to
feel caged.'

'I guess there are others that feel caged, as well as you,' said
Aaron.

'I guess there are.'

'And maybe they haven't a chance to get out.'

Lilly was silent a moment. Then he said:

'Well, I didn't make life and society. I can only go my own
way.'

Aaron too was silent. A deep disappointment was settling
over his spirit.

'Will you be alone all winter?'

'Just myself and Tanny,' he answered. 'But people always
turn up.'

'And then next year, what will you do?'

'Who knows? I may sail far off. I should like to. I should
like to try quite a new life-mode. This is finished in me – and
yet perhaps it is absurd to go further. I'm rather sick of seekers.
I hate a seeker.'

'What,' said Aaron rather sarcastically – 'those who are
looking for a new religion?'

'Religion – and love – and all that. It's a disease now.'

'Oh, I don't know,' said Aaron. 'Perhaps the lack of love
and religion is the disease.'

'Ah – bah! The grinding of the old millstones of love
and God is what ails us, when there's no more grist between the stones. We've ground love very small. Time to
forget it. Forget the very words religion, and God, and love
– then have a shot at a new mode. But the very words rivet
us down and don't let us move. Rivets, and we can't get
them out.'

'And where should we be if we could?' said Aaron.

'We might begin to be ourselves, anyhow.'

'And what does that mean?' said Aaron. 'Being yourself –
what does it mean?'

'To me, everything.'

'And to most folks, nothing. They've got to have a goal.'

'There is no goal. I loathe goals more than any other impertinence. Gaols, they are. Bah – jails and jailers! gaols and gaolers –'

'Wherever you go, you'll find people with their noses tied to some goal,' said Aaron.

'Their wagon hitched to a star – which goes round and round like an ass in a gin,' laughed Lilly. 'Be damned to it.'

Aaron got himself dressed, and the two men went out, took a tram and went into the country. Aaron could not help it – Lilly put his back up. They came to a little inn near a bridge, where a broad stream rustled bright and shallow. It was a sunny day, and Aaron and Lilly had a table outside under the thin trees at the top of the bank above the river. The yellow leaves were falling – the Tuscan sky was turquoise blue. In the stream below three naked boys still adventurously bathed, and lay flat on the shingle in the sun. A wagon with two pale, lowing, velvety oxen drew slowly down the hill, looking at each step as if they were going to come to rest, to move no more. But still they stepped forward. Till they came to the inn, and there they stood at rest. Two old women were picking the last acorns under three scrubby oak-trees, whilst a girl with bare feet drove her two goats and a sheep up from the water-side towards the women. The girl wore a dress that had been blue, perhaps indigo, but which had faded to the beautiful lavender-purple colour which is so common, and which always reminded Lilly of purple anemones in the south.

The two friends sat in the sun and drank red wine. It was midday. From the thin, square belfry on the opposite hill the bells had rung. The old women and the girl squatted under the trees eating their bread and figs. The boys were dressing, fluttering into their shirts on the stream's shingle. A big girl went past, with somebody's dinner tied in a red kerchief and perched on her head. It was one of the most precious hours: the hour of pause, noon, and the sun, and the quiet acceptance of the world. At such a time everything seems to fall into a true relationship, after the strain of work and of urge.

Aaron looked at Lilly, and saw the same odd, distant look on his face as on the face of some animal when it lies awake and alert, yet perfectly at one with its surroundings. It was something quite different from happiness: an alert enjoyment of rest, an intense and satisfying sense of centrality. As a dog when it basks in the sun with one eye open and winking: or a rabbit quite still and wide-eyed, with a faintly-twitching nose. Not passivity, but alert enjoyment of being central, life-central in one's own little circumambient world.

They sat thus still – or lay under the trees – for an hour and a half. Then Lilly paid the bill, and went on.

'What am I going to do this winter, do you think?' Aaron asked.

'What do you want to do?'

'Nay, that's what I want to know.'

'Do you want anything? I mean, does something drive you from inside?'

'I can't just rest,' said Aaron.

'Can't you settle down to something? – to a job, for instance?'

'I've not found the job I could settle down to, yet,' said Aaron.

'Why not?'

'It's just my nature.'

'Are you a seeker? Have you got a divine urge, or need?'

'How do I know?' laughed Aaron. 'Perhaps I've got a *damned* urge, at the bottom of me. I'm sure it's nothing divine.'

'Very well then. Now, in life, there are only two great dynamic urges – do you believe me?'

'How do I know?' laughed Aaron. 'Do you want to be believed?'

'No, I don't care a straw. Only for your own sake, you'd better believe me.'

'All right then – what about it?'

'Well then, there are only two great dynamic urges in *life*: love and power.'

'Love and power?' said Aaron. 'I don't see power as so very important.'

'You don't see because you don't look. But that's not the point. What sort of urge is your urge? Is it the love urge?'

'I don't know,' said Aaron.

'Yes, you do. You know that you have got an urge, don't you?'

'Yes – ' rather unwillingly Aaron admitted it.

'Well then, what is it? Is it that you want to love, or to be obeyed?'

'A bit of both.'

'All right – a bit of both. And what are you looking for in love? A woman whom you can love, and who will love you, out and out and all in all and happy ever after sort of thing?'

'That's what I started out for, perhaps,' laughed Aaron.

'And now you know it's all my eye!' Aaron looked at Lilly, unwilling to admit it. Lilly began to laugh.

'You know it well enough,' he said. 'It's one of your lost illusions, my boy. Well then, what next? Is it a God you're after? Do you want a God you can strive to and attain, through love, and live happy ever after, countless millions of eternities, immortality and all that? Is this your little dodge?'

Again Aaron looked at Lilly with that odd double look of mockery and unwillingness to give himself away.

'All right then. You've got a love-urge that urges you to God, have you? Then go and join the Buddhists in Burma, or the newest fangled Christians in Europe. Go and stick your head in a bush of Nirvana or spiritual perfection. Trot off.'

'I won't,' said Aaron.

'You must. If you've got a love-urge, then give it its fulfilment.'

'I haven't got a love-urge.'

'You have. You want to get excited in love. You want to be carried away in love. You want to whoosh off in a nice little love-whoosh and lose yourself. Don't deny it. I know you do. You want passion to sweep you off on wings of fire till you surpass yourself, and like the swooping eagle swoop right into the sun. I know you, my love-boy.'

'Not any more – not any more. I've been had too often,' laughed Aaron.

'Bah, it's a lesson men never learn. No matter how sick they make themselves with love, they always rush for more, like a dog to his vomit.'

'Well, what am I to do then, if I'm not to love?' cried Aaron.

'You want to go on, from passion to passion, from ecstasy to ecstasy, from triumph to triumph, till you can whoosh away into glory, beyond yourself, all bonds loosened and happy ever after. Either that or Nirvana, opposite side of the medal.'

'There's probably more hate than love in me,' said Aaron.

'That's the recoil of the same urge. The anarchist, the criminal, the murderer, he is only the extreme lover acting on the recoil. But it is love: only in recoil. It flies back, the love-urge, and becomes a horror.'

'All right then. I'm a criminal and a murderer,' said Aaron.

'No you're not. But you're a love-urger. And perhaps on the recoil just now. But listen to me. It's no good thinking the love-urge is the one and only. *Niente!* You can whoosh if you like, and get excited and carried away loving a woman, or humanity, or God. Swoop away in the love direction till you lose yourself. But that's where you're had. You can't lose yourself. You can try. But you might just as well try to swallow yourself. You'll only bite your fingers off in the attempt. You can't lose yourself, neither in woman nor humanity nor in God. You've always got yourself on your hands in the end: and a very raw and jaded and humiliated and nervous-neurasthenic self it is too, in the end. A very nasty thing to wake up to is one's own raw self after an excessive love-whoosh. Look even at President Wilson: he love-whooshed for humanity, and found in the end he's only got a very sorry self on his hands.

'So leave off. Leave off, my boy. Leave off love-whooshing. You can't lose yourself, so stop trying. The responsibility is on your own shoulders all the time, and no God which man has ever struck can take it off. You *are* yourself and so *be* yourself. Stick to it and abide by it. Passion or no passion, ecstasy or no ecstasy, urge or no urge, there's no goal outside you, where you can consummate like an eagle flying into the sun, or a moth into a candle. There's no goal outside you – and there's no God outside you. No God, whom you can get to rest in. None. It is a case of

> Trot, trot to market, to buy a penny bun,
> And trot trot back again, as fast as you can run.

But there's no God outside you, whom you can rise to or sink to or swoop away to. You can't even gum yourself to a divine Nirvana moon. There is no goal outside you. None.

'There is only one thing, your own very self. So you'd better stick to it. You can't be any bigger than just yourself, so you needn't drag God in. You've got one job, and no more. There inside you lies your own very self, like a germinating egg, your precious Easter egg of your own soul. There it is, developing bit by bit, from one single egg-cell which you were at your conception in your mother's womb, on and on to the strange and peculiar complication in unity which never stops till you die – if then. You've got an innermost, integral, unique self, and since it's the only thing you have got or ever will have, don't go trying to lose it. You've got to develop it, from the egg into the chicken, and from the chicken into the one-and-only phoenix, of which there can only be one at a time in the universe. There can only be one of you at a time in the universe – and one of me. So don't forget it. Your own single oneness is your destiny. Your destiny comes from within, from your own self-form. And you can't know it beforehand, neither your destiny nor your self-form. You can only develop it. You can only stick to your own very self, and *never* betray it. And by so sticking, you develop the one and only phoenix of your own self, and you unfold your own destiny, as a dandelion unfolds itself into a dandelion, and not into a stick of celery.

'Remember this, my boy: you've never got to deny the Holy Ghost which is inside you, your own soul's self. Never. Or you'll catch it. And you've never got to think you'll dodge the responsibility of your own soul's self, by loving or sacrificing or Nirvanaing – or even anarchizing and throwing bombs. You never will ... '

Aaron was silenced for a moment by this flood of words. Then he said smiling:

'So I'd better sit tight on my soul, till it hatches, had I?'

'Oh yes. If your soul's urge urges you to love, then love. But always know that what you are doing is the fulfilling of your soul's impulse. It's no good trying to act by prescription: not a bit. And it's no use getting into frenzies. If you've got to go in for love and passion, go in for them. But they aren't the goal. They're a mere means: a life-means, if you will. The only goal is the fulfilling of your own soul's active desire and suggestion. Be passionate as much as ever it is your nature to be passionate, and deeply sensual as far as you can be. Small souls have a small sensuality, deep souls a deep one. But remember, all the time, the responsibility is upon your own head, it all rests with your own lovely soul, the responsibility for your own action.'

'I never said it didn't,' said Aaron.

'You never said it did. You never accepted. You thought there was something outside, to justify you: God, or a creed, or a prescription. But remember, your soul inside you is your only Godhead. It develops your actions within you as a tree develops its own new cells. And the cells push on into buds and boughs and flowers. And these are your passion and your acts and your thoughts and expressions, your developing consciousness. You don't know beforehand, and you can't. You can only stick to your own soul through thick and thin.

'You are your own Tree of Life, roots and limbs and trunk. Somewhere within the wholeness of the tree lies the very self, the quick: its own innate Holy Ghost. And this Holy Ghost puts forth new buds, and pushes past old limits, and shakes off a whole body of dying leaves. And the old limits hate being empassed, and the old leaves hate to fall. But they must, if the tree-soul says so . . . '

They had sat down again during this harangue, under a white wall. Aaron listened more to the voice than the words. It was more the sound value which entered his soul, the tone, the strange speech-music which sank into him. The sense he hardly heeded. And yet he understood, he knew. He understood, oh, so much more deeply than if he had listened with his head. And he answered an objection from the bottom of his soul.

'But you talk,' he said, 'as if we were like trees, alone by ourselves in the world. We aren't. If we love, it needs another person than ourselves. And if we hate, and even if we talk.'

'Quite,' said Lilly. 'And that's just the point. We've got to love and hate moreover – and even talk. But we haven't got to fix on any one of these modes, and say that's the only mode. It is such imbecility to say that love and love alone must rule. It is so obviously not the case. Yet we try and make it so.'

'I feel that,' said Aaron. 'It's all a lie.'

'It's worse. It's a half lie. But listen. I told you there were two urges – two great life-urges, didn't I? There may be more. But it comes on me so strongly, now, that there are two: love, and power. And we've been trying to work ourselves, at least as individuals, from the love-urge exclusively, hating the power-urge, and repressing it. And now I find we've got to accept the very thing we've hated.

'We've exhausted our love-urge, for the moment. And yet we try to force it to continue working. So we get inevitably anarchy and murder. It's no good. We've got to accept the power motive, accept it in deep responsibility, do you understand me? It is a great life motive. It was that great dark power-urge which kept Egypt so intensely living for so many centuries. It is a vast dark source of life and strength in us now, waiting either to issue into true action, or to burst into cataclysm. Power – the power-urge. The will-to-power – but not in Nietzsche's sense. Not intellectual power. Not mental power. Not conscious will-power. Not even wisdom. But dark, living, fructifying power. Do you know what I mean?'

'I don't know,' said Aaron.

'Take what you call love, for example. In the real way of love, the positive aim is to make the other person – or persons – happy. It devotes itself to the other or to others. But change the mode. Let the urge be the urge of power. Then the great desire is not happiness, neither of the beloved nor of oneself. Happiness is only one of many states, and it is horrible to think of fixing us down to one state. The urge of power does not seek for happiness any more than for any other state. It urges from within, darkly, for the displacing of the old leaves, the inception of the new. It is powerful and self-central, not seeking its centre outside, in some God or some beloved, but acting indomitably from within itself.

'And, of course, there must be one who urges, and one who is impelled. Just as in love there is a beloved and a lover: the man is supposed to be the lover, the woman the beloved. Now, in the urge of power, it is the reverse. The woman must submit, but deeply, deeply submit. Not to any foolish fixed authority, not to any foolish and arbitrary will. But to something deep, deeper. To the soul in its dark motion of power and pride. We must reverse the poles. The woman must now submit – but deeply, deeply, and richly! No subservience. None of that. No slavery. A deep, unfathomable free submission.'

'You'll never get it,' said Aaron.

'You will, if you abandon the love idea and the love motive, and if you stand apart, and never bully, never force from the conscious will. That's where Nietzsche was wrong. His was the conscious and benevolent will, in fact, the love-will. But the deep power-urge is not conscious of its aims: and it is certainly not consciously benevolent or love-directed. Whatever else happens, somewhere, sometime, the deep power-urge in man will have to issue forth again, and woman will submit, livingly, not subjectedly.'

'She never will,' persisted Aaron. 'Anything else will happen, but not that.'

'She will,' said Lilly, 'once man disengaged himself from the love-mode, and stands clear. Once he stands clear, and the other great urge begins to flow in him, then the woman won't be able to resist. Her own soul will wish to yield itself.'

'Woman yield – ?' Aaron re-echoed.

'Woman – and man too. Yield to the deep power-soul in the individual man, and obey implicitly. I don't go back on what I said before. I do believe that every man must fulfil his own soul, every woman must be herself, herself only, not some man's instrument, or some embodied theory. But the mode of our being is such that we can only live and have our being whilst we are implicit in one of the great dynamic modes. We *must* either love, or rule. And once the love-mode changes, as change it must, for we are worn out and becoming evil in its persistence, then the other mode will take place in us. And there will be profound, profound obedience in place of this love-crying, obedience to the incalculable power-urge. And men must submit to the greater soul in a man, for their guidance: and women must submit to the positive power-soul in man, for their being.'

'You'll never get it,' said Aaron.

'You will, when all men want it. All men say, they want a leader. Then let them in their souls *submit* to some greater soul that theirs. At present, when they say they want a leader, they mean they want an instrument, like Lloyd George. A mere instrument for their use. But it's more than that. It's the reverse. It's the deep, fathomless submission to the heroic soul in a greater man. You, Aaron, you too have the need to submit. You, too, have the need livingly to yield to a more heroic soul, to give yourself. You know you have. And you know it isn't love. It is life-submission. And you know it. But you kick against the pricks. And perhaps you'd rather die than yield. And so, die you must. It is your affair.'

There was a long pause. Then Aaron looked up into Lilly's face. It was dark and remote-seeming. It was like a Byzantine eikon at the moment.

'And whom shall I submit to?' he said.

'Your soul will tell you,' replied the other.

FOR THE BEST IN PAPERBACKS, LOOK FOR THE

In every corner of the world, on every subject under the sun, Penguin represents quality and variety – the very best in publishing today.

For complete information about books available from Penguin – including Puffins, Penguin Classics and Arkana – and how to order them, write to us at the appropriate address below. Please note that for copyright reasons the selection of books varies from country to country.

In the United Kingdom: Please write to *Dept E.P., Penguin Books Ltd, Harmondsworth, Middlesex, UB7 0DA.*

If you have any difficulty in obtaining a title, please send your order with the correct money, plus ten per cent for postage and packaging, to *PO Box No 11, West Drayton, Middlesex*

In the United States: Please write to *Dept BA, Penguin, 299 Murray Hill Parkway, East Rutherford, New Jersey 07073*

In Canada: Please write to *Penguin Books Canada Ltd, 2801 John Street, Markham, Ontario L3R 1B4*

In Australia: Please write to the *Marketing Department, Penguin Books Australia Ltd, P.O. Box 257, Ringwood, Victoria 3134*

In New Zealand: Please write to the *Marketing Department, Penguin Books (NZ) Ltd, Private Bag, Takapuna, Auckland 9*

In India: Please write to *Penguin Overseas Ltd, 706 Eros Apartments, 56 Nehru Place, New Delhi, 110019*

In the Netherlands: Please write to *Penguin Books Nederland B.V., Postbus 195, NL–1380AD Weesp*

In West Germany: Please write to *Penguin Books Ltd, Friedrichstrasse 10–12, D–6000 Frankfurt/Main 1*

In Spain: Please write to *Longman Penguin España, Calle San Nicolas 15, E–28013 Madrid*

In Italy: Please write to *Penguin Italia s.r.l., Via Como 4, I-20096 Pioltello (Milano)*

In France: Please write to *Penguin Books Ltd, 39 Rue de Montmorency, F-75003 Paris*

In Japan: Please write to *Longman Penguin Japan Co Ltd, Yamaguchi Building, 2–12–9 Kanda Jimbocho, Chiyoda-Ku, Tokyo 101*

CLASSICS OF THE TWENTIETH CENTURY

The Outsider Albert Camus

Meursault leads an apparently unremarkable bachelor life in Algiers, until his involvement in a violent incident calls into question the fundamental values of society. 'The protagonist of *The Outsider* is undoubtedly the best achieved of all the central figures of the existential novel' – *Listener*

Dark as the Grave wherein my Friend is Laid Malcolm Lowry

A Dantesque descent into hell: into Lowry's infernal landscape of Mexico – the Mexico of his masterpiece, *Under the Volcano* – and into Lowry's own personal abyss, reverberating with mental terrors and spiritual chasms.

I'm Dying Laughing Christina Stead

A dazzling novel set in the 1930s and 1940s when fashionable Hollywood Marxism was under threat from the savage repression of McCarthyism. 'The Cassandra of the modern novel in English ... reading her seems like plunging into the mess of life itself' – Angela Carter

The Desert of Love François Mauriac

Two men, father and son, share a passion for the same woman – attractive, intelligent and proud, but an outcast from respectable society because of her position as a 'kept woman'. 'He writes with an intense, almost tempestuous force about the life of the emotions' – Olivia Manning

The Expelled and Other Novellas Samuel Beckett

Rich in verbal and situational humour, these four stories offer the reader a fascinating insight into Beckett's preoccupation with the helpless individual consciousness, a preoccupation which has remained constant throughout his work.

Chance Acquaintances and Julie de Carneilhan Colette

Two contrasting works in one volume. Colette's last full-length novel, *Julie de Carneilhan* was 'as close a reckoning with the elements of her second marriage as she ever allowed herself'. In *Chance Acquaintances*, Colette visits a health resort, accompanied only by her cat.

FOR THE BEST IN PAPERBACKS, LOOK FOR THE 🐧

D. H. LAWRENCE

D. H. Lawrence is now acknowledged as one of the greatest writers of the twentieth century. Nearly all his works have been published by Penguin.

NOVELS

Aaron's Rod
The Lost Girl
The Rainbow
The Trespasser
Women in Love
The First Lady Chatterley
The Boy in the Bush

Lady Chatterley's Lover
The Plumed Serpent
Sons and Lovers
The White Peacock
Kangaroo
John Thomas and Lady Jane

SHORT STORIES

The Prussian Officer
Love Among the Haystacks

England, My England
The Woman Who Rode Away

Three Novellas: The Fox/The Ladybird/The Captain's Doll
St Mawr *and* The Virgin and the Gipsy

TRAVEL BOOKS AND OTHER WORKS

Morning in Mexico *and*
  Etruscan Places
Sea and Sardinia
Selected Essays
Studies in Classic
  American Literature
Apocalypse

Twilight in Italy
Fantasia of the Unconscious *and*
  Psychoanalysis and the
  Unconscious
Selected Letters

POETRY

D. H. Lawrence: The Complete Poems Edited and Introduced by Vivian de Sola Pinto and F. Warren Roberts

PLAYS

Three Plays: A Collier's Friday Night/The Daughter-in-Law/The Widowing of Mrs Holroyd